# HUNGRY WATER

## BOOK 1 OF THE RIVERINE RESISTANCE

## K. E. LANDRY

*For BK and EEK,*
*who taught me the best things come before we think we're ready*

*Hungry Water,* \ ˈhəŋ-grē ˈwȯ-tər /, *n.*

*Disrupted river flow with excess energy, prone to causing erosion and structural instability.*

# EXCERPT FROM THE SECTOR KEYSTAR
# ANNUAL REPORT

*Season of reaping, seventy-three years since the uprising.*

With the supply of hydro from *The State*, Sector Keystar is nearly self-sufficient in factory-to-table food production.

Experiments gardening in the dry harbor continue, with the citizenry providing home-recaptured hydro to grow the plants. There is small evidence of insect lifeforms reproducing, but the gardens themselves have produced no measurable harvest. Even with guard patrols, the meager produce output disappears before it can be added to our tallies.

Until we have a stable hydro supply for citizen consumption and food production, we must request a small increase in State-supplied resources.

The tables on the next several pages break down our food reserves by category and hydro required to continue production in the coming year. We have no hydro reserves.

# 1

---

I haven't dreamed since my release. The first few nights, I'd wake up every hour on the hour, startled by a change in the light, or nothing at all. I've been sleeping longer the past two weeks, but still no dreams. Not real ones, anyway. Sometimes, I'm standing in a field of mist. I look around, but the mist is so thick I can't even see myself.

Tonight, I followed the same routine before bed as I have the last three weeks. Check locks. Shower. Brush teeth. Check locks again. The psychiatrist they're making me visit says I'm developing a healthy routine. The consistency will help me get more sleep. She's been right about that so far. When I told her about the mist, she told me, "Good, good. We're making progress." It didn't matter that there wasn't anything else in the dream—the mist itself was a dream and my own way of processing what happened to me. She's wrong.

I release my thoughts for the day and inhale deeply, relaxing as much as I can in the too-soft bed in my apartment. *Breathe out. Breathe in. Breathe...*

*The mist sends its heavy green tendrils through my mind, trapping me in sleep. I'm dreaming. It imprisons me in my own mind while I'm trying to rest, keeping me lucid, teasing me. The mist is hiding something from me.*

*Tonight's different. Though I still can't see anything, there's a sound.*

*Gravel crunches under light footfalls. Someone is trying to be quiet, but the stones betray them. I can't move, and I wouldn't if I could. I have to know what's going on. The sound grows louder—closer—but then it disappears. I'd groan in frustration, but apparently I can't even make a sound in this dreamscape.*

*Through the cool mist, someone's breath warms the back of my neck.*

*"Run."*

My eyes snap open. The sound from my dream is down the hall and all around me. Heavy boots rhythmically strike the floor, shuffling into some kind of formation. I throw back the covers and tiptoe to the window. Easing up the sash, I peer to the ground. Guards, everywhere, patrolling like ants on a cake crumb.

I crawl onto the fire escape and lower the window behind me. I won't look over the edge. *I'm on ground level. I'm on ground level.* I try to believe the lie so I can get out of here. Flattening myself against the building, I sidestep to the edge of the iron landing. They'll be monitoring the bottom of the ladder, so I need to find another way out. I climb over the side of the platform and find a toehold in the crumbling decorative molding. I test it as best I can, unsure if it will support my weight. *Too high, too high, go back!*

Screams startle me from my hesitation, and the percussive bang from a flash grenade goes off somewhere inside the building. My instinct to flee conquers fear. I take my chance and scurry to the corner, heaving myself around the wall to the other side. My grip is death-tight and, luckily, the wall bears my weight.

*Don't look down.* My resolve weakens as the old mortar crumbles under one of my hands. People shout below. I sneak a peek. The guards are busy chasing hordes of residents streaming from the exits. More guards follow, and the cacophony of their orders carries over the screams.

One of the emerging guards yells to the team behind the building. "She wasn't there. Someone must've tipped her off."

"Clear the area."

"Are the civilians out?"

"Eh, if they're still hiding in the building, they're acceptable casualties."

They're going to blow the building. I don't know how I know it, but I do. I shimmy back to the fire escape and head down five flights as quickly and quietly as I can. I want to go faster, but I'm fighting myself every inch I descend. *They're just stairs. Pretend you're inside the building.* I'll deal with the guards if I have to, but I've got to seek cover as soon as possible. Fourth floor. Third. Second.

The leader starts a countdown. "Five, four, three..."

I'm out of time. I fling myself over the edge toward the outline of a hulking dumpster below. A couple of heavy black bags break my fall, their contents launch skyward at the same time an explosion rattles the sides of my new metal cage. Clouds of dust and debris gather overhead. They're smaller than I expect.

"Move out."

Boots march away. I'm lying on a bed of empty hydropacks and Nutripaste wrappers. The corners of the cartons poke me, but I don't dare shift my weight. I can't make a sound. The vestiges of the Nutripaste coat me with sticky, smelly vital nutrients. The coating glues the odds and ends of special rations to me in a disgusting stew. Some rotten celery stalks. Tomato tops. Bread some rich slob made and couldn't be bothered to eat before it went moldy. I breathe through my mouth for the next fifteen minutes, then pull myself out of the garbage.

The imposing giant of my building still stands, to my surprise, but it has not made it out unscathed. In the side, right where my apartment used to be, a gaping hole opens into the night. The remnants of my tattered bedsheets flap in the cool evening air like a flag of surrender.

I ALMOST WISH for rain to scrub the stench of sour milk and rotting meat from me, before dissolving me into a giant puddle of goo and making me one with the garbage itself. The air is unusually cold for the season of growth, and the dampness from the decay I've inadvertently bathed in intensifies the cold. I've been wandering around for the last two hours, sticking to the side streets, staying in the shadows. I roll my shoulders, and the left one contracts. Garbage is not as soft as it seems, and this chill isn't helping. For once, I'm glad I sleep in my boots. My feet are the only part of me with some approximation of warmth.

At the end of the road, a streetboard glows yellow and orange. Mom, Dad, and a kid eating a cozy dinner at a round table. The meatloaf in the center explodes with a shower of sparks that align to form words: *Protecting your lifestyle for the last seventy-four years.* The image transitions to a group shot of guards proudly saluting.

No one can remember a time without the guards, and no one alive remembers the uprising they were created in response to. We get snippets in school, or from stories told by our parents, as told to them by their parents and back. I've heard variations on the story from all my foster moms—at least the ones who cared enough to tuck me into bed.

The world's still an unequal place, and it's a guard's job to preserve and protect everyone from those who would take too much. Every year, The State taps a certain number of citizens to become guards. How many they need changes, but the tapping is always the same. Guards keep the peace in each of the sectors to make sure that no sector attacks the others. Our sector seems to have gotten poorer over the seventeen years of my life. Another sector was hoarding their resources, but The State put a stop to it through the guards. That's why you never guard your own sector once you're tapped. You'd have too much of a stake in the game, and too many reasons to look the other way. The State shuffles everybody up when you're in service.

I can't remember what sector I served in, or anything else about my service. All I know is what the doctors told me: there was some kind of explosion or something, and I have partial amnesia. Everything between my tapping up until my release from duty is gone. I remember the scratchy industrial linens when I woke up, the cool sterile blue of the training quarter's health center light, the harsh antiseptic scent of cleansers stinging my nostrils. They asked me what I remembered. I told them I remembered being in school and being tapped, but that was all. They released me—I'm one of the few who ever qualified for a medical release—and I came back to my own sector.

They've been watching me ever since.

I can't find shelter tonight. For some reason, the guards are after me—that much is clear from the very targeted explosion in my building—and I can't book a hotel room without giving ID and putting a blinking red arrow up that says "target's here, guys." The best I can do is keep away from them tonight. The anklet they're using to track me isn't accurate to more than a block or two. In the morning, there should be enough people on the street that they won't be able to do anything overt to me. The State won't want to disrupt the illusion of normal life that daytime brings. It's the darkness that's dangerous.

## 2

The mist is back. In a sense, the green hazy blanket comforts me because I know I'm dreaming. My body is curled up in an alley service entrance ten blocks from my former apartment. My mind is stuck in this mist.

I blink hard, but the mist is still there. It stings my eyes, and I bring a hand up to rub it away. This is new. My body obeys my commands. Tentatively, I take a step forward. Fear and relief intermingle as I start to navigate this dreamscape. My steps are hesitant, and I teeter like a small child learning to walk a balance beam.

"Ohio." I exhale. Shaking off nerves, I walk with more confidence than I feel. This is my head. My world. I can do this. I walk for what feels like hours, but the mist is unchanging. For all I know, I'm walking in circles.

Boom. A rifle report cracks through the mist and echoes in the empty space. Instinctively, I hit the ground.

A man's voice barks in the distance. "Don't be afraid to unload on them. You've got plenty of ammo, and they breed like rats."

A cacophony of booms and cracks fills my mind, and I'm jolted awake, again, just as I'm starting to experience something in this nothingness.

Wind blows under the awning, chilling my already damp body. Thunder rumbles in the distance, threatening deadly rain. The gray skyline of the sector is tinged with deep purple pre-dawn light. I'm warm, warmer than I should be, but I start to shiver. Pulling my legs in, I ball myself up by the wall of the building and wonder what to do next. One thought replays itself over and over in my mind, but I can't even find the strength to stand.

*Go home, Bree.*

"I THINK SHE'S WAKING."

"Rise and shine, young one. Time and tide wait for no man—"

"No person."

"It's a figure of speech."

"I know that, dear, but that doesn't make it right."

The effort to lift my eyelids is exhausting. When I finally open my eyes, the room is grainy, like a picture from an antique book that's faded in places. I'd almost think it was the mist, but there are far too many sounds for that.

"Up and at 'em, kiddo."

Until it's unceremoniously yanked away, I had no idea I was covered with a blanket. I'm in a bed. I don't stink of garbage anymore. The room is bright with artificial light, and the first thing that strikes me is that there are no windows. I'm reflexively checking for exits, and the only one is a roughhewn door blocked by the two oldest people I've ever seen in my life. They must be pushing sixty-five. No one lives that long in this sector.

"Let me out," is the first thing I say to them, followed quickly in priority order by "Where am I? Who are you?"

The silver haired woman peers at me over wireframe glasses. "Funny, we've been wondering the same thing about you."

"But first, breakfast." The man smiles brightly, well, as brightly as his old yellowed teeth will let him.

He's got glasses, too, but his are black plasticine. He whips out a cracked tray with a few broken crackers and some kind of gray-brown protein paste that matches the color of his old man hair. His smile fades a little when I don't touch the tray for several seconds. Instead of eating, I try to swing my legs down out of the bed. If I move fast enough, maybe I can rush around them for the door. My legs barely obey me, and the best I can do is sit on the edge of the bed. The old guy takes this as acceptance and pushes the tray closer to me. I stare at him.

My stomach growls, breaking our odd standoff. He lets out a laugh and quirks an unkempt eyebrow.

"Here, I'll join you. You can call me the Professor." He winks at the woman.

Taking a cracker with his veiny wrinkled hand, he scoops some of the gunk in his mouth. For a second, he bends his knees like he's going to sit down with me on the bed, but my death stare keeps him standing.

"And I'm Doc," the woman laughs a tinkling laugh that makes her silver hair rustle like wind chimes. She winks back at the Professor like she's making some kind of private joke. "And you are?"

My stomach growls again. Without breaking eye contact with the man, I take a cracker and smear some paste on it. I crunch down, and warm richness fills my mouth, sticking to my teeth and tongue. I have trouble swallowing, but neither of us is dead from whatever that tasty gross mess is.

The man, excuse me, the Professor, smiles again, reading my face. "Sticks to your ribs as much as your mouth."

I unglue my tongue. "What is it?"

"Something like peanut butter."

My blank response urges him on.

"Peanuts were a crop grown a little south of here. Kind of like a bean, kind of like a pea. Delicious when roasted."

The salty, slightly smoky flavor rolling around in my mouth tastes nothing like peas, though I guess it feels kind of like a gritty sticky oil. Maybe that's the butter part.

"Best accompanied by a cold glass of milk, but this will have to do."

He produces a bottle of soy milk, sealed, and drops it on the bed. I crack the cap and guzzle it.

"Easy there," the woman—Doc—says. "We don't know how long you were out."

"How about you tell us what happened and why guards were circling the block where we found you?"

"I—I don't know." I stare into the empty soy milk bottle as though it contained my memories.

The Professor laughs. "Keeps her cards close to the vest, this one."

"Cards?" I'm confused.

Doc's stern but kindly eyes narrow at me. "Hmmm. I think we have something to show you."

The Professor offers me his arm. "Milady."

I'm at their mercy, so I play along. I lean more heavily on his arm than I'd like to admit, but he doesn't flinch. I want out of this room. We shuffle down a dark hall, small glowing bowls periodically showing the way. The light is so dim, I'd probably trip if not for the old guy's surprisingly strong arm. Doc leads the way at a sedate but purposeful pace. Of the two of them, she seems to be the one in control. I don't know why that matters to me, but for some reason, it does.

**3**

Doc opens a heavy metal door. "Welcome to the war room."

Shrugging off the Professor's arm, I walk unsteadily across the space.

The war room is a weird mix of old person's living room and office. I bypass a ratty orange couch and some armchairs along one wall and sit in a hard metal chair at a long conference table. Easier to bolt from a chair than a couch so old it might swallow you. Doc and the Professor follow suit and sit in the chairs across the table from me.

Giant screens fill one wall in three rows, some tilted at angles so their images almost reflect on one another. A huge black box with a really loud fan whirs underneath a small desk with a giant keyboard.

"It's modelled after The State's watch rooms," the Professor explains.

The screens at the top are labelled with a hand-written sign that says only "The Network." A bunch of words run across the top and sides of the screen in an incomprehensibly organized and specific way. I can appreciate the structure, but it doesn't seem entirely useful. The screens in the center are maps with a bunch of dots, and the ones at the edges and on the bottom seem to show live feeds from security cameras around the sector. The camera views shift periodically, but I can't tell who's changing them.

The technology looks really impressive and really illegal, and I continue to wonder what I've stumbled into here. They've given me a few minutes to take it all in but not really provided anything by way of explanation. Clearly, they're not with The State. And since The State's sent guards after me, I'm not with The State. Maybe this Doc, the Professor, and I are on the same side. Maybe they can help me figure out what's happening to me. Or at least fill me in on what side I'm supposed to be on.

"So, now that we've shown you something of ours, how about letting us in? Why were the guards after you?"

The Professor might be right. Maybe I should let them in. "I really don't know."

He taps one side of his nose with a long finger, "That, my dear, may be entirely why they're after you. You know something. They know you know something. But you don't know what you know."

I can't resist playing along with a smirk. "What if what you think they know I know isn't something that I actually know at all?"

The Professor laughs and pats me on the head like I'm a puppy who's done a party trick. I shrug out from under his offending hand.

Doc grimaces. "Walk us through your routine."

"I get up from bed at my now nonexistent apartment, look for a nonexistent job, go to my actually existing shrink, grab a cava and keep looking for a job, and go back home."

"Every day?" Doc asks.

I nod.

"Lather, rinse, repeat," the Professor says.

Doc shoots him a sideways glance as though her eyes are telling him to shut up. He cowers a little under that stare.

"Who's your psychologist?" she asks.

"Dr. Ableworth. Mid-twenties, about 5'3", 140 pounds or so. Could be pretty if she didn't have a pencil shoved up her spine." The pertinent details rattle off my tongue, though no one probably cares about them.

"When's your next appointment?"

"Noon tomorrow. Today?" I scan the walls for a clock. "What time is it?"

Doc looks at her watch for longer than necessary, pursing her lips in thought. "Ten thirty in the morning. You'd better get going to that appointment. I don't think it would do you well to miss it."

"But the guards—"

"We'll do some digging and get back in touch with you. In the meantime, play dumb at your appointment. Be honest about what you saw but nothing else. Nothing about here."

Obviously their war room is highly illegal, and they're trusting me with knowledge about it, for whatever reason. Maybe they want something from me. But I want something from them, too. I have to figure out what happened to me last year. Maybe they can help me get to the bottom of it. Gwock knows the shrink has been useless.

"How do I get out of here?"

"The Professor will take you," Doc says.

He gallantly offers me his arm yet again. "Mademoiselle?"

*Weirdo.* I take it, mostly because I'm feeling unsteady. His old wrinkled eyes droop with sadness.

"Sorry, Charlie."

"My name's not—"

Something pricks me in the back of my neck. My vision fades, and I have the sensation of being hoisted over a shoulder before my world goes completely dark. Can't even trust an anti-State, kindly old gray-hair.

# 4

I wake up in an alley, the rumble and beep of a delivery truck warning me to leave my temporary home and get moving. I stumble into an open doorway, and the truck bounces over my former sleeping area. My legs aren't working quite right.

"Missouri!" I yell at the sky and The State.

There used to be a time when there were a lot of states, spread out over a huge area. Now, there's only the one. The State. People used to be different, and grouped by their differences, and they lived in their states. They prayed to different gods like the Voice Mail and her sacred son, the tube videos, and the holy gwockamoly. The gods left after the Incident. Most of us don't pray anymore, and we curse the gods of our ancestors. If some do worship, they pray to time: to the times when there were differences, the half-remembered, mangled names of states their whispered supplications: *Massets, Marylan, O, home!*

"Missouri." I try to massage feeling back into my cramped muscles and remember how I got here.

Gradually, the events from last night filter into my foggy mind. The guards at my apartment, breaking down my door and destroying the room. Falling asleep in this alley. Meeting Doc and the Professor, and thinking that they might be allies before they drugged—

"Son of the VM!" I'm going to be late for my State-mandated appointment.

Fury at Doc and the Professor fuel my stride, and instead of being late, I get to the shrink's office twenty minutes early. I bet they wanted me to think it was all a dream, but I don't dream anymore. Fooled them, the old corpses. *But they fooled you, too. They got you in there and out of there, and you couldn't do a gwocking thing about it.*

The receptionist isn't even at the desk, that's how early I am. Dr. Ableworth comes out and scribbles on a paper, muttering a quick hello.

"I can wait. Shouldn't you be in with another patient?"

She mumbles something about finishing early and takes me right back to her office. She seems rushed for someone who's running ahead of schedule, fixing her hair in the hallway on the way back.

"I don't mind waiting until time. It's no problem."

"No, no, it's fine." She rummages around in her desk for note-taking supplies.

We sit down in her office. Then the standoff begins.

The rhythmic tapping of her pencil on the edge of a yellow notepad has a calming effect on me, at first. Its steady pace, heartbeat-like, is a metronome I can sync my breathing with. Dr. Ableworth stares at me, willing me to say something. I squirm a little on the leather sofa, stopping when it squeaks under me. *Focus on the tapping, Bree. Breathe. When being interrogated, stay silent.* The thought sounds like someone else's in my mind.

We're about three minutes into the silence now, and I can tell Dr. Ableworth is losing patience with me. She breaks.

"What's happened to you?"

I give in, cautious. "What do you mean *happened*?"

"You're different today. You usually talk to me." Her body is still, but her squinty pissed-off eyes betray her agitation.

A hundred thoughts pass through my mind each time she taps the pencil. How normal is normal? What does she know? How should I feel about what I think she knows but may not know?

"I don't know where to start," I say to fill the space she's left for me in between the incessant pencil wagging.

"How about you start with where you were last night."

And I know she knows. She knows about the raid. She doesn't know about Doc and the Professor—she's fishing for that.

"I was out walking, mostly."

The pencil stops. She settles back in her chair, and her face has lost a little of the pinched-pissed look. "Walking," she repeats, an invitation to continue.

"Yeah. I was walking, and I sat down someplace to think, and next thing I know I'm awake and it's time to—"

"Where?"

"—come here. Where was I walking?"

She ignores me and follows immediately with another question. "So you never went home?"

She could be working for anyone, and the urge to conceal is strong. I trust my gut. "No, I fell asleep on some random stoop."

"That's not healthy." Her judgement is sounding less and less shrink-like and more and more...something else-like.

"I was fine. It was chilly, but I was fine."

"You have a perfectly good apartment to sleep in."

She's watching me carefully, watching my reaction to her mentioning my apartment. I've got to sell this, play it up. I lean forward, and my shoulders droop. I shield my eyes with my hand so she can't see me too clearly.

"It's hard, you know? I'm trying to be tough, but I couldn't sleep. I mean, I started to, but the dreams. Not having them keeps me up like a little baby. Nightmares would be better than that green nothingness." I sneak a peek at her, and she's buying my act. It's not hard for me to act tough. Harder to show weakness, even pretend.

"Are you starting to see anything in your dreams?"

I pause, for maybe a half second too long. Her finger inches toward the pencil.

I blurt, "I see the mist. That's all."

"I can give you something to take the edge off. Help you to stay asleep."

"I'm not sure about medication." My hesitation is real, but I have to play this right. I finally look at her and allow my words the barest hint of a quiver. "Maybe it would help."

"Excellent." She smiles as she grabs a pad from her desk and scrawls something on it. "You can pick this up from the pharmco at 28th and Hill. They're pretty quick, and there's a nice park across the street if you want to do some walking."

"What I really need is a cup of cava." No lies this time. I'm exhausted after the late night raid, and then meeting Doc and the Professor.

"There's a cava shop near there as well."

"Thanks." I try to make my eyes well with tears, but they don't obey. Probably for the best.

"Are you okay?"

I blanch, but I don't think she's figured out my game. "Yeah. I mean, I guess so."

She rips off the scrip and hands it to me. "Same time tomorrow. Let's check back in about your sleep. I don't want you letting this go too long."

"No problem." I give her a grin and all but run out of the office.

"Bree." Her calling my name doesn't stop me so much as the resumed pencil tapping.

I feel like she's pointing a gun at my back. I have to make

myself keep my arms down at my sides rather than raising them in surrender as I turn back to her.

"Yeah?"

She cocks her head. "Enjoy the cava."

"Yeah." I skedaddle out of there as quick as I can without further raising her suspicions.

## 5

I sit by the glass window sipping from a steaming mug, watching the passersby. The glass isn't really glass—too breakable—but the material is clearish. Everyone hurries around, heads down, their darkly blurred outlines blending in to the shadows they cast on the crumbling pavement. The wind buffets a page of the sheets down the street. I can't make out the headline nor any images. Not that those pieces of the propaganda machine are worth reading.

I've angled myself in the corner of the shop. I've got the useless Jobs section in front of me, but I barely read it. I can see the customers reading comics and other shorts at their tables, the people outside through the window, and the door. The wall is reassuring at my back, but I'm still nervous, scanning for a second set of doors or some other egress.

Something's not right with me. Normal people don't think this way, and I have no idea why I do. The hair on the back of my neck has been glued upright. I am wary and constantly alert. I don't know what else to do, so my subconscious becomes my conscious, and I scan.

The tall guy reading the sheet runs his hand through his hair, knocking his glasses askew: not a threat. The woman muttering to herself, jiggling her leg and pitching her voice low to avoid anyone else overhearing: not a threat, at least not to me. The guy wiping down the counter—

A man flops into the chair across from me. "Hiya Bree."

"Gwock!" I sputter, knocking my chin against my cup. The hot liquid arcs and scalds my cheek and arm, but I barely register it. I'm on my feet in an instant and bring my hands up in a guard.

"Bree, it's me. 'Laska, man. Chill."

He's familiar, but my adrenaline makes swiss cheese out of my rational brain. I try to place him while the other patrons stare at me. Not what I want right now.

I shake my scalded hand as a kind of explanation. "Burnt myself. Cava's hot." I lamely lower myself into my seat. Everybody goes back to their business. Tall sheets guy never even looked up in the first place.

This guy laughs a little and gestures toward his goatee then grabs one of the twists of hair framing his face like a beaded curtain. "I probably look a little different than the last time you saw me." His face sobers. "Before the tapping."

He shifts in his seat. The chair tilts, and he catches himself right before he falls to the floor. "Close one," he mutters.

"Spyder?" I say his name as a question.

The guy in front of me is as awkward as the kid I grew up with, but this guy almost looks like a man. I take a closer look at his scraggly facial hair and realize he's further from a man than I thought.

"You remember!" Spyder sounds delighted.

"Of course I remember, idiot, we only went to school together for like four years."

"Four years, three months, and four days. Well, I guess it depends on if you count a school year as a full year. Maybe we should just go by days. With holidays and both times I was sick—you never got sick—782 days."

I smile, the first real smile I can remember giving in the VM knows how long. He may look a little older, but his personality is the same. "You haven't changed."

The tips of his ears turn coral. "Yeah."

"What brings you around this stone of the mountain?"

Spyder stares at me intently, almost as though he were puzzling something out. His awkwardness is kind of charming— he always geeked out over comps in school but never really people so much. Unless they were into comps.

"Our, uh, mutual friends asked me to track you down."

My heart starts to race in my chest. I went to high school with Spyder when I was with the Blanks. They were all set to adopt me when I was selected in the lottery and auto-aged out due to tapping. I don't want them drawn into this, especially not Em, my foster sister.

"You need to leave."

"It's cool—they just want to see you again."

I would like nothing more than to go back to them and pretend I never got tapped. "I can't." I can't go back when someone is after me. "I'm not sure what's happening to me, but you have to trust me, Spyder. Please."

The tall guy reading the sheets stiffens a little and raises his arm over his head in a weird jerky stretch.

My breath catches. "*Down!*"

Glass arcs over us, shards pelting us in a deadly rain. Screams and spilled drinks continue the chaos. Spyder and I lock eyes under the table for a fraction of a second. Metal cans clatter to the floor.

The cava shop fills with smoke, and guards pour in from the entrance and kitchens.

"*Go! Go! Go!*" I shout in unison with their squad leader, though they're heading in, and we've got to get the gwock out. I leap from under the table and use it as a springboard to vault through the open window.

Boots pound like drums, the glass under them a gravelly counterpoint, following their leader's command. My throat is thick as I run, tasting the acrid smoke. My mind is clear in the chaos, running through a series of ordered questions without breaking my stride: *Where do I go? Is there cover? Are they following me?* I run past a series of crumbling buildings and turn down the first alley I find.

In my periphery, a streak of denim blue and black gains on me.

"Bree," Spyder stops me midway through the alley. "Quick, put this on your ankle monitor."

He holds out an adhesive strip that looks like a cartoon vomited on it. I don't question him but apply the freaky decal to my anklet.

"Follow me." He jumps impossibly high and uses his weight to pull down the ladder on a fire escape. I climb after him as quickly as I can. When we reach the landing, he pulls the ladder up after us.

"Quietly," he says.

We continue climbing upward, like the reverse of last night when the guards came to my apartment building. I hope I don't end up in a trash heap again. He's much faster than I am, and not just because I hate climbing in this stupid upward direction. He's pretty fit. The metal ladder creaks, sounding its age out into the day, regardless of how lightly we step.

Spyder pauses and thrusts his hand back at me in the universal signal to stop. Not a second too soon, as two guards round into the alleyway. A blonde female—petite, less than 5'5", maybe 115; hard to judge up here—leads the way.

"She's got to be around here somewhere," she says to her patrol partner—male, average height, about two-thirds heavier than she is.

I risk shifting my weight to look up at Spyder. The metal stays silent. He puts a finger to his lips.

*She*, the female guard said, not *they*. They're not after Spyder —they may not even realize he's here. Once again, the guards are trying to capture me. Or worse.

The pair of guards halfheartedly patrol the alley, kicking at trashcans and nudging piles of detritus—tattered cloth, shredded plastic, and stray pieces of the sheets—that seem to collect in the pockets of potholes and crumbling architecture. These buildings were beautiful once, before the wars, or even longer ago. The columns have crumbled, the rose lintels rotted. All that's left are me and Spyder, strange gargoyles in our ghostly city.

My life is at risk, and my fingers burn in resistance to this contemplative stillness, but being stationary is the smart move. The tingle spreads to my shoulders. Only two of them. I could take them. I know I could. The woman breaks out a radio.

"Nothing here except a pile of trash. No sign of a rat."

What's that supposed to mean?

Garbled noises on the radio.

"Did you get that?" the woman asks her partner.

"No clue. Probably saying that some other team got her. Gwocking traitor. I hope she doesn't make it back to HQ. This sector's infested with 'em. Dirty rats."

They laugh.

That word, again. It bothers me worse than them calling me a traitor, like an itch between my shoulder blades, in just the right place that I can't scratch it. I roll my shoulders, and my hand slips on the metal bar. With the hollow whisper of skin on metal, the laughter stops.

"Sorry, Spyder," I whisper.

I unhook the ladder, and our combined weight sends it clanking down into the alley. I drop the last few feet to the ground.

I roll into a crouch, but the element of surprise is not quite on my side. The man is slightly slack jawed, but the woman is ready for me. I spin around behind the man, taking his knee as I go. The pop is loud; his scream, louder.

"Perry!" The woman sounds like she's more pissed that the man got taken down than worried about his health.

I keep Perry's body between me and the woman. I'm ready for her.

She doesn't come after me right away. We move in parallel for a few steps, keeping the same distance between us, readying ourselves for battle. A hiss of static penetrates the tension. Without breaking eye contact, she raises her radio and says firmly, "Man down, I have—"

I lunge at her, but I'm too late. More will come soon. I yank the radio from her hands and slam it into her jaw with a satisfying crunch of plastic and metal on bone. She sways on her feet. I slide my hand around her neck and turn her head upwards. She's now totally off balance. With my hand on her opposite hip, I spin her into the ground, taking out her knee along the way. They're both down now, but the woman is tougher than her partner. She reaches for something, and I pin her hand, snapping a couple of fingers. That ought to do it.

I scramble back to the ladder. Spyder's still at the top, and he's hugging himself in some weird defensive posture. I hope I didn't scare him too badly. Shouts ring out from around the corner, and a phalanx of guards enters the alleyway.

Orders are flying, and I climb.

"*Stop!*"

The telltale whine of a weapon charging urges me on. *Stupid, stupid, stupid.* My chant sets the tempo for the climb. But I know it's no good. They have the range, and I'm a gwocking rat in a cage. I stop climbing and do a quick scan. The weapon is ready and pointed in my direction. If I jump at just the right time, at just the right angle, I can avoid the blast and maybe take a few of them out. I'm not that high. I could maybe even get away.

The weapon fires, and I leap toward four guards clustered just west of the ladder. The shot misses, and I'm bracing for an impact that never comes.

My shoulder is wrenched from its socket as something, someone, catches me and swings me over the alley. We swing up now, up, up. I'm tracking the guards below as they scramble to change position when I'm hoisted over the edge of the roof of a neighboring building. I finally have a chance to look at my rescuer: Spyder. He gives me an uncharacteristic wink as he unhooks a line from a harness he wrapped around himself at some point.

"Don't leave home without it. Climb on." He points to his back. "I've got lines rigged up for a ways. Let's get you out of here."

I don't even have time to be afraid of how high we are. The guards know where we are. I scramble on his back like a kid, and I can't tell if I'm annoyed because he's treating me like one or if I'm just annoyed with myself for getting guards on us in the first place. I put my hands on his shoulders, ready for my piggy back ride. He takes one of my hands and wraps it around his chest. I do the other myself. Adrenaline and effort have made him warm, and he smells like cava and cinnamon. I grab my own elbows to secure the hold—he's still got that narrow geek body.

"Trust me," he says.

I do, and we fly.

The high from fighting quickly wears off as Spyder swings me through the air from building to building, rope to rope. *Are we done yet? We're too high. The ground.* The ground is so far away, but it shouldn't get closer. I should be on the ground. *Too fast, too fast. Are we done yet? I'm going to puke. I'm going to puke.* I close my eyes. Breathe. *Don't puke. Don't puke. Don't puke. By the VM, are we gwocking there yet?* Breathe. *No, wait don't puke. Don't—*

We land on some roof, and Spyder takes a few quick steps forward. The momentum carries him toward the edge. I let go of him and roll sideways. He looks back, surprise on his face as he disappears over the edge without me.

I puke.

In less than a minute, he swings back over the edge, coming from a different direction. I don't even want to know how he made the circuit. Stepping away from the lunch I left on the ground, I hold up my hands as a barrier between us.

"Thanks for the ride, but I'm done."

"We're not there yet."

"I'm where I'm going."

"Where's that?"

I cross my arms over my chest. "Here."

"And where's 'here'?" He mimics me. The jerk.

"Doesn't matter. I've got to double back anyway."

"Double back? Double back to what?"

I don't answer him. Instead, I walk closer to the edge of the roof, trying to get my bearings and figure out where we've ended up in the sector. We're high. I want to see more of what's below, but I can't force my feet any closer to the open air that drops straight to the hard, hard pavement below.

"I got you out of there, and now you want to . . . what? Go back and mix it up with twenty guards? Get yourself killed?"

"I have to know why they're after me."

"What are you going to do, beat them up then ask their broken bodies, 'Please, can you tell me why you're chasing me?' That makes a lot of sense. Anyway, you seemed to have a pretty good idea of what was going on in the cava shop. So let's keep going."

"You've got a lot of nerve."

"I've got a job to do." He's in my face like he wants to get physical. "So let's get going."

"I'm done. I'm tired of this. I'm going to go find out what's going on. And if you don't step back, you're going to end up like the two guards back there. I swear I don't care what you did to help me."

And just like that, Spyder gives up. Like someone shined a light on his namesake, he scurries for a dark corner.

"I'm sorry," he says more like a breath than words, slouching, defeated. "I can't make you do anything you don't want to do."

"Thank you for your help." I'm stiff, formal. The easy camaraderie between us was so quickly destroyed. "Why don't you go program some comps or something. Leave the fighting to people who can handle it." I don't know why I said that.

*Don't trust your opponent, even when he's down. You must destroy him.*

"Whatever. I'll tell Doc you can't make it." He vaults over the edge into nothing.

Doc? I thought he was with the Blanks, but did he mean Doc and the Professor sent him to look for me? I lean over the edge, battling the dizzying height long enough to croak out a weak, "Spyder, wait," before collapsing back on the safety of the roof.

Great. How do I get down from here?

# 6

I've always hated health centers, but right now it's the best place for me to find information on why the guards were after me. The whir of machines and rhythmic beeps provide cover for me as I make my way down the hallway.

I swipe a folder from the door and peek at the name. *Gynnifer Evans.* I flip through it briefly while no one is around, then continue down the hall. The smell to this place is so strong I taste it—like cleaning fluid that's been sprayed in layers on itself, slightly different scents every time, so thick the fumes seem to grow on my tongue. It's so clean, it's dirty. The walls are a light olive, not so sterile as the scent, but just the right shade to hide all but the bloodiest of stains.

I can't remember too much of the last time I was in a real health center. It was my last visit to the Electrician—I was maybe eleven, twelve? Right before I ended up with the Blanks. The building is designed to be forgettable. But I can't forget him.

Besides tapping us for service in the guards, the other thing The State does is monitor our locations, all day every day. Rich parents have their kids chipped. That way, they have the illusion of freedom, even when they're being monitored. The rest of us wear these clunky bracelets around our ankles.

When you're a kid, they're especially annoying. You bump against them all the time, and they get tight—you have to visit the Electrician to have them re-sized or order the next size up.

The anklets are subsidized by The State. They used to make us pay for them, but some parents couldn't afford it. The anklets would cut off their kid's circulation, and their feet would get infected. Some of them had the infected foot cut off, but mostly they just died. So now The State pays, and everybody's happy.

I stopped growing about two years ago, so I shouldn't have to visit the Electrician again unless I get fat or have a kid of my own. That guy gave me the creeps. He's tall and has a potbelly with greasy handprints all over his shirt. He smells of rancid meat, and he always tried to be alone with me, even when I was a real baby. Sometimes, my foster moms would protect me. They knew. If I never see him again, it will be too soon.

*"We're going to pop the old one off, and then we'll pop the new one on."* He smiled at me. *"How does that sound?"*

*Even then, I knew I didn't have a choice. I nodded.*

*"We've grown a lot, and this has gotten pretty tight."* He used a screwdriver, a key, and some kind of laser-y looking device to open the initial lock. A port opened, and he plugged a wire into it, then typed some things into his comp.

*"We'll feel much more comfortable with the new one on, won't we?"*

*I nodded.*

*He took off the old anklet and rubbed slow circles on my foot. "Let's just check our circulation. We've grown so much."*

*Even then, I knew I didn't have a choice.*

A loud clatter of metal from around the corner startles me. I shake off the memories and round the corner, hoping for the best.

A nurse in a blue uniform squats on the floor surrounded by meal trays. She's older than me—not a gray-hair by any means but as close as I've seen these days. Not young enough to be by the book and not so worn she doesn't care. Perfect.

"Let me help." I squat next to her and pile the remnants of food and flatware onto the cart.

"Thanks," she says with a warm smile.

We quickly finish the work, and she starts to wheel the cart away.

"Hey," I say. "Maybe you can help me."

"What can I do for you?"

"I'm a little lost. My brother's here, but I can't find the room, and I don't want to go all the way back downstairs."

"What's the room number?"

"I think it had a two in it. Maybe you've seen him, though. Perry." I describe the male guard I took down a few hours ago.

Her eyes narrow. She's catching on. Play it right, Bree. Play it right.

"And he's a guard." I finish, my voice quavering a little.

"Civilians are not allowed access to the military component of this health center." Her voice is as crisp as the creases in her starched white cap, but I can see the uncertainty in her expression.

I try to turn on the tears. My eyes well, but I can't cry. I hope my display is enough.

"I'm sorry. He's not my brother. He's my fiancé. We met when he got stationed here. His unit sent a message to let me know he was hurt, but they wouldn't tell me anything. I just have to see him and make sure he's okay. I'm sorry I lied. I'm sorry." I manage to squeeze a tear out.

The nurse looks around the hall. I've got her.

"Come with me." She opens a wooden door and takes me down a side corridor. We stop in front of a big metal door with a heavy latch and a scanner. "Shift change is in fifteen minutes, which is always a little chaotic."

I know. That's what I'm counting on.

"Be out in ten, or I can't say what they'll do to you." She swipes her badge, and the door pops open. "I think yours is the first door on the left. Ten minutes, remember."

I pitch my voice higher with false brightness. "Thank you. Thank you so much!" Inwardly cringing, I give her a hug, and I try not to be too stiff about it.

She pulls away. "Nine and a half minutes," she says with a whisper and a wink.

Oh, yes, we're the best of friends.

"Thank you," I say, and I mean it.

She disappears on the other side of the metal door, and I take a quick look around. I spot the nurses' station not too far from a set of thick glass doors that must be the main ones. They're probably mirrored so folks on the other side can't see in, clear on this side so we can see out. There are a ton of nurses milling around, talking to each other and scrawling on whiteboards. I try to match their body language and walk with purpose down the hall to the first door. They shouldn't even notice me. I am one with them in rhythm.

The door is open, and a curtain is drawn around the bed. I duck into the bathroom, waiting.

I haven't really planned out what comes next.

A phone rings in the room.

"Hello?" The guard's voice is slow and sleepy, the result of rest and painkillers.

"Yeah, the little rat got me," he says. "I don't know what they did to her, but I've never seen anything like it. She dropped down and took me and Wynn out in seconds."

He laughs shortly. "Thanks for the heads up."

His voice changes completely. "Sir."

"Yes, sir." I can hear him wincing.

"No, sir."

"Sir."

"Yes, sir."

This isn't getting me anywhere.

I walk out of the bathroom and grab the phone from the weak guard who's too surprised to make a sound. The voice on the other end is male, deep, clipped and cold.

"If she comes anywhere near you, you are to contact me immediately. Do not engage. Do you understand? Soldier, do you understand?"

"What do you want with me?"

A moment of silence. "Well, hello. We knew you were in the area," he says with a weird note of amusement.

"Who are you?"

"Meet me and find out. Twenty-one hundred hours. The pathetic excuse for gardens downtown."

"Wait, what? What time?"

He pauses. "You're good. Tonight. Nine p.m. The gardens. Be there."

I'll meet him. I'll sneak out of this place and get some answers. If the nurses try to stop me, I'll play it lost and cool. *No worries, just visiting my friend Jen Evans. She's here for—*I didn't read that part of the folder on the door—*it's private.*

I toss the phone back to the guard. "Sorry about your knee."

SUNLIGHT FLOODS my room and I blink hard to shut it out. It burns through whatever mists of my dreams lingered and welcomes me to a new day.

I try to stand up to close the curtains and grab a few more peaceful minutes of sleep—VM, when was the last time I slept this well—when I realize I'm not at home. I'm in a rough gown, hooked up to some kind of IV. The rhythmic beeps on a monitor increase as my heart keeps time with my anxiety. Health center.

I don't know how I got here. The last thing I remember, I was —everything is gray. In my apartment? No. I was meeting someone. I don't know who. Not my doctor, someone else. I'd been somewhere, doing something, and I had to go meet someone—where? The work district? Maybe about a job?

A bang in the hall sends me into overdrive, and I leap to my feet, hand grasping the IV pole to steady myself or maybe to use as a weapon—I'm not sure.

A nurse cheerfully wheels in a clanking metal tray. "Rise and shine," she chirps. "You're already up, I see."

I don't hurt anywhere, but I must be a mess. Maybe they've got me on painkillers or something because I really feel fine. Maybe a little off balance but no pain.

"What happened?"

She laughs. "I think I'm supposed to ask you that."

I sit carefully on the edge of the bed and try to re-center.

"I can't remember."

"That's common with head injuries."

I don't find that reassuring. The nurse leaves the tray at the foot of my bed and comes around the side and checks the bag on my IV, then my vitals.

"You're doing well," she says. "You'll be out later this morning, I'm sure."

"But what happened?"

She sits next to me on the edge of the bed and leans toward me, almost whispering. "There have been a bunch of explosions in this sector in the last two days. Terrorists, they're saying in the sheets. You probably didn't know that before you came here. A bunch of you came in last night. They bussed you in from the blast zone."

"I don't remember." I'm calm, and the calmness feels strange. My brain is screaming at my body that I need to remember, but not remembering feels...normal.

"Your fiancé was discharged to military care last night, or I'd try to sneak a longer visit in for you."

Okay, that doesn't feel normal. "My *what*?"

"Oh, poor thing, you probably don't remember that either. You were here last night visiting your fiancé, before you went, well, wherever you went where you got blasted."

"I was supposed to meet up with somebody."

"Hey! Maybe you're remembering."

"Gynnifer Evans. No, that's not right." I have no idea who Gynnifer Evans is or why that name popped into my head.

"It'll come in time. Do you need transpo back home?"

"What sector am I in?"

I regret the question as soon as I ask it. Whatever medicine they're giving me must be making me loopy. No one travels between sectors anymore, except in service to The State. Why would I be in a different sector? Even I don't know. As far as I can remember, I've never been to another sector. The training grounds that I can't even remember are in the neutral zones between the sectors. But my memory is not the most reliable. The nurse looks at me strangely. Time to think fast.

"I'm a guard," I say, hoping my lie provides all the explanation she needs. It doesn't, but she helpfully fills in the blanks herself.

"Were you undercover chasing the terrorists? You weren't in uniform, or we'd have put you with the military patients." She claps a hand to her mouth. "I shouldn't have asked that. Please don't report me."

She's even given me an excuse not to provide more details in my lie. I may have lost more memories, but I'm lucky. "It's fine. What sector am I in?" I ask again.

"Sector Keystar. Do you need transpo to your base?"

I'm in my home sector, thank gwock. What was I doing here yesterday? "No, that's okay. I can make it."

"I'm sorry you don't remember your visit with your fiancé. You haven't seen him in so long."

I try to look dejected and figure out what the Kentucky is going on. "Yeah," is all I can say.

## 7

I'm discharged from the health center too late to make my therapy session, but I head there anyway. I have to go to an appointment every day, because—I can't remember why I have to go there every day, but I do. I did something. Or something happened to me. Maybe the doctor can help me remember why I'm forgetting. What I'm forgetting. I can't remember what I'm forgetting. I put my hands to my temples and try to massage the information back in.

The receptionist doesn't look up when I enter. "Can I help you?" she says.

"I'm Bree, I missed my appointment with Doctor—" I can't remember her last name. "With the doctor."

"Last name."

It takes me a minute to realize she means mine. "Oh. Carter."

She flips through a notebook, licking her finger with each page turn. Gross.

"Ms. Carter, you completed your course of therapy yesterday and have officially been discharged. Congratulations," she says with all the enthusiasm of a decorative plasticine plant.

"I don't understand. I don't remember that. Maybe I should be reevaluated."

"Ms. Carter, your course of therapy is complete at the request of The State. The notes on your file indicate you do not have sufficient funding to continue a private course of treatment. Have a nice day."

She presses a button on the side of her desk, and the auto door swings open behind me, ushering me out.

I walk home.

I should be upset, but instead I'm relieved. I'm trusting my gut here, since that's all I have without the memories of the last few days to guide me. My stomach churns when I try to fill in the bigger empty spots. I know I've been going to that doctor for weeks, so why can't I remember—him? Her? It feels right not to go, but it feels wrong not to remember.

My building is closed for renovations. A large plasticine sheet covers a gaping hole in the side. I guess the nurse was right about the terrorist attacks. I've got to find a new place to live, unless I've already found a place to live and I just can't remember where it is.

I ARRIVE at the front counter in a well-kept apartment building in the work district. As far as places to live go, this one's got to be outside my temporary housing allowance, but I have limited options. I don't even get a chance to open my mouth before the manicured attendant cuts me off.

"I'm sorry. We have nothing available presently." The man sniffs so hard, it practically lifts his giant head off of his body like a snobby helium balloon. Luckily the skinny black tie around his neck holds his blobby head in place for him.

I've been all over the sector trying to find a place to stay. At this point, I'll be sleeping on a stoop somewhere. My old building wouldn't even let me up to my room to pick up what little I own. It's fine, though. I'm used to being on my own with nothing. Feels familiar. Feels like home. I do need a place to sleep, though.

I try to puncture helium head. "Listing in the sheet says you have a vacancy."

"That has been filled. Welcome to *The Drake*." He greets the person behind me, simultaneously dismissing me.

"I'm not finished with you yet. Hey. Hey." I lean over the counter and grab him by the lapels.

A beefy guy in a metallic suit takes a step toward us. I release the twit, who gives the obvious security guy a slight shake of his head. He makes a big show of straightening his stupid tie and brushing invisible lint from his shoulders.

He lowers his snooty voice and deigns to talk to me as a human being. "We have certain standards to maintain at *The Drake*. We have a vacancy in our luxury suite, but that is reserved for the families of guards who have distinguished themselves in service. I can't help you."

"Thanks for nothing."

I rip a few fake green leaves off a potted plant and toss them into the dry fountain in the foyer. It may be petty, but it's the only revenge I have. I hope the imperfection drives him crazy.

I should never have stopped here. Even if I got past balloon-head, I'd never be able to afford it. This is the richest part of the sector, even richer than Happytown, where the lucky live. I'd lost the lotto when I was born and never had a chance to distinguish myself in the guards, since I was released for some still-unknown reason.

I've been to six different buildings today, and I got the same answer all over the sector. Nothing available. At least, nothing for me. One place offered to scan me. I let them. The girl scanning me told me what a cute decal I had and showed me her own anklet, covered in a bunch of chimeric fruits and vegetables. I suppressed a shudder but left my own hideous cartoon decal in place. No idea where I got the decal, but it felt wrong to remove it, even though I still throw up in my mouth a little every time I look at it. Eventually, the girl scanning me got really quiet and said she couldn't get a read on me. Whatever. I know the code for not wanted.

There's a whole section of town for the unwanted, and those who try to shield as much of their lives from The State as they can, so that's where I go now. The buildings fade from dingy to dilapidated. I travel along the gradient in the sector from the rich to poor. The fancy building with its plasticine plants and stone relic of a fountain—a remembrance of a time when water was so plentiful they could waste it on decoration—wanes to buildings struggling to stand. There's creativity here, amidst the ruin, but small things like fountains have long been destroyed.

Only the partial shells of buildings remain, with fewer walls and more holes than my sorry old home. This is where the wars wreaked the most destruction. This is where the outsiders live— outside, but still inside. This is who the guards protect us from. This is where I belong.

I walk the gravel streets. The main ones were pavement once, like Happytown and the work district, but the years have battered it down to black pebbles. Even in the rich areas, the alleys are ground to rocks. No one can afford to keep everything pretty. The difference is, they're open about the ugliness here.

I liked the outward beauty of Happytown when I first went there. I was with my second foster family. I thought they might keep me. They gave me my own room in this house with a light blue finish and a fence around the front that was so white, we had to wipe it down with rags to keep the street dust off. It seemed like I could play in that yard forever with the rag balls they gave me, but I guess I did something—I don't know what— because I didn't get to stay.

I didn't go back to Happytown until I landed with the Blanks. To my older eyes, it was much dingier, like they tried to paint the bad away, but the ugliness of some of the people still showed through.

No one is around here yet. Still too bright out, I guess, but the light fades pretty fast.

*Keep to the shadows.*

Undergrounders. That's what the people who live in this part of the sector are called. They don't really live underground, but they only come out when no one's around, and they stick to where it's dark. I guess that's why they got the Undergrounder nickname. They're not living and travelling in tunnels, but they may as well be.

I have nothing to worry about from the people here. I could take any one of them, and I have nothing they'd want to take from me. The guard patrols, though—I might have trouble with a full complement.

Last time I was here was right before I was sent to the Blanks. The family I was with before them, well, they weren't too bad I guess. They didn't really pay me much attention, and there was mostly food around for me. I'm not sure why I left. I wanted something better, I guess. I wanted control.

I made it through half a night the last time I was in Undergroundland. The State used my anklet to track me, then dumped me back into care. I was young enough that they minded back then. They don't care who ends up in Undergroundland after we're through school. Everyone gets a chance to be the best. That's what they say at the work placement ceremony at the end of school. Those who aren't the best...well, they have to live somewhere.

My instincts are better now. I walk by a couple of buildings that are in semi-decent shape. Missing windows, a few missing bricks, but the roofs hold, in mostly good condition. I pass these by. There's an order to this part of the sector, and I haven't fit myself into it just yet. Those places are the cream of the crop for an Undergrounder, and I don't need a sign or a snob to tell me they have no vacancy. I don't want to fight my way in. I have nothing against these people. I'm tired. I just want to exist.

A couple more blocks, and I find it. About a third of the roof is in good shape. The other two thirds are still sort of there but caved in on the upper floors. Building looks to be five or six stories high. The bottom is stone block and the top, wood frame and plasticine. The wood didn't hold out, but the stone should. The building won't fall down tonight.

The doorframe is mostly empty, the door itself long rotted away. I kick at a bunch of junk piled in the opening, intentionally or collected by the wind, I can't tell. The trash shifts a little, revealing buried pieces covered with slimy green film. I've got a couple of sheets in my back pocket from when I was looking for more traditional vacancies, so I use those to protect my hands and shift the contents. I enter. I scan. Piles of outdated sheets and cardboard near the entryway form a primitive shelter. Someone lives here.

The cardboard moves a little.

"A rat?"

Someone's raspy voice says the word as I think it. I hate that word. I don't know why.

The board shifts, and a matted head pokes through.

"A big rat."

I grit my teeth and try to figure out how to play this. I'm no rat.

He emerges from the cardboard, mostly naked. It's impossible to tell his age. He's very thin, and his skin hangs loosely on his frame, as though he were once a man of some substance. His eyes are wide, and he stares at me for a long time without blinking. He breaks eye contact and does a weird little dance around the pile of trash that is so clearly his home.

"Gotta get rid of the rats. Kill the rats in my house." He laughs, the dry cackle of a man not used to saying much.

I hold the rolled up sheet still in my hand. "I can help."

He laughs again and nods, beckoning me into his garbage pit.

Home sweet home.

# 8

I'm walking in a green cloud that obscures all sight, dampens all sound. My heartbeat and the rhythmic in and out of my breath echo inside my body, but the green swallows the sound as soon as I exhale. I've been here before. I know this, even as I know the cloud is really a cloak, and I need to break through to find what it's hiding. This is a dream.

I wave my arms and step forward to see what mysteries might be revealed. Nothing. I take the opportunity to reflect on my day, my life.

I was in school. I was tapped. I did my service. I was discharged. I am here.

The events of my life come to me like bullet points on a list. I feel no attachment to them. I cannot remember the details, and I'm comfortable with that.

As I accept it, the green foams like a deadly river, and I'm carried downstream, unconsumed. I flow into an eddy, where the green calms and dissipates, revealing a broken, beaten body lying supine on rough gravel.

The body is chanting, "He did this. He did this. He did this."

The body is me.

All at once, memories from the last few days flood in. The guards at *my apartment, Dr. Ableworth, Spyder, Doc and the Professor. Someone has been taking pieces of me, and they just tried to take too much.*

*I am not calm. I do not accept the events of my life. That is not who I am, and that is not me, crumpled and defeated.*

*"Get up," I tell the other me. "Get up right now."*

*She doesn't listen. I grab her and lift her into a sitting position, but she slumps back to the ground. I march around her, assessing the situation, my combat-style boots crunching the stone. She doesn't appear injured.*

*"You have to get up. We have to fight." Fight what, I'm not sure, but there's a sense of danger and urgency in the unknown. Green mist encroaches on us.*

*She starts to cry.*

*"You can do this. I know you can do this."*

*She shakes her head no.*

*"I'll help you. I've been where you are. We can do this together." I beg, I plead, and I cajole, but this other me won't or can't be convinced. The mist is getting closer, and I need to get her up and talking to me before it separates us forever. I do the only thing I can think of. I do what I'm best at.*

*I kick the crap out of me.*

*There's no satisfaction in beating someone who won't fight back, but I do it anyway. Other me moans and rolls around as I aim the toe of my boots into her side. The echo of her pain burns in my organs, and it only makes me wale on this wimp even harder. I yank her hair and get in her face, giving her one last chance.*

*"Get up."*

*She spits in my face.*

*"That's my girl," I say, just before I headbutt her.*

We wake up.

CONTRABAND IS EVERYWHERE in our sector, like a few maps I

found and memorized as a kid. These little bits connect us to our past, and people and families hoard them, keeping to themselves the precious nuggets of our golden history, as though sharing them would diminish them. Share with the wrong person, with someone connected or someone about to be tapped, and you could bring the wrath of The State down on your entire family.

Sometimes, though, people take a risk.

When we were thirteen, Spyder took that risk with me.

"I have something to show you," he said.

"What is it?"

He produced a couple of sheets and thrust them at me.

"Whoa." The news sheets had always been printed in black and white. Spyder's sheets were covered in colors more vibrant than anything I'd ever seen, making the colors in Happytown seem like pale imitations. Until that day, I didn't realize how gray everything was. The sky, the buildings, even the two trees left in our neighborhood were washed out and dim in comparison to the pictures on these pages. Only the comp screens had greens and reds this bright.

"You can't tell anyone," he said. "They're my dad's. They were my great-great-grandfather's or something. The pictures tell a story. They called it a comic, but it's not really funny."

"Is this real? Like our history?"

"I don't know, but it's pretty bad-laska."

A pale but colorful man in a funky blue and red dress flew through the images to rescue people. His super hearing heard when they were in trouble, and he rescued them with his super strength. Spyder's comics were missing the very beginning and most of the end, but it was pretty clear that the flying man saved the day.

"This is so cool."

"Here's another." He handed me one with black ink so deep it was like staring into an unlit, forbidden room. I'd never even seen the night that dark before. The hazy blue security lights outside made the night only a little dimmer than the day.

A bright yellow beam cut through the darkness, summoning the hero with a wild symbol.

"That's all? Where's the rest of it?"

"It's all we have. You can't tell anyone." He snatched the pages back from me and stuffed them in a drawer. "My dad would kill me if he knew I showed you."

"I won't tell."

And I didn't. At least, I think I didn't. I'm not sure what happened during my training, but I don't see myself selling out Spyder for one memory from so long ago. Besides, if I had, there's no way he'd have come to the cava shop.

Which brings me to where I am, right now. I need help, and I'm not too proud to admit that. I don't think I could luck into finding Doc and the Professor again, not that I'm sure I want to after they drugged me. Spyder, I've known for years. Spyder, I can trust. And if he trusts them... All I've got to do is find a way to signal him, and then he'll come and take me to Doc and the Professor, and then—I haven't worked that part of the plan out yet. But with his geeky comp skills, I bet he can hack into The State and find out something about why the goony guards keep coming after me. And Doc and the Professor know way more about how the sector works than they told me. If they can figure out peanut butter, maybe they can figure out me.

I grab onto a rung of a ladder and give it a small shake. The reverberations make my teeth chatter. Yeah, it's just the wobbly ladder. No nerves about climbing this rickety rust bucket or anything. Luckily, I've got some help.

"Do you think you can do it, Charley?"

He gives me a missing-tooth grin. "Easy freezy, lights are sneezy."

I've spent the last two nights sleeping in a room on the third floor of this building. Floor's probably too generous a term, as most of the ground is a giant gaping hole looking onto the second and ground floors. Charley, the guy in the cardboard pile I met when I came here, is my only neighbor. There's probably a reason for that: he's nuts. But he also leaves me alone, and he keeps the guards away. Even predators know you don't mess with crazy.

I've spent the last two days rigging up a signal for Spyder. I found some old board and cut patterns into it like in the comic he showed me years ago. I've tried the board against the footlights on the street, and it makes a pretty good pattern of light and shadow. I hope Spyder recognizes it.

The ladder leads through the third floor to the roof, through a lot of junk. On the ground floor, Charley stabilizes the bottom by sitting on the lowest rung, and I've got to climb up to the top from the third floor. Hopefully, Charley isn't distracted by imaginary rodents and he just stays in place. I spit on my palms and rub a little dusty grit from the broken bricks into them. I exhale and start the climb.

I've made it two rungs when the ladder starts to sway. The vibrations start at my feet and make it hard to keep my grip.

"Charley, stop moving."

"I ain't moving," he shouts back.

I close my eyes. I can do this. I jumped from a building to escape the guards, and I climbed a fire escape as high as this ladder the other day when Spyder and I ran from the cava shop. *Come on, Bree.*

The ladder sways more, and I barely hold on. I might be sick. I jump six inches to the ground and collapse, hugging myself.

After a minute, Charley pokes his head through the jagged floorboards.

"You alright there, Missy?"

"I need a minute. Ladder's not stable."

Charley, still on the ladder, gives it a good shake. "S'fine." The moving metal warbles out a sickening song.

I gag. "Please don't do that."

After a few minutes of silence and recovery, I give the boards to Charley with as simple and concise instructions as I can manage and send him up to the stupid roof in my place.

Dust rains down with each step he takes. I cough. My throat's even drier than when I was on the ladder.

"How's it going, Charley? Did you get the light signal in place?"

He stomps around, making the clay rain thicker.

"Charley?"

His foot thuds stop, and he lets out a whoop. "Woooeeee, they're gonna let the dogs loose. Hunker down, everybody."

In the distance, the raid siren wails. I scramble up the ladder to Charley, fear cutting through my aversion to heights like a sheet through the skin of an overworked delivery kid.

"Is it—?"

He points to a streetboard glowing red, with a single blinking word: BOUNTY.

Reflexively, I check my anklet. Still in place, thank the VM. I'd be an idiot to remove my anklet and face Bounty, but accidents happen. Since I'm up here, and my nerves seem to be at bay, I check the signal. The security light mounted to the roof casts a cool glow through the cardboard filter, making the light look like Spyder's eight-legged namesake. Hopefully, he sees it.

On the streetboard, the word "BOUNTY" dissolves pixel by pixel, and numbers slide across from right to left, disappearing as they reach the edge. 5, 4, 3, 2, 1.

As the one appears to fall off into the air, a name, Willen Todd, slides into place. No picture on the board yet, but a big empty square holds space for a headshot. I don't recognize the name. Last seen, though, is The Drake, the last building where I tried to find an apartment.

I don't like how connected I am to The State lately.

"You in on this, Missy?"

"What? No, I have nothing—I mean, it's not my thing."

"Whelp, pull up a chair, and let's watch the festivideos." He ambles over to the ledge and sits, swinging his legs over the roof edge and staring at the giant screen on the streetboard.

A few guard formations take shape on the border between Budgetville and Undergroundland. On the street below us, a few Undergrounders appear with sticks and chains. Bounty hunters.

"They're coming. That boy better run," Charley says.

This guy Willen Todd must not have a recent picture on file, because it takes forever for a grainy black and white surveillance camera image to load. The reward amount flashes underneath. Five hundred credits. A decent amount. The payout number holds steady for a minute before dropping to four-ninety. The Undergrounders below break into a run toward the work district where The Drake is and where this guy was last spotted. Four-eighty. That'll get them moving. The quicker someone is found, the bigger the Bounty.

On the streetboard, the last known location shifts: Centre Street and Park Avenue. Four-seventy.

"Oh-ee, he's in for it now!" Charley slaps his palms on the ledge.

Willen's headed toward Undergroundland. Big mistake. They won't protect him here. Bounty is paid out whether the person's alive or dead, so in general, anyone would rather be found by the guards. They're supposed to incapacitate only and remove the person from the sector for trial. Not that anyone wins at trial. Best case scenario is to be found by guards and immediately request Pilgrimage. Heading toward Undergroundland, which is teeming with bounty hunters, is an incredibly risky move. Four-sixty.

The streetboard goes all staticky, then switches to live feed from the cameras on the street.

Charley leans over the edge of the roof as if that could bring him closer to the digital action. "That's it. He's done for."

The streetboard shows Willen Todd surrounded by guards, the lucky idiot. He looks around wildly, then dives to the ground between two of the guards' legs. They pivot and are on him in a second. One holds his face in the asphalt with a worn boot. Another wrenches his arms behind his back. They lift him up. The streetboard doesn't have audio, but the camera zooms in so we can read their lips.

I mouth the familiar words with them. "Willen Todd, you have been captured and will stand trial at the mercy of The State."

Willen lifts his head and makes eye contact with the camera. "Pilgrimage."

The word BOUNTY blinks twice on the streetboard before dissolving into a weird animation of the word CAPTURED behind some pixelated bars. The image holds steady for a minute or two while the bounty hunters disappear into alleys, and VM-knows what other little secret pockets of the sector, like they were never out in the first place. The streetboard shifts back into a State-sponsored advertisement. *Nutripaste—Real nutrition for real families.*

"Sorry it took me so long," Spyder says, and I jump about a foot. "Hard to get anywhere with all the patrols and hunters out."

Charley claps with glee. "They got him! Didja see? Didja see?"

Spyder's dark jaw is firmly set. "I saw. Who is this?" he asks me.

"I guess you could say he's my landlord."

"What do you want, Bree? You've got to take this down." He's cold.

I know I left things badly between us, but I thought he'd be over it if he came. Spyder kicks the cardboard off of the lights so the pattern goes back to the normal glow, mottled in places where age has fogged the color or jagged where the globes have cracked in pieces. A trail of rope attached to Spyder's harness follows him, keeping him safe, even where the roof bends a little under his feet as he clears the cardboard.

The adrenaline from the Bounty is fading, and I'm suddenly aware that I. Am. On. The. Roof.

"Let's talk." I make for the ladder.

"You want to talk, talk." He widens his stance. "Up here."

"But the guards—" I say weakly.

"I'm not going to let you jerk me around, Bree. Not this time. There's serious things happening."

"I know. That's what I want to talk to you about. I don't know what's happening to me. What happened to me." He can't understand what it's like to keep missing chunks of time—to miss part of myself.

"We want to help you. But you need to realize you're not the most important thing in the world. Get out of your head, Bree, and get into the sector."

"What's that supposed to mean?" I clench my hands into fists. I want to pound something, soon.

Spyder senses my aggression. He'd better back down.

"I don't want to fight," he says.

"Me neither."

"Could've fooled me." For someone who doesn't want to fight, he's doing an awfully good job of it.

"What's that supposed to mean?" I say again.

"Did you really need to fight those guards outside the cava shop, or did you want to? Look, don't answer that. I'm here. I want to help you, but the guards are swarming everywhere, and your little lighting display could lead them right here. Be back here in the morning, about an hour before sun up."

"No problem. I live here." The jerk doesn't even care that I'm living in a trash heap in the middle of the Undergrounders' domain that the guards might invade sooner rather than later.

"To be clear: not here, this building. Here, on the roof."

Oh.

"I don't see why—"

"Scratch that. Don't meet me here."

Whew.

"Meet me there," he points to the roof of a building about a block away, a few stories taller than this one.

Jerk.

"You still have your decal?" Spyder asks.

"Yeah." I cross my arms, sulking. He's lucky I didn't remove the hideous thing during my last episode of "Bree's Lost Her Memories Again." I guess I'm lucky too, since it's helped me avoid The State. But I won't tell Spyder that.

"Well, whatever you do, whoever you choose to go out and beat up, don't take that decal off your anklet," he finishes.

"Fine. Okay. No problem. See you later." I turn my back on him, wondering why I'm hurt.

"Almost better'n the Bounty." Charley's long, dirty fingernails curl around my shoulder. "Good show."

I turn around, but Spyder is already gone.

# 9

I lay on the remnants of an old mattress, avoiding the springs poking up through decades-old fabric. I don't sleep much anymore, and I don't really want to chance sleeping through my meeting with Spyder. He has such a bad attitude, I don't know if I'll get another chance.

He's wrong, though. Nobody knew what that light signal meant but him. The guards came nowhere near here, but I was ready to rabbit if they did. I don't always have to fight. He's wrong.

I get up from the stupid broken bed and pace around the room. Not in circles—the missing wall and encroaching decay prevent that—but I pace in some kind of weird oval/triangle combination that defies definition. No sleep for me tonight. No dreams.

I might as well go to the other roof and wait, but who am I kidding—I'm not going to spend a second longer than I have to up there.

I replay the conversation with Spyder and wonder how he got so aggressive. When I left for training, he was a shy geek who didn't say more than a sentence or two at a time. He'd never have even thought about raising his voice to anyone, let alone make demands on where and when to meet.

I flop back onto the bed and wince. Stupid spring catches me right in the calf. I massage my muscle and take a closer look at the decal—the one Spyder said not to take off my anklet. What an ugly cartoon. A pale yellow smiley face on a pinkish-orange, gwocked-up sunset background. The girls at my school used to put these things all over their anklets. All kinds of stupid designs and imaginary creatures like lions and these stupid walking bird things in little suits. I never did, because why try to hide the stupid ugly thing? Drawing attention to the anklet just made it more obvious.

The edge of the decal is peeling, and I play with it a little. I lift it most of the way up before pressing it back down. I'm not oppositional for no reason like Spyder thinks I am. He's the one who was fighting with me for no reason.

This is stupid. Stupid, stupid, stupid. I've been fleeing for my life off and on for the VM knows how long. I can't even remember the last year of my life, and I'm worried about a boy. North Dakota that.

I'm going to this building and getting my answers.

It's dark, and the streets are alive with activities winding down. Even in this light, no one seems to want to be in the streets. They stay close to the buildings—a living shadow that flows like dark water. I'm new and not to be trusted, so I don't even try to engage. I walk down the middle of the street and try not to notice their illicit dealings.

Their movements still as I near and start up again as I pass. In my periphery, some of the goods change hands—small cans without labels, sturdy boots, the occasional corner of a glossy magazine cover from ages past. That's execution-worthy, but the collectors will always go for the contraband.

The block-long walk seems to take an eternity. My instincts are screaming at me to duck for cover in the shadows with the rest, but I'm safer in the open, for now. I don't belong with them. I don't belong anywhere.

A person in a long coat with a gray cloth mask stops me at the entrance to the building. Its crudely drawn features mimic some kind of animal I've never seen before.

"Anything for sale?" he or she grunts.

"I'm meeting someone on the roof." Apparently I passed a test I didn't know I was taking.

The person performs an elaborate gesture to usher me into the building. Inside the building's stone walls, the temperature drops, and the steady ping of dripping water into a metal container signifies that someone's making use of every available resource, safely harvesting the day's condensation in the cool night. Still, the sound of water is unnerving. The foyer is empty. All the inhabitants are tucked away into their rooms, or, more likely, roaming the streets for another couple of hours until daybreak.

With these thick walls, it's no wonder this building is still standing tall, even in this part of the sector. I'm surprised The State hasn't declared it a garrison for the guards. That would ruin the Undergrounders.

The temperature rises little by little as I climb the back stairs. My steps clang loudly on the metal-edged concrete—my presence is no secret. I'm getting antsy, and I start going two or three steps at a time. I'm not eager to be up so freaking high, but I *am* eager to have Spyder's help.

I'm not sure how best to approach him. I'm not a damsel in distress, but based on our last conversation, I can't be too forceful. As I contemplate my approach, I lose focus and slip on the crumbling concrete edge of the stair where the metal reinforcement has broken off. I hiss at the scrape on the side of my leg. It stings, but it'll heal. The scrape is not even crippling, just a nuisance. I'm annoyed and push myself to go up even faster. I'll show a minor injury who's boss.

The night air is cool and thick up here without a hint of a breeze, promising a warm, sticky day. I pace in place while I wait for Spyder. Got to get this nervous energy out somehow. The quiet hangs like a blanket, dampening all but the loudest sounds.

Then, something changes. A rumble in the distance, like thunder on the ground, stops me in my tracks. After a moment, the high-pitched whine of a charging laser plays counterpoint, until all of the sounds coalesce and culminate into the giant boom of a laser cannon hitting its target.

I can't not look over the edge.

Unlike the screams and cries I'd expect to hear from the normal parts of the sector at an attack, the Undergrounders stay silent. Already part of the landscape, they simply fade further into it. It's too dark to see much, but the tank that rolls through has giant floodlights mounted on top, illuminating the decaying streets and the figures that march through. Not terrorism. The guards. The State.

Buzzing fills the air. With a loud whoosh, four people dressed in head-to-toe black land on the roof. I crouch in a fighting stance, ready to take them out and flee before the rest of the guards arrive. It'll be close, but I can take four. They flank me, two of them going to the far edge to monitor the ground, two blocking the stairs. One at a time. I can do this.

"You've got to get out of here. Come with us." One of them steps toward me.

I maintain the distance between us. "Who are you?"

They don't have a chance to answer. The loud wail of feedback pierces the night, and a deep, mechanical voice echoes in the air.

"Little rat, we know where you are. Come down like a good girl, or we'll come and get you."

The arm of the tank pivots toward this building. On the top, riding astride like he's saddled up some kind of animal, is a giant man with a bullhorn. I can't make much else out at this distance, but I've got bigger problems.

"You're not with them?" I ask the black-clad strangers.

"We're with Spyder," the leader answers.

"Let's go," I say.

"Grab on," the leader says with a smirk, pointing to the straps of a harness I'm only just seeing. Great.

I swallow my fear, my pride, every emotion I can think of, and hold tight. "Let's do this." I say, closing my eyes this time.

WE LAND ON THE GROUND, thank the VM, and I almost fall down when I let go of the leader. Someone grabs me from behind and hauls me through a large doorway, practically kicking me down a set of stairs toward another door. It opens, and Spyder yanks me through. He ignores me and waits for the rest of his team to enter.

"I see you've met the mites." Without waiting for a response, he brushes past me to talk to the leader. The leader gestures angrily and stabs his finger in my direction, but I can't hear what he's saying.

Spyder's harnessed, like he was going to be one of the swinging acrobats that took me swooping around the sector, but clearly I wasn't important enough for him to deign to talk with me. I'm still get my bearings from that flight, but it only takes me a moment before I interrupt them.

"Why didn't you come get me yourself?"

"I'm working on things. I told you, I'm busy. The mites'll show you where to go."

I really wish he'd stop calling them mites. I'm having trouble not laughing each time. Spyder's mites.

"I almost killed your stupid mites. I thought they were some elite squad of guards, like weird flying Ops or something. They were this close to being toast." I pinch my fingers together.

"They were that close to being toast anyway." Spyder points to the mite leader. "He told me the guards were ready to blow the whole building. You're lucky they didn't follow through, or you'd be personally responsible for the deaths of everyone in that building."

"Me? In what world is this my fault? I didn't ask to be chased by the guards in some twisted game. I have no idea why they're even after me. Someone is messing with my memories, the whole mother-Californian State is after me, and you don't even show up."

"I got to you, didn't I?"

"Whatever."

"Right back at you."

He takes some kind of wand from a pocket in his harness and moves it over me. The wand lets out a steady beep as he goes.

"What's that?"

"A scanner."

"I meant, what are you scanning for?"

As I ask the question, the beeps blur together in a loud shrill. Spyder clenches his jaw so hard he could crack a rock, furious.

"I told you not to take the decal off."

"I didn't. I mean, I thought about it, not really my taste, but it seemed important to you," I halfheartedly joke.

"You almost got them killed. That decal is how we handle the tracking signals. We increase the margin of error in their positioning system. When you took it off, you led them straight to you...and my mites."

"I didn't take it off, I swear." I pull up my pant leg to check. The decal is gone, but there are scrapes along my ankle oozing blood from when I lost my footing on the stairs. "Look, see. I scraped my leg. It must've come off when I did that."

"Just another example of how you're careless."

"Why are you even helping me when you so clearly hate me? Why did you even talk to me in the cava shop in the first place?"

He'd seemed so nice when he first sat down, sweet and shy like my old friend. Amazing how in the space of minutes he turned into a first-class jerk and hasn't stopped since.

"I told you I was asked to contact you by our mutual friends."

"Right, and then you just assumed I knew who you meant. I thought you meant the Blanks at first, but then I realized—"

"He means us, dear." Doc and the Professor stand silhouetted in the open doorway. "Now if you children are finished arguing, we have work to do."

## 10

D oc and the Professor lead us through a series of tunnels—no decals required in their domain—to the quarters I'd visited earlier.

Along the way, the Professor explains, "This part of the sector was built during the riots. Not the riots in our history, but the time before that. We don't know too many details, except the police—that was their version of the guards—used them to make sure they could surround protestors on all sides. You'll see their fear reflected in the building construction as well—single doors, long narrow hallways. Inspired by the truly ancient times when a single archer could hold off an army."

The Professor says a lot of words I don't understand, but I get the basic gist. *Control the streets; control the people.* While we're under the sector, we're not too deep. People above us wake up and start their day. The tunnels lose the above ground demarcation between Budgetville and Undergroundland—we could be anywhere in the sector.

"Where—?"

"Shh." Doc cuts me off with a finger to her lips and points to a grate in the ceiling.

The noise from the street is louder now, carried down somehow through that grate. We keep walking through this oddly illuminated space, bulbs in metal cages casting prison bar shadows on the ground.

"The grates provide airflow within the tunnel and also allowed the police to monitor activity on the streets before deploying their forces."

Since silence is obviously no longer required, I say, "Police? Seems like these would be a pretty valuable tool for the guards."

"Of course," the Professor says easily. "If they knew they were here. That's the problem with ignoring history. They forget."

"Forget?"

"Ignorance is a weapon The State uses to control us. But to do that, they must also steep themselves in the same foolishness."

"But if they're just as ignorant as we are, how do they stay in charge?"

"You don't have to be wise to lead, these days. Only a little less foolish than most of those you lead." He pauses. "You wanted to ask something, earlier, when we were passing the grate?"

"Oh. I guess it was just, what are you doing down here?"

"Preserving what we can. Welcome back to The Bunker. Or as we call it, home." His lips quirk in a half-smile, and he gives Doc's hand a quick squeeze.

We pass another set of grates, and the mini-lecture is over for a time. I expect the Professor to pick back up when we're clear, but he doesn't, and I'm grateful for the silence to process the last several hours.

We arrive at their home, The Bunker, and we go straight to the war room they brought me to last time. Spyder shrugs off his harness and flops into the chair in front of the screens, tapping madly on a keyboard. The views on the screens switch too rapidly for me to process, but he seems to be taking it all in.

Doc and the Professor lead me to a ratty orange couch that sinks a little in the middle and ask me about my shrink appointment. It seems so long ago, but it was only a couple of days.

I don't answer them at first. I want to know more about them. I want to know if I can trust them. I want to know if they can help me.

The Professor breaks the silence. "I feel as though we should take a small step back, in order that we might take a giant leap forward. We owe you an apology after our last encounter."

"You mean when you drugged me and dumped me on the streets. No problem. Apology accepted." I'm dripping with so much sarcasm, I'm practically drooling.

The Professor winces. I don't want to let them off easy, but this is a good opening to find out more about them.

Before he or Doc can say anything further, I continue. "Where exactly are we?"

"Home sweet Bunker," the Professor says.

"But what is it? I know it's where you live, and you're clearly doing something against The State."

Doc and the Professor share a look.

"You've seen the tunnels leading here," the Professor says. "We built our home in large rooms connected to the tunnels. It's a bit like spokes on a wheel, except we have a few connected hubs. Together, we call the rooms The Bunker. It's a military reference—"

"I'm familiar." I cut him off, not sure what I'm looking for to know that I can trust them. "How many people live down here?"

"Oh, not many. Less than twenty."

"How do you survive without The State tracking you down?"

"We've been off-network for years," the Professor says.

Doc elbows him in the ribs, like he's said too much.

I change my line of questioning to keep him talking. "What's the network?"

The Professor steeples his fingers in an educator's pose. "The network is The State's positional tracking system. A combination of monitor signals and video feeds provide the accuracy they need for pinpointing a citizen's location at any given time."

A short and succinct name for how The State always seems to know where I am when I'm not wearing Spyder's fancy ankle monitor stickers. Speaking of Spyder, I sneak a glance at him. He's typing away with his face close to a screen like he's working extra hard to ignore me.

I turn back to the Professor. "I haven't heard of the network before. I guess I knew about monitor tracking and the cameras, but not together."

"The State may call the network something different. That's the term we use." He shrugs.

Doc clears her throat and changes the subject. "Dear, I'm sure you have a lot of questions, but we do as well. We'd really like to know more about your State-required therapeutic visits."

"Oh," I say. While I do wonder about their lives here, I have to admit my curiosity is as much about hiding myself as it is about discovering them.

"Please understand our reluctance to share information has nothing to do with you, personally—Spyder's vouched for you— but we have to protect ourselves. If The State has a particular interest in you..." She trails off.

"If The State has an interest in me, I could lead them right to you."

She smiles faintly. "Exactly. Not intentionally, of course."

"Of course." I wish Spyder would look up, say something, and give me some clue about how a teenage boy joined up with a bunch of gray-hairs to somehow take on our government. My eyes burn holes into his ropy hair. Nothing. I'm on my own, like always. I swallow hard and decide to trust them.

I tell Doc and the Professor and Spyder, if he's bothering to listen, everything that's happened since they drugged me and left me on that stoop. It's funny how I was furious with them for that right after, but the fury burned away in all the events that happened since.

I pay special attention to the new block in my memory, after the hospital, taking care to avoid the details of my dream where I beat the crap out of myself to get my memories back. That's private, and no one needs to know about it. I tell them about how I came to be with the Undergrounders, and I inject as much appreciation for Spyder and his mini-mites as I can muster. But even I don't buy it as I'm saying it. Spyder's typing speed slows for a fraction of a second, so he's probably paying at least a little attention. I hope he is, because that's as close to a thank you as he's going to get from me after the way he's treated me.

"You woke up in a health center." Doc chooses her words carefully, like she's processing the story by repeating it back to me. "But you didn't remember anything."

"Yeah."

"What's the last thing you remembered when you woke up?"

"I—I don't know. I remember knowing that I was released, but I don't remember being released. Probably the tapping, right before training. At least at first. Then things kinda trickled in. I remembered you, but it took...time."

"And that didn't seem odd to you?"

"It seemed..." It takes me a minute to search for the right words to explain. "Familiar. Normal."

"Oh, how very, very interesting." Doc leans forward over her knees, her face uncomfortably close to mine, as though she's trying to unlock the secrets of my brain through awkward eye contact.

"And how did you get your memory back?" she asks.

I have to tell her something. If she's going to help me, I have to let her in a little.

"I had a dream. I was fighting—someone, I can't remember who. All I saw was a person, nothing else. When I woke up, I remembered." Telling her I assaulted myself in the dream seems too weird.

"But not everything," Doc counters. "You said you were in the health center, but you didn't say how you ended up in a bed of your own after visiting that guard. What happened then?"

"I—I don't know."

"So your memory is not fully recovered."

"Let the girl breathe," the Professor interjects.

The aging springs protest as Doc sits back on the couch, assuming a pose of relaxation. She waits a beat before starting in again. "I'd like to take you to my lab, run some tests."

"Oh, no, you're not taking me to a lab to study me like some kind of—" I freeze, and my face goes cold as the blood drains from my cheeks.

"Like some kind of what?" Doc gazes at me intently.

"Like some kind of rat," I whisper.

The clickity clack of the keyboard stops, and for the first time since we've been here, Spyder looks at me.

"I think we better go to your lab after all," I say.

## 11

Doc's lab is adjacent to the room they had me in when they found me after the guards attacked my apartment. Spyder stays in the war room, still doing his comp thing. We pass three unoccupied health-center-style beds and head to a small door with a tiny window to the lab. It's like the door to a closet, if the closet were massive and filled with different kinds of machinery. The door is nearly as thick as it is wide, and it takes both Doc and the Professor to pull the heavy slab open.

There are a few comps in here and all kinds of important looking equipment. Needles, IV-style bags, tubes, and pills—these are the only things I recognize. A giant mechanical arm hangs suspended from the ceiling with a weird metal looking soup can on the end. Nearby, there are some glasses and lab coats. I guess I recognize those, too.

In the far end of the room are a couple of huge cylinders with black cots in front of them.

"That's where I'd like to test you." Doc points to the machine on the left. "That one there."

"What does it do?"

"This device measures your brain activity. You'll have a little jab, tiny prick, nothing to worry about, and then I'll ask you some questions and show you some pictures. I'll measure your responses here." She sits down at a comp and pulls up some pictures. "This is what I'll see—a picture of how your brain responds to different kinds of stimuli."

"What's the jab?" I ask suspiciously.

"It's a kind of tracer that binds to the cells in your body."

"Cells—like a prison?"

At my frown, she sighs. "I hate that they don't teach science anymore. Cells are the tiny bits that make up you. Think of a building made of stone or brick. The building is you, each stone or brick making up the building is like a cell. The tracer will adhere to your cells and let us see what lights up in that brain of yours."

This can't be real. "You're going to...color...my brain."

"In a sense. Hopefully, we'll be able to get more information about your memory troubles."

"Hopefully?"

"There are no guarantees."

I appreciate her honesty. "That's good enough for me. All I want is the chance."

She injects the tracer then and there, and we wait awhile for it to take effect before I go into the tube. The initial jab stung, but the pain fades quickly. I thought I'd feel the goo as it bound to my cells, but I'm the same as always. Surprisingly, climbing onto the cot in the tube is the weirdest part. Since Doc only needs to look at my brain, I don't have to go all the way into the tube. Just my head and neck—lucky me. Still freaky.

"I'm going to say some words or phrases, and measure your responses to them," she calls from the other side of the room. "When we're finished with that, the Professor will show you some pictures. Don't move, and think about whatever comes naturally."

She talks with an almost mechanical quality, pausing for a few seconds between each word, "Blue. Cat. Red. Dog. Yellow." Her pause is slightly longer this time. "Rat."

No, I'm not thinking of anything in particular, not at all. If I were, it'd probably mean I had my memories back.

The words she chooses take on a more pointed quality, before going back to the neutral "Guard. Sergeant. Two plus two. Washington, D.C." When she says the city's name properly, I flinch. Not many people know the real names anymore. Doc continues, "Ten minus four. Ladybug. Light. Spyder. Shadow."

"You're doing very well, Bree. We're going to switch to pictures now. First one's just to get a baseline, so you can get used to the image quality."

The Professor inserts the first photo in the tube and holds it very still. The shot is blurry, grainy and dark, but it's easy to make out the edges of the building and windows. The blue safety light in front is a glowing, thick, wavering line.

And then the images come fast and furious. People mostly. I barely have time to tell gender, let alone figure out if I recognize anyone. The Professor sends them flying faster than a crooked dealer in an Undergrounder's poker club. Within what feels like seconds, he's finished.

"We're going to do some more words now."

The Professor withdraws the images. Doc runs through the same list as before in that machine voice, with maybe one or two differences in the words—I can't really remember exactly what came before. She pauses a little longer between them.

When she's finished, she says normally, "Wonderful job, Bree. Now let's have a little chat."

I slide out of the tube, and Doc calls out to the Professor, "Separate images three, six, ten, and twelve please, my darling. Now come over here, my dears."

The three of us sit on one side of a square folding table in some plasticine chairs. The Professor lays the images out. I can look more closely at them now and see what they actually are.

While the pictures all contain people, the people in them aren't always the most remarkable feature. My eye is immediately drawn to a striking woman who appears to be posing next to a Christmas tree. Her red hair cascades over her shoulder in stark contrast to the olive green of the plasticine tree. The picture is of better quality than the others, like part of a streetboard ad.

"Is she a model?" I ask. "I've seen her somewhere, but I can't place her."

"Of sorts," Doc replies. "We can't say too much at this point, as we don't want to corrupt any emerging memories."

"She kind of looks like Dr. Ableworth—my shrink. But younger and prettier. Maybe related?"

One of the photos is an older man, not yet a gray-hair. He's staring straight into the camera with his mouth quirked in a half smile and eyes that want to wink at someone.

"That's you." I turn to the Professor. "Or was you."

"A long time ago," he says with the wink he couldn't give in the photo.

"We needed to test your responses with familiar, or partially familiar, images." Doc slides the next photo toward me.

What happened to not corrupting my emerging memories? The picture shows a woman at a distance, in profile, walking into a food shop.

"Mrs. Blank—that's my old foster mother. How did you know about her?"

"Spyder told us a little about you at our last leadership meeting."

I'm being manipulated. I tamp down my natural impulse to resist and ask, as neutrally as I can, "Leadership?"

"We'll talk more about that later, dear. Last photo, please."

There's a man, shielding his face with a large hand. The top of his head is weirdly lit—shiny, almost. But it's that hand in the foreground, with a huge skull-shaped ring that extends from knuckle to knuckle on his ring finger. My heart feels like it's trying to beat its way out of my body, and my hands start to shake.

"What's happening?"

The Professor sweeps all of the images from the table.

Doc rushes to my side, shines a light in my eyes, and starts checking my vitals. "Breathe," she says.

I calm pretty quickly once the photos are away. The rhythm of Doc's brief medical examination is soothing and familiar.

The Professor is quiet. "You know him, don't you?"

I hold back tears and answer honestly. "I've never seen him before in my life."

DOC LEADS me through a warren of hallways. Walking is calming, and my steps give me a rhythm to breathe by. We enter a room I haven't been in before. There are photos on the walls like I've never seen before, realistic looking images of orange dirt with huge spikes and flattened spears or giant expanses of blue water straight out of some child's imagination. There are pictures of people, too, fading images lovingly framed with blackened cardboard. This is clearly part of their personal quarters.

I sit on a sofa that's of even worse quality than the one in the war room, afraid to lean back lest the whole thing collapse. Doc and the Professor each sit in faded fancy high-backed chairs across from me, flanking me. I think they're trying to give me space, but it feels more like they're going to attack me.

Doc shows me the picture of the man with the ring again. "We call him Cueball. We've never seen his face—"

Here comes the first assault.

"I said I don't know him."

"I believe you," she says simply and lets the statement hang. She gets up and disappears into another room for a moment. She returns carrying a tray with glasses and a pitcher.

"Lemonade?" she asks.

"Yeah, sure. Thanks."

She pours me a glass, and I drink. It's sour, nothing like the lemonade we had at school, but the finish is sweet. I must have made a face because the Professor laughs.

"I haven't seen a lemon in years, but she gets the acidic component just about right in that lab of hers. Much more refreshing than that sickly sweet corn water they serve up there." He points to the ceiling, to the sector above us.

Once again, I have no idea what he means, and I nod along. "Why do you believe me?"

Doc peers at me over her glass. "Why shouldn't I?" She takes a long sip of the tart drink. "The State has done so many things over the years that I've seen firsthand. I have no reason to trust them. And you've given me no reason *not* to trust you."

"Those photos—were they of people with The State?"

"At least one of them was, and you picked him out of the lineup."

"But I don't know him."

"But you do."

"You said—"

"Let me tell you about the test I just gave you." She raises her hand and looks at the ceiling briefly, like she's composing her thoughts. "There are different areas of your brain associated with different memories. You access the memories through different means, like seeing a familiar face or smelling something that has a strong association. For example, if we didn't take the trash out for a few days, the smell accumulated, and you walked into this room, you might wonder what was going on. It might also trigger memories for you from a few days ago when you were hiding from the guards, smelling like you just came out of a dumpster. Make sense?"

I nod. "Or that weird fruity clean smell that always makes me think of the heath center."

"Precisely. Now, when you hear a word you recognize or see a picture, lots of different areas of your brain light up, because you're constantly making connections between things. This is the science of our ancestors. They were just starting to gain a deeper understanding of the brain when the Incident happened. Unfortunately, a lot of their science was lost at that time, but we apply what we can, and we're still learning."

"Why can't I remember?"

"We can't tell why you can't remember, but if it helps, we can tell that there are things you can't remember."

"But I already knew that." I wish she would just get to her point.

"When we give you the more neutral words or images, all sorts of different areas of your brain light up. The same areas of your brain light up when you see the images you don't remember. There's nothing wrong with your memory structure."

"But I can't remember, and you said you believed me. You—"

"Listen, please. The memories are there, but I believe you can't access them. Think of a room. How do you get in the room?"

"I walk in, but—"

"Walk in through what?"

These interruptions are getting annoying. "Through the door," I say through gritted teeth.

"And what happens if there is no door? How do you get into the room then?"

"That's stupid. Of course there's a door. Otherwise, the room would be pointless, and no one would even know it's there."

"Exactly."

"So my brain is the room, and the memories are locked

inside, except not even locked because there's no door for a lock to be on?"

"Now you're getting it."

"I mean, that's great and all, but what do we do?"

The Professor answers this time. "I'm no doctor, but it seems like we need to make a door."

## 12

D oc spends hours researching normal brain activity in her lab. They let me stay the night, in one of the health center beds, while she continues her work in the lab next door. I can hear her shuffling around, the thud of heavy books landing on her work table, the tapping of her keyboard. What use are walls and doors when the sound carries through the cracks?

I'm exhausted. Spyder had me up at the buttcrack of dawn to meet him, and I haven't slept since. I can't sleep with all this activity and the potential promise of restored memories. I want to punch a door into my brain with my fists, open something up any way I can. There's got to be a way. There's got to. There's got...

*Boom.*

*Thunder, in the distance. No, that isn't right. That's a large weapon discharge. Bursts of smaller weapon fire fill the air. Someone yells close by. All of this happens all at once, and the sounds jolt me from sleep. I think I wake up, but my eyes don't seem to work. Am I hurt? Dead? The blackness clears suddenly, and the green mist is back, my shroud.*

*This is a dream. What were the sounds? The boom, the yelling? What was she saying? She—it was definitely a woman. If I can hold onto that, maybe I can follow the thread back into the memory. I wave the mist around, making it swirl, trying to clear it out. I blow on the mist, do I everything I can think of to move it away, but it thickens into a dense vibrating screen. The light green coalesces to a darker green, and I can't even see the swirls anymore. It solidifies into a thick jade wall. No door.*

*I raise a boot and try to kick the wall in. I can barely move my leg. I'm pinned by the air itself. Powerless. I can't beat a wall in. All I can do is drift.*

*"Do you really think that'll work?" The woman asks, shielding her face with the sleeve of a shiny black jacket.*

I gasp, and I am awake. The sounds, the woman. Did I see her face? No, but maybe her eyes. She was near me—beside me? I run over and over the details, burning them into my brain before the torch is extinguished and I drift again, into dreamless sleep.

THE PROFESSOR FLICKS on the bright overhead lights, startling me from sleep in the narrow health-center-style bed. "Rise and shine, early bird. Lots of worms to catch."

"Is it morning? I can't tell down here."

"Time and tide wait for no man."

Whatever that means.

"Or woman," Doc interjects, coming out of her lab.

"Good morning my love, my fair one." The Professor practically dances to her and kisses her cheek. Okay...

"Good morning, dear." Doc gives him a quick peck back. She turns to me. "How did you sleep?"

"Okay, I guess. I thought I dreamed something, but there wasn't much to it. Some loud sounds. A woman said something to me."

"What did she look like? What did she say?"

"I can't really remember." The lie is small, but I already

decided with the last dream I didn't want them knowing too much about them, until I could remember more myself.

"Hmmm," Doc says. "As much as we've enjoyed having you here, it's time for you to be getting back home."

I don't really have a home.

"Spyder can take you," she continues. "It's going to be a while before I can be of any real help to you. We need to reestablish your neural pathways, but I'm not sure how to do that just yet."

Goody.

"I have some ideas, but short of immersing you in experiences that might trigger the memories, we don't really have a good path forward."

"What kind of experiences?"

"There's a possibility if you were tapped again, if you went through the same training, it might bring back the memories of your first training. We don't know for sure, though. There's also the potential of some drugs, combined with electrical stimulation—"

This time, I interrupt her. "Sounds like you've got a lot of work to do. How can I contact you again?" I'm tired from listening to her research, and I can't make it through a full recap.

"A few friends are getting together in two days. Spyder will give you the details. We'd like you there."

Cryptic. I like it. "No problem. And, thanks for trying to help me."

"Not for ourselves alone are we born," The Professor quips.

Obscure. I don't get it.

Spyder doesn't even say hello. He just mumbles without making eye contact and thrusts a decal into my hands. "Put this on, and don't take it off or lose it or whatever this time."

It's a hot pink cat on top of a rainbow. Disgusting. Not my taste at all.

"You got anything a little less...vomit-inducing?"

"Sorry." He shrugs.

I can't tell if he means it. It annoys me that he hasn't risen to my bait.

"Even a tech geek like you can see—"

Doc cuts me off. "Now children..."

"Be a gentleman, and escort the lady home. Be a lady, and accept the gentleman's gift." The Professor says.

"Whatever." I slap the decal on my anklet.

The Professor ignores my mood. "The technology isn't perfect, but the theory is sound." He looks at me sternly—well, sternly for the Professor—over his glasses. "I want to make sure you understand the risks and benefits. Think of yourself as the center of a circle, extending thirty feet in every direction. The State knows you're in that circle. Sometimes, they know you're in the center of the circle. But their technology isn't perfect, especially when there are a lot of signals gathered together, with the effect that, sometimes, they only know you're somewhere in that circle. These decals extend that radius up to tenfold. You could be two blocks away from where they think you are."

"I get it. Thanks." I'm short, and I regret it, but he's so long-winded. I turn serious. "Thank you. For helping me try to remember. And for the tech to not die in the meantime. I do mean it, even if vomit-kitty is possibly the ugliest thing I've ever seen in my life. Seriously, I didn't think you could make one uglier than the last one."

Spyder ignores my jibe. He leads me through a maze of hallways that all look like the ones we came in through. I can't tell if he's trying to confuse my sense of direction, or if all of this is really required to exit this little compound. Bunker. He's different than he was when he swung me out from the guards. Quieter, maybe. And not just because he's not saying anything. He's taking up less space somehow. I wonder if he's okay, but I don't know that I can ask him.

He stops in front of a thin metal door, shoulders hunched and staring at the ground, and gestures for me to leave.

"Spyder..." His name is an invitation for him to at least look at me. "I really mean it. Thanks. For everything."

He speaks so low I barely hear him. "You're welcome."

Before I wimp out, I rush through a request. "I was wondering —maybe—if you still have contact with the old crowd from school, could you maybe make Em a decal? Tell her to meet me someplace near that cava shop in a couple of days. I haven't seen her since...before...and I want to make sure she's okay. I obviously can't go to Happytown, so I was thinking, maybe—she's the closest thing I've got to..."

He still won't look at me.

"Could you just do this for me please? I know I've been a jerk, but really you have too, and I just want... Please?"

He nods once and opens the door for me. "Two days."

I rush past him, laying a hand on his shoulder in thanks. My version of a hug, I guess. He flinches under my hand, but then he waves to me as I head out into the light.

**13**

---

"**Y**ou're weak. Get up, runt."
*Hazy green light fills the makeshift ring. The color goes well with my nausea. I pull myself to kneeling, barely. A heavy boot connects with the side of my head, sending me sprawling on concrete. I slide, scrapes on top of bruises, but I won't say a word or make a sound. I try to get up again, but the pain is too much, and I pass out.*

I wake up. A dream. No, a memory.

Before I fell asleep last night, I did some exercises. Nothing specific to training—because I don't remember training—more of things that felt right, like they'd make sense for a guard to do. Some basic sit-ups and pushups and then a few jabs at my shadow. I can see myself in that fighting ring from my dreams, but I can't remember any details about other people who must have been there.

The room felt unofficial, maybe like a club or an afterhours workout space. Actual training must've had more people, and this felt private. But, then again, this is all supposition until I get my memory back. I run through the same exercises as last night. Doc said simulating training might bring back memories, and I had my first whisper of success. If you can call a boot to the head a whisper.

What would they have taught me in training? Physical conditioning would have to come first. Fighting, for sure. The training is in my muscle memory; I took down those guards after Spyder and I left the cava shop. The routines and patterns of the guards are in my body, if not my brain. I can feel them, but I can't think them. Somehow I've got to turn my brain off so it doesn't get in the way of my body remembering.

I start in on some jumping jacks to get my blood moving. I'm not looking for a memory now, just a way to bring more of them back. I work through the problem, bouncing possibilities around my brain as my feet bounce on this creaking floor. The wood gives, and I try to lighten my impact. In and out, in and out, until I'm completely out of breath and fall to my knees. But it works.

The way I see it, I've got two options. I can keep doing these exercises and hope they trigger more memories. Or I can find someone to fight. Someone who might use the same training I had against me. The same moves that I might somehow remember.

Oh, gwock. Might as well do both.

I HATE RUNNING FLAT FOOTED, but the thick soles of my boots won't allow anything else. Each time my feet hit the ground, the reverberation echoes through my spine up to the top of my head. The air is warm and humid today, and the sun is shining as brightly as it ever does, casting a thick orange glow over everything. Sweat beads on my back as I push myself forward, trapped by the thick shirt I'm wearing. If my aim is to be as miserable as possible, I'm succeeding.

I run down the center of the street, hiding from no one. I'm deep in Undergrounder territory. Same as the other day, no one is out, or at least visible. *Keep to the shadows.*

Not today.

I stop for a moment, trying to slow my breathing by counting, prolonged inhales and exhales that my body fights. Not my first fight of the day, and it won't be my last. The guards don't generally patrol this deep in the sector, unless they have a reason to. Maybe today, I'm that reason.

I fiddle with the heinous decal on my anklet and wonder how the tech works. Before I can overthink it, I peel the decal off.

Almost immediately, I slap it back on and start running again. I'm not *completely* stupid. They sent a Georgian tank after me last time. I don't want to die. I want to remember who I am.

Regretting my momentary stupid impulse, I take a few turns down the side streets and alleys, losing myself in the rhythm of the run, and hopefully losing the attention of The State. For now.

For a moment, I wonder if I'm running from them. No. I'm running for them. I will run and run until I find them and make them give me back myself. I will run until I wheeze and fall down passed out, and when I wake back up, I will run again. I will run forever.

And then I'm flying face-first into the gravelly road. I brace with my arms and skid, trying to hold my head up. The stones cut through my long sleeves and pants, biting into my skin like a gargoyle's teeth. I register the sensation of tearing before the pain sets in.

When it does, all I can do is scream. "Son of the virgin!"

I curl myself into a ball and try to will the pain away. It doesn't work. When the throbbing becomes a dull part of me, the first thing I do is check to make sure the decal on my anklet is still in place. I won't make that mistake again.

Satisfied that the guards aren't going to come around the corner and haul me off, or worse, I haul myself out of the street to the shadows on the edges of the alley. I flick the loose gravel from my pants and start to work out the small chips that broke through my meager cloth defenses.

"Gwock, I thought you were Ops. My bad." A girl around my age materializes next to me.

If I weren't already on the ground, I'd have jumped at the interruption. "Who are you?"

"What are you doing out in the middle of the day? Alabama, are you new to this sector or something? Shhh. They're coming."

She switches from rapid fire questions to total silence before I can take a breath. She crouches next to me in tight dark clothing that emphasizes her athletic figure. Her sleeves are long, like mine, which means we're both covering up something in this hot weather. Unlike my heavy boots, her shoes are light and whisper-soft, like she'd dance through the streets rather than running.

She turns down the alley, passes me, and her ponytail brushes my cheek. She smells faintly of sweat and fruit syrup. She reminds me of the play period after snack at school, when we'd invent whatever games came to us with swing chains and foam balls.

"Could you run, if you had to? Not far, maybe thirty feet." Her question is a breath, not even a whisper.

Flexing my knees to test the pain, I nod.

Five guards enter the alley in a V-formation, weapons at the ready—some kind of ugly barbed clubs. Gravel crunches uniformly as they progress; they march as one.

We stay as low and close to the side of the building as possible before they pass. Neither one of us moves more than we have to.

They pass us and pause at the next intersection. The lead guard takes out a radio and barks out, "No sign of her here. Proceeding down the southwest route." He signals to the team.

They left face and continue marching down the next street.

"That was lucky. Come on." Fruity ponytail hauls me to my feet and braces me, sliding a surprisingly strong arm under my shoulder and around my waist. She's a little taller than me and lean enough that I'm surprised she can support me. "Yeah, no way you could have run. Let's get you inside."

My options are to hobble through the streets with the guard wandering around or go with this chick who's clearly trying to avoid them. *The enemy of my enemy is my friend.*

"Thanks," I grunt.

We walk a few feet to an open doorway, where a rusty metal door is propped open with a short length of pipe. She leads me down a set of stairs into a basement room that reeks of grimy bodies and dirty laundry. The light is dim down here, and it takes me a minute to adjust after the harsh daylight.

A raised square in the middle of the room covered with heavy black fabric takes up half of the room. Posts at each of the four corners, a frayed rope wrapped around them, further define the space. I've heard about these but never seen one—it's a fighting ring.

On two of the four sides, large metal hooks hang suspended from the ceiling with heavy black bags, patched in places with different colored cloth and thick twine. The other two sides have rows and rows of unmatched chairs. Some look like they belong at a fancy dining table, and others are metallic and institutional, interspersed with brightly colored chipped plasticine chairs. There must be about a hundred, so tightly packed the people who sit in them must be able to smell what their neighbors had for dinner.

The walls are black, like the fabric, and the chairs stand out in the space, like the ring is some giant mouth about to devour them. The whole place is a little creepy. At night, it's probably filled with the worst of the Undergrounders. I wonder if it's less creepy then.

"Come to the back, and I'll get you patched up. We've got a few supplies we can spare before the next run." She pulls me toward the training area. "Oh, wait. Shoes off on the mat, please."

I start to bend down, but the movement strains my raw skin. "Can I at least sit down?"

"Sure, sure. Yeah, that's probably better. I'll get the stuff."

She disappears through a dark door that blends in with the rest of the wall. I gently lower myself into one of the metal chairs. No cushion, but that makes it cleaner than some of the others. I keep my shoes on since it's just easier that way. She reappears through the invisible door with gauze and a brown bottle.

"Disinfectant and these." She pulls a pair of tweezers from her back pocket. "Should do the trick."

She crouches down and pours a little from the bottle onto a piece of gauze, wipes the tweezers, then dabs the gauze on my skin through the holes in my pants.

"You want to take these off?"

"Not unless you buy me a meal first." The joke is older than our grandparents would be, but she smiles and winks at me.

"Didn't think so." Her delicate fingers dance over my scraped skin, deftly removing the loose stone. "It's not starting to scab yet, so this shouldn't hurt much."

It doesn't. I can barely feel the lightness of her work. A slight tingle trailing her touch is all that remains.

"What's your name?" I ask.

"Lex. Yours?"

"Bree."

She stops her work momentarily to look up at me. "Hello, Bree," she says with a half-smile.

We sit in silence for the next few minutes as she finishes her ministrations. When she's done, she wipes her hands on her tight pants and stands. "Sorry about that."

"What? No, you're fine. Thank you."

"Ah—least I could do was fix you up." She pulls me to stand when I'm not quite ready. My feet are tangled, and I lean into her. It's almost like a hug, if I were the hugging kind.

"I have a confession to make." Her lips buzz by my ear.

"Yeah?" I straighten up.

"You fell for me."

"Huh?" I'm pretty sure my face is bright red at this point.

"Because of me. For the club, I mean."

"I don't understand." Is she trying to be cute?

"We've been getting a lot of patrols around here, which is unusual to say the least. There's nothing for the guards to protect here, and we mostly keep to ourselves. But I'm not one to let an opportunity go to waste, and neither are my employers, so..."

"So?"

"So we set traps to catch the guards where we can. We take whatever we can off of them. Supplies. Med kits, weapons, that kind of thing."

"I was running. I didn't land in any kind of trap."

Lex holds up a metallic spool and unwinds it a little. The wire is so thin, I can't see it in this dim light.

"I set up a trip line. I knew the guards would be coming, but you got here first. I'm glad I got to you before they did."

"Me too, I guess." I'm not mad, but I *am* confused. That's pretty normal for me lately. At least she hasn't drugged me or taken away my memories. Yet.

"Were you running from them? The guards?" she asks.

"Not *from* them. I don't think I could take five, though, so I'm glad I didn't find them."

"You wanted them to catch you?"

"No—it's a long story, and no offense, but I don't know you."

"You could." She draws out the word, teasing me, I guess. When I don't really react, she continues. "I know we just met."

"What is this place?" I'm not so off-balance around her any more...now that I know she off-balanced me in the first place.

"The club?" She seems surprised. "You haven't heard of the club?"

"I mean, I've heard of the concept, but I didn't know this particular one existed."

"This is the only club in the sector. There were a few more a couple years back, but this is the only one left. They come from all over to watch the bouts."

"I was away for a while." I immediately regret my admission. No one goes "away."

Her eyes narrow like I just gave her the key to understanding my entire life.

"Oh. Okay," she says calmly. She's excited, though, bouncing lightly on the balls of her feet. "Do you by any chance need a job?"

A job? That's the last thing I need right now. Credits and another way for The State to track me.

"No thanks."

"Probably not like you're thinking, not like a job-job, but a job." She points toward the empty ring. "In there."

"You want me to fight?"

"Yes. Certain...types...always put on a good show."

What type is she talking about? "I'm not who you think I am."

"I don't think anything about you." Lex crosses her arms in front of her chest. Her fingers worry the seam of her shirt, right where a guard's insignia would go.

"You think I was a guard? Well, I wasn't."

"Oh." She deflates.

I take a hard look around the room. Something about the ring calls to me, reminiscent of the whisper of a memory I dreamed this morning. "But, actually, now that you mention it... I wouldn't mind a good fight. If you could teach me the rules."

Her smile is the only answer I need in this moment. Hey, a girl's got to eat and access her lost memories somehow, right?

## 14

"*One, two, three, four, five, six, seven, eight, nine, ten.*"

*We chant in unison. I'm in a room with a thick padded floor and mirrored walls all around. The reflection of the space is blurry, like looking through a window clouded by age. But it's accurate to what I see around me—dark shapes that melt together in movement.*

"*One, two, three, four, five, six, seven, eight, nine, twenty...*"

*My body aches from the repetition. I strike with each count, just as everyone else in the room does. We're aiming for each other, though we do not touch. Contact at this point would mean punishment. On and on we go. Tiredness breeds sloppiness, and we're not getting out of here until someone makes a mistake. It's part of the ritual, the routine. There must be a mistake and a punishment.*

"*...one, two, three, four, five, six, seven, eight, nine, one hundred.*"

*The leader calls out, "Rotate partners. Begin again."*

*One, two...*

I gasp and wake up. That was a dream, a real, honest to the VM dream without any mist or anything. More than that, it was a memory. The running worked. And soon, once I go back to the club, I can start some real training and unlock more memories, useful ones.

I bolt out of bed, buzzed and a little anxious, like I've had too much cava.

The scrapes on my legs and arms aren't too bad, but Lex still wanted me to give it a little time before working out at the club. The only reason I didn't argue with her was that I was already tired from running. Little kids get hurt worse on ball courts than I did when she tripped me.

I do my morning exercise and head to the cava shop. If Spyder's as good as his word, it's time to see Em. He was supposed to give me details on some meeting, too, but he never did. Maybe he gave Em a note or something. I hope he doesn't show up, too.

When I leave Undergroundland, I keep to the side streets and shadows as much as possible. The cava shop's in an average area of town in Budgetville, so it's a nice central meeting place for me and Em. The cameras work around there, though, so even though I've got Spyder's puketastic decal confusing my ankle monitor, I've still got to avoid showing up on some overeager guard's security feed.

I can't be off-network like Doc and the Professor, but I can make it as difficult as possible for The State to track me. The State can't watch everywhere all the time, but it would be my rotten luck to have them looking at me at just the wrong moment. I will meet them on my terms, and my terms include keeping them as far away from anyone I care about as possible.

The cava shop's got a big wooden board where the window that the guards blew up used to be. It's cool, though. They've painted the wood black and drawn all over it in chalk—mugs and bread loaves and the daily special in cool big scripted letters, hanging over one of the mugs like steam. In messy scrawl in the bottom right, someone added, "10% surcharge added for all members of the guard." I snort, but The State probably wouldn't think it's as hilarious as I do. The shop could probably claim vandals since the handwriting is different, but the display is pretty brazen.

I've avoided crossing the street so far, but I have to in order to get to the cava shop. The street is exposed, no cover from cameras or the wrong kind of passerby. I'm quick.

Em's in the shop, alone, sipping on some green sludge that I hope isn't the daily special. I don't go over to her right away. I haven't seen her in over a year, and I take this opportunity to drink her in. It's a cava shop, after all. We look a little alike—we both have dark hair and similar face shapes, but that's where the similarities end. Even seated, I can tell she's still small. Her feet barely graze the floor, and they're bouncing excitedly with that pent-up Em energy.

Em's the most impatient person I've ever met, and my complete opposite, personality-wise. She's a firecracker. Short, scrawny, and, like a puppy, willing and able to knock anyone on their butt in a matter of seconds with her own excitement. I'm more filled out and cautious on the approach. I have to be.

I slide calmly and casually into the seat across from her. "Hey."

"Bree!" Em squeals and launches herself across the table at me.

I give her a quick squeeze before pushing away. She feels thin to me.

"Your mom feeding you enough?"

She smiles. "You know it. Growth spurt. Mom says the rest of me hasn't caught up yet but not to worry. I'm just glad I'm not picked last for ball anymore."

"Uh huh. Stand up."

She not only stands, she twirls and flops back into her seat.

"You *have* grown," I say.

She's still on the short side, though. Knew it.

She laughs. "You're such a liar, Bree."

"No, really. You're like, a quarter of an inch, maybe half an inch, taller than the last time I saw you." I choke back a laugh but can't hold it in.

"Your face." She points, and now we're both cracking up in the middle of the shop.

Em wipes the tears from her eyes and says through laughter, "I missed you."

It's like we've been doused with a bucket of icy cava.

"Me too."

"What was it like?"

"I don't remember."

"Are you okay? Did something happen?"

"I don't know. I'm working with some people to try to get my memories back."

"Maybe you hit your head or something. They didn't tell us much, but they told us you were released. Mom tried to find out more, but they said they couldn't tell us 'cause she wasn't your guardian anymore."

Mrs. Blank, Em's mom, was my foster mom for a while until I was tapped. As part of my service, The State emancipated me.

"Why haven't you come back to us?" Em's pleading stare is like a punch to my guts.

"Honestly?" I would never lie to Em, but I draw the word out to buy some time to compose my thoughts. "I don't really know. It doesn't feel safe. I feel...different. I'm constantly on edge, and I see threats everywhere. And a lot of those threats have turned out to be real so far. I guess I didn't want to bring that to you."

"But we're together now."

"Spyder fixed it so The State doesn't know. That's the only reason, and I really wanted to see you."

"He gave me this." She pulls up her pant leg and shows me a decal of a kitten riding a unicorn on top of a rainbow. "'Lorado rad, isn't it?"

I pretend to throw up, and we both laugh again. "He give you anything to give to me?" I ask, thinking of that meeting Doc wanted me to go to.

"Nope. Why?"

"Doesn't matter." If they want me, they can use their tech to find me. Not my problem. I've proven I can get memories back without them.

"He said I'm only supposed to wear it for an hour. Something about signal syncing and cameras and a network. You know Spyder."

Only too well.

"Only an hour? You should be getting back. We can't chance going longer." To cut off temptation, I get up to leave.

"But you haven't even had a drink yet."

"Doesn't matter. This is serious. I'll be in touch. I'll find a way." I hesitate. "Tell your mom I said hi."

Em springs up and wraps me in a tight hug.

I give in and rest my chin on my almost-sister's head. "Miss you," I whisper into her hair. I can tell she heard me, because she squeezes me tighter.

I push her away and leave the shop without looking back.

I CHANGE behind a curtain into the workout clothes Lex gave me. They're tight, like what she was wearing the day I met her, but a deep purple instead of the cool black she wore. I don't object because colorful clothing is so rare, and it's amazing how rich the purple is, like the evening sky after a deadly rain. Not really my style, though, especially because the stretchiness of the fabric gives them a weird sheen. I leave my boots on, which look ridiculous with the skintight outfit, but they make me more comfortable.

Lex greets me as I walk into the training area. "No shoes on the mat."

"Come on," I say.

"Safety reg. Can't have our equipment getting damaged."

"Fine, fine," I grumble and toe off my boots. I didn't really think she'd let me keep them on.

"I want to get an idea of where you are. We'll start with an open workout, and when I have a better idea of your skillset, I'll direct you into some targeted drills. Sound good?"

"Sure."

She puts me in front of one of the hanging bags and instructs me to hit it however I'm most comfortable. I act on instinct. I use my fists, open hands, elbows, legs, every part of me I can to send the bag flying, swinging away. I relish it coming back so I can strike again. I sense the rhythm of its oscillations and time my strikes nearly perfectly to really feel the connection as each blow lands. This is the most satisfied I've felt since my release.

Going with my impulse, I dodge the bag as it swings toward me. I spin in a tight circle and let loose a heel kick that sends the bag flying off its hook and crashing onto the mat on the other side of the room. Small stones spill out from a new rip in its side.

"Nice one. Hang tight a second."

"Thanks." I'm panting a little. This has been a good workout.

Lex fiddles around in the corner of the room and pulls out a square of cloth and some cord. "You rip it, you stitch it."

WITH MY BACK against the ring, I sit on the floor, sewing up the bag. It's taking forever, and I've pricked my fingers at least a dozen times.

"Ouch," I yelp at the latest and stick my finger in my mouth.

"Y'know, most people bleed here because someone's hit them."

"Consider it a donation."

"We're not a health center."

"Ouch."

"Seriously? Again?"

"Shhh. I've got to finish this." I smile and try my Dakotaest not to poke myself again. The back and forth is easy with Lex, like we've known each other for a long time. We sit in silence as I finish stitching, and that's easy, too. It's nice.

When I'm done, I toss the heavy bag at her, rocking her stance a little. Good.

"All done. You said something about drills?"

"Yeah. Unfortunately, there's a meeting here soon, so we've got to clear the training area."

"Oh." I'm disappointed. I haven't felt so alive as when I was literally kicking the stuffing out of that bag. "Want to scrounge up some food or something? Since we have to get out of here?"

"Thanks, but I actually need to go to the meeting."

"What's it for?"

"Just some setup stuff and member debrief for the owners. Most boring part of my job."

"What exactly *is* your job?"

"I'm a coordinator. I actually wanted to talk to you about that —" A beeping near the back entrance by the lockers interrupts her. "Gwock! That's the owners. See you later."

She practically pulls me to the door and shoves me through the front. "Hey—my stuff."

"Sorry, they really don't like non-employees around for these meetings. You can get your stuff next time. Besides, you look great." She looks up and down my body, and it catches me off-guard. "Like an old-time superhero or something."

I flex a little inside my workout clothes, feeling almost as pumped as when I was working the bag. I'm on the verge of striking some ridiculous pose like in one of Spyder's comic books, but reason quashes the impulse, thank gwock. The backdoor beeps again, and Lex slams the heavy, rusted front door in my face.

"Okay, bye," I say to the air. Weird.

The door reopens. "Knew you couldn't stay away." I almost smirk before my boots are unceremoniously tossed out and the door slams shut in my face once again. Well, fine. "Couldn't have given me my normal clothes, too?"

I pound on the door and wait for a minute to see if they'll be delivered in the same way. Nothing.

What to do now? I was planning on spending the day training. I guess I could go back to the crumbling building where I live with the crazy hobo and—do more jumping jacks? Fix the holes in my floor? Try and fall asleep so that I might have another dream? I don't like having nothing to do, so it's time for me to find...something.

A job is out. Clearly. Not through the normal channels, anyway. There really aren't any jobs that The State doesn't track. Credits are tracked, and there's no real way to trade for anything when you have nothing. I could try to find some odd job doing yardwork or cleaning for a crappy Nutripaste sandwich, but there are enough places that give those away for free. Charity is the work of the Carolinnyites, so called because they believe in the tales of southern hospitality. They have orders all over the sectors.

I've got a place to live, and if I need food, I can get it from them. The only price is listening to them talk about their values. Besides, at some point, fighting will be my job—once I finish showing Lex what I can do. If I get the chance to. Getting kicked out stings, but I get that everyone needs to be careful. Guards are everywhere.

So I guess I'm back to my primary task: getting my memories back. I've tried running and working out the way I probably had to during training. I'm on the path to fighting, but the club is closed. Maybe it's time to find a new opponent.

## 15

I head to the very edge of Undergroundland, which borders with the part of the sector where most people live and scrounge to make ends meet. We call it Budgetville. On my side of the street, the Undergroundland side, total squalor. On the Budgetville side, faded, crumbling brick and stone, but at least there aren't any holes.

I head into a clothing shop that boasts "Five Different Shades of Green" next to a brown colored shirt in the window. A bell rings when I walk in.

Without looking up, the woman behind the register says, "Can I help you?" She keeps flipping through the sheets.

"I'm good, thanks." I walk among the racks, brushing past a mix of men's and women's clothes in the five shades of "green."

From what I can tell, there's brownish green, really brownish green, dark greenish brown, and that's about it. I can't resist needling the bored cashier. "I thought there were supposed to be five shades. I only see three."

"We're out of stock."

Too easy. She's had practice.

I grab something at random. "Can your order me this in one of the other shades?"

"We get what we get. State rations." She pushes the sheet to the side and pulls a piece of string from underneath the counter. She winds it around her fingers in a complex pattern.

"Okay, well, I guess I'll take it in this color." I open the door. The bells ring again, and she still hasn't looked up. "And by take, I mean I've picked something up, and I'm going to walk out of the store with it."

She shrugs. "Suit yourself."

"As in, without paying. As in, I'm going to steal this."

"Thank you for shopping at Clothing Remainders. Have a nice day."

With my hand on the door, I try one last time, "Maybe you should call the guards or something? Let them know there's a robbery in progress?"

She waves me out of the store.

I walk outside with my free, greenish—I finally look at what I picked up—extra large pair of men's underwear. Joy. Couldn't even accidentally on purpose steal something useful. A few passersby stare at me but quickly turn away when I make eye contact. I must look like a crazy person in my shiny purple training suit waving giant underwear around like a sick green flag.

If I can't get the guards called on me, then I'll go find them. I stuff the underwear behind a bin on the corner. Maybe I'll come back for them on my way home. A present for Charley, because what says "I care about my landlord" more than a useful pair of boxers three sizes too big for his emaciated frame.

I could try some vandalism. Throw some rocks at a window or break something. I kick at a concrete curb until my toes go a little numb. With one more solid kick, a couple of chunks break off. I heft the largest and bounce the rock around a little in my hand.

I go back to the bin, grab the underwear, and head back to the clothes shop.

Bursting through the door and talking over the stupid bells, I say, "It didn't bother you that I took these? I don't want them anyway, take them back." I throw them on the ground and leave.

I take aim at the stupid five shades of green sign in the glass window. *Do it. Do it. Get the guards here, fight them, and remember.*

I can't. Who am I kidding? I can't do it. I can't willfully destroy someone's place of business, someone's livelihood who never did anything to me. They may sell State-issue goods, but so does everybody else. Whoever the owner is, he or she is not responsible for my missing memories and doesn't deserve to be drawn into this. Unless the owner is that annoying register clerk, and then maybe she does.

The concrete chunk falls from my fingers and tumbles a few inches. I watch the edges crumble from the slight impact, and, as seems to be my constant state of being, I wonder what I'm doing. I sit on the curb and fiddle with the decal again. Maybe if I peel it off just for a little while, the guards will come like they did outside of the club. It worked once, but I'm hesitant to try my network-luck in Budgetville where there are more cameras for them to track me, even if my signal is bouncing around everywhere.

I don't want to die. I only want to remember. I get this feeling in my stomach that there's a fine line between the two, and that's the only thing stopping me from peeling off this cutesy stupid sticker and letting them come to me. A strong gust of wind blows my hair forward. I push it back, and look to the sky. The weather doesn't change much in the sector. Though the sky is always gray, the subtle outline of gathering clouds drives me to my feet.

And then the rains start.

A man about a half a block away feels the first couple of drops. He screams and drops to his knees, clawing at his face.

A woman covers her child's head with a dish and runs into the nearest building.

More screams fill the air. The streets are in chaos as we all scramble to find cover. A couple of drops land on my arm, melting through the fabric. I ignore the burning and run for the closest building: the clothes shop.

The woman behind the counter finally looks up to find me spitting on the burned spots on my sleeve.

"I've been patient, but I've had about enough of you."

"It's raining."

She bolts from her chair and runs for the window. She peers out, panicked. "This isn't glass—it's plasticine. Help me."

We pull down a rolling metal cage from the ceiling. The bars are designed to stop robberies, not rain, so it will provide little protection if the wind shifts.

A young father and his son come out of one of the back dressing rooms, drawn by the loud groans of metal.

"Everything okay?" he asks.

"It's raining. Help us." We pull racks of clothes over and stack them in front of the cage.

"Stay back," he orders his son. He pulls yards of rough fabric from the bulk bins at the front and quickly weaves the cloth between the bars at the top of the cage.

"How's the roof here?" I ask.

"I'm not sure, but there are three floors above us, so that should be enough."

"Daddy? What's going on?" The little boy's voice trembles. His father quickly finishes with the fabric, then runs back and scoops up his son.

"We have to stay inside for a while."

"Are there bad men outside?"

"No bad men. You know how every year there are a few days when we have to cover up because the sun gets really hot? It's kind of like that." He kisses the top of the boy's head.

"Is the sun out?"

"Not today. Today it's raining."

"What's rain?"

"Rain is like when the sun burns, but wet like a drink from a hydropack."

The boy probably wasn't even born the last time it rained. I remember my first rain. I was older than him, maybe eight or so. I was in school, which was probably the safest place for us to be. A lot of the buildings in that area still had glass, and the schools are one of the most heavily patrolled areas by the guards, so vandalism is at a minimum. A bunch of kids were whining about no recess, because we could see the rec yard outside through the thick glass windows.

A row of trees bordered the back of the metal-framed climbing equipment. They were the first to go. At first, it seemed like the leaves were disappearing—not floating down to the ground like in the season of reaping, which would have been in a few weeks—but there and then not there. Branches broke off and crashed to the ground, where we couldn't really see them anymore. Last to go were the trunks, which sort of seemed to invert on themselves, collapsing inward and then down in a gooey mess with floating wood chips that looked like pictures I'd seen of sinking ships.

When the metal climbing frame twisted on itself and started to sink, the kids who'd been whining about no recess started to cry. I didn't cry. I was used to having nothing.

Here, in the store, we huddle in a back corner, as far from the windows as possible and near to the counter in case we need one last layer of defense. The sirens start wailing, a relic from our ancestors. Now, they only sound when it rains or if there's some kind of attack. This is the third time I've heard them. They sound like a machine crying.

"I'm Shyla," the clerk says.

"I'm Michael," the man says. One of the old names. "And this is Vin. He's grown a lot in the last month. We were getting him some new threads before the next class cycle starts."

"I see that a lot. Hi, Vin." She smiles at the boy.

"Bree," I say.

No one seems to be paying attention to me.

Vin says, "In school they told us when the sirens go off we have to get under our desks, but there aren't any desks here."

"That's why we have this." Shyla thumps the counter. "Sturdy, like a desk."

The roof creaks above, a few floors up, and feet pound as people run overhead to shore up their protections. Vin stares at the ceiling, and his father and Shyla do their best to distract him.

To pass the time, they make up a strange game involving the string Shyla was playing with earlier and rolls of socks from a nearby bin. I follow the action as they invent the rules. Vin seems to be winning, but only because his additions to the newly minted game serve his immediate point total. They don't invite me to play, and I wouldn't. It's dumb. The boy sends a sock flying and lets out a loud whoop when he scores a point. A muted scream carries down to us, but the ceiling is holding.

Vin's elation turns somber as he moves away from the field of sheets and wastebaskets.

"Are you scared?" he asks me.

"What? No."

"You're really quiet. Sometimes I get quiet when I'm scared. It's okay."

"I'm not scared of the rain."

The boy scoots close to me so that our legs are touching. "But you're scared of something."

"Vin…" his father warns.

"No, it's really okay. You're right that I'm scared of something. And you know what else? You're right that it's okay to be scared."

The boy nods.

Something, or someone thumps the ceiling. A loud crash that

sounds like a tray full of dishes breaking and some yelling make us all jump. Vin leaps into his father's lap.

Michael strokes his hair. "We're fine, buddy." I notice he doesn't say the people upstairs are fine. "Sounds like someone dropped something."

He stares at me and Shyla, as though daring us to contradict him.

Shyla tosses a roll of socks into the air. "Do you want to play some more?"

"No, thanks," Vin says. "I'm scared of the rain. It sounds bad. You must be scared of something *really* bad if the rain doesn't scare you." He stares at me, wide-eyed.

"I can't remember why I'm scared," I say.

"Like a bad dream? Like when you wake up and you know something bad happened, but you can't remember exactly what?"

"She doesn't want to talk about it, Vin."

I ignore his father. "You're a smart kid," I say.

"I'm second in my class. So far. I have to beat out Jade to be first."

"If you work really hard this year, then maybe you will."

"I know. I bet if you work really hard, you won't be scared anymore. You know what else I know? What we can't see is scariest. We can't look at the rain 'cause it'll hurt us. That makes it worse somehow, you know." He points to the ceiling, where all is now quiet.

"Uh huh."

"So sometimes we just have to do things anyway, even though we're scared."

"You sure you're not first in your class?"

"Not unless Jade got stupider over break."

We sit there for hours, listening to the rain hiss down. Vin falls asleep, and the rest of us are tempted to out of sheer boredom. We can't be fully bored though, not when there's the threat that the water will bore through the building. Waiting gives me plenty of time to think, and I'm so tired of thinking. I can't help but think of Spyder, Doc, and the Professor. I hope they're doing okay in The Bunker. With the grates in the tunnels, the rain must pour down on them.

"Take these." Shyla hands me a stack of clothes. "You'll be more comfortable in them."

I'd almost forgotten about the shiny purple workout suit. Dark neutrals are more my style, but this green-ish beige is better than nothing.

"I can't pay you," I say.

"Consider them a gift. We'll all be more comfortable if we stick to regulations, even when it's just silly little clothes."

I gag at her prim tone. "Thanks."

She's just lucky I hate bright purple. I throw the clothes on over my workout gear.

"I don't like being cooped up." Michael paces circles around the shop. He walks within a few feet of our makeshift wall, but he doesn't touch it. For the most part, he avoids looking at the fabric-enforced gate altogether.

"If you want, I can get the guards here for you. After the rain," Shyla says to me.

"You've got a funny way of being nice to someone."

"You seemed to want them here earlier. I didn't want to help you hurt yourself, but if that's what you want—"

"I don't know what I want."

Michael sits back down. "Stay as far away from the guards as possible. They're not like us."

"Shhh." Shyla points to a security device in the far corner of the room.

"It's not like they're surveilling during the rain. Even The State has better things to worry about right now," Michael says.

Shyla's low whisper is urgent. "You can't know that—and they might take Vin away from you."

"They won't," he says. "People pay attention now. The State

keeps talking about how the other sectors are a threat to us, but the guards they give us are from those other sectors. People notice."

"Not everyone can be bad," Shyla says. "You know they take the good ones out and make them Lifers. To protect us. They tell us that at the tapping."

"Have you ever talked to a guard?"

"Of course! Every two weeks when they come by to check the devices and conduct the interview."

"No, I mean really talked with them. About their lives, anything."

Shyla is silent. I watch them both.

"I thought so. You don't know them, and they don't know us. Aren't you tired of living like this? Selling these things?" He grabs one of the greenish shirts and shakes the material in her face. "As though it's what you want to be doing, as though you have a choice, as though we have a choice in what to buy? Eating the same rations day in and out, hoping that with a miracle allotment of some special ingredient and some cooking skills you can make Nutripaste taste like anything other than the dirt it is?"

Shyla motions at the security box. "Be quiet."

"He's right," I jump in. "Something isn't right, and not just with me. Something's wrong with this entire sector. There's no point to any of the stupid regulations."

"Yes, there is," Shyla hisses. "Keep your voices down. That, that sleeping boy right there is the point. And if you're too busy looking for someone outside of your sad life to blame, then maybe they *should* take him away from you. You don't deserve him."

"Maybe he just wants better for him," I say.

Michael tosses the green shirt over the rack. "You don't like what I'm saying, that's fine. But ask yourself: When was the last time you had a real, honest to the VM conversation with someone who didn't spout the sponsored State lines?"

"You don't know what you're saying," Shyla says.

"Maybe I don't." He waves his arms at the rows and rows of clothing racks. "Or maybe the rain burns through all this crap so we can see the real crap underneath everything."

In the corner of the room, a wooden piece of furniture crashes through the ceiling, taking out the security box, and landing in a tangled mess of wood and wires on the floor.

"Daddy!" Vin wakes, screaming.

"Under the counter," Shyla orders.

We obey, huddling together. Water drips onto the mess, hissing, burning. A sharp smell weaves its way through the room and stings my nose. It smells like concentrated health center cleaning fluid.

"The rain will stop soon," Michael whispers into Vin's hair.

For all of our sakes, I hope he's right.

## 16

The pounding, hissing rain dulls to a deadly patter against the sides of the building. Our makeshift wall holds as the storm quiets. The scrape of furniture on floorboards above breaks the silence.

A woman's voice calls through the broken ceiling, "You folks alright down there?"

"We're okay. How are you up there?" Shyla says.

"All fine on the upper floors, but there's a hole that must be clear through to the roof. Our best guess is that there was a blockage in the gutters or a piece missing from the last storm, and the water flowed right into the side of the building."

"Lucky we weren't underneath," Michael says.

"We're all lucky. Report from the top floor is that the rain seems to be tapering off, so we can all get out soon and start fixing this mess."

"Thanks for the news," Shyla says.

True to the word from the top, the rain soon lets up. I wonder how Undergroundland fared, and if my building made it through. I hope Charley's okay. Cardboard won't protect anyone from this.

We take our time clearing the cloth from our makeshift barricade with metal poles from the clothing racks. We can't touch anything wet with our hands, so we have to work together to use the poles to pinch the cloth and pull. Where it still exists, that is. Portions of the cloth continue to disintegrate as the wetness wicks inward. The wetness smells sharp. Its caustic tang burns our noses, which makes it even more important to clear the cloth and vent the shop.

Shyla directs us, and we assist without complaint or questioning her orders. Except for Vin, of course. He sits under the counter ignoring the piece of string from earlier, silently watching us. Shyla and Michael's earlier argument is not forgotten, but the amount of work ahead of us keeps disagreements on the back burner. Besides, none of us owe any of the others anything, except all of us need to help to get out of here.

We carefully move the damp and sopping fabric to the pile in the corner where the ceiling crashed in to keep any further damage limited to one area. When we fully uncover the metal gate, it's mostly intact, though the sample clothes in the window and the window itself are gone. We can't roll the cage back up, because some of the joints have become twisted from contact with the acid.

"We could leave it up for a little longer," Michael suggests. "There may be some looting later, and this could protect the store."

"We'd be sitting targets," I object.

"And the guards won't be able to get in when they're deployed," Shyla says with steely focus on Michael. "The State will protect the store from looters."

"It's your merchandise. You can lose credits if you want to," Michael says. "Oh, wait. The clothes aren't yours. They're on consignment from The State."

Before another argument can fully erupt, I say, "Let's get out of here. We all have others we'll need to check on, so let's just go."

"Fine." Michael rattles the cage with a pole. "We can't get this back up, so it'll have to come down."

We wind dry cloth on our hands for protection and find safe places on the metal to grab.

"On three," Shyla says, back in charge.

We pull, but aside from some dramatic rattling like a ghost in chains, the gate holds.

Shyla drops her grip. "This isn't working."

I bite back the retort I have for such an annoyingly obvious statement and throw a dirty look at Michael before he can start another fight. He's actually not paying any attention but jabbing at the corners of the gate with his cloth-covered fists.

It gives me an idea. "What if we hit the weak points?"

"You mean bash them uselessly like he's doing?" Shyla punches at the air with a mocking expression on her face, as though she's making a point.

Michael and I ignore her.

"We hid from the rain—what if we use it now?"

They quickly catch on, and we tie some of the damp, dissolving cloth to a couple of rods that have broken off from the center of the gate.

"Ouch!" Michael hisses as the cloth burns his hands.

"Let me see." Shyla examines the wounds. "Rinse this off in the back sink. Through that door. There's a couple of hydropacks underneath. Use what you need to before that gets any worse." I guess she does have a heart.

"Thanks." Michael jogs to the back and rejoins us in a few minutes. His palms are streaked with pink—superficial damage only.

"I'm glad you got the water off in time," Shyla says. Their earlier fighting seems totally forgiven. "Let's all check our hand wrappings before we try this again. Once the wet cloth is on the poles, we should change the dressings on our hands immediately, before the rain burns through."

"Agreed." Michael nods.

"No argument here," I say.

We fix up the poles and hold them high against the gate. It takes a while for the acid to do its work—much longer than it took to burn Michael's hands. The metal is strong, and what we're using is probably on the weaker side since the cloth is still partially intact. Holding these poles in the air for fifteen minutes is a great upper body work out, but it's tiring.

Shyla's arms start to tremble first, and Michael's arms go wobbly shortly after. I could do this all day. Direct result of the training I can't remember, no doubt.

*Know your squad. Lead your squad.*

"Let's try pulling down again," I say.

We carefully stow the poles so the wetness is away from the main area and recheck our protective cloth bindings. Another count of three, and we pull. A low moan turns into a high-pitched squeal as one of the bars near the top grinds on itself and gives way.

"It's working," Michael shouts.

We keep pulling, but the rest hold fast.

"Should we put more of the water on it?" Michael asks.

There's no way he and Shyla can hold the poles for long enough.

"I think we need to alter our approach," I say.

Shyla sits on Michael's shoulders, and I carefully hoist some of the wet cloth up to her using one of the poles.

"Steady," I say to them both.

Shyla takes the cloth and wraps it around the poles at the top of the gate. After a few applications, she tosses her protective cloth down and asks Michael to lower her so she can reapply fully dry cloth. A few rounds of this, and we've got the top of the gate completely covered.

"Now what?" Michael asks.

"We wait."

Michael curls up beside Vin, who's fallen asleep again during all of this, either because he's young and needs the sleep or from boredom. Michael throws a protective arm over him and closes his eyes. It's probably only around two or three hours after when evening mealtime would be, but the stress of the day makes everyone tired.

Shyla and I sit on the other side of the room so as not to disturb them. She hands me a couple of Nutribiscuits and a hydropack.

"I believe in The State and the system," she whispers. "The State is all we have to protect our families. You must believe that, too, or you wouldn't have wanted the guards here earlier."

"What?" I say as neutrally as possible, because I have no idea what she's talking about.

She grabs my hand and squeezes tightly. A single tear rolls down her cheek as she nods at Michael and Vin. "He's given up, but you haven't. The State is here to help us all. I don't know what you need, but I'll do everything I can to help you."

"I—I don't know what to say." This woman is crazy, and I'm not going to say anything to make her more upset.

"I can help you apply for services—housing, food or clothing allotment, whatever you need. If you need a job assignment, I can try to reserve you for a few hours a week here. The work would only be part time, but it would be something."

"Oh," I say, but Shyla nods as though I'd said "okay."

"All I ask in return is your testimony."

"My testimony?"

"We've got to keep that boy safe. Vin needs to be separated from Michael. He's young enough there's still a chance for him."

"I don't know." I do know this woman is crazy. There's no gwocking way I'd help her.

"You could change his life. You could change *your* life. Turn things around and save both of you."

"I'll think about it." I'll think about it as I try to get as far away from this shop as possible. Finding the guards has not been one of my brighter ideas.

"That's all I ask."

Our conversation fades after that, thank the VM. I'm not sure how long we need to wait for the rainwater to do its work, but I check the gate periodically. If the metal is as weak as the ceiling, it'll just collapse, but at this point I'm happy to hurry the destruction along.

After another couple of hours, Michael rouses himself, and the three of us work together to bring down the gate. We work almost silently. The tension has grown between Michael and Shyla, and I really don't want to involve myself. I wouldn't be surprised if Michael overheard our conversation. I hope he knows I wouldn't do anything to take his son away, but there's no way I'm going to bring it up while there's still no way out of here.

I position myself on one of the ends, Shyla on the other. Michael takes the center, and we pull. The gate releases with a grinding groan, with Michael supporting the bulk of the weight. Grunting, he pushes the metal toward the outside. Stray pieces of metal fall against the window, dislodging the melted hunks of plasticine that remained, sending a mess of debris spewing into the darkened streets.

Air rushes in, warm and humid, like daylight giving its last breath before the night. For the first time I can remember, the blue street lights aren't on, the bulbs having been dissolved in the acidic rain.

The clatter echoes in the empty streets. Vin awakens, scared.

"Dad?" His voice is sweet and thick, like the sugar syrup that Mrs. Blank would pour on our breakfasts on special occasions.

"I'm here." Michael scoops him up and cradles him, creating a barrier against Shyla with his entire body. "We're going home."

He ignores both of us and walks out of the shop, grinding pieces of State-issue cloth under his heel as he walks.

I follow them.

"Wait!" Shyla grabs at my sleeve. "Are you going to help?"

"Yes," I say. "I'm going to help them by getting away from you."

I turn my back on her and walk out of the shop.

"I already have his chip ID from the payment system. I don't need you," Shyla yells at my back.

I hope she's lying.

## 17

My walk back to my decrepit home from Budgetville is unusual. I no longer have to keep to the shadows, because the entire world is in shadow, the tall buildings hiding what little light there is from the slivered moon. In spite of this, I am more vigilant than normal. Repair crews are out, efficiently replacing tracking cameras and their housings and security lights along the streets. Other crews must be working on damage to the power grid; I can only assume that's why the new lights are not yet operating. The workers largely ignore me, though. Either I'm too stealthy for them to notice, or they just don't care.

The guard patrols are trickier. They're out in force, no doubt as a peace keeping mission. I've passed three different units in only a few blocks, each on hyper alert. They've got giant flashlights, and they sweep the lights in a huge arc as they walk. Each time I potentially enter their range, I stop and time the sweeps. As long as I stay out of the flashlight beam, the dark night conceals me. Movement will only attract the guards' attention.

Shyla was worried about looters, but I haven't seen any so far. Tonight is perfect for a little stealing, and I'm tempted to go after some of the little luxuries The State holds so dear. I've got a brand new outfit, courtesy of Shyla's bribery—I mean, generosity —but, gwock, it would be good to eat something other than the tasteless vita-rations I've been scrounging for in Undergroundland.

I alter my course a little so I pass down grocers' alley. With a few exceptions, like the ancient mall, The State keeps shops of the same type together. Supposedly they simplify supply lines, which cuts down on costs. Keeps the shop operators honest with prices, too.

"Curfew is in effect," a voice blares out on the sector-wide com system. I guess they've gotten that part fixed first, as none of the lights are yet on. "All citizens are to remain indoors. If you need assistance, please place a yellow indicator in your door slot. Units are patrolling to provide help as needed. Again, curfew is in effect and will remain in effect until the damage from the rain can be assessed and abated. Remain in your homes until further notice. Curfew is in effect."

A series of noisy blasts echo in the streets, and the message loops after a minute or two. Just another courtesy of The State for any citizens trying to grab a little sleep tonight. Underneath this noisescape, the buzz of a radio gets louder as I creep down the street.

"Roll call." A whispering, disembodied voice breaks through the static. "D1 reporting clear," "D2 reporting clear," "D3 reporting clear." The voices of the guards start pouring through, making it easier for me to pinpoint the location of the guard with the radio in the dark.

Unlike the patrol units, his flashlight is off. He's leaning against a building on the corner, so still he's like part of the building. He's armored—any residual wetness from the rain will not go anywhere near his skin.

I've made a mistake coming this way. In addition to the

patrols, each of the shops has a guard posted to every door on every building. I'm sure there are plenty inside, too.

I backtrack. None of them seemed to have spotted me. I can't be sure where the stationary units are posted, but my gut tells me to avoid the biggest streets. My heartbeat is loud in the night, and each exhalation of breath announces my presence to the careful listener. I tense, ready to fight an enemy I cannot yet see.

Light floods the streets as the lamps come back on, and I am flooded with relief. Though I am illuminated in the bluish glow, the guards are as well. It's back to the shadows for me.

The patrols thin out a little in the residential neighborhoods, called to other duties or no longer as necessary with the lights (and presumably security cameras) back on. A few guards cluster on the unofficial border to Undergroundland, but they dwindle to nearly nothing when I cross the line toward home. Keep the Undergrounders in—no one cares what destruction we wreak within our own borders.

The buildings are all still standing. I don't know what I was expecting, but some obvious degree of destruction. I find the damage when I enter my building.

Splintered wood and concrete dust cover the stacks of cardboard Charley's accumulated over the last however many years. The stacks themselves have toppled, and a few are soggy, melting messes. Sheet pulp and normal building materials mingle in a soupy, smelly mess. Hunks of metal flotsam are sprinkled throughout like seasoning on a gourmet meal. The gray of old wood and concrete too bland? How about a few rusty nails partially dissolved on top for a warm coppery glow.

The tangy aroma of rain and destruction burns my nose and throat as I call out, "Charley? Charley?"

My voice is swallowed by the debris. I wade through the room, careful to avoid anything damp. "Charley," I call again.

"Don't think this gets you out of this month's rent." Charley pops up coughing from underneath a pile of sheets. Some kind of metal bowl is on his head, sprinkled with holes too uniform for the rain to have made.

I knock the bowl off his head, and it lands with a thunk on top of a large piece of wood. "Rain's stopped. And I don't pay you any rent."

"Yeah, that's what you think. For now." He snatches the bowl back and places it firmly on his head.

"You talking about the rain or the rent?"

He laughs. "Welcome home, girly. Good luck getting up there." He points up through the floors. I can see the corner of my bed hanging over the edge.

"Great." Just what I need. More open space, up nice and high. Sweet dreams, Bree.

FIRST THING IN THE MORNING, I head to Lex's, ready to fight. The club is dark and smells like dirty socks, slightly damp and mildewing from being in a laundry pile too long. I'm beginning to feel at home because of the girl standing across from me.

"Welcome back," Lex's lip quirks in a not-quite smile. "Nice outfit."

"What, this old thing?" I've paired the purple training shirt Lex gave me with the surplus pants from Shyla's store. I look a little ridiculous—the pants are a half size too big and baggy, and the shirt is skintight. But I'm much more comfortable.

"You do okay with the storm?"

"It was fine. Got caught out which was kinda annoying, but I slept like a baby last night." I had, with no dreams to bother me, or help me remember. "You?"

"Stuck in that meeting. The rain was basically over by the time we were done."

"Must've been a long meeting."

She changes the subject. "I was thinking we'd move on to

some partner training today. You hit the heck out of that bag, so let's see what you do to a person."

I remember the literal stuffing everywhere and draw back in surprise. "You want me to do that to a *person*?"

Lex's chest pulses with laughter, deep and throaty. "You are so literal. Too funny. We'll be using protective training pads, but we can hold back a little if you're worried."

We? Does she mean *she's* going to be my opponent?

She tosses me a few pads and bangs two gloves together. "Let's see what you got."

This could be interesting.

We circle each other in the ring. Lex's feet barely graze the mat as she dances along the ropes. She's nimble, light, and delicate, and I can't land a blow on her, which is frustrating as heck. She floats by me. Her jab brushes my cheek as she passes, more an annoyance than a real strike. I swipe at her arm, but she's already gone. My sad attempt to block pulls me a little off balance, and she lands a kick with a little more power right in my exposed ribs.

I wince and grunt a little. "Nice one."

"I could do this all day." She winks and prances around the ring.

She tests me with a few more jabs, and I don't chase her punches again. She's not going to be able to use the same trick on me twice.

She unleashes a flurry of light blows, and I raise my fists to cover my face. Suddenly, I'm on the ground with a sharp pain in my leg. While I'm on the ground, Lex drops her guard and waits for me to get up. She doesn't even offer a hand to help me.

"Seriously, you kicked me? How is that fair?"

"Street rules. This is a fight, not a sport."

I'm pissed, because we didn't talk about rules beforehand. Massaging my calf, I stand and test my weight. It's a wicked charley horse, but the pain will pass.

"Ready?" Lex asks.

"Bring it."

She keeps dancing around, but I know exactly what I'm going to do. The next time she throws one of those stupid little jabs, I smash my head into her fist. The surprise of the impact interrupts her timing, and I catch her arm, pulling her head down and exposing her side. I thrust a kick into her ribs, and all the air rushes out of her.

She bends further over, and I'm ready for my next move: destroy her stupid arm, and then destroy her. A quick pop, and I dislocate her shoulder. She screams and drops to her knees, exposing the back of her neck. I—I don't know what I'm doing.

"Crap, Lex, I'm sorry." I drop beside her. "I don't know what's wrong with me."

"Put it back in," she says through gritted teeth.

"What?"

"You popped my shoulder out, you put it back in. Now."

"I don't know how—"

"Shove it, really hard."

"I don't want to hurt you...more."

"Just do it."

"Okay."

Tears leak out of the corners of her eyes. She jams a glove into her mouth and bites down. Blood's dripping from somewhere on my face where she punched me. I didn't even notice. The blood mixes with her tears, running in pink rivulets on her cheeks.

"On three," I say. "One—" I push really hard to shove her shoulder back into its socket.

Her glove muffles her scream. After a minute, she rotates her arm in a circle. She wipes her face dry with the back of her glove. "Good as new. What happened to three?"

I hesitate, because I'm not sure how to read her. "I thought it might be better if you didn't know exactly when it was coming."

She laughs. "Back on your feet. Let's finish this."

I'm relieved...and confused. "What?"

"We're not done yet."

"No way—I took you clean out. That's got to end the fight."

"Ends when I say." She shrugs—with both shoulders—and offers a glove to help me stand. I grab on and use her stability to bring my whole body close to hers.

"No." I'm in her space and firm.

"What's the matter? Scared?" Our noses practically touch— she's not backing down.

"Yes," I say honestly, because I really think I could have killed her. And I think she knows it, too. I'm not sure what her game is, but this round has got to be over.

We stand there, millimeters from each other, when Lex lets out another laugh, breaking the tension. "Fine, fine. You win. Match is yours. Besides, we need to keep you ready for your first real bout."

She ducks under the ropes and starts shedding pads. Underneath, her workout shirt is damp with sweat and clings to her body. She heads into the locker room. I follow her without taking the time to remove my pads.

"Bout?"

"Yes—that's what we do here, remember? You want to work out here, you've got to fight for the privilege. Tomorrow night, an hour after sundown. Plus, you'll get a little something extra."

She peels off those dance-like shoes and shimmies out of most of her workout gear. My face heats up. We stand there for what feels like forever, and I have no idea where I'm supposed to be looking or what I'm supposed to do now. I settle on gazing at the corner of a stall, but I sneak glances from my periphery. Lex is long and lean—no wonder she's so light and graceful. Her muscles are taut and run in beautiful, uninterrupted lines down the length of her. When she moves, without clothes to impede her, she is pure water and probably just as deadly. But I'm not looking.

"I'm talking about credits." She grabs a pack of cleansing wipes and takes her naked body into a bathing stall, pulling the curtain around her. "You'll get your fair share if the betting goes well."

I can focus more now that she's in the stall. "I can't use credits," I say.

"Off-network? Most of us here are too. We can fix you with a temp ID, or you can just give me a list of the things that you'd buy, and we can run the account here. My employers are used to it."

"I don't know." Maybe fighting would help bring back my memories, like Doc said. Experiences close to what I probably went through in training. But The State seems to have given up chasing me the last few days. Maybe I'm better off not remembering and starting some kind of new life. But to start a new life, I need credits, and I need something to do besides avoiding the guards.

"Bree, I can smell your brain burning." Lex whips the curtain back and tosses the cleansing wipes at me. "Your turn to clean up. Think about it. Maybe just try once, and see how it goes."

I head into the stall in full workout gear and draw the curtain.

"Helps to take the training pads off first." Lex opens the curtain. "Need some help?"

At least she's dressed this time, but I'm not. "Get out, and let me think." I throw my gloves at her and push her out of the stall. I can see the hurt on her face before I close the curtain again. "Sorry," I mutter.

"I hope you fight," Lex says. "I kinda like you, and I'd miss you if you didn't come around anymore."

By the time I'm clean and changed, she's no longer in the locker room, and the training room is empty. I walk along the ring, trailing my finger on the ropes. A fighter.

Some kids grow up to be teachers, shop owners, or custodial guardians in the youth programs. I never really had an idea of what my work assignment would be, and I didn't really have to worry about it once I got tapped with a year of school left. At the time, I thought I'd figure my future out while in service. Since then, I've been so busy running from and chasing the guards, I haven't really had a chance to think about it.

Maybe I *had* thought about it, though. Maybe I'd figured life out and made decisions, and The State robbed that from me when they took my memories. Somehow, I doubt it.

I could be a fighter. I might hurt someone worse than I hurt Lex, but a professional would expect to be hit hard. That's the risk they'd be taking. That I'd be taking. I could fight and make a real life here in Undergroundland and stay far away from The State forever. As long as they stay away from me.

## 18

My fingers tingle as I curl them into fists. I am electricity —I pulse, and energy is mine to harness. The rest of the world travels in slow motion while I move with the speed of pure power. I am ready.

*I walk from the hallway into the arena. The lights would be blinding if I were not one with them. No longer in the shadows, I am pure brightness.*

*My opponent is a form without feature, the outline of a person in my harsh light. I will destroy him. I will win. That is my training. That is my job.*

*A heavy hand claps my shoulder.*

*"Finish it."*

When I wake up, I'm not sure if it was a dream or a memory.

I WALK around Undergroundland scrounging for a few supplies and learning about my new home. I've got most of what I need, but Charley could use a new shirt or maybe a coat as the weather starts to cool. He's the only thing between me and being homeless, and I feel obligated to keep him safe.

With the rain gone, the air is thinner and less heavy. Breathing and moving are easier, and I direct my extra energy into helping Charley. I can't tell if he really likes being alone or if it's easier for him because no one shares his reality.

The shops are out. Part of me wishes I'd thought to ask Shyla for something for Charley, but that would mean telling her something about my circumstances. No thanks.

There are places in the sector you can go to find almost anything without a credit trail, for the right price. The markets are deep within Undergroundland, where The State doesn't care enough to patrol. When I was in school, kids would tell stories about going to the markets to get things that were the stuff of legends: intoxicants. They'd have great stories about their heroic journey to get the goods, always successfully, of course. Mysteriously, the contraband was always consumed before they came back to our part of the sector.

It only took a few months before I realized they were full of crap. Youthful naiveté. I never tried going into the markets back then, but now, illegal shopping might be a normal part of my life. Especially if I fight for Lex. Gotta spend all those illicit credits somewhere.

Because it's still daylight, the streets in Undergroundland are empty.

To find the mysterious markets, I do what I do best: I hide and watch, waiting for someone to follow. In the normal parts of the sector, empty streets are standard. The streets are clear in the day during work hours, except for the rolling proscribed half hour lunch break. Everyone's too busy, with too much to do. Daily recreation hours are mostly spent shopping, staring at entertainment screens or sitting in cava shops. People are really only in the streets to move from one place to another. There's no spontaneous conversation. You might nod an acknowledgment to a classmate or neighbor, but no one wants to stay on the streets too long. Dilly dally, and you might get selected for random questioning.

Since no one in Undergroundland has an official job or residence, there's no reason for any of us to be in the streets whatsoever. At least, that's what the posted signs say. Most of them disintegrated during the rain, but a few under cover still remain.

TERRORISM BEGINS IN THE STREETS. PROTECT YOUR HOME BY STAYING INSIDE.

Underneath the thick black letters, a faceless guard in silhouetted profile stands proudly against a grayscale backdrop of our sector's flag, a triangular starred banner.

So, everyone here is expected to stay in the non-existent homes they don't officially live in, and some poor sucker is stuck monitoring dots on a screen to make sure we don't wander too far from where we're supposed to be.

I catch movement out of the corner of my eye. A man across the street darts from building to building, pausing to check his surroundings at each stop. He's well-dressed in tailored dark navy, not in the standard gray-green State-issue clothes and not the uncoordinated castoffs belonging to the Undergrounders. He's got credits to burn and enough authority to get what he wants.

He's probably paid off some low-level State employee to ignore his signal on the monitor for the shift. But he can't walk brazenly through the streets, because it's not expected. Or because he's having more fun creeping around this way.

What an entitled jerk. I'd like to kick the crap out of him. But first, I'll follow him.

He has no idea how obvious he's being. At least the dark color he's chosen blends with the shadows, but his quick movements are easily tracked. I move at a more sedate pace, allowing the distance between us to widen. I trust that I won't lose his flitting figure in the empty street.

The man pauses in a doorway and kneels as though he's tying his polished loafer. I take the opportunity to gain ground, never taking my eyes off of him. He pulls out something tucked in the leg of his pants.

I freeze. Did he spot me? Is that some kind of weapon?

No, he's not paying any attention to me. I'm directly across the street from him now. He waves whatever he pulled out near a doorframe, and with a loud *click*, the door unlatches and swings wide open. I get a glimpse as he rushes in—people mill around between rows and rows of tables. I run across the street and grab the handle to the door right before it latches behind him.

I'm about to stroll in when a heavy hand drops on my shoulder. In surprise, I let the handle go, and the auto-lock snaps back in place.

"What're you doing, Bree?" Spyder asks me.

"Gwock it, Spyder. I was about to go in there."

"Sorry." He says unapologetically and very annoyingly. "You've got an appointment."

# 19

The metronymic ticking of some health machine keeps better time than the sector's clock. I drum my fingers to the rhythm as Doc fastens thin cables to various boxes.

"Your turn." She holds up the ends, which are attached to thin silver discs about the size of the opening to a hydropack. "Shirt off. No need to be shy—just us girls here. And undergarments can stay on."

I shrug out of my shirt, fold it, and lay it neatly on the cot beside me. This is the most Doc's said to me since Spyder delivered me to the health room and disappeared without so much as a goodbye. Or even a wave.

The only reason I'm doing this is that Spyder interrupted me from going into the market. If he could interrupt me at any time, so could The State. Just because they've not bothered tracking me down for the last few days doesn't mean they won't again. Plus, I've had Spyder's handy signal bouncer on, so who knows if they've really been trying. I'll get Doc's treatment, then go to Lex's for the fight, balancing my new life with memories of my old.

"You were a topic of conversation at our last leadership meeting—which we were hoping you'd attend."

I'm about to protest when she continues, "Don't worry, dear. Spyder confessed that he forgot to give you the information. Something tells me you'll have another chance."

"I guess. I mean, I'm kind of busy…"

"Whatever you say, dear," she says absentmindedly.

I'm a little curious about their organization, but I'm more curious about my own mind.

She picks up a tube and squirts a thick liquid in generous dollops all over my chest and back. "This will be a little cold," she warns after the fact.

Placing the discs on top of each dollop, she secures them with a thick band of black tape.

"There." She nods in satisfaction and fiddles with some knobs and dials on the boxes. Whirs and beeps join the ticking and my drumming, creating a medical musical. It's almost enough to hum to. Which the Professor does as he walks straight into the room.

"Oops." He averts his eyes. "Sorry about that."

Doc tosses me a piece of cloth to drape around myself.

"No big deal," I say. "I had an undershirt on, and I'm covered now."

"All quiet on the testing front?" he asks Doc.

"We haven't started the pill sequence yet. I need to get a few readings first."

"Excellent. What happened to you?"

He steps into my space and touches my forehead. I wince.

"That's a nice shade of purple."

"I walked into something." Yeah, Lex's fist.

He peers at me over his glasses. "The rains do funny things to people."

"Yeah." If he wants to think I was caught in the middle of a looting party or something, so much the better.

"We fared well here, underground. Of course, we had to avoid the tunnels. Water gushed through the grating system. That was our first warning the rains were here, that diabolical dripping from the broken drainage system. I can remember our first rain, when we didn't know what that meant. Some got caught in the storm." He shudders. "There but for the grace of God...."

He looks at me expectantly. He's shared his story, and now he wants something in return. I'm not playing.

"Is this supposed to itch?" I scratch at one of the discs on my chest.

"Careful," Doc says. "That needs to stay in contact with your skin."

"Hmmm..." The Professor pushes his glasses up on his nose.

"Here we are." Doc produces a series of cups, some with pills in them, others with colorful liquids. "You'll need to take these in sequence. We'll monitor as we go and see what happens. Have you had any dreams since you were last here?"

"I'm not sure—I can't tell if they're memories or just dreams."

"These will open you up a bit more." She holds up a set of thicker cables. "I've got two more to attach to your head. You'll feel a little," she hesitates, "buzzing with these."

"Buzzing?"

"The combination of the drugs and electricity should stimulate your cerebral cortex, providing you the ability to rapidly create new synaptic connections to access your memories. Theoretically, of course. You're an *n* of one."

I'm only slightly confused. My lack of response gives Doc the opportunity to attach the cables to a thick headband which she straps around my head.

"Okay..." I finally say as a couple more discs poke me in the temples.

"Here we go." Doc hands me the first cup.

Liquid nearly sloshes over the brim. I sniff, but it smells like nothing. I down the contents in one big gulp, and it tastes like a hydropack, thin and bitter. In a few minutes, my body starts to relax. The discs warm on me, and I can't tell if they're reflecting my own body heat or if Doc is sending a little jolt through them. It doesn't matter either way. I'll be fine. I'll be fine. I'll be—

The noise of the machines fills my body. My heart thumps in time with the ticks, and my blood pulses with the rhythm. At times a cup is held to my lips.

"Open." The instruction reverberates like glass near a speaker, and I obey.

One of the pills sticks in my throat. I try to cough, but I can't dislodge it. I want to wave my arms to signal to Doc that something is wrong, but I'm so relaxed and loose, my arms don't want to leave their comfortable position at my side. One of the machines goes into overdrive, and a high-pitched alert fills the room.

I taste sharp rubber, and a gloved hand sweeps the pill out of my mouth. "We'll adjust dosage for the next set," I hear.

At this point, I realize I can't see. One of the drugs has so totally relaxed me that I can't bear the weight of my eyelids.

I want to throw up, and I want this to stop, but I can't do anything.

"Please," I want to say, but my body does nothing to indicate that my brain is connected to it. As my panic increases, the rhythm on the machines increase and fill me further. I cannot sense anything in the room around me. The bed that I am lying on has disappeared, and I am floating, weightless in my mind.

The beats are no longer distinct. My heart is a buzzing blur, summoning green to the edges of my black vision. The mist is here, like a shroud descending to cover and reveal me.

"*Stop!*" The Professor breaks through the veil, and I am nothing.

⌇

I AWAKEN IN THE NIGHT, sheets tangled around my feet. I kick at them before standing—the last thing I want is covers sending me spiraling through the broken floorboards to broken bones below. When I stand, I'm on smooth cement, and I remember that I'm in the small ward at Doc and the Professor's bunker, being monitored. The darkness could be night or day. With the lights off underground, no one can really tell where the basement blackness ends and the day begins. The floor starts to roll underneath me, and I sit back down, hard, on the edge of the bed.

A light switches on in the corner, one of those table lamp things that passes through the generations. Its warm yellow glow illuminates the Professor in a tall cushioned chair.

"Rise and shine," he says.

"Good..." Morning? Evening? "Good to see you. How long have I been out?"

He checks a band on his arm. "Oh, about a day or so. Day and a quarter."

"I've been here over twenty-four hours? I've got to get out of here." Just as soon as this room stops spinning.

I've missed the fight. Lex is going to be so pissed at me, if she even talks to me.

"You don't remember? Curious." He fiddles with the band, spinning it in circles on his arm. "I don't know if Doc was expecting that."

"Where is she?"

"We've been taking turns monitoring you. You had a bad reaction partway through but seemed to overcome it, so she insisted that we continue." There's a hard edge to his voice, at odds with his bemused smile. The tone is nothing like I've heard from him before.

"But I'm fine, right?" I test my weight again. This is so oddly reminiscent of how I first met the Professor that our conversation doesn't seem real.

"I think, my dear, you'll need to tell us that." Doc stands silhouetted in the open doorway.

"She's been stirring for the last half hour or so but only fully awake for minutes," the Professor tells her.

"Thank you," Doc says to him. "You can go now."

"I think I'll stay. I'd like to hear the results of this experiment firsthand."

"Absolutely." Doc gives him a tight smile.

"What do you want to know?" I ask.

"What do you remember?" Doc says.

The question is loaded, but the truth is easy. "I remember the first drink you gave me. Everything is hazy after that."

"Nothing else?"

"Not really. I mean, there was the sensation of being in this room and something happening, but that's really all. And, actually, I have somewhere I was supposed to be, so if you could just give me my clothes—"

"We need to monitor you for a few more hours, and we should discuss some things." Doc checks my vitals.

"You tried your best. I get that, and thanks. But this took a lot longer than you told me it would, and I have a life. I'm fine."

"You really need to stay." Doc turns her back to me to open the door of a supply cabinet.

Hot fury boils my goopy brain. How dare she turn away from me?

"I'll go in this if I have to. I'm out of here." I rip the monitoring discs off. Anger steadies my balance as I move to the door.

"Stay." Doc moves between me and the exit and puts a hand to my chest.

"Take your hand off of me."

"Oh, for god's sakes, just tell her that she remembered. This corrupting memories nonsense will cost us everything," the Professor thunders, breaking our brief standoff.

"Remembered what?" I ask, cautious. Then more firmly, I demand, "What did I remember?"

Doc sighs. "When you were tapped."

## 20

In the war room, Spyder manipulates screen images according to a list Doc's provided him. He changes angles and zooms in on various locations. On the wall adjacent to the screens, the Professor pulls down hanging maps until he's found the one he's looking for. He mutters to himself and smacks the map with a long stick.

Doc and I sit at opposite ends of the conference table. She places a sheaf of sheets in front of her. Handwritten notes, drawings, and arrows abound, but I can't make out the contents. Her handwriting and personal shorthand are unintelligible.

After Doc's bold pronouncement that I'd remembered something, she and the Professor propelled me into this room without giving me a chance to ask any questions. At least they let me put my clothes back on first, but I had to carry my shoes with me. With Spyder added to the mix in the war room, the three of them look like ants building a nest in front of a food factory. And I don't much like being the food to the busy workers.

"I think you'd better start talking," I say.

None of them look in my direction—they keep scurrying around.

"Hey," I say a little louder. "Hey!" I bang my hands on the table.

I hate being ignored. From my lap, I take one of the shoes they didn't even give me time to put back on, and I hurl it toward the screens. My shoe crashes dead center into a screen. Sparks rain on Spyder, who turns around, radiating fury. Oops.

"What the gwock do you think you're doing? Do you have any idea how difficult and expensive it is to get these?"

"I didn't mean to—" I don't mean that as an apology.

"What were you thinking?"

"I don't *know*. That's the whole point. My memories are gone. You brought me here, and you've kept me here for longer than you said you would, like I don't have a life—which I do. Just because I can't remember anything from before doesn't mean I haven't started trying to rebuild something now. And then you tell me that I remembered something, but you don't tell me what, and when I *bother* you by asking you about myself—about who I am and what I remembered and what is mine, you all *ignore* me. I'm tired of being ignored. I'm not some stupid science project. And I'm furious because I thought you were supposed to be my friend and you didn't seem so bad either." I address Doc, Spyder, and the Professor in turn.

Spyder's turned his back on me again, sweeping up the shards from the screen. My anger's burnt out, and now I'm only disappointed in him. But I will have what's mine. I'll be gwocked if I got a memory back and they have it, not me.

Doc peers over her glasses at me. "I've told you why I think it's a bad idea to tell you your memories instead of letting you rediscover them yourself."

"I don't—"

"But..." She holds up a hand to interrupt me. "What you remembered is important to what we're doing here, and I think you need to know."

"Finally." The Professor steals the word right from my lips. He straightens his final map and sinks into a chair, giving Doc a small smile and a wink. Whatever argument they were having seems to be over. As if I cared.

"But we need to know if we can fully trust you," Doc says.

"With my own memories?" My anger rises again.

"Not just that. With us. With what we're doing here."

"I don't know what you want from me."

Spyder empties the dustpan into the trash. At the sound of the tinkling glass, Doc coughs pointedly at the screen I destroyed.

Spyder finally looks at me, and he doesn't break eye contact as he says, "You can trust her."

The Professor chimes in, "'In thy face I see the map of honor, truth, and loyalty.'"

"That's good enough for me," Doc says.

"What did I remember?"

"I wish we'd had some way to capture images like that." Doc gestures to a frozen image of some buildings on a screen. "But we'll have to rely on the few State recordings we've been able to access. You didn't remember in any particular sequence, so the Professor and I tried to capture as much as possible in our notes. We took turns watching you and piecing these together."

"Tell me."

"I don't know what you're expecting—" Doc begins.

This time I'm the one to cut her off. "Just start. Now. Please."

"You were tapped. You went in for training. While in training, you were identified as being particularly suited for combat. There were some trials, some discussion of which sector to send you to in order to best utilize your skills. You and another quickly rose to the top of your training class, and there was some competition between you—formal competition, I mean. A contest. The winner was to be selected for special duty on the Bridge."

"Pilgrimage." I exhale the word as a prayer.

"Precisely."

Pilgrimage, our one chance to leave the sector we're born into

—unless we're tapped. Pilgrims journey on their own to find new life and connect with our ancestors. No one knows what they find —they are forbidden from returning. Only the bravest go on pilgrimage, or those without any hope. The start to the pilgrimage is always the Bridge, where the pilgrims cross into their new life, with nothing but the clothes on their backs and whatever they can sneak past the guards. No one has ever seen the Bridge. Except me, and I can't remember it.

"Do you remember?" The Professor asks.

"It's like a story of someone else's life."

"I'm trying to keep this vague enough to preserve the integrity of your memories should they begin to re-emerge," Doc says.

"I can live with that," I say. "But none of this explains anything."

"You won the competition and were assigned to duty on the Bridge. Presumably, something happened, and you were released. Perhaps The State had second thoughts about your release and are working to nullify any threat you pose."

"Presumably and perhaps you're jumping to conclusions," Spyder interjects.

"It's a logical explanation," the Professor says.

Doc nods in agreement. "Bree's memories are incomplete or still re-emerging. Until we have the full picture, we must infer conclusions from what we know of her past, both in training and more recently."

"'Nullifying a threat aligns with my recent experiences," I say drily, imitating Doc's med-speak. "In other words, they're trying to kill me."

"Yes," Doc says.

"But you're in luck." The Professor claps his hands. "They're trying to kill us, too."

"Whoopee." I give a sarcastic clap but quickly get back on track. "I could have figured this much out without you," I say.

"Maybe not the part about the Bridge, but everything you're telling me is so sterile. Generic."

Doc picks up a pen and stabs the air in my general direction. "I'm giving you the facts, only the facts, so that your memories will remain yours. I could go into a little more detail of what you remembered, but then your memory would be of me telling you, not of the experience itself."

"I get it." She's only said the same thing about a dozen times, and that pointy pen of hers is really pissing me off. "What does this have to do with you? What did you ever do to The State?"

"Have you ever noticed how young we are?" Spyder asks. "All of us, I mean. Present company excepted." He gestures toward the gray-hairs.

"Of course." But I haven't thought too much about age. Doc and the Professor are pretty much the oldest people I've ever talked to. Everyone else is parental age or younger.

"You ever wonder why that is?"

"Not really. It's always been that way. Cats and dogs live to ten or twelve. People live to forty or maybe forty-five. I guess it's just our species. I think we learned that in school." As that last sentence leaves my mouth, I realize that the assumptions I've always held have been spoon fed to me on a bed of Nutripaste. The aftertaste is foul.

"It wasn't always that way," Doc says.

The Professor leans back in his chair, like he's settling in for a story. "Perhaps, for a time, but then science and medicine restored the discordant elements. Then people lived to be far older than we, into their eighties or nineties. And now..."

"And now?"

The Professor stares off into the distance, like he's trying to see through the walls to what's on the other side. "And now, we are returned to our former disorder."

Enough of this talking in riddles. "So why is The State trying to kill *you*?"

The Professor gives one of his annoying enigmatic smiles, and before he even opens his mouth, he's set me on edge. "'Dissensions, like small streams, are first begun. Scarce seen they rise, but gather as they run—'"

"Let me stop you right there. The rhyming is nice and all, but why the heck are we talking streams, and exactly who is running?"

"We are the Resistance. We are The Riverine," Doc says. "And you are welcome to join us."

I have no idea what she's talking about. "Yeah. I guess maybe."

"Your enthusiasm is underwhelming," Doc says drily.

The Professor paces, gesticulating wildly and staring at the sky as though he's composing and conducting a piece of music all at once. "We are The Riverine Resistance. We resist through flow. Like the water of old, we wend our way through the sector, carrying life to all who live here, building and growing until, like the water of today, we will rise up and destroy The State."

He looks at me expectantly. "Umm." I'm not sure exactly what he's talking about, but it sounds like an uprising. "Will getting my memories back make all this make sense?"

"I hope so."

"So, maybe let's get on track with that, please." These gray-hairs meander in and out of time like a lesson so boring I'd doodle in the margins. I get that they're opposing The State and all, but they really can't seem to focus.

"Teenagers." The Professor clears his throat. "While we don't have the ability to record and store information, The State does," the Professor says.

"And?"

"And, with your young gentleman at the keys, we can access stills of just about anything."

Spyder slumps in his chair but flexes his fingers. "Ready when you are."

The Professor consults the map. "Pull up location Alpha, second in the season of preparation, eight a.m."

"We're going to show you a series of images that relate to what we know of the experiences you had—being tapped, training, that sort of thing. While the images will be generic, my hope is that the visual stimulation, coupled with the memory fragments from the protocols we executed over the last twenty-four hours, will lead you into conscious recollection of those events."

Wordy, but I get the idea. The pictures will get me my memories. A crowd appears on the lower left screen. I move my chair so I'm closer.

"Full view," Doc says.

The crowd magnifies, taking over the entire wall. I can make out sorrowful faces, pinched eyes and drawn lips. The thick black bars of each screen break the image oddly, dividing faces and families with inky pillars. There's transpo in the background— old buses and vehicles like we see mostly in school or on special patrols.

A line of people wait in front of them, and a few are taking their first steps onboard. I can't see their faces, but there's a set to their shoulders, a rigidity that's more than the stillness of the image. There are some in the crowd who've got their arms folded, as if to stop themselves from reaching out to those boarding the transpo.

"Where are they going?" My fingers itch to trace their profiles.

"Training," Doc answers. "They've been tapped."

Most people in the sector have seen this firsthand. When someone is tapped, they're sent a pass for someone to come with them to see them off. That person becomes their primary contact while in training and service—the only one they're allowed to communicate with from home. Some people trade or sell their passes. A big red pass with a space to write down someone's name and address came with the letter they sent me after I was tapped.

I burned it.

"You're quiet," the Professor says. "What do you think?"

Doc leans forward, eager. "Are you remembering something?" Her pen is poised on the edge of a sheet, ready to write notes.

"Not really. Thinking about before. I was tapped, but I still don't remember anything past the night before I left."

Doc nods to Spyder. The screen goes gray and wobbly, like it's covered in electrified dryer lint.

"Did you know they send training patrols into the sector?" Doc asks.

The Professor points to a spot on a map. "Location Beta, last year, thirtieth in the season of growth, three a.m."

While Spyder taps away on the keys, the Professor connects the two points on the map with a thin red line. After a few seconds, the image appears. The picture is grainier than the first and very dark. It was clearly taken in poor lighting conditions— the blue lights must've been out. A formation of guards in strange looking uniforms hold black batons across their bodies, their faces hidden by the shadows from their weapons.

I touch the uniforms onscreen. "These should be darker on top, with patches on the shoulder here and here."

"They haven't completed their training. Are the training patrol uniforms at all familiar to you?" Doc asks.

"No."

"This isn't going to work," Spyder mumbles.

"What?" I lean forward, getting into his space.

"Next location, please," Doc says.

"No, wait. Do you not want me to get my memory back?"

Spyder shrinks in his chair. "Sure. You're not you without them. But—"

"What do you mean 'I'm not me'? Of course I'm me." I leap from my chair and slam it back into place at the table, sending Doc's sheets fluttering to the floor. Twin dents from where the arms impacted the cheap metal will mark my place here forever.

Spyder flinches but stays seated, the coward. I pace alongside the short wall like a rat in a cage. No. I am *not* a rat. I will not be a rat. I can leave this room whenever I want.

Doc starts to rise, and the Professor quickly takes her arm and leads her out of the room. I barely notice them through my fury, but I register enough to realize they're going to let us have this out. I'm going to squash Spyder. Finally.

But before I can, his hurt voice cracks as he says, "You weren't like this before. Fighting all the time. You're so angry and suspicious now. You were always kind of a loner, but you let people in. Em. Me...almost."

"Don't you think I know that? Do you think I can't feel it? I'm so frustrated all the time, and the only way to get it out is to hit something or run away or do *something,* because I can't just sit around and pretend I'm okay. Because I'm not. I sense things, and I feel things, and I react in ways I don't understand, but it's my body moving, and it feels good to move—so much better than sitting and staring at the walls all day."

He stands and shrugs into one of his stupid flying harnesses. He wears it like armor as he approaches me. "I get away from these screens, you know. Or did you forget who rescued you when the guards were after you?" He holds up a short length of rope with a carabiner attached.

"That's not what I—can we please not do this? This isn't the point. None of this is the point." I can smell that cinnamon again, the same as when we met in the cava shop. His scent is warm, welcoming, annoying.

"It *is* the point. *We* are the point, you and me, and everyone else in this world. I left school after you got tapped—did you know that? Did you care? Did you ever think to ask, 'Hey, Spyder, what's happened with you in the last year?'"

"I did! In the cava shop, before the shooting started."

He is quiet.

"I think I did. Didn't I?"

He shakes his head. "You were on such high alert, you barely recognized me."

"Of course I recognized you. It's been over a year—you've changed!" He's more man than boy now, and we both know it.

"Yes." He squeezes my hand. He's in my space, and the heat from his entire body radiates along the length of me. There's a slight pull between us, like magnets that are just far enough away from each other that they don't stick. But when he speaks, it's like a switch is flipped in me, reversing my polarity. I don't know who I am, and he names me. "Bree," he whispers.

"No." Without hesitation, I answer what he will not ask, and he drops my hand as carelessly as he steps off of building roofs.

Hopefully his harness will catch him now.

## 21

I'm alone in the war room with the blinking network and camera screens to keep me company. The streets are empty this time of day, so the camera feeds of emptiness amplify my loneliness.

Spyder is my friend. I can't deny that I'm drawn to him, but the timing isn't right. I clench my jaw, furious that he'd try to insert himself in my life when he knows I'm working so hard to get my memories back. I'm not the girl he went to school with.

The war room door creaks open, closing my thoughts on Spyder as Doc and the Professor return. Doc sits in a chair across the table from me, while the Professor keeps a respectful distance and lounges in one of the corner arm chairs. Doc's cheeks are practically puffed out with the words she's holding in. I'm silent. I wonder how long she'll be.

Less than a minute.

She leans forward in her chair and gestures widely with her hands. "We need your help. If we can unlock what's in your head, you may change everything."

"I'm sorry. I can't help you. Please, try to understand."

"To be completely honest, I don't."

"She wants a life," the Professor says in the corner. "Who can blame her?"

"What kind of life will any of us have if The State continues to rule over us?" Doc snaps back at him.

He gives a wry smile, "That, my dear, as the kids say, is not her problem."

"It's not that I don't care," I say.

The Professor shuffles over, nearly tripping over ancient, flapping blue slippers. He blocks my view of Doc and pats my hand. "Forgive a few gray-hairs. You deserve your own life, whatever you choose to make of it."

Coming to this decision wasn't easy, but it was fast. I knew before Spyder even left the war room that I couldn't stay here. I can't help them fight an enemy I don't know or understand when I don't even know or understand myself.

"I'm not saying forever—just for right now," I say.

"It's not you; it's me," the Professor says with a wink.

"Huh?"

Doc pokes her head around his side. "Don't worry about him. At least stay the night. Have dinner with us, and we can talk again in the morning." The offer of food tempts me. I'm still tired from the treatment and hungry, too.

I'm careful to agree to dinner and a room for the night but nothing else. Doc leads me through a maze of corridors to a big open room with rows of long metal tables and an assortment of plasticine chairs and benches. There's a long range of stovetops on one end, with a huge oven big enough for me to climb into. Large, dented metal pots hang on the walls with an assortment of long handled spoons and knives on big blocks of wood. The room is kind of like the cafeteria at school mixed with the parts of eateries no one's allowed to see but that you get glimpses of when someone barrels through a big swinging door.

About fifty people could fit in here, but besides us, there are only five men and women clustered at the far end of one of the long tables. Their heads are down, long hair obscuring their faces. They murmur to one another and rise, dumping plates into a sink the size of a wagon before ducking through a set of double doors on the other side of the room.

"Who are they?" I ask.

"Late diners. No one you need concern yourself with," Doc says.

"Ask not what you can do for your country. Ask what's for lunch." The Professor waves a fist in the air.

I bristle at his stinging remark. He said he understood why I couldn't help.

He hastily adds, "It's a silly old quote. We're having dinner," but he doesn't make me feel much better.

"Please, sit," Doc says.

The Professor opens a tall white storage cupboard and pulls out a short stack of plates and utensils. He opens the door to one of the warming ovens and pulls out a big pot. Doc opens her mouth to make conversation with me, but nothing comes out.

Normally, I'm fine with awkward silences, but this dinner was probably a mistake.

"A lot of people live here?" I ask.

"More than you'd think—not as many as we'd like," she answers.

"I thought it was just you, the Professor, and Spyder, so pretty much anybody other than that is more than I'd think."

"Spyder doesn't live here." The Professor balances bowls in the crook of his elbow and serves us with a flourish. "Stew. Don't ask about the ingredients, because there's no telling."

I poke at the gray lumps, and my stomach growls. "Better than Nutripaste."

The stew is hot and tastes like it's been cooking so long, all the flavors have melded into one. Different than Nutripaste, not necessarily better tasting, but the stew wins on temperature and texture.

"Where does Spyder live?"

"With his parents," the Professor says with a laugh. "He's only seventeen."

Right. Still a kid. Just like I should be.

I'm quiet, and the Professor sobers. We eat the meal quickly and in silence. As the Professor clears our plates and starts scraping the dishes left in the sink, Doc clears her throat. "I won't say anything more after this, but it would mean a lot to the people who live here if you'd change your mind. We need all the help we can get."

"I'm sorry."

She nods, a bit sad. "I'll take you to a guest room." She walks to the Professor and touches him lightly on the elbow. "Just be a minute, darling."

I go with her, wanting to be home in my own rickety room, wishing I had never agreed to stay. If I've learned one thing in my life: wishes don't come true.

## 22

I'm not sure where to go—no one is. We mill about a large room with high ceilings like an old indoor ball court. The floor is wooden, springy, and scuffed, with faded painted lines. Half of the floor is set up with rows of chairs. We dump our bags into the empty side of the room. As more time passes, pockets of conversation develop. I ebb and flow in and out of discussions, never contributing, picking up themes of home and family. Not much I can say on the subject.

An old door squeaks open, and a man so tall and wide he has to duck and practically turn sideways comes in. He's in uniform, and he looks like he's in charge. The chatter dies to mutters, and the groups cluster tighter, as though for protection. The man stands in front of the rows of chairs, silent and strong as a statue. We watch and wait.

He looks us over, makes a noise of disgust, and his voice thunders through the high rafters, shaking the beams. "Sit. Down!"

We instantly obey, scrambling and plopping down hard into metal chairs. Spittle sprays those in the front row, and his own shirt is spattered like he got caught in a rainstorm. But instead of dissolving into a gooey puddle in the rain, he's dissolving us instead.

"My job is to turn your sorry behinds into a force to be reckoned *with. I don't fail, but some of you may. Fail me, and I'll see that you spend the rest of your service in refuse and sewage treatment.*

*"Patrols will be hard, but your training is harder. I will hone you into the weapons the sectors need. Are we clear?"*

*We stare mutely. I catch my neighbor's expression out of the corner of my eye. His mouth is hanging open, just a little.*

*"Are we clear?" the behemoth of a man yells again.*

*"Yes," some of us say, some of us stutter.*

*"Are we* clear?*"*

*"Yes," we respond, a little more forcefully this time.*

*He sweeps a few of the empty chairs in the front row with his giant arm, sending them to the floor with a crash. His voice rings out well over the noise. "Are. We. Clear?"*

*"Yes!" most of us scream in response.*

*"It's 'Yes, Sir,'" he says calmly, spins on the heel of his boot, and exits the room back through the giant door.*

～

*I'M CRYING, curled on the floor. Horrible pressure compresses the side of my face. I can't see, and all I taste is rubber and boot leather.*

*"No mercy," Sarge screams, and the pressure is lifted from my face. The heavy toe of a boot slams into my kidney, and I throw up a little before passing out.*

～

*"CONGRATULATIONS, Blue Squad. Bree Carter, with me." Sarge's mouth twists like he's eaten dirt—he can't stand that I've led my squad to victory.*

*I follow him down the corridor to his office. I'm not going to lie; I'm quivering in my boots just a little. The adrenaline from the training exercise has started to fade, and my tired muscles tremble.*

"Trainee Carter." Sarge is almost cordial as he holds the door open for me.

I enter the office and stand at attention. A giant desk nearly fills the small room, with several yellow files and a large comp screen. You don't see too many of those here. Gently closing the door, and further disrupting any sense of ease, Sarge sits in an equally giant chair behind the enormous desk.

"Please, at ease." He gestures to a small wooden chair facing the desk.

"Sir." I sit, and I can barely see over the edge.

"Congratulations, Trainee Carter. You've won the spot."

My heart sinks.

"But don't get too cocky. Masters will be joining you to keep you in line."

To torture me, is more like it.

"Thank you, sir."

Sarge grabs one of his file folders and a pencil and flips through the contents, making a few notes here and there. He hasn't dismissed me, so I stay seated in this too-small, hard, uncomfortable chair, trying not to fidget. He keeps me there for what feels like hours, until he finishes whatever he's doing. When he looks up, he pretends to be surprised to see me.

"Dismissed, Carter." He waves toward the door, light flashing on his large, silver skull ring. "See you on the Bridge."

"Yes, sir." I walk out of the office and into my future as an elite guard.

A MASSIVE STRUCTURE of metal and plasticine repair patches stretches across the inky water. I have never seen anything so large in my life. The beams dwarf the tallest buildings in our sector, and the entirety seems to fade into clouds crossing the dangerous flow. Thick spikes of some material I can't identify support the structure, disappearing down, down into the churning, deadly water.

About fifteen of us gather near the water's edge, staying as far back as the boundaries will allow. The dirt is different here, fine and soft and almost like a kind of water itself as the powdery grains shift and move every time one of us steps. The Lifers at the perimeter laugh at us.

"Sand. It's called sand." One of them chuckles.

His partner quiets him with a nudge of his rifle stock. "He's coming."

The sand firms and crumbles beneath Sarge's heavy boots. For the first time, I see him smile. "Welcome to destiny's gate. The fate of the world is in that Bridge."

I should've known that smile portended nothing good. Sarge haunts my dreams and my waking with every training exercise.

"Gentlemen, observe," he says.

It doesn't bother me anymore that he refuses to acknowledge some of us are female.

Sarge holds up a Nutripaste packet and a small glass of green-brown water. The color matches our uniforms. Slowly, he removes the mush from the packet and drops it into the glass. The water splashes a little, but he holds the glass out with a straight arm, never wavering. The water hisses and bubbles, and the paste sinks, smoking all the way down. For good measure, Sarge shoves the metallic wrapper in, and it flames a little on the surface of the glass. He tilts the glass so we can all see the thick, burnt sludge it has become.

"Masters," he calls. "To me."

"Sir." Masters leaps to his feet and stands at attention.

"Take the glass."

Masters grabs the glass and hisses with pain, dropping the deadly container onto the training floor. The glass shatters, and the sludge slowly spreads. Something strange has happened to the water, though, *because the floor stays intact. Somehow, the water has lost its power to dissolve.*

*"It was hot, sir," Masters says lamely.*

*Sarge slaps him across the face, sending him sprawling next to the ooze. "Get out of my sight."*

*"Sir."*

*"But not before you clean up your mess."*

*"Yes, sir." Without hesitation, Masters drops and starts wiping at the possibly-still-acidic-sludge with his sleeves.*

*"No, no." Sarge reaches into his pocket and pulls out a shiny spoon. "Eat it."*

*"C*LIMB UP THERE, SOLDIER.*"*

*I'm paralyzed at the gates to the Bridge. The first few feet are solid, but just a few steps out, the sides drop away to the nothing beneath. I try to will my feet forward, but I can't go.*

*"Up, up!" Sarge screams in my ear.*

*My paralysis lifts long enough for me to sink to my knees. I can't, I can't, I can't. It's too high, and if I fall, the water—it'll eat me alive.*

*Sarge aims a kick at my behind, and I'm sent sprawling forward. At least I'm closer to the ground now. I claw at the crumbling pavement so hard my fingertips bleed. I will not break this connection to the safe, secure ground.*

*T*HE INSTRUCTOR SMACKS *a diagram with a thin flexible rod. Each time she strikes, the rod snaps back with a high-pitched ping.*

*"These are our entrances. In the event that the targets overcome the initial obstacles, these are where we'll enter. There are choke points here" thwack-ping "and here" thwack-ping. "If they make it past us*

*here—and they won't—we can remotely control the last several obstacles. All of this will be part of your training.*

*"Remember that this is a spiritual journey for those who undertake the challenge. Our aim is control, but that doesn't mean we can't give them a good death."*

*"Death?" I can't help but interrupt. "I thought this was Pilgrimage."*

*A couple of people snicker.*

*Masters coughs and clears his throat, then says under his breath, "Late to the party, Carter."*

*The snickers turn into outright laughter.*

Thwack-ping. *The instructor brings the rod onto Masters's desk, less than a finger's-width from his hand. The laughter stops, and she continues her lecture.*

*"A pilgrimage is a journey to a sacred place. There is no place more sacred than that where this life ends and the next journey begins. Everything we do, whether on the streets of the sectors or on this Bridge, is to that end. We preserve life as we usher others into new life."*

*"These are the best. Don't fill their heads with crap." Sarge's hulking form fills the doorway.*

*The instructor glares at him and brings up the rod, filling the space between them like a sword. "Get out of my classroom. You'll have your chance in practicals."*

*Sarge holds up his hands in mock apology. "Fine, fine."*

*"IF YOU CAN'T FULFILL your duties as a guard, I have no use for you." The head of the training program is one of two gray-hairs I've ever seen.*

*The other was much younger. She lived because her condition was diagnosed at the health center as "premature." All I can see is the top of his gray head. He's too busy scribbling notes to bother looking at me. Sarge stares at the bridge through the window in the training center, listening.*

"I'm afraid of heights. I'm sorry."

"I have no use for fear."

"Can't I just go be a normal guard in some sector somewhere?"

"You were chosen as an elite trainee to live up to your full potential in the highest honor of service The State has. No more than twenty trainees are selected each year, and only forty percent of those succeed."

"Then I'm just part of the sixty percent who failed. I can live with that."

"They don't."

"I don't understand."

He takes off his wireframe glasses, rubbing at his eyes. "They don't live. Sixty percent of trainees selected for Bridge duty don't survive the training period. And that doesn't include normal casualties in the tour of service. You can't simply leave the program."

"I could—I don't know, be a cook or a janitor or something."

"We share those duties among the team. The work is too secret to trust outsiders. You'll have to continue."

"We do need a little lab rat," Sarge cuts in.

"I'm sorry, sir?"

"An old expression." The gray-hair bites his lip. "And now that you've mentioned it, Sergeant, this trainee might be suited for a new duty. We may even be able to waive the physical Bridge requirement."

"Thank you, sir." I try to maintain my military bearing as relief courses through my body.

"Project Praetereo," he says to Sarge.

"Excellent idea, sir." Sarge cracks his knuckles, and the light from the setting sun reflects off his silver skull ring, putting a creepy glint in his eye.

~

I'M IN A HEALTH CENTER. The light is bluer than the safety lights in the streets, and I've got wires and patches all over me. A light flannel blanket covers my naked body. My hair feels thick and matted, like I've *been sleeping poorly for days and my nightmares have started to lock it.*

*"Hello?" My voice creaks with disuse, and my tongue feels thick and heavy and sore, like my mouth is swollen from a thousand tiny sheet-cuts. A small cup rests on the bedside table. I down the bitter liquid and try to clear my throat. "Hello?" I call out louder this time.*

*There's no one near. I climb out of the bed, using a nearby chair for support, and pull myself to the paneled door with a narrow window. I peer through, and the lights in the empty hallway flicker with the same eerie blue glow.*

*I crack the door and whisper into the emptiness like some small child, afraid of what will answer me back. "Hello?"*

*No one comes. My legs buckle underneath me, and the weight of my eyelids feels like the world itself.*

*I crawl back into the bed and pull the covers over my head.*

*"Hello-o." The nurse's cheer rouses me. "Good morning to my favorite patient."*

*"Why am I your favorite patient?"*

*She jumps about a foot, banging her knee into a table with a bunch of small instruments. "You're awake—they weren't expecting that for... Nevermind. I'll get the doctor."*

*"Please don't leave me alone."*

*She pushes a button on her necklace and sits at the foot of my bed. I want to ask her so many questions, but I don't get a chance before an entire medical team comes barreling in.*

*The leader is easily identified in the crowd of white coats. Bright red hair cascades down her shoulders like fire on ice. Besides me, she's the only one the rest of them look at.*

*"Where am I? What happened? Am I okay? I feel mostly okay, so why am I here?"*

*"There was an accident—"*

*"The tapping. Is everyone else okay?"*

*"What do you remember?"*

*"We got on the bus yesterday—maybe a couple of days ago. What day is today? We were headed to the training grounds. There were a lot of people on the bus. I didn't really know them, but I hope everyone's okay."*

*"Good, good." The doctors furiously scribble notes, and the lead ignores me for a moment and says to them, "Regression is normal and expected in cases like these. We'll continue to monitor to see if she makes any progress."*

*"Not in here. Don't monitor me in here," I interrupt. "I want to go home, or wherever I'm supposed to be staying during training."*

*"Ms.—" The doctor consults the chart. "Bree, your training concluded several months ago. What you're remembering, the tapping, took place nearly one year ago."*

*"A year? No, that's not possible."*

*"There was an accident."*

I INHALE a scream as I wake from the dreams. My head feels too full, like when I was sick as a kid and the pressure built and built and built. I won't get better this time. Whatever Doc did—the memories are there, but they're too much, and they're all jumbled up.

Every muscle in my body aches, as though I've relived my entire training and service in however long I've been asleep. I want nothing more than to go back to sleep, to heal and let my body and brain process this deluge of new information, but I'm taut and ready for the next assault. Mental, physical—I can take on either. I won't be sleeping any time soon.

I turn on the light. The bed is too soft. The mattress sinks where I sit on the edge, and the faded floral covering doesn't hide how garish the comforter must've been when it was first made however long ago. I ball cloth and punch into a rose, trying to find some release. A cloud of dust rises, and I sneeze. A hundred years ago, maybe.

I have to get out of here.

I still don't know where Doc put my clothes. An old wooden bureau contains drawers of State-issue clothes in various sizes. Somehow, they seem out of sync with the antiques in the room. I put on whatever's closest to fitting and wend my way through the corridors, doing my best to re-suppress my memories, at least for now.

They come anyway. I remember the halls of the training facility, sneaking through them at night, trying to find the kitchens in the beginning when everything was new and we still thought we could have some fun. We liberated some fresh fruit once and gloriously feasted on apples, eating the cores and the stems so there wouldn't be any evidence. My training partner got a horrible stomach ache and almost gave us away when—

*Shake it off, Carter.* By some miracle, my feet take me back the path that Doc led me on, right to the cafeteria. The doors buzz with the people inside. I bypass them and keep moving. If I can find the war room, I think I can find my way out. I take a deep breath and try to leave this underground maze.

*"They're a bunch of rats, and you're the obstacle. We're going to take turns practicing, but if you want to flush them out, you've got to get them where they live. And remember: they don't deserve to live. If you let them, they'll breed like the rats they are, chew through all the supplies in the sector, leaving everyone else with nothing. It's not right. It's not fair. Eliminate them. Go. Go. Go."*

*We rush the training grounds with clubs, no lasers this week. We fight, hand to hand, with the instructors wandering among us. When I make a mistake, the bruises form immediately. The longer we fight, the sloppier we are. I taste salt as sweat runs in my mouth, and the sweet tang of blood when my opponent grazes my nose. I'll get him for that. I attack.*

*"There's a delicate balance in our ecosystem, and your job is to maintain the status quo. Preserve. Protect. Kill."*

*"Kill," we scream. We fight harder.*

*I launch a perfect swing, and my opponent drops to the ground.*

*"Preserve. Protect. Kill," an instructor shouts.*

*"Kill!" I raise my club high.*

I want to throw up. I fall to my knees, disgusted with my past self who has become so present. What did they do to me? What are they doing to all of us?

That's how the Professor finds me, curled in a ball near the doorway of the cafeteria. Closing the door, he rams the bolt so that others will have to leave another way. He sings me songs from another time and smooths my hair, holding me as I sob and try to forget who I am.

## 23

D oc gives me something to help me stay calm. She can't, or won't, take the memories back, but she'll, in her doctory vague way, "try to make me as comfortable as possible."

I don't think I'll ever be comfortable again. The drugs help my body—my heart beats at a more normal pace, and my muscles don't feel like they're going to jump out of my body and leave me a walking skeleton—but they can't help my mind.

This time, when I tell her I need to leave, that I need some time to myself, she doesn't argue with me. She knows I'll be back.

"This can't happen again," I tell her. I'll help them in whatever way they're opposing The State, but I have my own request as well. "We have to stop the tapping."

Doc gives me a sad smile, and I wonder how much she knows about what happened to me. I wonder what I said out loud when the memories started to come back—in that space where not remembering and remembering blur.

"We will." She and the Professor hug each other and send me out into the harsh light of day.

I don't know how long I've been with them, only a few days,

but I know I need to start living my life the right way, the way that meshes with who I was and who I am. I've got to apologize to Lex, and I can't fight for her. Not for fun. Not for profit.

I don't want to let her down, but my new self is too fragile. I can't let *myself* down.

"Drive carefully," the Professor calls after me.

Doc elbows him in the ribs, but his nonsense makes me smile.

"I will," I turn and promise, and he gives me a wink and a smile.

"Do be careful," Doc says. "Today's the Day of Obligation, so be mindful of the parades."

"I will." I'm glad the medicine Doc gave me will soon be wearing off. I'll skip the next dose, maybe take the meds again tonight to sleep easier.

The crowds are already starting to gather for the afternoon parades to welcome the guards home. The Day of Obligation is the day when separated families are reunited, when we count supplies, and when we begin the process of readying ourselves for the new year.

A long time ago, when the weather got cold each year, people harvested food. Our lives and traditions are different now, but we respect the ancient customs. We wear costumes and celebrate into the night with bright lights. Spending energy on the bright lights reminds us that we have enough. The costumes are to honor the traditions of our ancestors, who dressed in strange brightly colored garments and masks to make their harvests. This is what we're taught in school. My new memories hint that these are lies.

As I hurry toward home, I try to recall something specific, any lessons about the Day of Obligation, but I don't have the familiarity with my own life to recall exactly what I want. Mentally, I'm staring at a shelf full of books, and the fact I want is in one of them, but I can't just grab the correct book and leaf to the page I want—my arms won't even obey my command to reach. If I think through something happening now, a memory might pop in, unbidden. I think that might be how this works, but I think a lot of things. I'm so frustrated. I want my recovered memories to become part of me, but I still can't really remember them.

The Day of Obligation ushers in season of reaping, so the next tapping is about four months out. The State is never too specific about the date, but tapping always occurs in the transition to the season of preparation. The State says that the date is governed by a mathematical formula affected by the supply tallies we all submit, date of the last rain, and temperature cycle. No one can really figure out the formula, and the explanation feels like a lie, too.

I can barely tell that it rained only a few days ago. The damage has been repaired or hidden, and the only sign of change is the shiny new posts and boxes for the lights and cameras dotting the streets. The sidewalks are thick with costumed people. I have to walk in the streets to get anywhere. The parades will be starting soon.

Because we don't have many colorful fabrics left, people use texture in their costumes. They sew together sleeves or pants from different garments, dark brown and light green together, or make their sleeves and pant legs comically long or short. Fringe abounds. Thick and thin strips of fabric line people's spines like ancient animals or are woven through their hair like ribbons.

Now and again, there will be a pop of red or purple—fabrics of the wealthy passed down through generations that are lovingly cared for and only come out on parade days. Those are the stories they tell, but those who have the means can always find caches of ancient plasticine fabric, like the purple workout suit Lex gave me. I guess my workout shirt is still at Doc and the Professor's.

Tomorrow, all citizens begin the process of cataloging their lives and reporting their material possessions to The State. Every piece of ancient red fabric, every leftover ounce of grain or paste in their larders. We must have enough, and no one wants to trigger an audit. The State says they make "reasonable allowances for mistakes," but a mistake is grounds for extended service and rehoming families.

I won't report this year. I have nothing but the clothes I'm wearing, and even they don't belong to me. Though every citizen is required to report, I should stay clear of The State based on recent experiences. And also based on experiences from the last year, which I'm just starting to figure out.

At least these crowds are good camouflage from the network. The State tracking screens are probably going crazy with everyone out in the streets. Our State-issue colors all match, even if mine are less ornate than most people's. No way the cameras are picking me up on a day like today.

In the distance, drums pound. They're deep, resonant, and semi-irregular, like different stampedes converging on one location. The hiss and whine of the speakers on the streets joins the music, and a crackling voice announces the parade will be in our location in minutes.

No time, then. I won't get back to Undergroundland before the festivities start. I've got to fade into the crowd and watch, let the movement carry me in the direction of my new home.

The drums grow louder. Hundreds of pairs of boots crunch the weathered asphalt, marching around the corner like an animal with a rigid military exoskeleton. The speakers crackle again. Brassy music pipes through the streets. The guards shuffle a little to adjust their timing to the new beat.

One of the guards breaks formation. He steps forward, and the others fall back behind him in a triangle position. He is the head of their human spear, and he brandishes an iron baton covered in streamers.

"Who are we?" he shouts

"Sector Keystar," the guards answer in unison.

"Who are we?"

"Sector Keystar." The second response is nearly inaudible from the whoops and hollers in the crowd.

I join with them, raising a fist to blend in, but my cheers are hollow.

We dance around the guards to welcome them home. Most guards ignore us, trained to stoicism in their years of service. A few can't resist the allure of being home after so much time in barracks and on patrols. Pictures pinned to their chests and back flap as they join us in celebration. The pictures show those who didn't make it, those who gave their lives in service to The State. There are more pictures than guards who made it home.

Occasionally, one of the men or women marching on the edges will grab the arm of a child and pull them into a short spontaneous dance. One little girl ends up on the shoulders of an especially tall guard. She gets the best view of the parade for half a street before her mother catches up to them, and the guard tosses her into her mother's arms. Her shrieks of delight drive the crowd into more of a frenzy.

Someone slams into me.

"Watch it," I snap.

Energy carries us apart before he, or she, can acknowledge the accident. A few people shoot me dirty looks. I'm killing the positive vibe.

"Sorry." I shrug, and some of them smile at me.

I'm carried away by the momentum of the people in the streets, and for a while, I decide to let myself float in the crowd, like I'm part of a twisting, churning storm cloud. The movement is not relaxing, but the chaos is exciting.

I would have been in a parade like this if I'd stayed in service and made it through. I'd be marching right where these men and women are—no, that isn't quite right, either. Memory teases me, on the edges of my consciousness.

*The room is darker than any street in the sector. A single bright*

*bulb illuminates the instructor's face at the front, so bright that the tiny
light deepens the darkness. The instructor rings a bell.*

*"We are the few. The chosen," she intones.*

*She strikes the bell again.*

*"We are family. We are your lifers."*

*Once more, the bell.*

*"We live to serve The State, and The State serves us."*

*Abruptly, the light winks out.*

I'm not sure if the dark is a metaphor for another mental
block. I feel separate from it, like the memory belongs to
someone else or is a story I've been told. In this moment, I'm not
present in the memory.

Nor am I present in the streets, until the crowd pauses and
seems to open. Without its motion, I'm not sure which way I'm
headed.

*Whump, whump, whump.*

Not a memory, but a real sound in the skies overhead.
Everyone stops to gaze at the choppers joining the parade. Choppers are a rare sighting in the sector, unless there's a Bounty. I
tense and check the nearest streetboard just to be sure—no, no
Bounty.

The choppers fly low, angling between the buildings and
shining their spotlights in erratic patterns. Each spot is a different
color, and the red, green, and blue lights make beautiful patterns.
We *ooh* and *aah*, and I don't have to pretend enthusiasm anymore.
The colors are amazing, and the flying is remarkable. Navigating
the tall buildings and staying in formation with the other choppers
requires the best of the best. Pilot duty was easily the hardest for
those lucky enough to be selected. Except for Bridge duty, of course.

The head of the parade calls a stop, and the guards join us
watching the show. The drum beats fade to nearly nothing. In
this moment, we are unified—those who left to serve, those who
stayed at home, and me, somewhere in between.

The music on the speakers intensifies to cover the crowd's silence, and the brass pierces my ears uncomfortably. I'm not the only one. Several of us cover our ears and wince at the high pitched whine.

"Bree Carter," a loud, booming voice cuts through the higher tones.

I freeze. I know that voice.

Ropes drop from the choppers, and guards dressed in black with their faces covered drop into the street and head right for me. These are elite. These are Ops.

There's nowhere to run. There are too many people on the streets, people who haven't done anything wrong. So I do the only thing that makes sense. I plunge into the middle of the parade. Well-trained or not, the element of surprise is on my side. Plus, those parading are not the guards that patrol our sector— these are our people, home from their duty stations elsewhere. They won't be so quick to go for me.

Or not. Someone grabs my arms and wrenches them behind my back.

"Wait a second," he says. "Do they want you?"

"I don't know. I've got to get out of here." I'm not tracking the Ops team, but they're going to be on me in seconds.

He loosens his grip and turns me around to face him. "I don't know—"

One of the Ops team reaches us. He throws a punch, and I duck, heading toward the home guard who stopped me. The Ops guy shifts his weight to try and follow me with the blow, and he lands his fist. But not on me. The punch catches the home guard on his shoulder and sends him spinning.

In that moment of chaos and confusion, another Ops team member grabs me. He's incredibly tall, about a foot taller than me, and there's powerful force in his bruising grip. I aim a kick at his legs and use the surprise to twist loose.

The home guard gets to his feet and roars. "Hey, that Ops guy hit me!"

The home guards closest to him leap to his defense, and the Ops team retreats a few feet. I try to slip through the fighting, but more Ops are streaming in, like ants to a sugar wafer. As they fight the home guard, they maneuver themselves into a circular perimeter with me and a half dozen of the home guards inside.

"Gwock!" I'm not sure what's next, but this isn't good.

The Ops team passes a thick coil of black rope among themselves. As one, they stop fighting those trying to break in and out of their perimeter and attach the cord to their uniforms. They unfold thin metallic shields and hold them in front of their bodies, clicking them together to create a solid circle of metal.

"Activate," the Ops leader orders.

They set their shields down, forming a three-foot-high metal wall. They turn inward to face us.

The music stops, and a command echoes through the street speakers, "All citizens, return to your homes immediately."

The citizenry are confused. The fighting has stopped, but the air is thick with tension. No one wants to move, because moving would spark the next round of conflicts.

"Give us the girl," the leader says. "You have served honorably, and this girl is wanted for State questioning. Do not throw your lives and service away for an Undergrounder."

The home guards do nothing. They don't fight, but they don't move to give me up. There's debate written on all of their faces—the cowards.

One of the home guard outside the Ops perimeter breaks the tension. She charges, and the wall drops her with a pop and a crackle. They've electrified their shields somehow.

"You'll find that touching one of us will cause the same damage." The leader flexes his fingers, and sparks arc between them.

"What the gwock?" The home guard who originally stopped me is shaken. "What do we do?" he whispers.

"If you're going to take me, you're going to have to let us out of this electric cage," I say to the leader.

"No problem, rat." The leader unhooks himself from the cable and approaches me.

I tense, weighing my options. Going peacefully isn't one of them. I have to fight. I have to—

A thousand stinging needles penetrate my body. They're on my face, my chest, my hands. I wipe at them, but the pain only intensifies. My back arches, and I scream. When I hit the ground, the pain of the impact is a relief from the fire that courses through my nerves.

Through the veil, someone yells, "Stop!"

The immediate pain ceases, but its echo lingers as I try to stand. A tangled web of wires on my clothes and exposed skin snares me. I don't even know how they got there, and the leader holds up a small remote.

"You will make no defense," he says simply, and holds the button down for a split second.

The quick burst of pain sends me sprawling on the ground.

"You think this is the worst that can happen to you? You know nothing of pain. Before we're through, you'll hurt in places you didn't even know you had, in ways you didn't even know you could hurt." Though his words are menacing, his expression is blank.

"Stop," I whisper as I stagger to my knees. "I'll come with you."

"Good." The leader aims a kick at my head.

I fall.

I wish he'd knock me out, but he knows too much about controlling the pain, about taking the agony just far enough, just like—

A series of blows to my ribs, then my back, as I curl to protect myself from the onslaught.

"I'm sorry," the home guard says to me, but he doesn't even try to stop them.

It doesn't matter. They'd kill him. They might even kill him anyway.

I'm limp when the Ops leader slings me over his shoulder. The choppers circle back and drop ropes. The rest of the Ops team detaches from their human electric fence and attaches themselves to the choppers. With a whir, they're gone, leaving only me and the leader surrounded by their charged shields. Two lengths of thick rope comes down, and he makes a coil around both of us with one of them.

I puke, and it splashes on the leader's mask. He'd probably hit me again, but we're about to take off. He makes like he's going to kick me, but only wipes his boots on my pants.

"Can't stand the pain?" He sneers.

"Afraid of heights." I won't give him the satisfaction of knowing just how much I ache.

He hooks the makeshift wall with his gloved hand and secures it to the other rope. He tugs on our rope, and we fly over the sector.

We're about six feet in the air when I finally, gloriously, pass the gwock out.

## 24

# THREE MONTHS LATER

"I think she's ready to try again," says the doctor in the hall. I hear a murmured response, but the buzz of conversation fades to near-silence. They must have remembered that I'm not deaf.

I'm in a State-run health center, but the room I'm in is designed like a home, and the décor is oddly reminiscent of the room I stayed in at Doc and the Professor's. There's lace on the bedspread and floral curtains at the windows. I've got a small desk with a couple of books and a glowing lamp. The food isn't that bad, three squares with only a little Nutripaste. Guard rations were way worse, but the food can't compare to the magic Mrs. Blank was able to work with her limited pantry.

I pace circles around the bed, waiting for the doctor to come in. Maybe I should seem calmer. I flop into the chair at the desk and leaf through one of the books. My leg jiggles, and I clamp my hand down to stop the shaking.

They've changed out the books a few times when I've asked them to. This one's pretty juvenile. Some imaginary creatures like tigers and elephants forming a society. The elephants keep trampling the tigers, and the tigers keep eating the elephants. They can't figure out how to stop hurting each other, so they set up a special animal police force to keep everyone in line. Then they're happy forever, and no one gets eaten or trampled anymore. The end. Standard State propaganda.

The doctor comes in. She's got beautiful red hair that cascades down her back like flames, like someone I used to know, sometime. "I'm glad to see you're resting." She wheels in a chair from the hall and sits, facing me.

"Hello, Dr. Fire," I say.

She smiles faintly. I was disoriented when they brought me here; I have no idea if that's her real name or what I call her because of her hair.

"What's your name?" she asks me.

"Bree."

"Bree..." she prompts.

"Carter. Bree Carter."

"Birth day?"

"Fifth, in the season of preparation, fifty-eight years since the uprising."

"Good, good. Now that we've established I'm talking to the right person," she shrugs and smiles, as though she hasn't made this joke every day for months, "Let's get started."

"Okay."

"How old are you?"

"Sixteen." The first question's always the easiest.

"What day is today?"

"I'm not sure exactly, but we're almost in the season of reflection or maybe a week or two in."

"Good. Where do you live?"

I gesture around the room. "Here, I guess."

"Before you came here."

"I—I guess I was with the Blanks."

"Now, Bree. We've talked about guessing before."

I correct myself. "I was with the Blanks."

"Who are the Blanks?"

"My foster family."

"Good. Good. Now, how did you get here?"

"I guess I—" Careful, Bree. Careful. "I mean—I was hurt."

"Hurt?"

"Something happened to me. I didn't feel good. I was outside, and the air was cold, but then I felt too warm. And I woke up here."

"You mean you were sick."

"Yes, yes, that's right. I got sick."

"And you were so sick that you couldn't remember much about yourself at all."

"No, I couldn't. Because the sickness hurt my head. Inside, in my brain."

"That's right. And are you all better now?"

"I feel better, but you're my doctor, and you're helping me. You'll tell me when I'm all better and I can go home."

"Very good, Bree."

"Thanks." I drop my head onto the desk, glad to have passed another test.

"Does your head hurt now?" The doctor puts her hands on my back, then my neck.

I sit up, trying not to tense too much. "No. But trying to remember is hard."

"Yes, it's very hard. And I've got some other hard things for you today. Do you think you can listen to them?"

"I gue—Yes."

"Great, Bree. You're doing great." She motions to the hall, and an orderly wheels in a large comp-like device with an oversized screen. A dozen thin wires hang from one side, and the doctor attaches them to the semi-permanent ports on my body.

"I'm going to tell you some things, and we're going to measure your body's reaction. I'll stop if things get too hard for you, and this machine is how I measure if things get too hard, okay?"

We've only done this for weeks. "Okay."

"Bree, you're right that we're in the season of the harvesting, but you're not sixteen. You're seventeen, nearly eighteen." She watches the screen, not me, at first.

When she looks at me, I wrinkle my brow. "But we've only been here for a few months. Right? You haven't been coming to my room for a year."

"You're absolutely right. You had a different doctor before me, but you wouldn't remember him. Do you know what a coma is?"

"I think so. You sleep for a long time, but I didn't think people woke up from them." I curl my toes, trying to tense up where she won't see. The screen gives a beep, and I peek around. The graph shows giant spikes in my pulse rate. As the doctor would say, "good, good."

"Take a deep breath," she says.

I relax and breathe deeply.

"Good, good." She watches the spikes on the screen even out. "People don't usually wake up from comas, not anymore. In ancient times, they used to. You're a special case. You woke up. That's why we have these conversations, to ease you back into life."

"So I was asleep for a year?"

"Essentially, yes."

"I was hurt so bad, I slept for a whole year?"

"You weren't hurt in the traditional sense. You were sick, remember?"

"Sick. I was sick. I remember."

"Exactly. And now you're better."

"I'm better. Does that mean I can go home to the Blanks?" I push her.

She stares at the screen, ignoring my question. "You're doing really well."

"I want to go home."

"You will, you will. We need to take things slowly. I think

that's enough for today. We've made great progress, and we'll make some more tomorrow, okay?"

"Okay," I've long since learned that compliance is my best shot at success. "Can I have a different book?"

"I've got a special treat for you today." She smiles as she efficiently detaches the wires and wipes the ports with a sterile cloth. Underneath the machine, she pulls out a tray with some sheets and charcoal. "Drawing supplies." Her smile gets bigger as she lays them out on the desk.

I finger the charcoal and wipe at the dark smudge on my fingertips. "Thanks."

"I'd like for you to draw me a picture." She takes a piece and draws a line down the middle of the page. "On this side, draw what you last remember. On this side, draw what you imagine home to be today, over one year later. Do you think you can do that?"

"Yes," I grip the charcoal so tightly it breaks in my hand.

She notices my white knuckles and gently pries the pieces out of my hand. "Remembering will be hard at first, but tomorrow, we'll talk about what you've missed while you were sick. Does that sound okay?"

"Yes." Remembering my manners I add, "thank you."

"Good, good. You're making great progress, Bree." She wheels the machine out and leaves me alone, in peace.

I don't know how much longer I can play a childish fool, but I guess it's time to draw a picture.

MY ARTWORK HANGS on the wall. The doctor was really pleased with the buildings I labelled "home" and "school" on both sides, like she was surprised I could still spell. I'm playing my role well here. Over the last week, she's caught me up on life "outside" and tells me they have a special job lined up for me that's really important. I'll be helping unclog lines in the sanitation department.

Because that's where a rat belongs, in the sewers.

I remember.

Some things are still tantalizingly out of reach, waiting for me to make the inevitable connection, but I remember. They've been experimenting on me for the last two years, and this is only the latest round. They've manipulated my memories, my sense of self, my everything. I don't know who I am because they haven't let me. Each time I get a glimpse of myself, they start again. Not this time. I won't start over again.

After Ops captured me, they brought me to a health facility. They wanted me to drink medicine. When I refused, they held me down and poured the meds down my throat. I screamed and choked until a nurse came in and asked them what the gwock they were doing. But she wasn't on my side either. She didn't like the noise and jabbed a thick needle into my thigh.

I woke up confused, disoriented, and that's when they started playing their little game. "You're sick," they told me. "We're trying to help you." I drank their concoctions and took their pills... or pretended to when they stopped paying close attention.

They told me their truths, but they can't strip my truth from me. I've worked too hard to remember.

## 25

I sneak out of my room and crawl on the floor toward a large conference room. There are no cameras here—the staff are arrogant enough to think they can monitor me and anyone else who might be here. The rooms in my hall are all empty, though. The conference room door is open a crack. No one is worried about eavesdroppers because there are no patients here. Except me. I peer through the crack. Ten men and women gather around a table, looking at a large graph.

"Project Praetereo going well." The red headed doctor stands at the front of the room presenting to her colleagues. "Subject A has been a challenge, but I believe we've found the right timing and dosage to control the memories."

Project Praetereo. I'm part of the project. I was assigned after failing miserably at Bridge duty, but I can't remember my role. I want to scream with frustration, but I keep quiet and listen to the conference, hoping to figure out what's going on.

"Can you target the blocks?" A man in a dark suit asks.

"We can't remove a specific event, but our biggest successes have been in removing durations of events. For example, we have precisely targeted the tapping when working with Subject A."

A frisson of fear stops my breath: my memory loss since the tapping. I am Subject A.

"And she doesn't remember anything?" a woman in State-issue brown asks.

"Nothing that we can tell, and we've been very thorough in her examination. Once this treatment is complete, she shouldn't need further dosing."

Not as thorough as Doc, or her dosage wouldn't have been so off, but I had been ready for them this time. I am ready for them.

"I'm pleased with your work." Mr. Dark Suit says. He's clearly the one in charge.

"Good, good. I expect we can begin a larger trial in the next several months."

"Excellent. We have several sectors in mind. Captain?"

The woman in brown answers, "Once the target sector is chosen, we can deliver the compound in the normally delivered rations."

"I've been thinking about that." Another woman speaks up, this one in tailored black jacket that's shiny and unlike any material I've ever seen. But I've seen her before, somewhere. "Would it be possible to deliver the compound in a mist or vapor form? If we utilize rations, the subjects may not consume the doses simultaneously. That could result in confusion in the sector."

My doctor answers, "Theoretically, we could, but we've only tested ingestion and injection as methods of delivery. We'd need to run more tests."

"We don't have time for more tests," the man in the suit snaps. "We've been patient for years now, and things are getting...tense... in Sector Keystar."

"Then I suggest proceeding with the original plan," the doctor says coolly. "In my expert opinion, you'd be introducing a significant risk."

"And reducing the risk of a significant riot," the woman in the black coat retorts.

The woman in brown shrugs, unwilling to enter the fray. She's not in charge here.

"The committee will meet again to discuss before the final decision is made," the man in the suit says.

I regret the day I ever agreed to be part of Project Praetereo. Not that I had any other options when they released me from service. I know that now, with the memories I've managed to hold onto since Doc helped me. I will not lose them again.

I'll play their game for now, but once they let me out, I will find my way back through the mazes they've created, I will stop their plan for Sector Keystar, and I will destroy every last member of The State who imprisoned, tortured, and experimented on me.

"Hello, Bree." Dr. Fire catches me in the hallway. She cocks her head. "What on earth are you up to?"

"I—"

"No matter." She advances on me.

The last thing I register is the jab of a thick needle in my thigh.

"Hello, Bree." The doctor greets me warmly, in my room.

"Hello," I give her a big smile. My head is fuzzy from something—a needle? There's something about Sector Keystar I'm supposed to know, but the memory is just out of reach. I remember the one truth I hold on to: They're experimenting on me, and that must stop. "I'm going to miss you."

"What?" She's confused.

"When I have to go to work. I'm going to miss you. Will I live here? Will you come see me every day when I get home?"

"You're a big girl, Bree, and I think this proves that you're almost ready to try living out there." She points to the window. "We have a special house where you will be checked on to make sure you're safe, and you'll be helping the Blanks and everyone in the sector when you go to work."

"I want to help them." I don't add, *by dismantling the evil structure they don't realize they're imprisoned in.*

"Good, good," the doctor says.

Four days later, Dr. Fire shows me the "special house." The building is outfitted with security sensors and cameras on all egresses. Spyder's puketastic pink decal is long gone from my anklet, so The State will be able to see me at home and track me everywhere I go. For now.

The first day on the job, they don't use my name, just a number. "34891, please report to line A, section C." The work is dirty, and I smell sewage all the time, even when I go "home" to the house that's been provided for me. I guess it's a good thing, because the smell doesn't overpower me when I'm at work. At least the air is warm down here. This season's been particularly cold, and the ground insulates us.

I work in a crew of six. We don't bother with the full numbers, because nobody can bother to remember more than their own. I'm Three to these guys, which is about as high as most of them can count. If I ever wondered where the slower kids ended up after leaving school, I don't now. They're here, with me, digging through poop balls. At least they're nice and more honest than the good, good Dr. Fire.

In the old days, water was safe, and people used the surplus to flush their toilets. Now, workers run a special chemical through periodically to flush the systems. The chemical can't break everything up, though, so that's what we do. Go into pipe access and poke people's turds with sticks.

Besides work, I don't really get to go anywhere, except back to talk with the doctor. Fresh clothes and food are delivered to my little house twice a week. I don't even have to cook or do laundry. There's probably another crew entirely devoted to doing the sewer workers laundry. That job would only be slightly better than this one. After two weeks, the routine almost seems normal. That scares me.

I'm poking at a particularly nasty clog—is that animal hair in there?—when Seven, one of my crew mates, pokes me with her poop stick.

"Three." Seven's loud whisper echoes in the tunnels.

"Yeah?"

"You got any friends?"

"Used to."

"Me too."

"Want to be my friend?"

"Sure."

"Okay. Here." She hands me a Nutribiscuit wrapper. "Found this on the streets yesterday. For you. Friends give each other things."

"Yeah... Thanks, Seven." I fiddle with the wrapper, tempted to give it back.

"Friends also do things for each other."

"I guess."

"Okay, I gave you the wrapper, now you have to do something nice for me."

"Depends."

"That's how a friend is."

"What do you need?"

"Can you kill that spider? I don't like spiders." She shudders and pulls a yuck-face.

I smile. "Sure. Where?"

"It crawled down there." She points to a tunnel spur. "I don't like spiders," she repeats.

"I'll take care of it." I shove the wrapper in my pocket and head down the tunnel.

I figure I'll enjoy the break from digging in the lines for a few minutes, pretend to kill some spider, and head back to the crew. There's no way I'm going to see a tiny spider in a hole this dark, big enough for me to stand up in.

Except it's not a tiny little spider. It's a giant spider, literally half the size of a tank, with the fuzziest arms I've ever seen and two fangs, long knives in its gaping killer mouth.

"Holy Fargo." I try to stay calm, but this thing can't be real— the massive bug is straight out of one of the comic books I saw growing up at—

"Hey, Bree."

I jump and bang my head on top of the shallow tunnel. "Spyder."

He steps out of the spider costume, helping one of his mites out of the other side. "Thanks, man." He slaps him on the back and sends him scurrying back through the tunnels with a harness on. VM knows where he's going to find a place to swing around underground.

Spyder saunters over to me and says, "You want to get out of here or what?" He slaps a lime green decal in my hand, some kind of a piece of fruit with a weird face on the front. "You know the drill. Slap that on your anklet, and let's get out of here."

"What about my crew?"

"They'll be fine. You can visit later if you want."

I shrug. "They probably won't remember me enough to miss me."

"Speaking of—did you?"

"What?"

He leans in and whispers, his breath hot on my ear, "Did you miss me?"

"Spyder..." I trail off, his name a warning.

"I'll take that as a yes. I missed you, good buddy." He punches me on the shoulder with enough force that I'm rocked a little off balance. "You look okay."

"Thanks? You're such an arrogant creep when you're away from your comp."

"So you like the geek in me?"

"Come on—yeah, I guess."

"I'd like a little geek in you."

"*Spyder.*"

"I'm kidding, I'm kidding. Sheesh. Sound carries down here. Can't a pal kid around? We should probably split." He laughs like he's proud of himself, but there's a weird edge in his voice. "Suit's two halves—you want the left or the right?"

"A giant spider. Is that supposed to be some kind of camouflage?"

"Yeah. Color and texture blend in and keep us off of the odd camera that still works down here. Shape is just for fun," he shrugs. "I'll take the left."

"Sure." I climb into the right half. "You're gross, you know that?"

"Yeah, but you kinda like it."

"Kinda. You're a good friend."

"I know. I'm a friend. I know, Bree."

## 26

The war room hasn't changed much over the last three months, but there are some new pictures on the walls. A few faces I don't recognize, a shock of red hair—my doctor—and a slew of partial maps of the sewers and utility tunnels. The maps look mostly correct, but I spot a few mistakes on the sewer connections. More people live down here in The Bunker now, too. We passed a few on the way in. Some pretended to ignore me. A few whispered and pointed at me.

Some bright white poster boards lie on the table. They must've used some kind of chemical bath to make the sheets that white. I pull a poster out of the stack and flip it over to read the writing on the other side.

Large letters at the top read: TAKEN. There's a picture of me underneath, one of my school pictures from a couple of years ago. I'm young, but I still look like me.

"What the Wyoming?" I say through gritted teeth.

Underneath the picture, the text continues, *Bree Carter, beaten and abducted by The State on the Day of Obligation. Protect your family. Oppose The State.* It's not even a catchy slogan.

Doc and the Professor come in. He throws his arms wide like he's going to hug me. "It's good to see—"

I wave the poster in their faces as an accusation. "What is this? Have you made me the literal poster child of your revolution? What the gwock?"

"I see you haven't changed." Doc tugs the poster from my grip. "Are you going to give us a moment to explain, or would you prefer to jump to your own conclusions, as you seem to have a habit of doing?"

"I'm tired, and I'm covered in crap, so why don't we pile a little more on?"

"Easy, easy," the Professor says. "Look at me." He takes my two hands in his and squeezes slightly, taking a deep breath and looking straight into my eyes. "'The countenance is the portrait of the soul, and the eyes mark its intentions.'"

His hands are warm and dry. I find myself breathing deeply, matching my exhalations to his. Somehow, this silly old gray-hair melts the anger from me. "I'm sorry. I haven't had a chance to be myself...in a really long time."

"And your self is angry. I understand, and you should be angry," he says. "Would you like something to eat or drink?"

"No, thank you."

"I have something better for you." The Professor retrieves a thin towel, dabs his own hands, and gives it to me.

I've never wanted to be clean more in my life. I wish I could strip down and burn these clothes, but there's no way I'm getting naked in front of people. Lex wouldn't have any problem—Lex. The thought of her makes me warm from the inside out, like drinking a cup of cava on the coldest day of the year. I wonder if she's thought about me, if she's worried about me. As far as she's concerned, I completely disappeared. I could go to her, but the timing isn't right. I've got to put my own wants aside and figure out how to stop whatever is happening with The State.

I scrub furiously at muck from the sewer and ball the towel in my fist. Holding the offensive cloth with two fingers, the Professor chucks it out of the room, and the three of us sit down.

"I suppose I should begin," Doc says, "as this was largely my idea."

"News of your capture spread quickly, once the parade finished. The people were a little unsettled, especially the home guards who had just been released. As we agreed when you left here, we were looking for a way to stop the tapping, but instead of merely stopping something, we started something: a movement.

"The State began actively sending guards to round up anyone who expressed the least doubt about our government. That's something they've always done, but there have been more doubts lately. The displays of power had begun to be more frequent, and when they were so brazen as to attack a young girl on what should have been the happiest celebration day of the year..." She trails off, leaving me an opportunity to draw my own conclusions, or ask a question.

I wait for her to continue instead.

"We had an opportunity to do more than stop the tapping. The Riverine Resistance could become something real, a powerful force. You, your face, became the banner behind which we could unite the sector. We've been able to recruit some of the released home guards and others based on your story."

"You're raising an army."

"Yes," she says. "And you're the figurehead, come back from the dead."

On my way out of the war room, I stop by a partially ajar door and peer in the crack. Looks to be a small access room with yet more comps and screens. Inside, Spyder's geeking out, typing. I nudge the door fully open.

"Hey, Spyder."

"Hey." He keeps typing. Probably prepping for some meeting or something.

"Thanks for the rescue. How've you been?"

"Thanks for asking." The look he gives me over the screen is loaded. I bet he's thinking back to our fight, before I got captured. I hope I can treat him with a little more respect now.

"So? How are you?"

He pushes back from the comps and shifts awkwardly in his chair. "Good. Mostly staying with my parents these days. Trying to be a kid as long as possible, sorta."

"In between when you fly through the air and overthrow the government, right?"

"Sure, sure," and he looks at me so hopefully I want to cry. Staring at the ground, anywhere but me, he gets up, takes my hands.

I let him.

"How are you?" he asks.

"Honestly? I have no idea. I feel like I'm always trading one prison for another: foster care, training, the creepy health center sewer house, here. I had a few days that were my own in Undergroundland. I need time for me—to figure out who I am."

His face changes, like he's cracked some tricky comp code. "You can go back there, you know. They won't be able to find you as long as you keep that decal on. Take some time, like I'm taking the time at my parents. Then, maybe..." His thumbs caress the backs of my hands.

"Maybe," I give his hands a slight squeeze, unwilling to reject him completely. We're finally getting to a good place, and I don't want to ruin that progress.

"Hey, can I tell you something?"

"Yeah..." I'm cautious.

"Promise not to read into it?"

I nod, unwilling to trust myself to speak.

"Bree..." He exhales, like he's going to turn this into something romantic. "You smell like crap."

We collapse into giggles, friends again, finally. And for a moment, I am home.

## 27

I spend the morning getting caught up on the last several months. Doc and the Professor show me sections of the sheets with articles purporting terrorist attacks and thinly-veiled praise for the almighty State who protects us all.

For each article, the date and some key information on place and timing have been circled. Spyder brings up the footage real-time of the incidents in The State's own video record banks. Guards fill every last frame, assaulting my neighbors in the name of peace.

*It's not their fault. They don't know any better. They haven't been raised the same way we have. We have to protect them from themselves.*

The memory of rationalization pops into my head unbidden. I wonder—if I had completed training, become a normal guard in another sector, would I be doing just as these guards are doing? Would I be so brainwashed that I wouldn't see that The State had been feeding me lines and lies through my training?

The Professor picks up another sheet and reads the contents aloud. A stabbing in front of an entertainment screen.

"Enough!" I cut him off. "I get that things have deteriorated. I don't need any more of the blow by blow. How many are we talking overall?"

Doc points to a couple reports. "Most of the incidents are small. Less than a hundred dead, but many more wounded. Three, maybe four, skirmishes a week."

That's the kind of information I need. "I think we should go after the guards."

"They'll only send more of them." The Professor gathers the sheets into a large stack. He's finally ready to talk beyond the reports. "You know as well as we do, they'll send suppression units and further increase the presence."

"No—I mean, we should try to talk to the guards. Convince them that what they've heard about our sector is wrong. Stop them from continuing these attacks. Get them on our side."

"We've tried," Doc says. "We've lost some friends that way. The guards are highly suspicious and have been engaging in combat on approach. We can't talk to them anymore without them assuming an act of aggression."

"We should still try. The State talking points during training convinced us that everyone in the other sectors, everyone different from us, was inherently dangerous. If The State can talk them into it, we should be able to talk them out of it."

Doc focuses on me like dinner snared in a hunter's trap. "Your point of view is slightly different from the masses, Bree, but I appreciate your opinion. And I agree with you. Which is why I think you should be the one talking in the next part of our plan."

Great, I've walked right into their crafty gray-haired trap. I try to tamp down the suspicions I had of these two when we first met —we're friends now. "What plan?"

"We're going to stop the tapping in Budgetville and Under-groundland."

"You are? We are? What happened to growing a movement instead?"

"We can do both."

Stopping the tapping is all I ever wanted to do in the first place. No one should end up like I've ended up. No one.

Doc continues, "And we need you, my little figurehead, to spread the word."

I've stepped into it now. Speaking of crap. "Great," I say. "Can I bathe first?"

Doc laughs and leads me out.

I'VE BEEN WORKING on a stupid speech for hours in the gross floral room I stayed in before I got captured. Doc wants me to inspire their new recruits. Speech is probably an overstatement. I've got a few words written, but they have no shape to them. State, bad. Stop tapping, good. I think that gets the point across. I'm literally banging my head on the desk with such force that I almost don't hear the knock on the door over the thumping of my own skull against wood.

"Just a sec." I breathe and stretch to compose myself, but I still feel like I've traded the prison with the redheaded doctor for prison with Doc and the Professor. Whatever, any interruption is welcome. I open the door.

"Em!" I fold her tiny body in my arms and hug her, hard. "What are you doing here?"

"I'm here to see you, duh." She hugs me back harder than I'm hugging her, if that's possible. One of us is going to break a bone.

I give in to the hug for a moment, then hold her at arms' length. "Seriously, what are you doing here? This can't be safe."

"Mom and I are helping. We were so worried about you." She flits around the room, lifting the corner of the floral bedspread with a wrinkled pamphlet, leafing aimlessly through the sheets of abandoned starts to this VMforsaken speech on my desk. "Ugh! How can you work in this space? It's hideous. I mean, maybe Mom would like this junk, but it isn't you at all."

"Total gray-hair space," I say. We both laugh a little. "But, Em..."

She flops down in the desk chair and spins a little. "The Bunker's safer than the streets are. You hear what's been happening?" Following the twelve lines of Em's conversation is always a challenge, but I've gotten the hang of it over the years.

"Yeah, they caught me up. Doc's running a few tests on me since I got back, but she says I can go live on my own again soon, if I want. Trust me, I want."

"Oh! And Spyder gave me this wicked decal. Check it." Em's folding and fiddling with some of the sheets, but she stops her work to lift her pant leg and show me the artwork. Who knew cookies, cars, and unicorns went together?

"It's...nice."

She snorts. "Who do you think you're fooling? But I like the colors." She fumbles in her pockets. "Mom gave me something to give to you. For protection."

She hands me a rock, silver-gray and sparkly. I turn the small flat stone in my hand.

"Doesn't feel heavy enough to throw at someone."

"Even light things can be thrown." She crumples one of the folded sheets and tosses it in my direction. "But the stone's not for throwing. Mom found a lumpy rock when she was little and carried it forever until it got smooth. She gave it to me when I was like ten. Now the stone's for you, so you know we're always with you, no matter where you go."

"That's sweet, Em."

"I know." She wrinkles her nose at the patterned curtains covering a non-existent window.

I hesitate before asking, "How's she doing?"

"Okay, so far. She's just Mom."

Mrs. Blank is getting up there. Close to forty, and most don't live past forty-five. There are exceptions, though, but no one really hopes they'll be one.

"Good." I lay on the bed and throw an orange-shammed pillow at Em. "I mean, look at this stuff."

"We have got to get you out of here." Em runs to the door and rattles the knob.

"Soon. But not soon enough."

## 28

I have a reprieve from the orangey floral nightmare of my room in The Bunker—Doc and the Professor have agreed that, as a test, I can wander the streets. I wear one of Spyder's decals, but I'm still going on my own, so as not to put anyone else at risk. They've trusted me enough to give me the basics of the tunnel schema that lead into The Bunker, so I even get to do this gloomy walk by myself. The deep dark of the tunnels, broken by the occasional glow bowl, matches my mood. I welcome the solitude.

We all want to see how close an eye The State is keeping on me, now that I've escaped from sewer treatment duty. I'm still not sure why they wanted me to believe I was sick or what Dr. Fire was doing to me, but I know it wasn't good. Doc's best guess is that they were checking to make sure my memories haven't returned and to see how malleable my mind is. I still don't know why The State removed my memories in the first place. I must know something they don't want me to know. If I just had the right experience, I know it would trigger...something and give me the clue I need to piece all of this together.

I'll wander in the morning. Then the Professor is going to

keep going with my "formal education." I was never a big fan of school, but he says he'll be an easy grader because life is the real test. The State teaches us to their benefit, but they leave so much out and twist the real truth. The water—that poisonous danger that keeps us all in place—they made it that way. The State triggered the event that killed most of our ancestors. They supply hydropacks and food and clothes because they owe us, but they hand them out in limited number to control us.

I won't be controlled.

I emerge from The Bunker tunnels in Budgetville and step into the light. On high alert, I look left and right. The sidewalks are clear. Scanning the windows, doors, and roofs of the buildings, I make tentative progress down the street.

My breath swirls into frozen fog with each exhalation. Dangerous, but not deadly. I shiver and pull the bulky beige State-issue coat around me. I lost so much time with Dr. Fire and in the sewers that we're now deep in the season of reflection. I try not to let my mind wander too much and refocus on my immediate surroundings.

The early light plays games with the shadows, deepening them in the spaces between buildings, providing ample hiding spaces for guards or Ops teams. The basic guard patrols would be way more obvious, marching down the street to confront me head on.

But the streets are still empty. There's no guard, no citizens rushing to school or work. The day is too early for most. I am alone.

My eyes are drawn to the corner of a black dumpster, poking out from around the corner of a building across the street. Some sanitation worker didn't replace it properly—it shouldn't be in full view from a main street. I can't pull my gaze from the hulking form. I remember the first time the guards chased me, when I jumped into the garbage to escape them. I cross the street.

As I walk closer to the dumpster, my nerves tingle, and my

hands start to shake with excess energy. Why should a dumpster be misplaced? Is something hiding in the alley? Maybe this is a trap, and I'm about to spring—

A cat leaps from the blackness, landing on all fours in front of me with a yowl. I stifle a scream, then a laugh.

"I'm sorry to disturb you at home." I lean down to pet him, but he withdraws, hissing and barring his teeth. "My mistake." I laugh.

He turns in the cat version of a huff, his tail raised and lashing, and dismisses me.

Yes, I'm on high alert. Boy, I'd better protect myself from a stray cat. To appease myself, and without further disturbing the feline Lord of the Alley, I check behind the dumpster. Nothing there. I'm tempted to try and push it back into its proper location, but reason wins out, and I keep walking.

I walk and scan, scan and walk. I'm hoping to burn off nerves and the excess energy from confronting that cat, but the longer I walk, the more likely the long arm of The State will crush me.

The sector is waking. I get a few queer looks as people head to the streets to waste another day of their lives. They lift their chins and watch me from the corners of their eyes as though they can smell the sewer gases that no longer leak from my pores. Before I can think of anything to do to stop their strange looks, I'm in Undergroundland, alone again.

IN THE THREE hours I've been walking, I haven't even heard a whisper of a guard's boot on asphalt. Apparently, The State doesn't care about me, or Spyder's decal is doing an even better job than I thought. But then again, the last time I thought The State wasn't tracking me, I ended up captured by an Ops team. I'm tempted to go home, but I don't want to risk bringing guards to Charley until I'm sure no one's going to come after me.

Charley can't take care of himself. But I know someone who can...

Life is funny—I only lived in that building for a couple of weeks, but the partially-intact third floor feels more like home than anyplace I've ever lived. I feel guilty about that, like I'm a traitor to the Blanks who were the best family I almost had, but being on my own is the only thing that makes me feel like I really belong in this world.

I know where I have to go. I know where I want to go.

I knock tentatively on the rusted metal door. No one answers, which isn't really surprising. No one could hear that weak knock from the deep basement. I slap my palm on the metal with a stinging but satisfying clang.

No answer.

"Hello?" I call. "Lex? I wanted to tell you that...I'm sorry. I don't know what's going on in my life right now, but I didn't mean to let you down. I'm sorry I missed the fight, and I'm sorry it's taken me so long to get here to tell you so. Maybe..." I trail off, because I'm not sure what I'm going to offer her, and I don't know if I could keep any promise I might make.

I try the brass knob. The old metal squeaks but gives, and the door creaks open.

"Hello?" I head down the stairs to the basement.

Instead of the dark mats and rows of chairs I expect, there's nothing but junk. Pieces of broken sofas and empty Nutripaste wrappers litter the bare concrete. In the corner, a few small stones on the floor are the only clue that a heavy bag once hung from the crossbeams above.

I wish there was a clue, a message, any hint about what happened here. The State found the location. That much is obvious. Maybe everyone got out, moved the equipment to open the club somewhere else, or maybe...

The State takes people. It's no secret. I should have known when I found this place—too organized. Too professional. Too much of a threat to allow it to stand. They would have sent a platoon for a place this size, with known fighters opposing them. If they didn't die in the stand-off with the guards, The State would make sure they did later. After a trial, of course. If it did happen that way, if it all ended with fighting, I hope that's how Lex went down. She wouldn't have wanted to be captured.

I stare, defeated, and ready myself to go back to The Bunker. There's nothing left for me to do but fight The State and officially join the Riverine. No. I straighten my shoulders. That's not nothing. That's important. That's a purpose.

I try to forget that I may never see Lex again as I head back to The Bunker. But trying to forget her stings worse than any hit I might've gotten in the fight ring.

## 29

I stand when Doc gestures for me to. We're in a small room with some metal folding chairs. Maybe about ten people total, including Doc and me. I wanted the Professor here for support. He's more comforting than Doc, and they both know he's the warmer of them. The idea is to get me used to being uncomfortable, though, so I'm stuck with Doc.

Today, my official journey as a figurehead and leader of the Riverine Resistance begins. I won't lead dangerous missions or fight any guards. You know, the stuff I might actually be good at. No, instead, I have to talk to a bunch of strangers.

In the room, moisture hangs in the air, and the wetness makes me shiver. Water is dangerous, unless it's specially treated in packs. I've known that my entire life, but water is impossible to avoid in our climate, and it's even more impossible to avoid underground, like we are right now. We're deeper than where Doc and the Professor live, deeper even than the utility tunnels.

The walls are a mix of dirt and stone, and water beads on the rocks. When we went through the small hewn doorway, I nearly brushed up against the wet rock. Naturally occurring condensate is supposed to be safe, but alarms still sounded in my entire body.

The small hairs on the back of my neck wanted to stand up, but I willed them down just in case they'd wick that terrifying liquid against my skin.

But I'm supposed to say something now, out loud, to this group gathered here in this cave. They know all about me. I know nothing about them.

"Uh, hi." That's a really good beginning. "I'm Bree."

They smile to encourage me, but the rows of gleaming teeth could devour me. I stare at the cracks in the floor and continue.

"I'm here to talk to you about tapping. Tapping is when The State selects people for service. We become guards in other places. Mostly other sectors, but sometimes other places. I was tapped, but I never became a guard."

Oh, VM, kill me now. Everyone here already knows what tapping is, so why am I explaining it to them? I sound as idiotic as when I was talking to the red-headed Dr. Fire, but I'm not pretending now. If only I could hit something. That would be easier than this slow torturous death by talking.

I chance a quick glance up to see how my imbecilic words are going over. I'm going to assume Doc is trying to smile at me encouragingly, but her expression comes off as a tight grimace. I look at each person in the circle in turn. I'm brave enough for that.

Their kind faces are expectant. One man is even leaning forward in his seat, arms braced on his legs like he's so excited he might just snap up to standing. He's about five or ten years older than me, but so eager he seems...younger. A memory pops up, unbidden, but welcome. There were those in training who were eager, too. He needs to understand. This isn't a game, or easy. The memory fuels me, and I do the only thing I can: I tell him what I remember.

"After they beat me," I say quietly but powerfully, "they pumped me full of drugs that made me feel like I was floating. Which was a good thing, because before that, I could feel every bruise and broken bone in my body throbbing. They took so long to set the bones, they had to rebreak some of them. Then they gave me different drugs and hooked me up to a machine that made me convulse. I sweated and cried until they left me a huddled mess, covered in my own drool and crap. That is the reality of what we're facing. They've been killing people in the streets? Those are the lucky ones."

Eager Beaver leans back in his chair, stricken.

I can't finish. "I'm sorry. I have to go," I say mostly to Doc and push through the circle and past the dirt walls threatening to cave in on us all, to the exit.

I GATHER every scrap of notes from my desk in The Bunker and shove them into a cardboard box I found near the cafeteria. I will destroy the sheets later, once I'm away from here and safely anonymous again.

"That was brilliant." I jump as Doc barges through the door and grabs both of my hands. "You were wonderful."

I practically shove her across the room to get loose and keep stuffing my writing away.

"A few more of those speeches, and you'll be ready for a bigger crowd."

"I'm not your puppet. I'm not The State's puppet. I need space."

Doc waves her hand dismissively and prattles on. "Of course, of course. But the emotion in you, when you spoke, it was so beautiful, so inspiring. I was a little nervous at first, but you dug deep. You *felt* what you were saying."

"Of course I felt what I said. That was my life!" I explode. "This isn't some academic exercise in brainwashing people into doing what you want. For a doctor, you're so gwocking detached from anything real."

I blow past her with my box, leaving the cold doctor slack jawed behind me. I've got to get out of here.

The Professor is in the hallway. He holds up a decal in an understated black and white design. "You're going to need this, if you want to move about safely."

"Thanks." I hold the box on one hip and balance to slap the decal on my anklet. My anger burned out as quickly as a flash grenade, since Doc is still out of my sight in that floral nightmare. "I'm not—I mean I am going to help stop the tapping. It can't happen. But I can't be here either."

The Professor nods sagely. "That inward eye which is the bliss of solitude."

"I guess."

"You kids today. Be careful. Find what you need, and visit often. And remember, as a very wise man once said, the best way to find yourself is to lose yourself in the service of others."

"I'll be back in a few days."

And I come back. And I give more speeches to more and more people. And I hate talking to groups, but they listen to me. And with a few words, weeks have passed. I am a true leader in the Riverine Resistance, and I am about to give The Speech That Will Change Everything.

## 30

# FIVE WEEKS LATER

I wake to a thud and sit bolt upright in a tangle of covers. The bed is to the right of me; the thud was me falling. Landing, rather. I shiver and pull the blankets close. I try to remember the dream that's got me in this state. Flashes of white swirling in green mist. The Bridge again. I hate this dream. I've had it ever since I got away from Dr. Fire. I don't have my memories fully back, but that's become less important than the work I'm doing with the Riverine Resistance. The State hurt me, and I've got to stop them from hurting anyone else.

Doc says with time and patience, the trickle of memories will become a flood. Right now, I'd settle for a stream. Tonight's dream was different, though. I run through the scenes—glimpses, really—trying to pick out whatever my brain has latched onto.

The middle of the Bridge. An aerial view, which I know is impossible, because I can't fly, and there's no way I'd have gone up willingly in a chopper. I clamp down on the nausea that being so high brings. The bridge runs like a swirl of white chocolate through dark—it's beautiful. I close my eyes and hold the image in place, zooming in closer. Almost there. The pure white fills my vision.

There, on the side edge of the bridge, I see an aberration. A speck of red. Closer. The red expands, in a pattern, and I can make out hand and footprints coming from a giant puddle of the stuff. Even closer, and the red on white overwhelms my vision. Now there are specks of black throughout, and I know they're flies, and I know this is blood. All I see is color. Now fully awake, I crawl hands and knees and blankets to the jagged edge of the floor; and I throw up into the nothing.

Heaving, I take deep breaths and try to stop shaking. The floor creaks underneath me, and I move back from the jagged, wall-less edge. I'm home, in Undergroundland. My bed is on the third floor. High up enough that I'm not worried about the gangs of thieves, Undergrounders like me, that roam looking for easy pickings. Low enough that if things got tight, I could jump out the window and survive. Probably. I might break a few bones once I landed, but I'd be free and alive. Probably.

My life is based on probablys. I'll probably get more sleep tonight. I'll probably wake up tomorrow. I'll probably find something to eat. I'll probably survive one more day, until the day I don't. The only thing that's certain here is the uncertainty. That's what The State wants. Keeps us in line. Keeps us out of their kind of trouble. Keeps us in our own troubles.

The Professor's lessons and my own experiences with contraband have completed my real education. When I was eight or nine, I found an atlas in my foster mother's attic. Most of the pages had crumbled to yellow dust, but the index was still intact. I didn't tell anyone what I'd found. If I had, they'd have destroyed the atlas and taken me away. Instead, I memorized the true names of the states. It was my first act of rebellion.

When I was finished, I destroyed the atlas myself. It's safer this way. Spyder and his family can keep their comic books, but some types of history are more dangerous than others. The pages may be gone, but the knowledge is still inside me: *Massachusetts.*

*Maryland. Oklahoma.* On nights when I can't sleep or when the dreams get too bad, like tonight, I recite their names.

I crawl back to the mattress, but I can't bring myself to climb onto the rickety metal bed frame. Instead, I grab the pillow and bed down underneath the box spring. Cocooned in blankets, I exhale the forgotten names and pretend I'm somewhere else: a cave in the mountains where no one will ever find me, in Arizona or Oregon or whatever states had mountains.

I'M AWAKENED ONCE AGAIN, this time by a shrill scream and a weight pressing down on my midsection. I groan and poke my head out of the covers. The screaming stops.

"Hello?" A familiar voice says from on top of me.

"Get off me," I grunt.

"Bree?" My name in a hushed whisper. "Are you a ghost?"

"You're standing on the bed."

A sharp intake of breath, then an awed whisper. "You're a ghost that can see me."

"No, you're pressing the mattress on me. This frame is eight hundred years old, and I'm pinned underneath."

"Oh!" Two rainbow-stockinged feet appear over the edge of my bed.

"Hi, Bree!" Em wriggles her toes in hello and leans down to look at me. "Whatcha doing down there?"

"Not sleeping," I yawn.

"Rough night?"

"Could you just get off the bed so I can get up?"

"Sure. Sorry." She pops off the bed and kneels on the floor to face me. "Need a hand?"

Before I can answer, she's hooked me under the shoulders and is yanking me over the splintered flooring. I wince as a rough board scrapes my elbow. As soon as I've cleared the bed, I grip her forearms, lift my hips and flip her neatly onto her back. Em's been learning some self-defense. She's starting to get the hang of it, and I can tell she's been working hard.

"You've been practicing."

She groans and massages the back of her head. "Thanks."

We lay there for a few seconds and both burst out laughing. I get up first, offer her my hand, and heave her to her feet.

"How're you doing, Em?" We both giggle as I hug her. She is the brightest spot in my existence and the closest thing I have to a sister.

"Better than you." She breaks the embrace and pointedly picks up the blanket from the floor. She starts to fold it but quickly gives up and throws it in a lump on the bed.

Em's enthusiasm makes me nervous. I've loved spending more time with her over the last few weeks, teaching her to defend herself just in case, but her undirected excitement could easily get one or both of us killed in the wrong place at the wrong time. The sector is a dangerous place right now.

"Big day today." She flops on the bed, sitting cross-legged.

"Yeah." I sit down on the edge next to her, knees bent, feet firmly on the floor.

"Gwock, Bree, you look ready to bolt."

"I've got to be." She must hear the steel in my voice, because she rapidly changes the subject.

"I have muffins! Mom made them." She reaches into her bag and pulls out a delicious smelling parcel. Steam rises from the cloth covering in the cold morning air; I will have breakfast today. Em works the knot with her quick fingers, and soon we're looking at a pile of crumbly mush.

"Oops." She shrugs her shoulders. "It'll still taste good."

I smile, because Em is Em. We peel the muffin pieces from the cloth and stuff them in our mouths.

I have never tasted anything as good as Mrs. Blank's cooking. I stayed with them the longest, mostly because of the food. Well, the food and Em. I bounced from home to home for a few years, but the Blanks felt right. I tried to tone things down for them. I didn't want to bring trouble down on them, and I didn't want to have to leave. I was there for about five years, until last year when I was tapped.

I haven't seen Mrs. Blank since. I haven't gone back. It's better for all of us this way. Safer. And I still see Em, and I still get to eat Mrs. Blank's cooking sometimes, which has to be enough. My life will never be normal—no one's lives are normal—and I couldn't go back there and pretend otherwise. Besides, The State would find me there and do VMknows what to all of us.

The thirty seconds of quiet are too much for Em. She breaks the silence with a mouthful of muffin mush, "Are you ready?"

I nod but don't say anything. Today is a big day for me. Out of all the work I've been doing, today's demonstration is going to be the most important. People on the street have been circulating the word for a while now, and everything comes to a head today. I've got the venue. I've got the speech. I'll have the crowd. I've got a couple of hackers who will keep us off the network. The pieces are coming together in a big and terrifying way. The State won't know what hit 'em.

The timing is perfect. Tomorrow is the next tapping. And I'm going to stop it.

## 31

E m's unusually quiet during breakfast, which suits me just fine. She knows how important today is. I need the time to think and center.

I've been giving speeches for the last few weeks, and Doc thinks I've got enough under my belt now to make a big push. We need to, if we're going to stop the tapping. The Professor's been helping me a little with the speeches since that first one, but not too much. They don't want me to lose the authenticity of me. I don't want to lose that either.

I've been doing more research, too, which is really different with Doc and the Professor than when I was at school. The Professor says that true history will give context to my experiences. I guess he's right. I resisted a little at first, because I thought lectures would be boring, like school. But the stories of our real history are much more interesting than the lies we're told when we're children.

Tapping started a long time ago, before The State existed. The government of our ancestors started the process. In theory, tapping was a great idea. A lot of people had all these expectations of services that should be provided to them, and there weren't enough people in paid positions to provide services. Volunteers started helping out, but eventually, there weren't enough of them either. People didn't want to lose services, so when they made a law enforcing volunteerism, no one opposed the legislation. Initially, everyone between the ages of 18 and 25 was required to spend a year in service. In those days, people did great things like build homes for each other, taught each other, grew food.

But then, the quality of life started to change. Our ancestors had so much, but they wanted even more. The people were like parasites feeding off of one another. Some took too much, and the killings started. The slide into violence was gradual, and the government had to compensate by adjusting the volunteer program even more. One year of service became two. Two became three. Corruption bred in the ranks of the officials, and the parents of the rich began buying their way out of enforced service. The poor revolted. Many were killed.

For a while, those deaths were enough to stave off the inevitable. Our people relaxed back into the system that was so comfortable, that could now support everyone. Eventually, we re-populated and put a strain on the system again. This time, the government was ready. There was an event we call "The Uprising," and everybody talks about it in hushed tones. That's when the water went bad. Back then, they called it war, and it's what I'm trying to start right now.

Out of the ashes, our current civilization arose. As far as the Professor's told me, not much has changed since. The State exerts as much control as possible over each citizen's life. The enforced volunteerism was kept, only they've expanded the age range and added a lottery. Tapping. The State likes to keep us on our toes, holding our balance right on the edge of a roof. A finger's worth of pressure, and we tumble to our deaths.

My speech today could change all that. I'm not naïve—I know that more than one person talking is needed to change things.

That's where Doc and the Professor come in. But I'm getting ahead of myself. We all have to act as one, to perform one simultaneous act of resistance and rebellion that will show The State we mean business.

Everything's got to go as smoothly as possible today, so soon after breakfast, I get rid of Em.

"Thanks for coming over," I say. "And thank your mom for the breakfast."

She smiles at that and throws her arms around me.

"No matter what, we're you're family. Biology can't change that. Neither can The State." She squeezes me tighter and lets me go abruptly. I rock back on my heels to keep my balance. "You'll do great, and I'll be right there with you."

"No. I don't want you there." The words are out too quickly and too sharply. Em recoils, and her eyes widen in that way that means she's about to start crying.

Damage control time. "I'll feel your support wherever you are. You don't have to be there." I want her there, but I'm afraid for her. She's so small. Too much can go wrong. The crowd could get rowdy before The State breaks things up. I can take care of myself, even if the guards come.

Em must sense where my thoughts have headed. Her next words should be a balm for my frenetic mind. "You can't stop me coming."

That's not quite right. You're supposed to soothe me now, Em.

"But..." Here it comes. Whatever she says next is bound to make my life easier.

"But, I will stay at the back, near an exit. If things get out of hand, I'll rabbit faster than you can say..." She trails off, mumbling unintelligibly.

"What?"

"Faster than you can say..." She mumbles something again.

"I can't say that. You're not saying anything real."

"Then I'll have plenty of time to get out of there." She throws me a cheeky grin, and I do feel better.

"Bree," she hesitates, and I am instantly on my guard. Em doesn't hesitate. She takes my hand. "You can only do so much, you know? You can only control so much. Do the best you can, and let that be enough. If the plan doesn't work, it won't be because you didn't do enough. It'll be because the rest of the sector isn't ready."

I nod. I don't trust myself to say anything.

She squeezes my hand and walks to the hole that used to be a door. "I'll be back in the afternoon with more food. Do you want anything special?"

"You mean your mom is taking requests for my last meal?" The joke falls flat, and I force a laugh to cover up the silence. The room is too quiet. Em's too quiet. I close my eyes, because it's all too much. "Pot roast, please. The meat can be substitute or whatever. But with real carrots." I whisper.

"I'll see if she can get some."

Then Em is gone, and I am alone.

I do some of the basic stretching exercises and martial arts patterns they taught me last year in training to clear my head and ready my body. I've had the most luck restoring physical memories. My body feels the echoes and the continuity from training, through my memory loss to now, when I'm in active rebellion. The consistency calms me. I go over the speech I'll be giving as I move. The movement helps cement the words in my brain. I know I'll be nervous, but these weird rehearsals I've been doing every morning for the last few weeks should help keep me on track.

I've been dawdling long enough. I've got things to do to get ready for tonight. Time for my last exercise, something they didn't teach me in training, but that I've been pushing on myself. I walk along the edge of the floor with my arms straight out, keeping balance. My stomach drops a few inches when I look over the edge at the floor thirty feet below, but the rush energizes me. *I will not be afraid of heights. I will not be afraid of heights.*

I lower myself over the edge, holding with just my fingertips and swing my body back and forth like a pendulum. I jump and land on the catwalk that used to be the second floor. From there, a few quick steps and hops put me at ground level, where Charley confronts me.

"Here." He rises from the depths of his cardboard and thrusts a piece at me. "You dropped this last night."

I take the cardboard and gag at the scent. My vomit from last night covers the entire piece. I drop it on the floor and back away.

"Very funny, Charley. I'm sorry."

"You don't want this back?" He picks up the cardboard and sniffs it. I almost lose the muffins I had for breakfast.

"Nope. But I'll throw it out." I try to close off my nostrils, and hold out my hand.

Charley doesn't move.

"Or...you can keep it."

He snarls at me and flings the cardboard a surprising distance across the room. "Why the heck would I want that trash?"

He gets in my face, and I can smell the alcohol on his breath. "You'll be replacing that, Missy."

"Relax. I'll see what I can find."

"Good cardboard is hard to come by, and insurance sure as heck won't cover it." He cackles at his own joke and starts wheezing.

"Good one, Charley." I slap him on the back a few times and surreptitiously wipe my hand on my pants as I walk out onto the street.

## 32

B right sun streams between crumbling buildings, but I keep to the shadows. I'd love to walk down the middle of the road and let its warmth hit me full in the face, but then a tank might also hit me full in the face.

The guards patrol the streets constantly now, even in Undergroundland. They've brought in even more guards to "protect against the high terror threat level." They're the ones terrorizing us. The network shows them *almost* exactly where every person of interest is at any given time, or when someone's loitering, or when unpermitted groups gather. They don't need to patrol. All they have to do is watch a comp screen. Unless they suspect someone has gone off-network. But when that happens, the person's usually submitted for Bounty and caught within the hour.

The magic decals Spyder made still work, but The State must have figured out we were using them. We found that out the hard way two weeks ago, when our sector's security measures were changed. Crews were on the streets for days amping up and adding to the cameras on the streets. There aren't many places left where a camera won't find you. Since most of my friends are clearly on a State watchlist, they expect us to appear on camera every so often.

One of Doc's assistants—some kind of nurse or medical tech, I never met him—was on a supply run when a Bounty was issued for him. We hustled around and figured out pretty quickly how to map out paths to avoid the new cameras. Not soon enough for the assistant, though. Couple of Undergrounders caught him. No chance for a Pilgrimage. The streetboard showed them presenting his grotesque head to The State for payment. I guess they thought that would teach us a lesson.

We've learned to hide in plain sight—except for Doc and the Professor, of course. We're conscious of being monitored but hopeful The State will lose us in the banality of life. They haven't pursued me since I left the sewer workers, which surprised me at first. Ever since I moved out of The Bunker, I've been ready to turn myself in and request Pilgrimage, but that hasn't been necessary—yet.

The Riverine's been acting in small ways throughout the sector, some petty theft here, a little property destruction there. The State's busy enough responding to those pockets of violence and staging their own cover-ups that they can't root us out. The State doesn't have the resources to worry about what we might be doing—they're too busy handling what we *are* doing.

I don't like that they can track when Em comes to visit me, though. We have to save our off-network time for when we're doing something really illegal. Like the giant unpermitted gathering where I'm giving the biggest speech of my life tonight.

The State monitors our whereabouts and displays them to the guards on a network map. Spyder has ways to jam the signal for short periods of time, but we have to be careful when we do that, because The State gets suspicious very quickly. A few seconds is fine—a natural blip. A few minutes could be too much. Anything longer than that, and they sound the Bounty alert. Your life isn't worth anything once that happens. If the guards find you, you face immediate trial. If the bounty hunters find you...

I know they're watching me on the network right now, so I keep moving. As long as I stay away from the cameras and move, they can never be sure exactly where I am. The system isn't too exact, thank the VM. Head down, I make my way over a couple of blocks, duck into an alleyway, and stand in front of a short wall of concrete. No cameras here. I approach the pair of bulkhead doors and knock three times.

With a creak, the door rises an inch. A single eyeball stares at me from the ground. "Who sent you?"

I sigh. "Seriously?"

The door slams shut. I bang as hard as I can on it. I hope his ears ring for a week.

"By the VM, Bree! What on earth did you do that for?" The Professor opens the door, rubbing his ears, and motions me inside.

I walk down the steps and squint in the dim light. My eyes got used to the sunglow far too quickly. Once I'm inside, I'm safe. State tracking doesn't work well underground, and the Professor can manipulate our signals for some time. The network will show me in a building close by, watching an entertainment screen. We have a few hours, but I have to resurface to let the security cameras pick up my actual image, or they get suspicious.

"I was just having a little fun, since this is a covert operation and all." He runs a hand through his thin white hair, standing the strands on end.

"It's not a joke, Professor." I want to be annoyed with him, but he gives me a sheepish grin, and my annoyance fades to affection.

"Let an old gray-hair have his fun, kiddo." He winks, and I wince.

We have so few like him left.

"Sorry," I mutter.

The State says tapping is for our own good, that we serve each other when we serve The State. The world we live in is not a safe one, and we have to protect ourselves and our government. The Riverine Resistance knows the truth: Tapping is a form of population control. With age comes wisdom, and a sage populace would never tolerate the tyrannical rule of The State. Few here live much past forty. Tapping wipes out a good bunch, and the guard raids always seem to result in the deaths of gray-hairs.

The State says they die because terrorists and young Undergrounders prey on the weak, the elders. They raid to stop the Undergrounders, and gray-hairs and innocent citizens get caught in the crossfire. Me, I have my doubts. Most of the gray-hairs I've met in the last few months look like they can handle themselves, with a few exceptions, like Professor. He and Doc, his wife, have managed to live to the ripe old age of sixty. They tell me there was a time when people lived into their eighties and even to a hundred. If they were anyone else, I wouldn't believe them, but Doc and the Professor have secrets of their own, which is why I'm here right now.

Doc and the Professor have heightened their defenses. We wind our way down the halls past piles of garbage, heading deeper underground. The garbage is all strategic. The trash nearest the door is where they dump their food and other bio waste. I hold my breath through the worst of the smell. There are rats everywhere and a few insects, but the garbage does its job. No bums or other Undergrounders have tried breaking in to make a home here, and if they ever found the tunnels, the guards would take one whiff and keep on going. I'm not convinced trash would fool an Ops team, but luckily, we haven't been tested.

The Professor leads with a glowing ball in his hand. The dim light catches the outlines of larger objects, leaving details obscured. We tread carefully. The sconces on the walls are gone now. Permanent fixtures would make it too obvious to anyone who broke through the cellar doors that someone lived down here. I breathe a little easier now that we're in the sheet waste area.

I point to a piece of broken down cardboard. "Hey Professor, can I have one of these boxes?"

"Certainly. We're not using them."

"Great. Thanks." I make a mental note to pick one up on the way out. That should appease Charley.

The last time he felt wronged by me, a couple weeks ago, I woke up in the middle of the night to a warm stream of pee right in my face. God knows how he got up to the third floor. I went off a little. Hit him once. I didn't really mean to. I know he's not all there, but I lashed out. I was covered in the man's piss for goodness sake. I'd like to avoid that in the future.

The Professor stops at a wooden door and knocks three times. A small panel at the top slides open, and an eye peers out, darting between us.

"Who sent you?"

"Not you, too." I groan.

The Professor ignores me and whispers back at the eye. "Joe."

The panel slams shut. With a creak, the door opens half an inch. I'm tired of games. I push past the Professor and barrel into the darkened room. The Professor tiptoes in behind me and gently latches the door.

As soon as the door shuts, the room is flooded with light.

"Honey, I'm home." The Professor walks toward Doc with his arms outstretched.

Laughing, they embrace. I'm slowly learning that gray-hairs are just like the rest of us, but the PDA still weirds me out.

"What's up, Doc? I brought company." He kisses her on the nose and then on the mouth. I turn my face away and cough. They'd better not involve tongue while I'm in the room.

"And here I thought you were just going to the store to pick up some milk, bread, and toilet paper before the storm."

"Gray-hairs are so odd." I can't help but roll my eyes at them. "You're in good moods."

"'Youth is a wonderful thing. What a crime to waste it on children,'" the Professor says. He gazes into Doc's eyes and ignores me completely.

I cough again.

"We are the keepers of lost eras. Permit us our indulgences." Doc pulls back from the Professor to look at me critically. "Hiya, Bree. You've lost weight."

"I had a muffin this morning."

"One of Mrs. Blank's?"

I nod. She scoffs, spins with her arms out like she's doing a crazy dance, and leaves the room. I have no idea what she's up to.

Doc's been weird since my first speech. She's in this strange, somewhat playful, pseudo-competition with Mrs. Blank, even though they've never met. Each thinks herself my mother in her own way, or Doc's just trying to butter me up for something.

She's less cold now. I like the change in her, but it throws me off balance. She's like a completely different person. She returns in seconds with a plate of Nutribiscuits and a small glass of soy milk. Not really cookies at all. Not even a little. Blech.

"You'll need to dunk the cookies in the milk for a few seconds. They're a little stale, but they're the best we could scavenge."

"Thanks." So, they're hard, *and* they'll taste like dirt. Health cookies are the worst. I take the food and sit on the edge of their brown leather sofa, avoiding the gash that runs through the center. As soon as I put my weight on the cushion, I sink nearly a foot. Startled, I drop the food.

"Looks like we blew a few more springs." The Professor sighs and takes out a notepad. "I'll add fixing them to my list of things to do this weekend. Right after I mow the lawn but before we overthrow the government."

I'm too tense for the Professor's whimsy today. I ignore his nonsensical comment and pick the cookies off the floor. I blow on them and put them back on the plate. Doc sits next to me but on the other side of the gash. She knows I like my space. I'm worried the sofa will sink again, but it holds its position a few inches from the floor.

Doc tucks a silver curl behind her ear and smiles at me. I like how that deepens the lines at the corners of her eyes. The permanence of the creases makes me feel safe. For a moment, I will breathe this musty air deep inside me and pretend this is my life, here with Doc and the Professor.

"Are you ready?"

My fantasy ends in a millisecond.

"No." My voice sounds strange and small in my ears.

She reaches across the gap to take my hand.

"Please don't." The strength returns to my voice, and I stand and walk away from her. "I'm not a child."

"No." She hardens a little, reminding me of her own callous strength. "What do we need to do to get you ready for tonight?"

"Let's go to the war room."

---

## 33

The war room is filled with distractions that allow me to focus beyond tonight. The security feeds and maps with people dots have been updated to show whatever the guards are seeing at any given time. Spyder helped the Professor with the hacking—the feed is actually the same as on The State's comp system. We can look at the rest of the data feed, but knowing what The State focuses on is powerful.

The screen at the very center is one of the most important. The Professor somehow figured out the frequency of the monitors for the guards and keeps track of them all. This way, we can see how and where they're deployed. He initially started the system to determine where and when to forage, but it will be even more useful as we ramp up our numbers in the Riverine. Unfortunately, we can't track Ops teams, but this gets us most of what we need.

Another couple of screens on the wall adjacent have been added recently. This was my idea. The concept is the same as the center screen, but we monitor friendlies rather than guards. My dot's on there, but the screen shows me about three blocks away, thanks to the bounce the Professor set up around this place.

Spyder's in his web, probably saving the world on his comp games or simulating scenarios for the next couple of days after my speech. I'm relieved Em's dot is near her house, along with Mrs. Blank's. Hopefully, they'll both stay there tonight.

Doc and the Professor don't have dots. That's one of the things that make them so special. The State thinks they're already dead. I've come to trust them more and more as they've opened up to me about their own history.

As the Professor once told me, "'If you do not tell the truth about yourself, you cannot tell it about other people.'"

Doc came up with the plan to fake their deaths, and the Professor figured out a way to implement it. There's some kind of bio-mechanism in the monitors that checks to make sure the wearer is a person. Anyone can disable their ankle monitors, but the Professor figured out a way to remove them completely without triggering a Bounty. Around the same time, they began building The Bunker and developing the war room.

Once they had everything set up, they waited for the right opportunity. Doc took the biggest chance at that point. She found two volunteers among her patients with terminal diagnoses. She convinced them to take off their monitors. Within a half hour, Bounty was issued for the patients. Then, the Professor and Doc took off their own monitors, and the two patients slipped them on to fool The State. The Professor and Doc gave chase to make it look like they were after the Bounty. To The State, nothing was amiss. Doc and the Professor—in reality, the patients wearing their monitors—were on the map. The two without monitors must be the ones with a Bounty on them. Smart plan.

The patients came into the building that used to be on top of this cellar, where Doc and the Professor live now, and where they had hidden weapons. The Professor made them based on drawings he found of ancient guns. Doc and the Professor sneaked down into The Bunker while their patients shot at the guards who were surrounding the building. Using the guns was key. Doc and the Professor needed enough time to escape, and they needed to draw the right reaction from The State. Their entire plan hinged on what The State would do in response.

Doc and the Professor watched from an early version of the war room. When they saw the guards enlarging the perimeter, and eventually retreating, they knew everything would be okay. Within moments, the walls shook around them, and dust rained from the ceiling. The State fire-bombed the building. Everything was reduced to ash—the two who went off network and, as far as The State knew, the couple of gray-hairs who were pursuing them. An acceptable casualty, as Doc put it.

Ever since then, Doc and the Professor have lived down here, monitoring life above and gathering knowledge of life before The State. The last few weeks have been cleansing for me—a re-education of the world and the history of our people. They've told me stories about dictators and the totalitarian regimes of old, the gods before the VM, and defining technology like television and computers. We've come up with a plan to take our society into a new era where those things are possible again. We are stronger together.

The Bunker is too small to house our growing resistance. Doc and the Professor have been building a new headquarters, a place where people can live without the interference of The State. They've used their knowledge and skill to make a self-sustaining refuge for the sector. They call it: The Station.

But to grow the Riverine and fill The Station, we're going to need volunteers. Besides stopping the tapping, I'm supposed to get those volunteers. We go over our plans one last time before the time it really counts: tonight.

"I finished wiring the building last night." The Professor has rigged the building where I'm giving the speech to throw a bounce on everyone's monitors. I should be able to finish my speech before the guards find us.

"How much time will I have?" I've asked him this before.

He sighs. "I can't give you an exact number. A few minutes at most. I've widened the perimeter a bit, and I'll bounce different sections to different locations. They'll have to search a wide area to find you, but I can't give you a firm number."

Doc butts in. "Keep the speech short, to the point, and rabbit down the tunnel. Meet us back here as quickly as you can."

"Do you think people will get hurt?"

"Your Spyder had best answer that question. He's run the models for weeks."

"He's not 'my' Spyder." I roll my eyes. "I don't want a comp answer. I want a gut answer. You two have the most experience with opposing The State. I know we're planning on getting people out before the guards come, but what if they come too soon?"

They look at each other. The Professor gives Doc the nod, as though I'll take the answer better from a woman.

"I'll be at The Station, ready to treat anyone who's injured."

I groan. Is she purposefully misunderstanding me?

"Keep the speech short. Get the blockers out to everyone. Ask for volunteers to join us. Get everyone out who isn't joining us, prep the rest to flee to the tunnels." Doc ticks off each sentence on her fingers, like she's going down a shopping list.

"I know the plan already. We drew the diagrams together. I want to know if we're missing something—if there's some hole we haven't thought about."

The Professor begins, "The Riverine Resistance—"

"Screw the resistance. We're all equals here, and now you're acting like you've got something to hide. My friends will be there, and I want to know if they could get hurt. How many could get hurt?"

"It's a good plan," Doc says.

"It doesn't sound like such a good plan anymore." All air has left my body, and these underground walls collapse my lungs. "My friends."

"We don't know how many might be injured. Hopefully none, if we play this right." Doc says. For some reason, I don't believe her.

The Professor winces, and I bury my head in my hands. My body shakes with tearless sobs. Doc marches over to me and grabs my face between her hands. I try to pull away from the contact, but she squeezes harder.

"You're nervous. Pull yourself together. You know the risks. Everyone there tonight will be an Undergrounder or someone who knows the risks. We all lead half-lives already. This is war. People sometimes get hurt. People sometimes die. We've taken every precaution so that life can happen. So that full lives can happen."

I don't want to think about death. I see death sometimes in my memories, and I've suppressed the most violent ones. I won't allow myself to fully remember. Doc says memory suppression is okay and natural in my situation, but with tonight's speech and what we're planning for tomorrow... I have to focus.

"Keep on keeping on." The Professor gently interrupts my thoughts, and I have no idea what that means.

My smile is tight-lipped as I rise and make my excuses. "I've got to get over to the web. Pick up the stuff for tonight."

"Ah, yes." The Professor stares down his glasses at me. "'The spider's touch, how exquisitely fine! Feels at each thread and lives along the line.'" He winks.

"I don't know what that means."

"It means be careful," Doc says. "I'm sorry we can't be there tonight, but we'll be there for you after. We will all be okay in the long run. Just remember that."

"And in the short run?"

"In the short run, stop worrying, and visit," she clears her throat, "*our* Spyder, my little insect. Want some cookies for the road?"

"No, thanks." I'd like to keep the rest of my teeth, thank you. I echo Doc's words. "In the short run, I guess I've got to run. See you tomorrow."

I make for the door, but she blocks me and wraps her arms around me really tight. The Professor comes at me from the other side, and I'm sandwiched between these two gray-hairs. Doc kisses the top of my head.

"Love," one of them exhales.

I let them hold me. I count my breaths and try not to feel trapped. If I close my eyes, I can almost imagine that these are my parents. This is my house. I'm on my way to school or something, instead of about to start a revolution. As if by agreement, they break from me as one.

"Get going." Doc swats my behind.

I have no idea what my face must look like. My cheeks are hot, and the Professor laughs and taps Doc on her bottom. "Too far, dear." Then they're both laughing, and I'm laughing with them. And then I leave them.

"See you tomorrow." We smile, and I climb out of their hole, back to the streets.

As before, I keep to the shadows. The State knows where I am because of this gwocking ankle monitor, but I don't want to be on their cameras any more than I have to be. I don't know what I'm afraid of. Maybe that they'll look at my face and somehow guess our plan.

## 34

Spyder's family lives on the other side of the sector. The "good" part, which basically means far away from the Undergrounders. He's in Happytown, near the Blanks. Bounty rarely happens in these parts. Parents live with their children, raise them, and have good jobs and all that. They ignore The State as much as they can and live their lives.

I've only been here a few times since my release, mostly to see Spyder and work on the plan. He's been hanging out with his family more and more and avoiding Doc and the Professor's. I think he knows everything will be different after tomorrow.

I lived in Happytown twice, with my second foster family and then with the Blanks—though technically they were on the border to Budgetville. Things did seem happy for a while, mostly outside of the house. But I learned. The arm of The State is long.

The buildings change as I move through Budgetville into Happytown. First, there are more of them. There aren't as many crumbling piles of rock and cement like where I live in Undergroundland. They're also tended to more than the buildings in Budgetville. I like to run my fingers along the brick as I walk into Happytown. The surface is so smooth, because the facing is so old, but also because of the fresh paint. The sector is like a garden here. Yellows and pinks and greens. The pavement is almost dirt brown instead of the dull gray where I live, and these painted behemoths stretch toward the weak sun like giant flowers. It's amazing what credits can buy.

I pass a woman with a stroller. She smiles uncertainly and nods. I never did fit in here. To make her more comfortable, I become painted like the buildings. I stretch my mouth into a red and white crescent. The smile never reaches my eyes, but the woman doesn't notice. Satisfied, she continues on her way. When I look at the baby and offer a wave, he begins to cry. Children always know.

I'm almost to the web. I pause in front of a cava shop where women with glittery eye shadow and tight aprons squirt dollops of soy cream onto mugs before handing them over to businessmen looking for a mid-day pick me up. I decide not to enter through the front and duck down the alley to the fire escape. I've been pushing myself more and more with heights. Luckily, it's a short trip up, but it still feels like forever.

Spyder's family lives above a small eatery, but I've never been anywhere except his room—the web, as he calls it. Wires stretch from their apartment into the neighboring building, obscured by hanging laundry. I dodge graying shirts and duck through a mess of crisscrossing cords as I climb the steel escape to his window. My sweaty palms slip a little, knocking into a nest of wires, but they, and I, hold. I hope to gwock Spyder doesn't have some sort of weird password like the Professor. I don't want to be out here any longer than I have to.

No code—the window is open by the time I finish my slow climb up. Spyder's nowhere to be seen.

I stick my head in to chastise him. "You should be more careful about—"

Something grabs me by the shoulders and yanks me into the room. I topple down. The window slams shut, and a curtain blocks all light. A heavy weight on my chest prevents me from standing.

"Shhh." A finger presses against my lips.

"Spyder!"

"Be quiet. I'm listening. Were you followed?"

"No."

"Shh. I told you I'm listening."

"Then why did you ask?"

"*Shhh!*"

I give up and am silent. The weight of Spyder's lanky geek body doesn't bother me that much, but the physical contact does. I can't find a way to push him off, though—he's really tall, all arms and legs. Sometimes when he moves around, he really does seem like he's got eight of them.

"Okay. I don't think you were followed."

"Good. Me neither." I roll my eyes, even though Spyder can't see my reaction in the dark.

Even if I wasn't followed, The State knows I'm somewhere near here.

"I can hear you rolling your eyes, you know."

"You cannot."

"Can too."

Great, now we're in a five-year-old's argument. Dumb Spyder.

"Lucky guess is all."

"Whatever you say." He shifts his weight, and I can feel him shrugging in the dark.

I don't give in to the temptation to have the last word. Neither of us speaks for a few seconds, until I break the silence.

"Hey, Spyder?"

"Yeah?"

"It's good to see you, but can you please get off of me?"

For the most part, Spyder's been good about respecting my boundaries, but sometimes he pushes them. Like he's testing me, or testing us, I don't know. I don't want to fight with him anymore. We're in a pretty good place now.

"Sure." He takes his sweet time crawling off me.

"Can we get a light on in here, too?"

"Uh, sure," he says again.

A small lamp with all the wattage of a night light clicks on and casts the room in eerie shadow. One corner houses a smaller version of the war room but with only two screens. One screen has six sections. Spyder can highlight a section, and the image appears in full zoom on the second screen. That way, he can monitor a wide area and still catch all the details. There are about five other comp stations scattered throughout the room, and cracked open cases with green and gold innards dot the floor.

In the corner opposite the mini war room, Spyder has a small mat with a single blanket and no pillow. A book rests on a small table with a hot plate and another lamp. There's a pile of dirty laundry, harnesses, and cables next to his pallet. There's always a pile of laundry whenever I come here, and it's always the same. Probably because Spyder's always the same. Thick denim pants, black collared shirt. Never varies. Sometimes, he'll wear a shirt with funky buttons or one with a wide collar, but he usually wears a flat black shirt.

The ceiling of the web—now *that* is a sight to behold. Wires of all thicknesses and colors run throughout. Tiny ones disappear into small holes in the ceiling, feeding out to hidden antennae on the roof. Some lead out the side where I came in the window. Others connect to various machines and power sources in the room. They almost vibrate with energy. In a few places, I catch a glimpse of bare wire where Spyder has spliced two lines together. The metallic glint is beautiful in this low light. The ceiling is filled with a giant techno chandelier, which is the light of our revolution.

"I've got everything you need for tonight." He tosses a small box at me. "Those are yours to use for demo or whatever."

I pull a strip from the box in wonder. "It's so small."

"Just what every guy wants to hear." He laughs at himself. "No, really, thanks. In my line of work, the smaller the better."

"Are you sure this thing will work? Better than the decals?"

"Absolutely." He taps his ankle monitor. "Tested it myself. I'd say you could try right now, but you probably shouldn't take any risks before tonight."

I hate the lure of new technology. Although I'd really like to try, I agree with him. I can't take the chance.

"We've got several thousand of these puppies. I call them blockers. I've got them spread out among my guys, just in case something happens to one of them. I used the address you gave me and developed specific points of deployment." He goes to one of the comps, types a short command, and brings up a map.

"This is the building where you'll be speaking." He points to a yellow dot in the center of the screen.

"I created an algorithm based on the time constraints Doc and the Professor proposed. These blinking red dots are my guys carrying the devices. As you can see, they're pretty far out." He taps the screen, and the dots begin to move. "Periodically, these guys will move closer to your position. By the time your speech ends and the crowd lets out, they'll be ready to hand them out to everyone there." He leans back in his oversized chair, arms folded proudly across his chest.

"You're wonderful." I kiss him on the cheek and immediately regret the act when the tips of his ears darken.

He rubs at them. "Yes, well, you're important. I mean, it's important that we minimize risk. We have a job to do. Help as many people as we can, and protect as many as we can while doing it." His whole face turns coral. "Doing it. No, uh—I mean, helping them."

"Of course," I say lightly and change the subject. "Do you have the files for me to review?"

"The files! Yes. They're right here. I almost forgot about them because—But the files are just as important. Let me bring them up." He pushes himself away from the comp and rolls his chair to another workstation.

"I've got them on this system here. The one you'll want to pay attention to is Cueball. I don't know his real name, but he's very high up. You might recognize him now that some of your memories are back." Spyder chatters on as his fingers spin a digital web. He's in his element.

"The Professor couldn't even come up with a pic of this guy. Doc had me start looking, and I nailed him." He puffs out his scrawny chest like he's won a fight. "I hacked into several different systems to make a composite. This guy's hard to track. Impeccable record. Incredibly deadly."

He pulls up the composite, and I swear the temperature in the room has dropped about twenty degrees. I know this man.

"He was the commanding officer in charge of The Bridge detail." Spyder tells me things I already know. "He's a Lifer and a real SOB. He was in charge of training recruits for a while, but now it looks like they use him almost exclusively for mission work. I mean, he could still be training. I don't really know. But he's been on the streets in the area and always just before something happens—bombs blowing apartment buildings, people disappearing, that kind of thing." He shrugs.

"I nicknamed him Cueball because of his chrome dome. Baldy wasn't scary enough." His shrug turns into a shudder. "That is one bad dude."

I study the image Spyder has created and reconcile the picture with my memories. A seam runs down the center of his forehead. Another under his left eye. Spyder has done a decent job pasting all this together. The face is as hard as I remember. Not much in him has changed, but then, it's only been a year. The lower right quadrant of his face in the picture is the most complete. He slipped up with that one. Got a little too in the open. A little too close to the cameras.

*"Recruit, do you want to guard that bridge?"*

*"Yes, sir."*

*"The first step to guarding that bridge is guarding yourself." He swings wide. I do nothing to stop him, letting him bloody my lip. "Did you guard yourself just then, Recruit?"*

*"Yes, sir."*

*He laughs, a big bellowing sound. "That's right, you did. If you'd tried to stop me, I'd have beaten the crap out of you." He turns to the rest of my training squad.*

*"The first part of self-defense is knowing your situation and knowing the appropriate response. You don't respond the same way to a gray-hair trying to hit you as you do to a bad brawny dude with a knife. But you respect your opponent. Always. Watch your back.*

*"If you mean to kill, you do it, and you don't give the other guy a chance to kill you. Use whatever means necessary. You lie. You cheat. You sneak. You do whatever you have to do to stay alive and make sure the other guy ends up dead."*

I REACH out and touch the screen, tracing the visible scar along his jaw line.

"Guess I'm still learning," I whisper.

"What?" Spyder scans the image like he missed something.

"Nothing. Just memorizing his face. He doesn't look like someone I'd want to get caught by."

"Definitely not. You see this guy, something bad is going down. Problem is, you won't see him until it's too late. That's his job."

"Lucky for me, I've got you." I bump shoulders with him and knock him sideways in his chair. From there, just a little shove sends him to the floor, and the chair is all mine. I settle in, now in control. Powerful.

"Hey!"

"You're so nice to me. Keeping me safe. Giving up your chair for me. Such a gentlemanly thing to do."

"Awww." He gives up surprisingly quickly. "I've got a series of other photos that may be useful, but I'm not sure how much." He reaches over me and clicks the mouse a few times. "These are the guards that normally patrol the area. You probably recognize some of them 'cause they're on your home turf. No one here to watch out for, really. They're a little tougher than the ones around here because it's your part of the sector, but they're nothing you're not used to."

I study the faces. Nobody looks terribly familiar. I mean, I've seen the guards around, but it's not like I interact with them on a regular basis. I try my hardest to avoid them.

A few more clicks, and Spyder's back to the map. "I've been diagramming their patrol patterns. We've got the diversion in place. Once the guards congregate in this area, we can start bringing people in for your speech. Timing is everything here."

Spyder's getting nervous, just like Doc and the Professor were. We've been over this dozens of times. In a way, we're like actors before a show. We've got the stage set. We all know our parts. We've done a dry run without any explosions or other people. Unfortunately for us, we don't get a dress rehearsal. We practice as much in our minds as possible, but we've only got one shot tonight.

"Do you have the ear—?"

I don't get to finish my question, as Spyder has tipped the chair over. I tumble down and bang my elbow on the comp. The screen goes dark.

"Oh, well done," I say. "That's just great."

"No problem. No problem." Spyder rights the chair, plugs a few things in, and starts typing away. In less than a minute, he's got the system fully restored and his chair back.

"Do I ever get to ask you a question without you physically assaulting me?"

"I don't know what you're talking about, but I think you just did." He sits smugly in that dark chair.

"Ha ha ha." I scowl. "What I was saying before you rudely stole my chair is—"

"Your chair? I was rightfully reclaiming my own property."

"Whatever. Anyway. Do you have the earpieces ready?"

"Yeah. Didn't Doc and the Professor show you?"

"No."

"Theirs were delivered this morning. I've got yours right here." He hands me something like a tapered wad of gauze with a clip. "They're not exactly stealthy, but they'll do the job. Try it on."

I hook the clip over my ear and tuck the tip inside. "Seems snug."

"If you pull your hair forward, I don't think the earpiece will be visible at all," he suggests.

I finger comb my hair and look in the small mirror near his bed. He's mostly right. Except that I look like I've got the world's worst hair dresser and a major case of bed head—the hair by my ear sticks out a good couple inches.

"Maybe not invisible, but better than nothing," I say diplomatically.

Spyder nods. "They're not live yet, but they should work. We've done limited testing. They'll go live a few hours before your speech. I'll turn yours off once the speech begins so you won't be distracted, and we'll reconnect after."

Comp models. Limited testing. I'm incredibly uncomfortable with the number of untested variables in this plan. Hands steady, I remove the piece from my ear and breathe out slowly.

Spyder wraps his hand around mine holding the earpiece. "It'll work. You trust me, right?"

I give him my best Happytown smile, and he laughs. "Oh, ye

of little faith." He's been hanging out with Doc and the Professor for too long, picking up on their odd expressions.

"We'll do our part. You do yours. Worse comes to worst, we'll end up dead. Not like we wouldn't anyway."

"Thank you, Spyder. You always know just what to say to calm my nerves. You're better than pills."

"That's the magic of the Spyder's venom." He wiggles his eyebrows.

I groan. "You know I don't feel better at all, right?"

"Let a guy dream. I'm your big bad protector."

"Nope. I'm yours." And I wheel the chair out from under him.

His butt conks on the ground, hard. Laughing and rubbing the tender area, he stands. "Fine, fine. You can take care of yourself. But we'll all be watching out for you anyway."

"I know. I've got to get going."

"Okay." He shuffles his feet. In a move so quick I barely have time to react, he leans in and gives me a brief hug. "You're ready," he whispers.

This emotional stuff is killing me. I could handle Doc and the Professor, because old people are grossly sentimental. Gray-hairs go weepy at the slightest thing. Because there are so few of them left, they're always thinking about their own deaths and living on through the young or something. But with Spyder, he's one of my own. A year or two older than me at most, he should be able to control his emotions. He'll get the feelings beaten out of him someday.

I hold my back as straight as possible, which is a trick because I'm climbing through a window, and I leave Spyder. When I'm barely through, the window slams shut behind me, hard enough to shake the tangle of wires I'm now navigating through. Being shut out feels normal, and the abruptness tempers the annoying way people keep fawning all over me. I need more normal today... and fewer hugs.

## 35

The Professor told me once that the citizens who live in Happytown base their lives on images from the middle-to-late twentieth century. No one really knows what life was like back then, so I'm sure it's not completely accurate. But the attempt is kind of quaint. All the shops are in one area, and people try so hard to be friendly. I don't know how they can forget about The State, but they do.

But The State doesn't forget about them.

They walk along with their jobs and their families and their friends, and they ignore the fact that their lives are at the whim of The State, until they're forced to remember. People in these parts have a lot of children—usually around six, if they live long enough. If they have more children, they won't feel the hole as much when some are tapped and one or two don't survive. That's my theory. Big families help them to pretend.

Mrs. Blank and Em live on the edge of Happytown and Budgetville. They've got the best of both worlds that way. When they want to pretend, the shops of Happytown are only a short walk away. But most of the time, they live in the real world. Mrs. Blank knows what's important, and she knows how to survive. I was lucky to have her as a foster mother. For me, as the Professor would say, the third time really was the charm.

I cut through the rest of Happytown as quickly as possible—I don't want to pretend anymore. I detour a little ways to pass by the Blanks' brownstone. I won't go in. I won't expose them to any more danger. I'll just watch. Check in. See what could have been if I'd been born in another time, in a safer place.

Gray laundry flutters in the breeze on the second story. The front stoop is crumbling around the edges, but the construction is generally solid. The neighbors are out playing ball in the street. Their faces are pinched around the eyes, but their smiles are real when they catch the rubber toy. I'm drawn to the balance here. Wariness and happiness coexist. This is what I'm fighting for. Real people with real lives, who pay attention to each other and the world around them. With people like this, we can achieve real change.

I will be the catalyst, and they will transform the world.

THE REMAINDER of the day passes in a blur. I head back home to practice my speech, yet again, and prepare for tonight. I pass Charley on the way in. Shoot. I forgot the cardboard. I duck my head and walk quickly, hoping he's sleeping off his afternoon.

"Don't think I've forgotten about you, Missy."

I keep walking. "No, Charley." I sigh.

"You owe me."

"I know. I've been looking today. I've got something lined up, I promise."

"Don't let them cheat you. Good board can be expensive." He raps a hand on the structure he's created, and a piece flutters down. "Darn it." He turns his back to me and fixes his card house. When he reaches up to place the piece that fell, another falls, smacking him on the head.

"Stupid," he grumbles, continuing his work.

Having avoided a huge confrontation with the crazy man who lives downstairs, I gratefully tiptoe up to my floor. I toe off my boots and begin stretching as soon as I arrive. I can't help but be tense. My calves are wound tight. Ready to spring all day, I finally relax and pound the tension out of them with my fists. Massage will only do so much. As soon as I leave here for the speech, the tension will return. In a way, tension is good. I'm ready for anything, ready to move. Right now, though, I'm mostly tired.

I sit on the edge of the bed, and the cover pulls from the makeshift pillow, revealing something lumpy on top and a note.

"Knew you'd be back. Mom sends this with her love. Keep your strength up."

I uncover the savory dish. Sweet, delicious, melt-in-your-mouth stew, so tender it falls apart when I try to lift a piece of soymeat with my finger, and with huge chunks of sweet carrots. I wish there was bread so I could scoop the stew into my mouth. I lift the plate into my lap. There's another message underneath.

"P.S. Sorry, no bread. I gave it to Charley."

I swear under my breath and turn the note over.

"What? He was hungry. Use the fork."

I laugh out loud and pick up the fork lying underneath the note. Eating heartily, I smile and think of Em. She knows me too well.

Too soon, the meal is over, and I sit in silence with nothing to do. Once again, I go over what I'm going to say. I'm about two-thirds of the way through my rehearsal when the ear piece in my pocket crackles to life. I jam it into my ear.

"...I say again, Spyder checking in. Report."

"Bree reporting."

Silence for a few seconds, then he says again, "I say again, Spyder checking in. Report."

"Bree reporting," I say a bit louder.

"Shoot." He fumbles. The loud static crackle makes me flinch. I pull the piece out.

I hear him again, from a little bit of a distance. "Spyder checking in. Report." I nestle the bud back in my ear and don't say anything this time. I should have at least heard Doc and the Professor reporting. Something's not right.

"Oh!" Spyder says in realization. "I think I forgot to tell you. You have to press the button in on the side when you talk to transmit."

Thanks, Spyder. I press the button and say for the last time, "Bree reporting."

"Gotcha, Bree," he replies.

The Professor's lilting voice comes through next. "A very wise man once said, 'Insanity is repeating the same thing over and over and expecting a different result.'"

Ha. I think he just called Spyder nuts. Or us nuts for listening to him.

"We're all on line," Doc says. "Bree, your transport will be there in about ten minutes to take you to the site."

"Okay," I say. "Wait, what transport?" I assumed I'd be walking to the site. I hate when they make plans without me.

"Don't get angry, Bree." She sounds like she's about to say something more when the Professor interrupts her.

"Bree, you know The State has an unusual focus on you."

Yeah, I know. Better than they do, I know.

"We don't want to draw any unnecessary attention to the location. So we've rigged up an alternative," the Professor finishes.

"And why am I just learning about this now?"

"The alternate is very simple." Doc's soothing voice makes me nervous.

"We're going to hack the signal from the monitor and blip it while you're in transit," Spyder techno-speaks. "The Prof and I figured it out."

"Great." I pace semicircles around the patchy floor. "What kind of transport are we talking? Some kind of scooter? It'll still take at least five minutes to get there. That's too long to be off network."

"You won't be off-network for that long," Doc promises.

"How?" I stretch the word out, suspicious of the answer.

"Don't get upset, Bree," Spyder pleads, which only makes me more upset. They've been making decisions for me behind my back, treating me like a child.

The Professor gets his lecture voice on. "Signal disruption does us no good if a Bounty is issued for you, or if you're caught by the security cameras en route."

I agree but not out loud. I'm not sure where they're going with this, but I'll hear them out. As long as they stop telling me not to be upset.

Spyder's voice sounds small in my ear. "The mites have agreed to transport you...above the cameras."

*No. No way.* No way in all fifty states. I've seen what those little bugs think is fun.

"If you're all worried about me not taking chances, walking is safest. I'll keep to the shadows. I'll be safer that way." I don't know if I'm trying to convince myself or them.

"In the short run, physically, you might be safer," Doc says. "But in the long run, if you're spotted, you will be putting everyone at risk."

VM be gwocked. I know she's right. And I know I'm playing right into her hands, but I have to agree.

"They'll be here in ten minutes?"

"More like five now," Spyder answers sheepishly.

I just ate.

"I'm counting on your guys, Spyder."

"We all are," Doc says.

"My mites will take it easy on you. Don't worry," he says in a way that makes me worry.

"Let us know when you're leaving. We'll reconnect after you arrive," the Professor says.

"Got it." I can do nothing more than wait for the mites. And practice some breathing exercises so I don't throw up.

## 36

S pyder's guys are almost as silent as he is. I almost don't notice when they repel down the walls like a bunch of wannabe vigilante superheroes from Spyder's contraband comics.

I wave to them. "Hi guys."

One holds a finger to his lips. I stifle a groan. There's no need to be silent here. Spyder's mites love their dramatics.

Another motions for me to stand and hold my arms out. They fit a double harness around me, and one of the mites steps into the other part. The little sucker still doesn't say anything. Exaggeratedly waving his arms, he pantomimes putting them around his neck. I sigh and comply. Essentially, this weirdo's giving me a piggy back ride. At least if we fall, he'll cushion the blow.

"Spyder told me you'd be nervous. I'll tap your leg twice before we start moving and twice more before we pick up speed. Three times means we're stopping," he whispers. I give him a thumbs up instead of verbally acknowledging him. He nods in approval.

The rest of the mites are busy with cables, carabiners, pulleys, and all sorts of odd contraptions. Some are suspended in the air.

Others are leaning forward over the edge of my floor, hooking things together. If Charley looked up right now, he'd probably have a crazy fit thinking someone was coming after him. The mites work quickly and all stop as one. The prep is complete. My mite bounces on the balls of his feet a few times.

"Go time," I breathe into the ear piece.

The mite taps my leg twice, and we're off.

Before I can exhale a single state prayer, we're on the roof. I squeeze my lips together and will the nausea to pass. My mite unhooks us and screws down another carabiner. The process takes all of five seconds. I barely have time to catch my breath before he taps me again, and we're off.

He leaps over the edge of the roof, and we free fall for a moment before the harness catches us. Then we're swinging through the air, building to building, a quick unclip and reclip of the safety is all that slows us. I take back my thought about the wannabe superheroes. These guys *are* superheroes.

In about two minutes, the mite taps my leg three times, and I open my eyes. We've arrived, and I haven't even thrown up. I disengage and step out of the harness.

"Thank you," I mouth.

He gives me a thumbs up, re-clips his carabiner, and with a salute, falls from the roof. The gesture makes me steadier, more in control. I head for the stairs and make my way down as fast as possible.

I tap the earpiece. "I'm in."

"You're back on network," Spyder says.

"And not a moment too soon," the Professor finishes. "This is where the timing gets tricky. I've started the signal bounce in the building."

I make my way downstairs to the ground floor. The room is huge, with a podium and microphone on a stage in the front and room for almost a thousand spectators. We're not expecting nearly that many, but we're prepared.

My boots echo in the nearly empty chamber as I check out the space. Someone's hung a bunch of red and white streamers near the front. Probably Spyder's touch. I brush them away like cobwebs and keep walking, scouting the exits, searching for potential problems.

"T-Minus 10 minutes until the diversion." Doc sounds chipper.

"My guys have just about re-configured," Spyder reports.

I don't know how he's talking to them when he's got our earpiece in. Maybe Spyder swung over there. Maybe they've got some kind of comp messaging system. Or maybe they're using their spider sense. I almost laugh out loud at the thought and realize how nervous I must be if that seemed funny. I head toward the front of the room, where I will listen and wait until the diversion is in progress.

There are two lengths of old curtain forming a backdrop to our makeshift stage. The blue and white form a parody of The State's flag. I part the curtains and step into what I'll be using as a backstage area. A metal folding chair sits in one corner with a rubber cushion on top. Another chair acts as a table. Instead of a cushion, a small lamp, a packet of peanut butter, and a hydropack rest on top. I smile. Those feel like the Professor's touches. I sit and close my eyes for a few minutes, trying to find center.

"We are go on diversion."

I'm not sure who said it, but my eyes fly open. I won't see anything of the diversion, won't know anything of its success, until people start arriving here. I'm sure Doc and the Professor will give me updates now and again, but their focus must be on drawing The State's attention and evading the guards that will inevitably be deployed. Spyder and the mites have been passing out two sets of flyers for weeks—one set to a targeted audience, the ones we want to hear me speak, but most announcing their upcoming spectacle.

Though I'm not there to experience the diversion, I imagine how the action goes down.

On the other side of the sector, near Happytown, Spyder's masked mites descend, swooping in front of the cameras before disappearing back into the heights. A crowd gathers to watch the acrobatics. The density of the population protects the mites. The State can't tell on the network who's a member of the crowd and who's swinging around.

The mites put on quite the show. They've been practicing in an abandoned warehouse for about a month now. The Professor says the show reminds him of things he's seen in entertainment archives: the circus. He called the warehouse the Big Top. No one knew what that meant except for Doc, but it seemed to amuse both of them.

So the mites are swinging around. No harnesses for this show. Safety is boring. Part of the thrill for the crowd is the sense of danger. If one of the mites is off by a hair's breadth, he could tumble to his death. The whole routine should take about fifteen minutes.

It's almost time for the finale. The Professor named the finale "Barrel O' Monkeys." Spyder corrected the name to "Barrel O'Mites." I've watched them practice a dozen times.

The mites form one long line, connected at the arms and legs. They swing like a pendulum, and every three seconds, they change contact points. If they were connected arms to arms, they're connected legs to legs, from two limbs to one, or one to two. On the three second mark, each and every one looks like they will fall, but just as quickly, they reconnect.

Without warning, the mite at the bottom scrambles up the others as though on a ladder and disappears over the edge of the roof. One after the other, the remaining mites follow suit until none remain.

Everyone in the street should be wondering where the mites went.

The fireworks start, and the crowd stops speculating. They marvel at the flaming flowers in the sky. The music starts, louder than the Day of Obligation parade, bold and brassy—one of Professor's favorites from the marching band era. Every time the cymbals clash, a new work of art lights up the sky.

No one's in the buildings now. All are on the street, gaping at the sight above them. Barrel o' Mites wasn't the real finale. Spyder worked for almost a week on this one. He couldn't ignite the powder right on cue, so he had to use some mini-screens and hack a streetboard. As the music crescendos, the last "firework" scrolls across the sky.

"Happy Independence Day!" Not that any of them will even know what that means.

Then we bomb their buildings.

We're not destroying anything. They're just smoke bombs, and we set off bottle rockets to add to the confusion. The Professor plays more of his recordings. Not noises this time but sounds of war. Sirens and air raid horns and cannon fire fill the air. The guards are probably on their way by now, streaming in from all over the sector, leaving the area around the warehouse where I'm about to speak unpatrolled. The crowd will scatter—no one wants to be there when the guards arrive.

All of this is happening while I sit here, behind the curtain.

"It's time," the Professor says in my ear.

I rise and walk through the curtain, up to the podium and face the people in front of me. I forget every word I've practiced.

## 37

I swallow, exhaling "Alabama, Alaska, Arizona" to calm myself as I step up to the microphone.

People are crammed in from the doors in the back to the edges of the podium where I'm standing. There are hundreds. Maybe a thousand. Their quiet weight presses in on me. They are motionless, awaiting my movement. My tongue is stuck to the roof of my mouth, like I forgot to soak one of Doc's horrible cookies before chewing it. My body just won't let me speak. My eyes widen, my breath quickens, and I try to will the fear away.

A loud squeak from the back interrupts the quiet. The sound draws my attention, and I see Em in the back. She's hoisted herself up on a support beam and runs the edge of her rubber soled shoe down the metal doorframe, drawing my attention. She sees me looking at her, gives me a quick thumbs up, and drops back into the crowd. She'll keep her promise and stay by the door. Good.

I'll talk to Em. I can't see her anymore, but a woman near where she dropped out of sight has a small child sitting on her shoulders. They're my landmark. There's my pretend-Em. I may not be able to talk to the hundreds of faces in this crowd, but I can talk to Em. The stone she gave me is in my pocket. I imagine throwing it in one of the old rivers the Professor's told me about, safe as a hydropack. Waves ripple out from me. Again, I find the child in the crowd, and I imagine Em's face on the girl's face, loosen my tongue, and begin.

"As I walked the sector this morning, I couldn't help but notice the brokenness of everything around me. Street signs, buildings crumbling to rubble, cracked furniture on the street corners. After a while, we don't notice what's broken. We get used to it.

"Some things that are broken, we can't see. We can't see what's broken in here." I tap my fist on my chest.

"But we feel it. And after a while, we don't notice that we're broken. We get used to it. I don't have a lot of time to talk with you today, but I want you to know something about me: I'm broken. And do you know whose fault that is?"

I stop and scan the crowd. No one offers a response.

"My own."

Now, they begin to mutter.

"Hear me out. It's my fault because I haven't done anything to change the way things are. As many of you know, I was tapped almost two years ago. The State declared me unfit to serve and released me. I'm one of the lucky ones. How many of you have been tapped?"

About a third of the arms creep into the air.

"Keep your hands in the air if you were hurt while in service."

No one lowers a hand.

"How many of you have a family member or friend who was tapped?"

The rest of the hands go up.

"How many of them were hurt during service?"

The hands stay up. I take a deep breath and say in a low voice. "How many of you know someone who was killed while tapped?"

Not a single hand goes down.

"Everyone here has lost someone. We are broken. The system is broken."

A burly man in a green flannel shirt pushes his way to the front of the podium stage. "And what are you going to do? There are terrorists everywhere and we barely have enough food and hydro to survive. The State protects us, so we serve The State."

"Sir, you have it backward. We protect The State. The only reason things don't change is because *we* don't change. We like everything to stay the same because we think it's safe. But look around you. How safe are we when we're dying? We don't have to die. We're not at war. They say we're battling the criminal element, that there are terrorists among the Undergrounders, but we *are* the Undergrounders. I'm seventeen years old. Do I look like a murdering criminal to you?"

The man folds his arms across his chest. I've got to reach him.

"We need to look out for each other, protect each other, not The State. We've got to show The State that we're not going to die for them anymore. We can do better. We can live. It's not an easy path. Many will get hurt. Some may even die. But isn't it better to die for your family and neighbors, the people who care about you, than to just die?"

He uncrosses his arms, but he's still scowling. I can break through.

"We all know the statistics, even if we don't talk about them. In a given year, up to sixty percent of those tapped do not survive. What if one of those is your son or daughter? What if it's your brother, your sister?"

I pick three people in the crowd and make eye contact. "What if it's you? Or you? Or you?"

A ripple of unease runs through them, and the entire crowd shifts uncomfortably on their feet.

"It's not an honor to be tapped. It's not your duty to serve. The State wants us to feel some kind of loyalty to them, when they're not loyal to us. Tapping isn't about service to country and fellow man—it's about control. Ever notice how people in Happytown don't seem to get tapped? Kill enough of the rest of us, and there won't be enough of us left to revolt."

"So what do we do?" Plaid Flannel Shirt yells. He doesn't know it, but he's my biggest ally tonight.

I hold up the device that Doc and the Professor designed and Spyder built—a little latex strip like a bandage. "We heal what's broken."

The crowd murmurs. I can tell they think I'm nuts. Time to get technical.

"This is a blocker. The State uses the signals from our anklets to enter us into a giant tapping lottery. Disrupt the signal, disrupt the tapping. The signal disruptor is located in the center of the strip." I lift my leg and demonstrate with my monitor.

"Place the blocker here, and you'll be out of the running. Because tapping is live, you'll want to do this only a few seconds before it starts. You must remove the blocker as soon as the tapping is finished. If you place the blocker on too soon or remove it too late, you'll be at risk for Bounty." I take off the blocker.

"If we do this right, only people in Happytown and the work district will get tapped. They won't be able to pretend anymore. Together, we can stop the tapping. Together, we can stop The State. Together, we can survive."

I raise my fist into the air, and the hundreds of people in front of me follow suit. I've got them. This is it. We will stop the tapping, for us at least.

Briefly, my thoughts go to those in Happytown and to the children of The State officials. I'm not totally heartless. I don't want them to die either. There will be a smaller pool in the lottery this year, so more of them will end up tapped. I don't know what The State will do, but I'm hoping their reaction is enough to pull Happytown into the resistance.

I focus again on the cheering crowd. This feeling is incredible. All this energy and even love pouring out of them, pouring into me. We can do anything. We can defeat anyone. We will be the masters of our own destiny, no longer living in fear of that ultimate disruption of our lives.

I need to pivot now—I've got them on the blockers, but I can't forget to ask for volunteers to join the Riverine and come live at The Station. We've got to have more recruits if we ever hope to confront the guards and get through to The State. And I've got to wrap this up before the guards figure out where we are.

The smile on my face is real. Adrenaline gives me a buzz. I stare into this mass of people. Now that my speech is almost over, I can relax into the moment. I scan for familiar faces, but I don't see many. I know Em's hiding in the back—or hopefully she's left by now. The Professor and Doc are out helping with the diversion. Spyder's lurking in the shadows somewhere.

Out of the corner of my eye, I catch a hint of movement. Something drops from the rafters, a rope probably, and disappears into blackness. Speak of the devil. Spiders always hide in dark corners. I take a deep breath, ready to ask for volunteers to join the Riverine. Then, in the opposite corner, a single lightbulb winks out. The hair on the back of my neck prickles. I've learned to trust the signs.

What do I do? Do I warn the crowd? Mass panic is the last thing we need. This facility is unequipped for rioting. I can't be sure of what I'm seeing. Still, I can't let them be caught unaware if there *is* something out there. Maybe I *am* just nervous.

The raised arms in the crowd have turned to arms around each other's shoulders, and the cheering has turned into a collective hum. A clear baritone rings out.

> *"This world is one great battlefield*
> *With forces all arrayed,*
> *If in my heart I do not yield*

> *I'll overcome some day.*
> *I'll overcome some day,*
> *I'll overcome some day,*
> *If in my heart I do not yield,*
> *I'll overcome some day."*

The grizzled man in the flannel shirt sings one of the ancient forbidden songs. His beautiful voice soars from within that rough exterior and alights in the hearts of everyone present. He begins the next verse.

> *"Both seen and unseen powers join*
> *To drive my soul astray,"*

When he breathes at the end of the line, expanding those giant lungs for the rest of the verse, he slumps. His neighbors rush to support him, but they can't prevent his weight from collapsing. A woman screams as she drops him and holds her bloodied hand high in the air. The humming turns to buzzing, and the crowd starts to make for the doors. Murder is not a foreign thing to them—they all know to scatter when the violence starts.

This isn't a random street crime. This is my worst nightmare. Doc was wrong about precautions. There is no exit. It's too late.

Bright lights flood the room. A collective gasp rises up, then silence. A staccato beat breaks in: Gunfire. Screams. Sobbing. I duck down behind the podium for cover, but I have no idea where the shots are coming from. There could be someone aiming at my back right now.

Smoke and the stench of burning flesh fill the air. I cough. I'm on sensory overload—all I can smell and taste is battle, and the lights have momentarily blinded me. I can't see, and I don't have a weapon. We're like animals in here. They're hunting us—

they've corralled us, and to ensure their victory, our enemies are spotlighting us. We don't stand a chance.

If I give myself up, maybe they'll leave the others alone. I'm the ringleader. Cut off the head of a snake... I know procedure as well as they do. If I stop, they stop. But there's no guarantee they're following the manual. They might make an example out of everyone.

A child's cry breaks through the logic of my strategizing, and I remember: Em is somewhere out there. I have to stop this now. I raise my hands above my head in the universal signal for surrender and slowly begin to rise from my crouch.

## 38

At that moment, amidst bright lights and gunfire, on the verge of surrender, the world collapses underneath me. I fall hard in a cloud of dust and smoke. My first thought is that I'm glad to be alive. My second thought is with Em. I wonder how many the bomb took out. My throat feels thick, and I can't swallow. That's when I realize it's pitch dark, and there's someone very alive right next to me. My nostrils flare, but I won't scream.

"Shhh," he says.

I nearly cry out with relief. I'd know that hush anywhere. I only heard it all day today when I was with him.

"Spyder," I whisper and hug him tightly. "What happened? How do we get out of here?"

"We're under the building."

"I figured. Is there a lot of debris over us?"

"What?"

"Debris. From the bomb."

"They didn't bomb us, Bree." Spyder can make even a whisper sound impatient.

"What? Then why did I fall? Why am I down here?"

"It's a failsafe. Doc and the Professor dug out this room in case we needed a closer escape. They connected it to the tunnels we were supposed to take the volunteers through. We put a trap door just behind the podium. If something happened, my job was to get you out. Something happened. So here you are."

"And everyone else is still up there?" I scoot away from him. "Being shot at? Being *killed?*" I rise and bang my head on a beam. Low clearance. Wincing, I feel around the ceiling for the way up. There are a few more beams, and the only opening big enough for me to stand in is under the trap door, too high for me to reach. Frustrated, I slap my hands on one of the beams.

"Shh. They'll hear."

"I don't think anyone is going to hear me over the bullet spray, Spyder. I've got to get back up there and stop this."

"No, you don't."

"Yes, I do. People will die."

"People are already dying. We accepted people could get hurt. But you're *not* an acceptable risk." He's talking as loudly as he can while maintaining a whisper.

"That's crap, Spyder, and you know it. We thought they might get hurt, not slaughtered! If we let them die, we're no better than The State. A sacrifice is a sacrifice, whether it's for The State or for us." I keep feeling along the ceiling for the seam to the trap-door, but I find nothing. Frustrated, I bang my fists against it and hope something will pop open.

"Stop it," Spyder growls.

"Let me out." I bang harder. "Let me out," I yell as loud as I can at the ceiling.

"For the last time, *shhh!*" Spyder yanks on my leg and pulls me to the ground. My ankle twists a little as I fall, and the idiot arachnid pins me. "I can't let you do it, Bree. I'm sorry."

"By the VM, Spyder. That hurt!"

"Sorry." I can tell by his tone that he's not sorry at all. "If I let you up, will you promise not to make noise and to follow me out of here?"

"If you let me up, I promise I won't beat your face in."

He thinks for a moment. "Not good enough."

"Okay. Then I promise not to beat your face in and also to give you one minute to explain yourself before I head back up there to salvage what I can of this disaster."

"Doc will kill me if I let you back up there."

"I'll kill you if you make me stay down here."

"Excellent point." He releases me.

"Your minute starts now. You'd better have a good explanation."

"Simple. As we were canvassing the neighborhoods, people weren't that interested in coming. No one wants to anger The State."

"So why'd they come?"

"They heard you were talking."

"So?"

"So? You have no idea, Bree. These people know you."

"I know, I know. I'm a figurehead. I've seen the posters, remember?"

"You're more than that. You're a hero to them. The little girl taken by Ops, who survived. At first I thought they were just curious about you, but listening to you tonight, winning them over—you're a real hero. They'll follow you wherever you lead."

"That's all well and good, but you forgot one thing."

"What?"

"I'm not a little girl. I'm a trained soldier. If I'm the general of this revolution, I lead the charge into battle, and I'm the last to retreat. Get me up there right now, Spyder."

He hesitates, says nothing. I can tell he's on my side. I stare at him in the darkness. He may not be able to see me, but he can feel how serious I am. I concentrate all my mental energy into my eyes and send my will out through them like laser beams, burning holes into his head and heart. He *does* understand.

I understand him, too. I'd do the same as him if it were Em. But for me, the stakes are higher here.

Spyder shifts. He's relenting. He steps over me and presses a panel on the side of the tunnel. A crack of light gleams through a slit in the ceiling.

"Just there," he whispers.

I rise to go to where I should be, where I should have been all along. My ankle gives a little underneath me.

"Dammit," I growl.

How ironic. Spyder hurt me while he was trying to protect me.

"What's wrong?"

"I don't hear anything," I cover quickly. If he knows I'm hurt, he'll stop me from going up. That's not happening.

I roll my neck and shoulders and inch over to the door, favoring my left ankle. For a moment, I wonder if the sounds of the blasts and the sound of my own fall have deafened me. I've lost my hearing before. In the heat of battle, after repetitive discharge, my ears went numb. The only things I could hear were the things I saw, and even then it was only the imagined remembrances of what I should be hearing.

"Spyder," I say out of the side of my mouth. "Do you hear anything?"

He's under the trap, so the light illuminates him slowly shaking his head back and forth.

"Give me a boost."

I offer my bad ankle, and step onto the bridge of his hands. I brace myself on his shoulders to keep some of the weight off of it, and he lifts me to the trap. With both feet planted on his hands, I slide my fingers into the crack and widen the gap. Spyder lifts me no further. Good. I'd rather scout before heading into the thick of things.

The light seems bright because I've been arguing in the dark with Spyder, but the spotlights up top are gone. Only the dim light from ambient glow bowls remains. I look toward the crowd, but the podium blocks my view. Although I'm loath to admit it, I'm comforted by the fact that no one could have seen me disappear. No one should be looking for me. Sarge shouldn't be looking for me, if he was part of this mission.

I tighten my grip and pull myself up through the trap. Once I'm up, I lie prone on the stage and scoot around the podium to form a plan. The first thing I look for is guards. None. The second thing I look for is bodies. Many.

I whisper an oath and crawl back to the hole.

"Spyder, I need you." I hook my legs around the podium and lower my upper half into the tunnel. He grabs onto my arms. I'm glad I've kept up with conditioning: I try a sit-up, to bring him up with me in a parody of acrobatics. The mites make this crap look easy, but I can't manage it.

His flailing legs make it impossible for me to lift him. "Stop kicking," I hiss.

He should know better from his aerial shows. He stills, and I'm able to lift him enough that he can grab the edge of the floor and raise himself the rest of the way.

He wheezes and looks around. "Holy gwock."

The room feels empty, but hundreds of people lie on the floor.

"We've got to help them." I limp off the platform and head into the crowd.

Spyder catches up to me and spins me around. "What's wrong?"

"There are hundreds of people out there, dead or dying. That's what's wrong."

"No, what's wrong with *you?*"

"Are we seriously going to have this argument again? The one where I explain to you that my life is not as important as the lives of hundreds of other people? Especially now. Are you insane? You're worried about a stupid little twisted ankle when you're surrounded by the dead." My veins pulsate in the side of my neck. I jab my finger into his chest, just so he's clear on the point. "Get your priorities in order."

I turn and head into the piles of bodies. I do not check to see if he follows. Instead, I go straight to work. I've got to hurry. The guards are gone. I remember enough about guard procedures to know what happens next. Something to this scale, they need to get rid of the bodies. I need to find and evacuate any survivors, right now.

I divorce myself from the human and instead concentrate on disparate parts. A wrist without a pulse. A neck without a pulse. A chest that doesn't rise and fall. A mouth that does not breathe. Eyes that do not see. I catalog these parts and move on to the next subject, looking for something, anything that will give me hope.

A sound.

As though in answer to my thought, a groan comes from among the bodies. I shift through the already-cataloged to find its originator. Nothing. There is no life here.

I've seen a fair number of bodies in my time, and the sounds a human no longer in this world can still make amaze me. I suppose it's the shifting of things. The soul leaving the body creates a vacuum that their organs rush to fill. All that moving around is noisy.

A feather-light touch on my shoulder, and I spin around in a fighting stance. I've pinned the arm and am about to deliver a strike when I realize my non-attacker is Spyder. Of course it's Spyder. I release him, but I can tell I've frightened him. Surrounded by carnage, my battlefield instincts have come back.

"They're dead." He wavers on his feet and gags like he might be sick.

"Maybe not all of them. We've got to finish looking." I move to the next group and kneel beside them, repeating the efficient routine I've established. Spyder doesn't move. "Come on. We've got to get through this and get out of here."

He shuffles over and helps me move through the bodies. His face is going from green to white at a frightening pace.

"Maybe you should—"

Once again, Spyder interrupts me. This time by fainting. He lands on top of a lady in a brown coat. I gently pull him off the woman and let him lie. They look peaceful together, like lovers resting. Bile rises in my throat. The woman is dead and, like a twisted artist, I arranged Spyder with her.

I make my way through the rest of the bodies. Dead. Dead. Dead. The guards have done thorough work.

*If you mean to kill, you do it.*

Sarge's words run through my head. If he had any part of this operation, I won't find anyone alive.

*If you mean to kill, you do it.*

I look down at the boy whose limp wrist I'm holding, measuring nothing. His skin is unusually pale. Under dark blond hair, his cold blue eyes cut through me, seeing nothing. He's all of about thirteen. Too young to be tapped, yet he came. The body next to him must be his mother's. Darker skin, tight brown hair, but those same blue eyes. The hand that I'm not holding encased in her larger one. They probably had dinner before coming here. Maybe she helped him with his homework. Threw a ball around. His dad used to do those things before he was tapped. He never came home, and now...

I'm losing my mind. I'm seeing people—seeing their stories. I can't even focus on the parts anymore. I can't look for life when all I see is death.

*If you mean to kill, you do it.*

I take a deep breath to calm my imagination and restore my senses. I have a job to do. A logical, methodical job.

I hear a whimper, and I'm restored. The sound isn't Spyder waking from his faint. It's not the gaseous sounds of the dead.

The sound is life. Somewhere, among these shells, there's someone who needs my help.

I limp toward the sound and find nothing but another pile of bodies. They're stacked almost as tall as I am. It's unnatural. There's another whimper, coming from behind this wall of the dead. I steel myself and begin shifting them to unearth whoever is making that sound.

I move a body, and the whole tower slides. Clothing whispers, and the dull sound of flesh thudding on the ground makes me shiver. A sharp intake of breath. I don't think it's mine.

Suddenly, the rest of the bodies come crashing down, and I'm faced with a very small group of very scared survivors. My wits are suddenly sharper, and I am light.

## 39

"Don't hurt them," a man's voice rasps. He's moving unsteadily to his feet. He's not very tall, and he doesn't look like he works much with his hands. More a comp type, softer around the middle, like how I expect Spyder will look if he ever stops swinging around and makes it to his thirties.

Because I didn't perceive him as a threat, I'm caught off guard when he rapidly closes the distance between us and puts his hands around my throat. I tap at the nerves near his elbows and hold him in a lock. But I don't hit him.

A woman, probably his wife, screams without breath. The agony on her face punches me in the gut.

"It's okay. I'm not going to hurt anyone." I release the man, and he sinks to his knees. The silent screamer runs to him and wraps her arms around him.

"How many are you?"

The man and the woman have formed a shield in front of the others, so I can't get a good look at them.

"First, who are you?" the man says.

I laugh at the absurdity of the situation. An hour ago, they were hanging on my every word, and now, they don't even recognize me. Fear affects people strangely.

I echo the words of my speech. "I'm the one who wants to heal what's broken."

The man is puzzled, but the woman's face lights up in recognition. She whispers in his ear, and relief and hope pass across the man's features.

"Thank the VM, you survived. We thought we were the only ones."

How long would they would have waited in the carnage before trying to escape back to their homes? I'm glad they waited, and I'm glad I've found them. I try not to let myself hope there may be others.

"How many are you?" I ask again.

The man and the woman part and reveal what they've been concealing. A few injured lay on the floor, tended by those able enough to put pressure on wounds and keep themselves awake. People all over the room start standing up now, looking at the bodies in the room, realizing now how lucky they were. Altogether, there are maybe sixty or seventy.

"We were pressed in tightly. When the shooting started, we grabbed the fallen and shielded ourselves." The man sounds like he's apologizing, when he's helped save himself and everyone here from near-certain slaughter.

"You did well," I say.

His face reddens, and the blush travels down his neck. "I did well?" he repeats. "You did nothing!"

His face contorts with anger. "You said we were going to stop The State. Instead, you just got us killed by The State. So we're not dead yet. So what? They know. They always know. We may be alive right now, but they know where we live, work, how we spend all our time. They can pick us off at their leisure."

"No, they can't." Spyder appears beside me, that sneaky little arachnid, and I have never been more glad to see him.

He holds up a pair of bolt cutters. "Let's get to work."

We'd been planning to clip the monitors of anyone who volunteered to join the Riverine Resistance at the new headquarters, The Station. Whether they know it or not, these people have just volunteered. It's the only way they'll stay alive. Spyder approaches the man and woman first.

"Hold out your ankle," he instructs. "Now turn your head."

As soon as each turns away, Spyder snaps the tool shut with an audible crunch. Plasticine shards fly through the air, and their ankle monitors fall to the floor in rapid succession.

"We've just signed our death warrants," the man says.

"Look around," I tell him. "You were the one talking about how The State can get to you at any time. Now they can't."

"But the Bounty—"

"They'll never put a Bounty on you. As far as they're concerned, you don't exist. You stopped existing the moment you came to this meeting."

"Besides," Spyder chimes in, "once we're through here, no one will ever know you've left the place. Except for us."

"What's that got to do with anything?"

"No time." Spyder presses on, snapping the ankle monitors off the group at record pace. I hop on the balls of my feet as I wait for him to finish, testing my ankle.

"Those whose monitors have been removed, please go to the podium as quickly as possible."

About half the group moves to the podium. One woman carries her young daughter. She covers the girl's eyes to shield her from the bodies and guides her to the podium. I recognize them. She was the child on someone's shoulders near where Em should've been in the back. I fight the urge to look for Em and instead hustle Spyder through monitor removal.

"How many left?" I turn my back to the group so they won't see our conversation.

"Maybe ten or so. I'm going as fast as I can."

"We both know what happens next."

"I said I'm going as fast as I can."

Outside, the raid sirens start wailing, like it's raining. The siren stops, and a mechanical announcement warns about ongoing terrorist attacks. I strain to hear the telltale sounds of approaching helicopters—nothing, but it won't be long. We have to get everyone out now.

"I'm going to take the ones who've been cleared down. We'll have to use the new entrance under the trapdoor. I don't think I can get them to the other in time."

"Okay. I'm two minutes behind you."

I leave Spyder and walk back to the podium. I keep my steps even, betraying nothing of the urgency of our situation or the injury to my ankle. When I approach the group, I cut off their questions and instruct them as quickly as I can.

"We've got to clear the building. There's a trap door that connects with a tunnel that will lead us to a safe house. I'll go first, and I'll help those who are too young or injured to go down on their own. Then the rest of you will follow. We'll wait at the bottom for Spyder and the others. He knows the way."

A few nod, but most of their expressions are blank.

I hop into the trap door and ease myself down using my arms. When I'm hanging by my fingertips, I swallow to prepare myself for the impact.

I drop no more than a couple of feet before I touch the ground, but my ankle screams with pain, and my leg collapses underneath me.

"Kansas, Kentucky, Nebraska," I swear and pray at the same time. I crawl around and find a large piece of wood covering the entrance to the tunnels. With a push, the wood gives and reveals the entrance. Doc and the Professor did well digging this route.

"You ready?" Someone calls from up above.

"Send them down," I say.

The little girl is first. They drop her, and I catch her. To be more accurate, my body breaks her fall. I'm now lying on the ground.

"Send the second strongest person you've got up there down right now," I yell up.

A pair of scuffed boots drops to the ground beside me. A perfect landing, full of grace.

"Lex," I breathe.

The woman attached to the boots chastises me. "You're in no position to be helping others when you can't even help yourself. You should've counted yourself among the injured." She shakes her head at me, disgust in her voice.

That hurts worse than my stupid foot.

"I thought I'd never see you again," I say. And then I get angry. "And what were you doing before I showed up? Hiding behind a pile of bodies? That was really working out so great?" I rub my ankle and scowl.

She ignores me and calls up to the others. "Start sending them down." Without looking at me, she adds, "I see you've still got some fight in you." She finally turns toward me and brushes at the dirt on my shoulders. "I like you better in purple."

My face flushes, but I have no time to really talk or process my feelings. I help people to their feet when I can, but I'm barely on mine.

There are more injured than I would have hoped, but at least they're alive. Lex moves rapidly and efficiently, catching the injured delicately and easing them to the ground before waving the next one down. I'm impressed, and I hate that I'm not helping more. She's faster than I would have been on two good legs. The most I can do is wave everyone through to the tunnels.

Soon, the injured are all accounted for, and the healthy begin dropping through. Spyder's the last, and he pulls the door shut behind him as he jumps.

In the startling dark, a child whimpers.

"Hold on," Spyder says.

We've planned well, though we expected to be leading volunteers instead of survivors. A small stack of shallow bowls waits for us at the main tunnel entrance. Spyder produces a few powders from one of his pockets and mixes them in one of the dishes. The light's not much, a dull phosphorescent green that provides more comfort than illumination.

"We'll use glow bowls to follow each other," he explains. "You may not be able to see everything around you, but you can see the little green light ahead of you." He distributes the bowls and powder among the recovered.

We pair the able-bodied with the injured, and Spyder takes the lead. Each pair counts off as they move. Forty-seven altogether. Ninety-four people. Not as many as we'd hoped would join, but The State didn't give them any choice. There are too many dead up there. We made a colossal mistake somewhere—I can't think about that. I've got to protect the living. We've got to move quickly. There's not much time.

I bring up the rear, and Scruffy-Boots Lex volunteers to accompany me.

"I'm fine on my own, thanks." We won't be able to walk the tunnels, anyway. If I can't crawl, I should be able to sit and scoot. She looks at me strangely and places a hand on my shoulder.

"Never put your pride before a mission." She drops to her knees and crawls after the rest. "You'd better hurry." Her mouth is set in a thin line. She knows what comes next, too.

## 40

I scramble to my knees and bring up the rear. I was wrong. I'm not fine on my own. My ankle throbs, and I'm unable to travel as fast as I'd like. Lex waits for me.

"Hurry." The word is at odds with her tone of voice. She is unreasonably, unnervingly calm.

I push forward as best I can. The glowing green dots grow farther away. The others can't be moving that much faster than I am, but they've had a head start.

I pick up the pace, but vibrations rise from the ground to my hands. The ceiling of the tunnel quivers.

"Cover," she shouts.

I hope her voice carries to the front of the line. We duck our chins and throw our elbows up to protect our faces. Debris rains on us in a fine mist. Lex hurls her body overtop of mine in the instant before the largest explosion rocks the tunnel.

*Preserve. Protect.*

The noise is louder than the damage done. Nothing around us has collapsed or fallen. Lex rolls off me, breathing heavily. I lower my hands from the guarded position and listen for the sounds of the others. Spyder should have ordered the count off by now.

"Twenty-four." The first pair I've heard faintly calls. I have no way of knowing if the ones ahead of them have made it.

"Twenty-five."

"Twenty-six."

One-by-one, the pairs ahead of us count off. Twenty-four and above have made it through the blast.

"Forty-six." The call comes from several feet in front of me.

"Forty-seven," I yell out. I close my eyes and roll onto my back for a moment. I reach for my leg. Luckily, I've always been pretty flexible. I raise my leg to my chest and check the tender spots around my ankle. No further damage, but I'm going to have to stay off my leg for a few days. Once we get out of here, and assuming the tunnel ahead hasn't collapsed somewhere around pair twenty-four, of course.

"You there, Bree?" Spyder's voice crackles in my ear.

The ear piece! He'd turned our units off during the speech se we'd have no distractions, but of course he'd have a way to reactivate them.

"Pairs twenty-four through forty-seven accounted for." My voice cracks with relief.

"Pair one through twenty-three accounted for," he replies. "I couldn't hear any after around thirty-five or so. I was worried about you guys closer to the blast site."

"We're alright. Keep moving."

I'm concerned some of the others may not be able to travel for much longer, physically or emotionally. They'll have no idea the noise they heard and felt was The State cleaning up its mess. We'll help them, once we're safe.

At least this part's gone according to plan. If I'd been able to finish my speech, anyone who didn't want to join the Riverine would have safely left the building. The volunteers would've stayed, and we'd have clipped their monitors, just like we did with the survivors. When the guards arrived, Spyder had a slew of recorded sounds and effects he worked on with the Professor. We'd have filled the place with smoke and made the guards think they were under attack while the new, unmonitored Riverine members escaped through the tunnels. The guards would retreat and bring in the big guns to destroy the building, thus destroying the monitors and leaving the Riverine members off The State's radar—a bigger version of the same plan Doc and the Professor used when they first went into hiding.

We're just lucky The State likes to dispose of bodies in the same way it deals with insurgents. Can't claim a terrorist attack with a bunch of bodies around wounded by guard weapons. Safer just to cover everything up with a bomb.

The bomb rattled the ground a little, but the walls around us have held. We'd never really worried about them being destroyed. Spyder and his mites prepped the route through the old utility tunnels. Faint glowing markers lead us through the tunnels to safety. They painted marks directly on the tunnel walls, out of the same dim chemicals that help light the way in our glow bowls. The markers will stay lit for a few hours, long enough to lead us to safety, fading to nothing to protect us from The State following.

The crawl through the remainder of the tunnel is agonizingly silent. Whispered conversations have ceased. Those ahead of me have confronted their own mortality twice tonight. I'm respectful of the quiet, though I have many questions for my volunteer partner. I'm sure she has some for me, too.

Lex is obviously one of the tapped—or was at some point in her life. She's got her own stories and her own sorrows. I won't push too much in that direction. She operates on a different level than many I've met. Her bearing and her attitude don't seem like that of a common sector guard. I wonder if she was on the Bridge, but I won't ask.

Instead, I focus on my body. I move as delicately as possible to avoid further strain on my ankle. Lex moves with a whisper, the same in combat boots as in those leather looking slippers she wore when I first met her. She is graceful and light, even in this darkness.

"Bree?" Spyder's voice in my ear snaps me out of my thoughts.

"Here."

"We've got a problem."

IT TAKES FOREVER to squeeze through the line and make my way to Spyder up front. Some can barely move because they're so injured. I crawl around where possible, but there are hisses and stifled screams of pain when I miss and land on an errant limb. They look like miners, covered in fine dust shaken loose in the explosions, eerily lit by dull green glow markers.

"What's going on?" I ask when I get to the front, but the answer is obvious.

A couple of large concrete chunks fill the tunnel. So much for the walls holding.

"We tried moving them," Spyder says. "We got the small piece to move a couple of inches, but even if we can move it, we've got nowhere to put it."

I look around, trying to get a bead on where we are, but the tunnels all look the same at many of the points. There were symbols etched on the walls long ago, but age and draining rain have worn away most of them. My brief stint with the sewage workers gave me the idea to use the utility tunnels for our inevitable escape.

The anti-riot tunnels Doc and the Professor use for The Bunker are larger, but they only run through a limited area of the sector. The utility tunnels connect everywhere. I did my best to make maps from memory with the Professor, but we didn't bring the physical maps with us in case we got caught before we got underground. We don't want The State to know our strategies.

I'm not sure exactly where we are. "We'll have to try one of the spurs," I say. "Let's double back about three hundred yards or so. There was a large offshoot there. You stay with the group, and I'll head a little ways down, see if I can figure out where we are."

I raise my voice so that as many can hear me as possible. "We've got to double back and take a different route."

Several groans and whimpers fill the air. Someone says, "I can't make it."

"We can make it."

The same person says almost the same thing. "I can't do it."

I've got to be the girl on the poster. I've got to inspire them. "You're right. You can't do it. Not on your own. But *we* can do it. We can make it together. We will make it."

There's a quiet sniff in reply, which is good enough for me.

I repeat the information about halfway back, to make sure all the pairs have heard. The second time, no one objects, thank gwock. Talking just slows us down, and we're moving slow enough already because of the injuries.

I get back to Lex and fill her in with a little more detail. "Tunnel's blocked. We're working on a way around, but we didn't plan a second route. I have an idea of where we might go, though."

We arrive at the offshoot, and I stop the group so I can head down and check things out. I speak lowly to Lex, "I'm pretty sure this is close to where a series of mains come together. Keep them quiet, keep the glows covered, and keep them calm."

"Not asking for much, are you?" Lex snorts.

"If I'm not back in ten minutes, proceed without me. You might have to try to get around the blockage on the surface somehow."

Lex's fingers twitch, as though she might salute. "Don't disappear on me again."

"I'm not planning to."

"Good. You owe me a fight."

"Count on it." I hope she can see my smile as I fade into the blackness.

I belly crawl down the spur for about fifty feet. Gradually, I stretch out as the roof starts to rise, and the tunnel turns into a large opening, big enough to stand in. I stay on hands and knees for now, to keep the load off my ankle. The room is like the hub of a wheel, with a couple of dim caged lights mounted on the walls, and about a dozen spokes poking out and heading in different directions. We've got options.

Too many options.

I tuck a glow bowl behind a small rock to shield most of the light, marking the tunnel I'll need to take to return to the others. I didn't work in sewage treatment long enough to make a full map of what's down here, but I understand the basic patterns.

A puzzle of crisscrossing pipes runs overhead, and I pick out a few of the larger ones and trace them to their respective tunnels. The bigger pipes are the mains. The tunnels they lead to would be easier to move through, but we'd have a higher chance of running into a work crew. I eliminate the mains as options. Three spurs left. I could try going down each on my own, or head back to the group, gather everyone, and take a shot.

"Are we there yet?" Voices echo from one of the tunnels. I can't tell which, so I back quickly into the closest spur, so low I kiss the ground, until I'm shielded by shadow.

Another voice answers. "I don't know."

A crew shuffles into the hub. A couple of them bang their sticks impatiently against the ground or their sides, sending brown flecks flying. Just my luck—Seven and Two are in the crew. I tamp down the guilt at leaving them to the sewage crews while I escaped with Spyder. I can't let them spot me.

"We go down here." The leader turns ninety degrees from where I am. "I think."

"Let me see." Seven grabs a map from the leader's hands. "No. That's not right. It's that way." She points 180-degrees to where the leader had indicated.

*Hurry up. Hurry up. Hurry up.*

The leader checks the map. "Oh. I think you're right. Maybe you should have that."

"Okay," Seven says with a big grin.

"But I'm still the leader."

"Okay," Seven says again.

The leader takes them into the tunnel. I wait until the first five disappear from view before calling out quietly, "Seven."

She turns back into the hub and whispers as loudly as a scream, "Hello? You better not be a spider."

I step into the light. "It's me, remember? We're friends. You gave me a wrapper, remember?"

"Spider-killer!" she exclaims. "They said you fell into a pipe and died. We all have to be extra careful." She points to a length of rope tied around her waist, though I'm not sure how that helps her. "I don't remember your name. Sorry."

"That's okay." My luck continues. "Can I see that map?"

"Sure! Friends share." She thrusts the diagram into my hands, and I scan the lines. We can head down the tunnel parallel to where we've been travelling and cut across the second small access to get back on track. Easy.

I give the map back to her. "Thanks. You should catch up to the rest."

She barely gets into the tunnel before I stop her. "Hey Seven —are you okay? You get enough to eat and everything?"

She nods earnestly. "Yes."

"And...are you happy?"

Her brow knits. "I don't know." She thinks for a beat before her face lights up. "I would be if you visit me again. Friends visit."

"I guess they do. I'll come see you again." If I have my way, the guards will be on poop-scooping duty, and Seven and the rest of the crew can take a nice vacation in a field of flowers. If we can find some flowers.

## 41

L ex and I and a few others stand guard at the other entrances to the tunnel hub while Spyder leads the group down the alternate route I found on Seven's map. When everyone's through, Lex and I retake our position at the rear.

"You doing okay?" she asks.

"I guess."

"Good enough. For now," she says. "There's a lot I want to know about you, Bree Carter. Fighter. Speaker. Riverine Resistance Leader."

If she knows the name, she's one of us. For the first time since I've officially joined the Riverine, I smile. I'm a leader.

"Back at you, fight club manager. Former guard? Riverine Resistance Member."

"Sounds like we both have some stories to tell."

"Can't wait." And I kinda can't.

When the glow markers reappear, I sigh with relief. I wasn't one hundred percent convinced of my detour route. We've been in the tunnels for a while now, and we should be through soon.

Just as quickly as they appeared, the glow markers ahead of

us veer to the left and disappear into blackness. A finger of fear uncurls along my spine. I shrug my shoulders and continue at pace. We're probably nearing our destination. I crawl and crawl, heading toward the glow marks on the left. The tunnel straightens, and flashes of light bounce from the walls, revealing no source. The start of a headache tightens at my temples; I can't tell if the light is real or a product of my stress.

We reach the end of the tunnel. A heavy felted curtain blocks our path. Lex lifts the fabric open for me, and I crawl after the others, into the light. She follows. We're the last. We're all through.

Doc and the Professor found this space years ago and slowly started converting the large open rooms into a self-sustaining habitable space. The walls are concrete, and the structure is about the size of my old school but totally underground. The Bunker, where Doc and the Professor live, can only house about fifty. Here, in what we've nicknamed The Station, we could house a thousand. Enough to start a small army.

I breathe a sigh of relief and take a good look at the group. I was so task-oriented in the tunnel, I didn't take them all in. Reality knocks into me like a guard to a thief. A man lies on the ground, covered in blood and barely moving. His partner kneels next to him, arms shaking. He must have dragged him through the tunnel.

The rest of the injured have culled themselves. They stand in a corner cradling their arms or heads or putting pressure on their wounds. There are a few children, tears having swiped clean paths through the dirt on their faces. Most are accompanied by parents, or what I assume are parents. They've adopted a protective stance. Their look is primal—step toward their children at your own risk.

For the most part, these are not soldiers. I make eye contact with Spyder, and there's a question in his eyes.

"Let's move," I say aloud.

"No," the man kneeling beside the bloodied man says. "He can't go any farther."

"He has to." I'm too tired for diplomacy right now, but I try anyway. "The main rooms are really not that much farther. There's medical help available when we get there. Clean beds. A doctor."

The man doesn't even look at me. He stares at his bleeding friend. The tremors in his arms grow in magnitude, until his whole body is shaking. "I can't," he sobs.

Lex marches over to him and slings his friend over her shoulders. "I can." She looks at me. "Where to?"

Spyder leads us through the descending maze of the building into the sub-sub-cellar we've set up. The damp clings to our bones, and a few of the children sneeze in the musty air. The rotting wooden stairs are easy to navigate, but the compact dirt of the sub-cellar floor jars my injured ankle.

I'm trying not to wince or whine, keeping any sounds of pain in my head. There are many who've sustained worse injuries than I have, both physical and mental, today. For a few, this will have been the first time they've seen The State in action, up close and personal. For some, this will have been the first time they've seen death.

Spyder stops the group and heads to a steel door. He raps three times and gives the password. "Joe sent me." There's no laughter on the other side this time.

The door opens with a click, and Spyder pauses before entering. "Injured parties to the right. Everyone else, straight ahead to the big room at the end," he calls over his shoulder.

Lex is first through, carrying the bleeding unconscious man. The majority of the group head to the meeting room. Curiosity winning out, those with minor injuries have decided to forego treatment for the time being to see what lies ahead. Can't say I blame them. I wait at the door to the medical wing to assist those more severely injured.

After the injured have filed through, I walk into chaos. I detach, more than I already have. I won't survive, otherwise.

Bunks line the walls, stacked five high. Spyder's mites crawl up and down ladders, rapidly bouncing from patient to patient. There's so many more injured than the hundred we brought through the tunnels. Lots of bumps, lots of scrapes, lots of blood. A few cradling obviously broken limbs. I lose sight of Lex and the bleeding man. Hopefully, he'll be okay.

I grab a mite carrying a tray and ask for Doc.

"She's in the theatre."

"What's she doing in the theatre when all the patients are in here?"

"No, no, the operating theatre." He points to a curtained off area at the opposite end of the room. "Scrub in. I'm sure she'll want to talk to you."

I have no idea what I'm doing. There's a basin, so I scrub my hands and face with cleansing fluid. A pile of old dresses sits by the sink. I throw one on top of my grimy clothes and cover my head with a mesh net. I grab a cloth face mask from the cupboard above and go into the theatre to talk to Doc.

She looks up briefly when I come in. "You're limping. Take a pain pill."

Doc doesn't miss a trick, and I don't protest—now that we've arrived at The Station, my ankle's throbbing even more. Someone thrusts a couple of pills in a cup at me, and I dry-swallow them.

"You and Spyder have to get out of here." Doc doesn't look up from the innards she's putting back together. I try not to look at the mass of intestines she's running through her fingers and concentrate on her words.

"Focus, Bree. Can you leave?"

"Yes."

"Good. Grab Spyder and go. You two still have monitors. The noise of the explosions has caused enough confusion that the Professor's been able to keep you off-network, but we can't risk that any longer, and we can't risk you leading The State straight here." She wipes her brow on her shoulder.

"Close him up," she says to a woman who was elbow deep in this guy's belly with her, before turning to a mite with a tray of equipment. "Bring me the next one."

Doc helps transfer the next patient to the table. She shoos me away. "What are you still doing here? Grab Spyder and go. I'll be in your ear later."

I suspect she's being vague because she doesn't want anyone to guess how we're communicating. I can't tell if she's being cautious or if she has a real reason to worry.

I back out of the operating area. "Later."

I strip the gown, mask, and hair cover as quickly as possible. I stop to re-cleanse. I shouldn't hesitate for anything, but something about that guy with his insides hanging out makes me feel unclean. I dart through the hospital area, dodging mites and patients testing their own strength. Following orders is something I'm good at, but I still feel guilty that I'm not stopping to help anyone.

I bust through the double doors of the meeting area where Spyder went with the uninjured and nearly interrupt a presentation the Professor's making. A few turn toward me, but most of the tired crowd slump in their seats and stare at a projection on the wall. The image is startling: tall rows of plants, heavy with fruit, side-by-side with a food factory. Re-education. As he's speaking, the Professor shoos me away. Spyder's hanging out at the back. I tug him outside.

"We've got to go."

"Huh?"

"We have to go right now. Come on."

We run back through the hall and up the rickety wooden stairs. Loud footsteps thunder up the stairs behind us

"Hey. Hey!" Lex calls.

"Who are you?" Spyder asks.

She brushes by him to face me unimpeded.

"Since when did you become so noisy?" I ask her.

"Huh?"

"You were kind of clunky on the stairs. Not like in the ring. You were always so graceful, like a cat or a dancer." I'm babbling and grateful when she cuts me off.

"Well, I was in a hurry."

She's a little out of breath from running, and her clothes are still covered in blood from helping the survivors. A few strands of hair escape her ponytail.

Without thinking, I reach out to tuck her hair behind her ear. My fingertips linger on her cheek. "Why?"

"I didn't get a chance to say—I'm glad you're okay." She presses her own hand on top of mine. Her palm is cold and a little damp. Heat rises in her face, and warmth spreads to match in mine.

"Lex..."

Spyder coughs, exaggerated and rude. "You said we have to get out of here."

"He's right. We've got to go."

"See you around?" she ventures.

"See you." I break contact quickly, like ripping off a bandage.

Instead of going back to the tunnels on this level, Spyder and I head up a normal set of metal stairs toward the streets of the shopping area. Before we open the heavy double doors to step out into the night, I look back toward Lex, only to find her still cradling her cheek where I touched her.

## 42

The air is freezing outside, partially because I'm coming down from adrenaline. The season of reflection ends tomorrow, but my breath still swirls in the air. Doc's pills have kicked in—the pain has faded to a dull ache. I stamp my boots on the asphalt gingerly, like I'm saying hello to the frigid weather. Spyder does the same. We're both uneasy, and I'm trying my best not to let Lex overtake my thoughts.

"Who was that?"

So much for not thinking about Lex.

"No one." My gut churns with the lie. "We've got to keep moving."

I tuck my chin into my shirt to block the wind and hurry down the street.

Spyder scurries after me. "Didn't look like no one."

I keep walking. "I met her while I was working out after I first got released. She's a friend."

"Oh. Like a gym buddy or something?"

"I guess."

"You're good at making friends, *pal*." He spews sarcasm like a weapon at my back.

I come to a full stop, and Spyder runs smack into me. "Seriously? You want to start this again now, when hundreds of people died back there, and hundreds more are depending on us? You want to get into this now?"

"I'm sorry." Spyder shrinks to half his normal size.

"We've got work to do, together. So forget it, and let's focus."

He nods, chastened, and immediately gets back on track. I admire his ability to switch gears so rapidly. We walk through alleys, staying where we know the cameras aren't, but we need a plan.

I talk through a plan, rapid-fire reasoning. "We need to keep things as normal as possible. Pretend nothing happened. We go somewhere we always go, and The State might think we weren't involved with the warehouse."

Spyder understands me immediately. He always has. "Where to? Web or your place?"

"Web." Spyder has comp equipment there. We can monitor The State monitoring us and see what they've figured out.

"Back way's faster." Spyder enters a narrow alley, the entrance wide enough for one person to walk sideways, and I follow.

Once out of sight of passers-by, we run, keeping to the shadows, ever-vigilant of cameras. We need to clean ourselves up before they get visual of us on the network. Soon, we're at the web. We go in the front door like normal people, through the eatery and up the stairs in the back.

In the safety of the web, I collapse on the ground, breathing heavily.

"Bree!" Spyder rushes to my side. "You alright?"

"Can you get me some hydro?"

"Sure. Sure."

The adrenaline spike from the need to flee The Station faded more and more the closer we got to the web. Whatever Doc gave me wasn't enough. Now that we're here and I can relax, the throbbing in my ankle has returned full force.

Spyder hands me some cleansing wipes, a hydropack, and a glass. I remember where I am.

I hold up the glass. "Is it clean?"

"Yeah. Yesterday or the day before."

I give the glass back, crack the lid on the hydropack, and drink directly from the container.

"I've got pain meds," he offers.

"I'd love a half dose. I want to keep a clear head." And I've already got some meds in my system.

"Gotcha." He rustles through his belongings and produces a couple of pills.

I take the smaller one. "I need to get my ankle checked out."

"You could always go to the health center," he suggests. "Nevermind. That was a stupid thing to say."

"I think I'd better wait for Doc."

"You're probably right." Spyder fiddles with a few of his screens and brings up the network. "Looks pretty quiet, thank goodness."

"Thank goodness," I echo.

I'm not sure how to handle this. I don't know how much violence Spyder's seen or if he needs to talk right now. I'm not a very comforting person, but he's my friend, and I want to help him if he needs me. I need him ready for whatever comes next. I decide to start with the violence he didn't see. Maybe that's easier.

"What happened?" I eventually ask. "With the mites and the diversion?"

"Everything went mostly according to plan." He leans back in his chair and laces his fingers behind his head, staring at the ceiling. "Except for the part where the crowd didn't leave before the guards came."

I wince. I have no idea how to respond.

Spyder keeps talking. "Aside from that, I think it went pretty well."

"There were a ton of injured people in there. Did the Professor tell you anything else?"

"He was about to when you dragged me out of there."

"I had to."

"You could have waited."

"I couldn't."

"I needed to know. I need to know. My friends were there. I saw some of them in The Station, but I don't know who's alive and who's..." He shakes his head and says forcefully, "We could have waited five minutes, so I could find out what happened to my friends. What difference would five minutes have made?"

"The monitors," I whisper.

Spyder is silent for a moment. "I'm an idiot. Of course, the monitors. I can't believe we didn't clip ours."

"No use worrying about it now. We weren't expecting... There was a lot going on. Still is," I say pointedly. When that doesn't seem to sink in, I literally point to the comp.

Spyder gets the message. With a few clicks of the mouse, he brings up the warehouse where I gave the speech. The building is gone. Totally demolished.

"It's nothing less than we expected." My voice is cold, even to my own ears.

"But we were supposed to get everyone out first. They weren't supposed to die." He sweeps his arm across the desk, and the mouse and keyboard fly across the room. He flips over the chair and starts pounding on the back like a punching bag. When that's not enough, he picks the chair back up and throws it toward his bed. His bedside lamp falls to the floor and smashes to pieces. The chair dents the wall and falls to the bed.

Spyder sits on the floor, breathing great gulping gasps of air. I place my hand on his back, but he shrugs me off.

"I want you to watch." Every other word is punctuated by an almost-sob. He staggers to his feet and reconnects the equipment.

"What?"

"I want you to watch." He punches furiously on his keyboard. Suddenly, the building is whole. He types some more. Bright flashes are visible in some of the windows of the building. The whole thing vibrates for a moment—perhaps only in my imagination because I can guess what's coming next. Wisps of smoke curl out the sides, and then the entire building collapses in on itself and fades away in a cloud of dust. The whole process takes no more than ten seconds.

"I'm so glad we got the survivors out."

Spyder ignores me. He stares at the comp screen. He's rigged the video on a loop. Again, the building stands tall. Again, it's destroyed. Whole and gone. Whole and gone.

"Spyder, stop."

"The destruction is kind of beautiful. Brutally efficient." He's mesmerized by the screen. Up, down. Here, gone. Beautifully destroyed.

"Spyder." I need him to refocus. I'm not sure what's going on in that arachnid brain of his, but we've got to move forward.

"You can't dwell on the dead, Spyder. We made a big gwocking mistake, but we've got to move forward."

"All that death…"

"Those deaths have to mean something. We keep on, and they mean something. We sit here staring at the past, and they mean nothing. They died for nothing. Don't let them die for nothing, Spyder."

He thinks for a moment. "No. But what do we do?" He sounds so lost, like a little boy in a crowd, separated from his parents. He's teetering on the edge, and I've got to help him walk the line.

A flash of inspiration strikes me. "How are we watching this?"

"The security cameras in-network. We watch this stuff all the time." He sounds confused.

"No, we watch what's happening *right now* all the time. This happened hours ago. We only get stills from past feeds. How are we watching that feed now?"

"Oh. I was testing a way to record. I tracked the cameras around the building for your speech and captured as much as I could."

"Do you understand how brilliant you are?" I grab his hands and squeeze.

He flushes. "No."

"We've got to go through the footage. We might be able to see the guards moving into position. If we can…"

"We might be able to stop them from doing this again, the next time we have a gathering." Spyder catches on quickly. "Let's get to work."

## 43

S pyder and I have been watching footage from a few different cameras for several hours. Nothing. Occasionally one of us will notice a flicker of movement. He backs the footage up, but we can never agree if we're actually seeing something or imagining.

The pain in my ankle has dulled again thanks to the half dose of pain meds he supplied me, but I'm getting antsy staring at this tiny screen. I yawn, because today has been one of the longest of my life, and the muscles in my face appreciate the stretch. I can't take it anymore. I have to stand. I pace the short circuit of Spyder's room while he watches the footage.

"This is pointless." Apparently he can't take the tedium either.

"What we don't see gives us as much information as what we do see."

Spyder gives me a sidelong glance. "You sound like the Professor quoting somebody."

I quicken my pace, relieved that my mind has something to occupy it. "No, think about it. If this was a standard 'send in the guards' thing, we'd see guards on the cameras. The fact that we don't see anything means The State planned this out—they sent an Ops team."

"You mean like Cueball?"

I stop pacing. He means Sarge.

Spyder's legs twitch under his desk. "I was just being paranoid when I made that image. Doc gave me a list of incidents to track. I was done with my other prep, so I made that composite. I didn't really think Ops would be involved today."

Spyder's naive. The mention of Sarge—Cueball—has reenergized me. I sit back down in front of the comp system.

"There." I point to the corner of the screen. "That's definitely something."

Spyder freezes the screen and zooms in. "It looks like... a shoe."

"Not a shoe, a boot. Standard State issue."

"You think?"

"Oh, yeah." I plop my leg on the table and lift my pants. "See? Looks just like this. You get used to them after a while. People wear them even after they're released."

"If lots of people wear them, how do we know this means anything?"

"Could be a random person. A random person wearing State-issue boots and staying out of sight of cameras. Or it could be an Ops team."

"I'll check the cameras on either side of this one. If we look closely at the shadows, we might be able to tell the direction the person came from, even if we don't have a full shot of them. Maybe we can track their movements and see if someone made a mistake somewhere."

This is too subtle for my skill set. While Spyder's working, I replay the incidents of the night in my head. The speech went okay. I make a mental note to ask Spyder if the blockers were distributed. I don't want to lose sight of that part of the plan in all the excitement. Oh, Holy Voice Mail. I lost sight of Em. Bile rises in my throat. Gwock, what was I thinking? How could I have forgotten about Em?

"Spyder, stop."

His fingers fly as he scans, zooms, and rotates images. "I'm working as fast as I can, Bree."

"Finish later. Switch to the network. Please." I can hardly string words together to make him understand.

"Bree, I'm working."

"Em," I whisper.

His fingers pause, hovering over the keyboard.

"Sorry?"

"Em," I say.

Spyder swivels in his chair to face me. "Are you telling me Em was there tonight?"

I close my eyes and nod, swallowing hard.

Wordlessly, he turns around and brings up the network.

"I don't know her frequency," he mutters. "The master list is in The Bunker. Stupid."

I can barely focus on what he's saying. I shake as I imagine where Em might be. "She should be home in bed now. She should be lying fast asleep, curled around Oscar the cat, his fur tickling her nose, his tail lashing as he chases the bad dreams away for her. Instead, she's…"

"We don't know what she is, so stop." The fury in Spyder's pace leaks over into his voice. "What was she even doing there?"

My heart races with guilt. "She was there for me. It's my fault. She knew I was nervous."

Spyder runs a hand over his head and rubs at his eyes. "It's not your fault. It's no use blaming anyone. Let's figure this out before we jump to conclusions."

I hear what he's saying, but I can't listen. In my head, I can already see Mrs. Blank standing by the open grave. I won't go to the funeral. I can't. I can't face what I've done to the survivors.

Maybe I'll say goodbye later, after they've laid the flowers and left. The least I can do is—

"I've got her."

—jump to conclusions. "Thank you." My breath leaves me in a whoosh of relief.

"I didn't do anything. I scanned the neighborhood footage. She's in her pjs with her mom in the kitchen. Caught her through the window on a camera near the house."

"All that matters is she got out."

"Bree, she doesn't know that *you* got out."

"That doesn't matter. She's safe."

"I'm sure it matters to her. I bet it matters to her mom, too. Just like it would matter to me."

"We're all taking risks. She shouldn't have come tonight. This was my risk. She knew my risk. I'll let her know I'm alright later."

Spyder sighs. "You really should go over there."

"No way. And lead The State right to them? I haven't gone over there since I was released, and I won't now. Doc was right. I had to get out of The Station to keep everyone safe, and I have to stay away from Em to keep *her* safe. I'll get a message to her that I'm okay, but I have to keep her away from me, at least for a little while."

"We should've clipped our monitors, too. Why didn't we do that?" Spyder paces a little, shaking his head so that his hair moves like his namesake's many legs. "I guess you're right. I don't like it, but you're right."

"I know I am."

"Let me get back to the footage. It's kind of a long shot, but I've managed to trace a variation in the shadows down the block. Unfortunately, the shadow is nearly out of the radius where I was recording, and we don't have a clear shot yet. Four cameras to go."

"You'll get an image. I can feel it."

Spyder has just started on the last four cameras when Doc's voice crackles in our earpieces. "Doc checking in."

"Doc!" I'm so happy to hear her voice that I forget to press the side button to activate my voice. I immediately realize my mistake, and I'd have realized without Spyder's exaggerated pantomiming in the background. I press the button this time, but some of my initial enthusiasm has tempered. "Doc."

"How are you? I'm sorry I had to give you the brush off earlier."

I don't care how I am. I care how everyone else is, the ones who weren't expecting the path their lives took tonight.

"I'm fine, but Bree's hurt her ankle," Spyder says.

I shoot him a dirty look, but he just shrugs. Doc already knows, but Spyder's too old to be tattling.

"I can walk. I'm fine."

"Probably just twisted. Ice is the best. Keep your foot elevated, and wrap the ankle if you can to ease the swelling. Come by the place tomorrow morning, and I'll take a look at it."

"Thanks, but you don't have time."

"I have time. You can't run around with a gimpy ankle," she retorts. "Come by tomorrow morning."

"Fine. Can we move on to the important stuff now? Like what the gwock happened tonight?"

Doc sighs. "I was hoping you could tell me."

"The State surprised us, and the guards slaughtered us. We clipped as many survivors as we could find and got out before the building was destroyed. The end."

"Bree," Spyder hisses at me.

"I'm sorry, Doc. It's not your fault." I rub my temples, feeling a headache coming on. "I'm not sure what went wrong. I got most of the way through the speech. If I had ended two minutes sooner, people would have been leaving, and this wouldn't be such a mess."

"It's not your fault either. There's no way we could have foreseen this. We knew the timing would be tight, that The State would show up eventually, but we couldn't have expected this."

"We should have." I pound my fist into my hand. "We should have known. We know they've been watching me for months. Why wouldn't they know about everything? They always know about everything."

"They don't. That's one of the lies they tell to keep everyone in line. They can't know about everything."

"Tell that to all the dead bodies over at the Edmond Street building. Wait, you can't. They've already been destroyed. Tell it to the air, then. Tell their ashes in the air that The State doesn't know everything. They won't be able to hear you, but The State will. They'll have a good laugh at us while they decide exactly how they want to kill each and every one of us and destroy everything we've ever touched."

"Calm down, Bree." Spyder holds out his hand.

"No, I will not calm down." The meds are wearing off again, but I pace the room, out of his reach, grateful for the twinge my ankle produces with every step. That shot of pain keeps me focused and energized. "The tapping is still going to happen tomorrow. We didn't even get the blockers distributed. This was all for nothing."

"Actually—"

"I don't want to hear it Spyder." Fury has been building in me all evening, and I'm not about to tamp down my anger now. Spyder and Doc can take it.

"But we broadcasted over the network," Spyder says.

"You did *what*?"

"We broadcasted your speech over the network. Not everywhere. Just in targeted areas of the sector where The State wasn't looking. I've got some of my less-acrobatic guys distributing more blockers now."

My limbs tremble, and I clench and unclench my hands. I need to hit something. Soon. My voice is low, and I punctuate every word like a punch. "Whose. Idea Was. This?"

"It was my idea." The Professor's voice chimes in my ear.

"Information is our most valuable weapon against The State. The dissemination of information protects us."

"Information didn't protect us. Broadcasting put us more at risk, and you should have known that. Broadcasting my speech raised the stakes. It forced a response from The State."

"The plan won't work unless enough people block their signals tomorrow during the tapping," the Professor reasons.

"Tell me you stopped the broadcast before the guards ambushed us."

"We stopped the broadcast before the ambush," the Professor says. "I was monitoring from a closed location and delaying the broadcast by about a minute so I could review before sending the footage over the network. The last thing the audiences at home saw was the first verse of the song."

"Nice pipes, by the way," Doc interrupts.

"Well, he's dead now," I say. "One of the first ones shot."

"I didn't know…. He had a beautiful instrument," Doc says.

"Are you sure the first round of sweepers didn't pull him out?" the Professor asks.

"What sweepers?"

"We sent a few of the mites in as soon as the guards cleared out. They got a few out before you found the ones who were hiding."

Ever-present, the load in my chest feels lighter now that I've learned more have survived.

"How many did they find?" I ask.

"Perhaps fifty or sixty."

I'm uneasy. I can't put my finger on what's wrong.

"What happened with the rest of the mites?" Spyder closes his eyes.

The lines are silent.

Spyder slumps in his chair. I simultaneously want to shake him and offer comfort. So I don't touch him. But if he's too afraid to do it himself, I'll get him an answer.

"Doc?" The weight has returned full-force. "Tell us."

"The diversion display started out very well," Doc says. "The mites performed beautifully. They captivated the crowd. Everyone stood on the streets, mesmerized by the incredible swoops, dives, and leaps. And the fireworks—most of them had never seen, let alone heard of, fireworks. A few were scared when that started, but when they realized it was a thing of beauty, of celebration, the joy was palpable." Doc's voice is warm as she recounts the event. She's stalling.

"Doc, please."

"It went wrong." The simple statement is loaded with regret and a hint of anger. "Everything was going according to plan. The acrobatics. The music. The fireworks."

"And then?" I prompt her.

"And then..." She trails off.

"And then all of our actions continued according to plan." She goes cold and hard. "We could not anticipate the reactions of the crowd."

"We should have," the Professor says. "'Once spirit was God, then it became man, and now it is even becoming mob.'"

"Enough." I bury my head in my hands. I can't listen to this, and I can't look to see how Spyder's taking this nonsense. "*Please*, get to the point."

"The mites made it out. All of them. But..."

Spyder lets out a strangled sound of relief. I squeeze his hand, glad his friends are okay but terrified of what Doc's about to say.

"The smoke bombs went off. The music changed. We made the illusion so real that the crowd didn't know they were being fooled. We thought so hard about tricking The State, that we forgot we'd also be tricking those on the street." Doc's honeyed voice finally breaks.

"They panicked," she continues. "They fought each other to get back to their homes, to get off the street. The guards came to restore order. Obviously, there had been reports about the light and the noise. What the guards found was a crowd that had turned in on itself and exploded outward with violence."

"Crowd control." I close my eyes, which is a mistake, because all I can see are the diagrams from training.

*"Disband crowds at all costs. The people shall not congregate. If you see a group gathering, you disperse it. If you cannot disperse, you radio for back up. If your fellow guards fail to individualize the mob, we employ the following maneuver."*

*Sarge flips over a white board, littered with Xs and Os and lines, like some kind of sports playbook.*

*"The Os are you. The Xs are your targets. Your objective is to separate the Xs."*

*"What do we do when we've got them separated? Do we take them in?" a trainee asks.*

*"No, son." Sarge smiles. His white teeth glitter in the harsh light. "They're Xs for a reason. You execute them. Crowd control." He throws back his head and opens his teeth wide in some kind of perverted pleasure.*

"I should have known. I should have remembered," I mutter without talking into the ear piece.

Spyder stares at me like he's never seen me before.

Doc keeps talking. "They fired into the crowd. People scattered. The mites were safe, up high. I was safe, tucked away, waiting and watching. The guards tried to separate families, friends, strangers, any remaining little groups. They took each person in that crowd, and they butchered them."

"All of them?" Spyder's eyes are so wide, I can see the red blood vessels running through the white.

"They got a piece of nearly everyone. Most, they left for dead. The guards set explosives and disappeared as quickly as they came. We thought fast and implemented the same plan as we had for the warehouse. The mites worked quickly. They cut their own monitors and came down into the crowd. I came out and told them who was worth taking. Triage.

"We split into two groups at that point and sent half the mites your way. At the diversion site, the mites cut the monitors on the survivors and passed them into the tunnels in a human assembly line. We left the ones with major injuries behind and came to The Station without delay."

Left behind—she means left for dead. Doc's monotone recounting of events makes her sound like a machine churning out a verbal report. These are people she's talking about. Every muscle in my body is tense, forced to stay still until she's finished.

"By the time we'd gotten the heavy door shut, the first of the explosions ripped through the area. We held our position. When the noise stopped, we made our way to the tunnel, and I started surgery. I finished up about twenty minutes ago."

I can't listen to this anymore. "This is my fault."

"You need to stop internalizing everything," the Professor chides me. "You give yourself far too much credit for things you have no control over."

"You're wrong. I know this procedure. I know how the guards operate. I know crowd control. I should have remembered. I should have come up with a different plan." My pacing has led me to Spyder's bed, and I pound my fist into his pillow. "I knew better."

"The plan was good, Bree. Not the best, but good enough to get the ball rolling. We had to start somewhere."

I wish the Professor would just shut up.

He keeps going. "You can't be expected to remember everything from training. We went into this knowing your memory was imperfect, that you still have gaps and may have blocks in place for self-protection."

"Again with the protecting me. My mind may be protecting me, but I keep putting more and more people at risk, and I don't even know I'm doing it. I'm too dangerous if I can't remember everything. I'm not reliable."

Spyder, silently listening with his big eyes, finally speaks up.

"Bree's right. Hundreds of people died tonight, and we're putting more at risk. Everyone we've taken off network is as good as dead."

"They're free," the Professor says.

"As far as I'm concerned right now, that's the same thing," Spyder says.

We're responsible for these deaths. We might as well have killed them with our own hands. But...

"We have to go through with the plan," I say.

Spyder makes a face at me like I'm crazy. I haven't had a change of heart. I hate the truth, but I can't lie to myself. "We've already handed out the blockers and encouraged people to use them. It's done. We can regret the casualties and hate ourselves, or we can use this as an opportunity to move forward."

"But, Bree—"

"We don't have time to mourn right now. The dead will still be dead when we get around to it."

Spyder cowers like I've slapped him. "You could at least *pretend* to have a heart."

His words drive deep into my chest and anchor there. I close myself off.

"I don't need one when I've got a brain. It's time to think smarter. I made a mistake. And I'm not talking about the speech or the diversion right now. I keep making the same mistake involving my emotions. This is war. Casualties are a reality." I'm cold like Doc, and I hate myself a little for it. But we have to move on. I have to move on. Many made sacrifices tonight— their loved ones, their lives. The least I can sacrifice is my emotions.

"I'm going home, Spyder. I'll see you at Doc's after the tapping tomorrow. We've all got a lot to talk about."

"And a lot to think about." Spyder's look pierces me.

"Bree, signing off." I say into the earpiece, remove it, and leave the web.

I am out through the maze of wire and on the street in no time.

The streets pass in a blur. I'm on autopilot. I feel no pain. I see no threats. I am invisible to the world, and the world is invisible to me.

I blink, and I am home. Time is unreliable: Today seemed weeks long, but the walk home passed in a moment.

## 44

When I see my building, I relax instantly. The sorrow of the day fades away, and I can crawl into my bed and stay there until the nightmares chase me underneath. I slip inside as noiselessly as possible—no sense in waking Charley—and head to the corner to scale what remains of the stairs. I pull myself partway up and test the load on my bad side. My ankle gives a little, but I can bear weight. I wouldn't want to be climbing a mountain right now, but the climb up to the third floor is doable.

I'm only about a foot off the ground when a hand covers my mouth, and an arm wraps around my waist and pulls me backward. I struggle, but the angle is all wrong. I'm leaning backward and completely vulnerable. Ducking my chin to protect my neck, I squirm and try to roll over to fight my attacker.

He holds me fast. The smell coming from his hand is horrible. He's drugging me. I've got to break his lock. I stop struggling and relax into him, counter to his expectations. My opposite reaction throws him off. Reflexively, his grip loosens, and I lash out. I catch him with my head under his chin, and I'm able to turn, throwing him to the ground. I pin him. He wasn't trying to drug me.

"Charley!" Before I can get another word out, he's stuffed his disgusting, dirty-gloved hand back into my mouth.

"They're here," he breathes more than whispers. "They came in and gave me a doughnut and told me to go to sleep. I said 'Yes. Yes. Yes. There's a hole in the middle. Part fell out. I have to find it.' I ran away from them to look for the hole. Stupid idiots don't even know the hole's supposed to be there. They take out the middle in the kitchen."

Charley glows with his success. "Come on, come on. We've got to hide."

He pulls me out of sight into his cardboard home, and we hide. I try not to gag at the stench of feces and urine soaking through the sheets.

"We'd have more space if you'd given me that board you promised."

"I'm sorry, Charley. I have the cardboard in a safe place. I'll get it to you as soon as I can."

"What did you do?" he asks.

"I can't stay here."

"I know. They'll spring the trap. I wanted to talk to you before you die. I was hoping to get that cardboard."

"They know I'm here."

"Yup. Will you tell me where you hid the board?"

"I can't."

"I'm sorry." He sticks his head outside the rotting structure. "She's down here," he yells. "I've got her trapped."

He pushes me outside his house and whispers, "run."

I do. A few quick leaps, and I'm in the alleyway. As I leave, I see Charley punch himself in the face a couple of times and howl.

"She hit me. That little brat hit me. Hurry, she's getting away."

Footsteps thunder on the upper floor, and shouts ring out.

Where to now? It doesn't matter. They're tracking me on the network. The safest place for me is in a group, some place where they won't be able to tell exactly where I am. Where that radius of signal works in my favor. I've got to get at least to Budgetville. I can't think much beyond that. Forming a plan only slows me down, and I'm already slower than normal because of my gimpy ankle. Until I find some kind of cover, this is a straight chase, and I'm wounded prey. I don't like my odds.

I get farther faster than I thought I'd be able to. No mites to rescue me, none of Lex's fancy trip wires to slow down the guards. Straight athleticism and sheer determination are my only allies. Trash cans rattle behind me, and heavy breathing and curses carry through the night air. I cut randomly through the streets, hoping to stay as far away from the clumsy guards as possible. I lose sight of them for a few minutes, but they close on me. I cut again, right into their field of view. Stupid.

An unfamiliar female commander gives the orders. "Split up. She's headed down the alley. Blue team, follow her. Red team, split down the side streets. Triangle formation. Go."

In a flash of inspiration, I feel around in my pockets. There. I've still got the blocker from my speech. I slap it on my monitor and run the last couple of blocks into Budgetville.

"We've lost her," the leader of the red team crackles on the radio. "Do you have contact?"

"We're in pursuit. I have visual," Blue leader replies.

They're close, but not for long. I have a few minutes to disappear. I spot my opening: a basement storm window down another alley is open. I jog around the corner and double back, disappearing into the building. Inside, I stand flush against the wall with the window. The guards swear as they run right past my hiding place.

I've got breathing room, but I only have a minute or two before the Bounty goes out. I need to remove the blocker. I can evade the guards, but I can't evade the entire population looking for me.

I make my way up the stairs and find myself on the lower level

of a 24-hour shopping facility. There aren't too many shoppers, a
few third shifters getting their shopping done before work, but
there are enough. The depth should provide some signal blockage, too. They'll get a read on me, but they can't pinpoint me.
They should have to search a few buildings. What a phenomenal
piece of luck. I couldn't have planned this better if I tried.

I think a quick prayer, *Oregon*, and remove the blocker from
my ankle monitor. When I'm not immediately surrounded by
guards, I allow myself to relax. I need a game plan.

I pace the racks and pick up random items, placing them back
on the shelves nearly immediately. A State-issue green scarf.
Pencils. A carton of hydropacks. I create the illusion of a window
shopper.

A clerk blocks my path. "You can either purchase something
or leave now."

"I'm just browsing."

"We don't want you here. Buy something and leave, or just
leave. Your kind are always causing trouble."

I bristle at that. Has the clerk recognized me? Will he call the
guards?

"I can escort you out, if necessary."

I pick up a bottle of pain meds and dumbly present them to
him. After an eternity, I finally find my voice. "I'll take these."

He leads me to a register to process the transaction.

I limp after him. "Wait—I don't have any credits. I'm sorry."

He rolls his eyes and looks at my ankle. Taking pity on me, he
opens the bottle and hands me two pills. He nods to the door.
"Now get out of here." As I leave, he mutters, "teenagers."

He didn't recognize me. He's just a grump. The corners of my
mouth twitch into a smile. I go down to ground level and re-apply
the blocker. I need another highly populated area, underground
would be best, but I'll settle for anywhere on the street.

Despite my appearance and ability to fight, I'm not a hood-
lum. I'm usually asleep at this time of night. I don't know what

people do at night. If they're smart, they stay home and sleep like me. If they're not smart, they go out and cause trouble—stealing, fighting, drinking.

A bar. Preferably, a row of bars. A real hole in the wall with a lot of regulars, that's what I need.

I keep to the shadows even at night, an unnecessary habit for this time of day. The cameras can't get a shot of me in this light, but some are equipped with heat sensing equipment.

I don't have much longer to find someplace. Maybe a minute and a half left on the blocker. I need a place to hunker down. The more I keep bouncing on and off network, the greater the chance they'll find me. I could make my way over to Doc and the Professor's, but if the guards end up searching the area, I could destroy everything they've built. I'm on my own.

Lucky for me, this part of the sector is an armpit, and there're two or three bars on every block. The first one I pass has a glass door. Inside, a set of stairs leads upward. That won't do. Next, I pass one where loud music makes the outer walls vibrate. Everything appears to be on the ground floor. Okay, but less than ideal. About four people are inside, dancing erratically. Not enough to mask. I need more of a crowd to blend in.

I'm coming up to the third bar now. The Professor's always saying third time's the charm, and he's right. I don't have any more time left on the blocker, so I go in. This bar's mostly on ground level, but about two steps lead down to the door. Could be better. The main advantage is that it's filled with people. More noise from the signals, as the Professor explained. Hopefully, pinpointing my location on the network will be harder for The State. Before I head to the bar itself, I visit the ladies' room and remove the blocker so no one sees what I'm doing.

I head out to the bar area. There are a couple of empty stools. I limp up and take a seat.

The barman takes one look at me and says, "You look like you could use one. First is on the house."

"Thanks. I'll have a hydro."

The bartender shrugs, and I hold up the pain meds. He nods in understanding and pours the drink. I fiddle with the pills. The running, even the fast walking, has been murder on my ankle. I'm afraid I've permanently damaged the tendons.

I dry swallow the pills and chase them with the hydro. A man on the barstool next to me sneers.

"Hydro? Whaddya think this is, a church? Have a real drink, girly. Get the kid a whisky," he says to the bartender.

"No, thanks."

"Whaddya standing there for?" He ignores me and talks to the barman. "I said get the kid a gwocking whisky."

"Did you want something?" The barman gives him a big grin.

"Liforney," the man swears, mangling the state's name. I'm tempted to correct him. "A whisky, please." The emphasis is on the last word, making the request sound anything but polite.

The barman pours a stingy measure into the glass.

"I ain't paying for that. Pour a full dram."

"That's regulation." The barman sets the glass in front of me. "Measure it yourself."

"Let me behind that bar, and I will." The man raises a fist threateningly. He braces his arms on the bar and pushes himself to stand. He wobbles a little and collapses back on the stool. "Maybe I should just measure from here."

"You do that," the barman says.

The man snatches the glass from in front of me and drains it in one. He smacks his lips together. "Like I thought. Short. You gonna make 'em all short, guess I gotta order a double. And a double for the little lady." He shouts the last part, raising his glass high to the whole room.

"Keep it down," I say.

"I always keep it down. Until the morning. Then sometimes it comes back up." He pantomimes vomiting, barks a laugh, and slaps his palm on the bar.

No wonder the only seats available were around this guy. And I had thought I was so fortunate finding this place. I've only got a few minutes to plan my next move. If I stay too long, The State will find me. Somehow, I've got to disappear.

The barman sets a glass full of amber liquid in front of me.

"Drink up, girly." My neighbor whacks me on the back and raises his empty glass to me.

"Drink it yourself," I retort.

"Is that any way to be treating me when I've been so nice to you? Buy you a drink, and you throw it in my face." He sighs, and stares into his own drink. "Kids today ain't got no manners." He leans his head back and howls, "drink up, girly," and collapses in a fit of giggles.

If we hadn't before, we've definitely drawn the attention of the other patrons now. I can feel their eyes on me. They're all very careful to stare without looking. I run my fingers down the outside of the glass, tracing patterns.

"There you go," he says. "Drink up. You need me to learn ya how?" He raises a finger, and the bartender brings him another drink. He raises his now-full glass to me. I hesitate, and the bartender throws me a big wink over the man's shoulder and nods toward my glass.

I clink glasses with my inebriated neighbor and take a small sip before tossing the drink back. I smile as I swallow. Nutrijuice.

"To the bartender." I raise my empty glass to him.

"To the bartender." My noisy friend echoes.

"To the bartender." A third voice chimes in. A man slides into the seat next to me. "Hello, Bree. It's been a long time."

I freeze like the crowd did when the spots shone in their eyes and keep my back to him.

"Aren't you going to say hello? That's sort of rude." I'm stuck on this barstool, and I can't move to save my life. Not that moving would save my life. Not if he's already here.

"I'll have what she's having." I see him gesture out of the

corner of my eye. The silver skull sits large and heavy on his ring finger.

The barman moves slowly, polishes a glass and fills it with hydro. He pushes the glass across the bar, keeping eye contact with me. He raises an eyebrow as though he's asking me a question, but I can't respond.

My newest bar mate sips with an audible swallow.

"Good. I don't have to cite you for serving a minor," he says. "The report form would be tedious. It would ruin both of our evenings."

"Now," he continues, talking to me this time. "Did you miss me?" His breath is warm and sweet on my ear. I suppress a shudder and will him out of my life.

"Come on. Say hello." His voice rises in pitch, needling me.

I don't know what game he's playing, why he doesn't arrest or kill me right now.

His voice drops dangerously. "Say hello. That's an order."

"Hello," I whisper.

He chuckles. "That's my girl. Never could resist a direct order, could you? But you didn't address me appropriately."

"I'm released."

"You're never released. Once in the guards, always in the guards. Look around, this bar is full of them."

I turn my head, careful not to look at him, and survey the bar. He's right. I was an idiot not to see it before. The way they hold themselves, protecting their drinks, eyes down to keep out of trouble: these are State-supporting ex-guards. The State protected them, and they continue to protect The State, even when not in service. It's safer that way. For them. I wonder if he found me on the network or if one of these rats called me in.

"You see now, don't you? Fear inspires loyalty. That's why they will always be loyal to The State, and by extension, to me. You puzzle me." He strokes the back of my head, brushing his fingertips along my hairline before wrapping his thick fingers around my neck and squeezing gently. The skull ring digs into my spine.

"You're afraid. I can smell it. I can feel it." He squeezes a little harder. "But you're not loyal. Say hello to me."

Spots swirl in front of my eyes. I only have a few seconds before he cuts my blood flow off completely.

"Hello, Sarge," I say, surprised by the venom in my own voice.

"That's a good girl." He releases his grip and taps me on the back of my head, snapping it forward. I stop my forehead from hitting the bar and rub at the back of my neck. The pain meds I took for my ankle have already kicked in; it's a nice bonus that they're now helping my neck.

"I'm glad you're still tractable, if not loyal." He drums his fingers on the bar. "I always liked a challenge." The back of his knuckles on my cheek are somewhere between a hit and a caress.

"See you around, soldier." The sound of the stool scraping along the floor seems to last minutes. When I finally get up the courage to face him, he's gone.

The drunkard next to me is white as a ghost. "That's one scary dude."

Privately, I agree with him. I nod to the bartender and leave. The guards won't be looking for me again tonight. I remember enough to know that Sarge has already started whatever game he wants to play with me. It's my move.

I head out into the dark, empty streets. Vestiges of cold float on the night breeze, refreshing and cleansing me. The season of preparation begins tomorrow, and we will thrust aside the rules of The State and begin our own training with the newly freed.

I round the corner and head for home. I'll think no more about battles and lives lost. For now, I will sleep.

## 45

I wake on the floor, smothered by covers. I thrash to free myself, the haze of the dream lingering.

*"Get up that wall, Trainee." I climb and climb but don't seem to gain any height. The vines enliven and encircle me, pinning me to the wall of the course.*

"Move, move."

I struggle, but the covers only wind tighter around me. I can't escape.

*"You want to guard that bridge, you guard yourself. You don't want to know what happens if you don't guard yourself."*

I'm skidding. I can't control the movement. My legs aren't working—they flail uselessly in the air. I have no purchase.

*I slide down the climbing wall. My jaw hits the divots, each sharp shock mocking me. I could have held there. Or there. Or there. I'm nearly down the wall when he appears.*

*"You're mine, soldier." The last thing I register before the blackness is those white teeth and that silver ring.*

IN THE LIGHTNESS, the first thing I register is that I'm wrapped in blankets, dangling over the precipice of what used to be where the floor and wall met, a giant butterfly mid-emergence from its chrysalis. Somehow, in the space between dreaming and waking, I've become tangled in covers and thrown myself out of bed. Terror wells inside me as I dangle unsupported. I can't climb. I can't move. I will the terror down, this time. I will not let fear overtake me.

I crane my neck to find the covers wrapped around the bedpost closest to me. Suspended here, I can do nothing but laugh. The bed begins to slide along the floor. My laughter dies, and I hold perfectly still. The fear rises again, like ice rain flooding my veins, paralyzing and consuming me. The bed stops.

"Did they do this to you?" Charley calls up from below.

My dreams did this to me.

"Can you get me down?" I try not to move my lips as I speak.

"Nope."

That's not helpful.

"Why not?"

"I'm not strong enough." Charley pushes back the sleeves of his heavy green coat. "I've got chicken arms. Bwak bwak." He laughs. "Chickens can't help you. We can't fly. We have to stay around here pecking for our food." He folds his hands into his armpits and starts scratching at the floor. "Bwak bwak. Bwak bwak bwak. I'm a chicken."

"But, Charley, a chicken is a bird." I'm getting desperate.

"So?"

"Birds fly."

He thinks for a moment. "Birds do fly. Chickens don't. Chickens must not be birds."

"Chickens have feathers. Birds have feathers. That means a chicken is a bird, right? Use your chicken feathers and fly on up here and get me." The bed slides again. Gwock. I moved too much while I was talking.

"I don't have feathers. I must not be a chicken." Charley kicks a tin can and sits on the floor, chin in his hands. I don't have time for him to pout.

"Please, help me."

*There's no one to help you here, soldier. You've got to help yourself.*

The memory rises unbidden.

"I'm not a chicken and I can't help you. I must be a person, and people don't fly. Hey!" He smiles, more toothless than toothy. "If people don't fly, and chickens don't fly, then I must be a chicken!" He walks away from me to his cardboard, contentedly squawking to himself.

"Washington, D.C." I moan to the ceiling. If I can just work an arm free, I might be able to climb up. Without breathing, I pull my arms in close, listening for the telltale creak of the bed. So far, so good. I pop my shoulder back and work my fingers toward my face. If someone walked in right now, I'd probably look like I was picking my nose.

I pull my arm all the way out and grab hold of the sheet above my head. The bed's not moving. Freeing my arm has created enough space in the folds of the covers that I'm able to get my other arm out. My legs are still partially wrapped, but I should be able to climb.

I hold my weight with my arms and begin to move upward. As I do, the line goes slack. The bed moves a little, and the line tightens. This is not good. I climb as fast as I can, and the bed creaks along the floor at a more rapid pace. I place my hands on the edge of the floor and hoist myself up, blocking the bed. With a groan, the bed stops, right at the edge of the floor.

Relieved, I untwist the rest of myself and sit for a moment, breathing heavily. I can resist the fear. I can save myself.

Today is the tapping. As I found out last night, the blockers will work—if people actually use them. I stand and stretch. There's no time to complete my daily exercises. I need to be over at Doc and the Professor's by noon. They'll have been tending to the injured in The Station most of the morning, but

Doc will check my ankle and we'll watch the tapping at The
Bunker.

I try to ignore Charley as I leave, but he gets in my face and
makes bird noises. I brush him away, but he is insistent.

"Hey, Charley, you know what tastes just like chicken?"

"Bwak?"

"You."

I make no sense, but he hears the threat in my voice and
backs off. I head to Doc's, taking a slightly different route than
yesterday. If The State's got a tail on me, and they probably do at
this point, I don't want to establish a pattern. I place my blocker
on for the last minutes of the walk. I want to confront The State
on my terms. I guess that makes me the chicken.

## 46

I reach The Bunker in record time and rip off the blocker before a Bounty can be issued. The security measures in place around The Bunker should protect me for now. The Professor ushers me down the corridor to the main living space.

"Doc's grabbing a quick cat nap," he says. "She was up most of the night. I think she would have kept working, except she knew you were coming."

"I'm glad she's sleeping. I could go."

"No, she really wants to take a look at that ankle of yours. Besides, we should all watch the tapping together."

"Good idea."

"We invited other guests as well."

I groan.

"Visitors' footfalls are like medicine—they heal the sick." The Professor laughs lightly. "Our guests will be Spyder and Em."

"Works for me." I'll be happy to see Em.

"Now about that ankle of yours…" The Professor opens the door for me.

"It's much better this morning. It can wait. We should let Doc rest until the start of the tapping."

The Professor agrees with me. "She'll want to be awake for that."

We head into the war room and stare at the screens. The Professor breaks the silence.

"It's for the best, Bree."

"What's for the best?"

"This. Everything. I know you wanted more of a leadership role in the training."

"And I'll have one. We're not there yet."

"Nearly so. And, no, you won't." His mouth is a thin, firm line.

"Yes, I will." If he wants to argue like a two-year-old, I'm happy to oblige him. "Just because you're old doesn't mean I have to listen to what you say."

"Really. And how do you mean to lead training when you can't be at The Station for more than a few minutes?"

"So you'll train them, and I'll lead missions."

"They have to establish teamwork. They have to lead each other and follow without question. If you come in at the eleventh hour, you'll throw the whole dynamic off."

"So what am I supposed to do? Sit around and do nothing?"

"You're the face of it all." The Professor claps his hands together and rubs them frenetically. "You're the reason we have so many. People flock to you. They like you. We can recruit more through your story. People know you. You inspire them."

"I'm supposed to provide warm bodies, then. Innocents, who have no idea what they're getting into. You want to make me into a salesman, selling this resistance to the masses. I can't be a figurehead anymore. I can't stand around talking while people get hurt. I'm a soldier."

"Not anymore." The Professor points his finger at me. "You're still a general behind the scenes. Your intimate knowledge of The State allows us to anticipate their maneuvers."

I wince and think of the dead at the fireworks show. The

Professor corrects himself. "We have a better but not absolute idea of how they'll respond. You are more valuable to us for your head and your heart than you are as a body on the field. Get used to it."

"I don't want to get used to it."

"Stop being such a selfish child, and think of the greater good. These people have a hard road ahead of them. We all do. You can refresh them."

Oh, goodie. I've moved beyond figurehead: I'm the Riverine Resistance's cheer leader and hydro girl. Excellent. I would argue more with the Professor, but at that moment, we're interrupted by a rainbow-colored whirlwind.

"Hi guys!" Em throws her arms around me. "Bree." She squeezes me and breathes me in. I probably smell like smoke, alcohol, blood, and Charley's urine, but Em sniffs so deep, like I'm her personal air freshener.

"Good to see you, too." I pat her on the head awkwardly.

She squeezes me tighter. "Mom and I were so worried."

This is why I couldn't stay with the Blanks. I don't think the same way they do. I was worried about Em last night, but it never even occurred to me to tell them I was okay. Spyder knew, but I was too stupid to understand. They don't need a defective person in their life making them worry.

"When we got the note from Doc, we were so happy. You don't even know the half of it. We sat at the kitchen table for hours and hours and hours. Mom kept getting up to clean things she'd cleaned five minutes before. Finally, we agreed to make cookies. I got the flour everywhere, but I made a mess on purpose, so Mom would have something to clean when we were done. Oh! I brought you some of the cookies." Em ceases rambling for a moment and fishes around in her pocket, producing a few crumbs.

"Shoot. I guess I ate a few of them on the way over here. These are still good, though." She shoves them at me.

I take them and place a few in my mouth to be polite. Em nods in satisfaction.

"Good, aren't they?"

I nod. The cookies dissolve in my mouth. Much better than the stale Nutribiscuits Doc scavenged.

"Where was I?" She licks the crumbs from her fingers. "I got the note from Doc. One of those leash guys brought it by—you know, one of Spyder's friends always swinging all over the place? Oh, yeah, mites—and we read the note, and it said you were okay, and it gave me directions to come here, and here I am. I'm so glad to see you." She hugs me again.

I relax into her. She smells of soy butter and laundry soap. Normal smells from a normal life.

"Is Em safe here?" I ask the Professor.

"For now. The State's a little preoccupied with the tapping today and the aftermath of last night's events. We're taking a little bit of a chance, but Doc and I agreed you both needed to visit."

"What happened to you last night?" I ask her.

We go over to the table and sit in a couple of chairs. The Professor excuses himself. It's nice that he's giving us this time.

She sits cross-legged in her chair and faces me. "I wanted you to see me last night," she explains. "I thought I could help you."

"You did. You helped me focus. The crowd wasn't nearly as overwhelming with you there."

She smiles happily to herself. "I knew it. You needed me. That's why I had to come."

"When did you leave? I lost sight of you almost as quickly as I saw you."

"I left almost as soon as you started talking."

I don't know why, but I'm disappointed by this. Leaving means she was safe, but I wanted her to hear my speech, tell her mom about how I did. They'd be proud of me.

"I missed the first part."

I know.

"But then I went to where the Professor was holed up, and I caught the rest of your speech. You did great."

Warmth blossoms in my chest and is extinguished as I realize the implications. Em sees something of my reaction in my face.

"He kept me safe," she says. "We watched on the screen as the broadcast went out on the network."

If she watched with the Professor, she saw the building past the one minute delay where the Professor stopped the broadcast. She was watching when the first shots were fired.

"So you saw," I say calmly, but my heart breaks for her.

A shadow crosses her eyes. "I'm glad you're safe."

I can see the ghosts of the crowd in her face. She's too young to have seen that. I should have insisted she stay away.

"You shouldn't have come to the speech."

"I'm not a kid anymore." Her voice is gentle. "You can't protect me."

"Sure you're a kid. I'm nearly a kid. I lost my innocence two years ago, and for what? Every day that I'm a part of this resistance, I lose a little more. I do it to keep you safe. I do it so you can have a better life."

"You're not my mom." Her words are even, though they seem a teenager's accusation. "Your job is to be my friend, not to keep me safe."

"I have to look out for you. I have to. They forced me to grow up when I was five years old. You should hold on to your childhood while you still can. Fight them by staying innocent. Be carefree in spite of The State. That's the worst you can do to them."

"I can't do that, Bree. The same way you can't. When you know what's happening, you can't forget and pretend everything is okay."

"Thousands of people pretend every day."

"Thousands of people aren't me. Thousands of people aren't you. Thousands of people aren't Doc or the Professor or my mom or Spyder or the mites or anyone else who's helping us. I have to help. That's why I'm here."

She's old enough to know her own mind. I can't change her. She has to be herself.

When I was living with the Blanks, Em got in trouble because she kept letting cats into the basement. She said she thought they'd be cold because it was the middle of the season of reflection. Mrs. Blank kept wondering where all the protein was going. At first, she thought we were just a couple of hungry kids going through a growth spurt. Then, the smell started. Twenty cats in a closed basement stink up pretty quickly.

Mrs. Blank opened the door to walk downstairs, and five or ten cats streaked past her, running wild through the house. Em and I chased them, catching them by the tails, corralling them back into the basement. Mrs. Blank chased after them in her nightgown like a gray-hair, swatting them with a broom. Em and I both got in trouble. It took us weeks to clean the mess out of the basement.

Some of the cats got pregnant and kept coming back, trying to get into the basement to have their babies. Mrs. Blank turned them away, so Em snuck the cats into an abandoned shed. She and I built a cat door for them, and she'd leave a can of food out there once a week or so. But her mom's a soft touch, so she got to keep Oscar. Em sleeps with him every night he allows. Cats.

"What can I do?" she says.

Em's always looked after strays. It's part of who she is, how she was raised. Mrs. Blank is the same way. I can't fault Em for wanting to help, but I can't stop being me, either. I've got to protect her. I'll find her a few tasks to do, safe ones that will help us without exposing her to any unnecessary risk.

"We've got a lot of people in The Station." I avoid calling them survivors.

"Yeah? But that's good, isn't it?" Em must be able to hear the regret in my voice or she wouldn't ask.

"Most of them are hurt."

"Does Doc need some help?"

"It's too dangerous in The Station."

Em gives me a look.

"I don't mean it's dangerous for you. It's dangerous for them—you're still being monitored. If The State picks up on the fact that you're helping, you'll lead them right to everyone. It would be an ambush. I'm not even going to The Station."

She nods. "I can understand that. So how can I help?"

"We've got a lot of mouths to feed."

Her face lights up in understanding. "I can do that. I can scavenge food and drop it off here. Doc and the Professor can ferry it over to The Station."

I'm relieved. This will keep her safe.

"How many people are we talking? I might need to steal a little to supplement."

Now this is less than ideal.

"We have some funds, and stealing is out of the question. If any kind of law breaking needs to happen, the mites will be in charge. They can get you raw ingredients. You'll just need to prepare it."

"Okay."

I use the same argument the Professor used on me. "And once more people are up and functioning, we'll turn KP over to The Station. They've got to become self-sufficient. We'll only outsource while they're injured."

"Got it." She's got the cheesiest grin on her face.

"Thanks," I add.

The door opens, and Doc and the Professor come in. Doc yawns and stretches her arms over her head.

Em bounds over and gives her a hug. "Morning, sleepy head."

"Guess you're not as young as you used to be," the Professor says to Doc with a wink.

"You're not so hot yourself, old man." Doc gives him a little smack on the chest.

The Professor wheezes and clutches his chest. "You'll give an old man a heart attack."

"Sure, sure."

We all share a smile. In the quiet, the smiles fade from our faces as we remember why we're here. I guess Spyder's not coming. I didn't leave on the best note last night. Sometimes, when his feelings are hurt, he hides for a while, until he feels safer. Kind of like his namesake.

I'll have to stop by the web on my way home.

"How's the ankle, Bree?" Doc asks.

"Good enough. It can wait. Tapping should be starting soon."

Doc opens her mouth to protest, but the Professor stops her. "It's just about time." He taps a keyboard and brings a few views up. We'll be watching two screens, primarily. The main sector screen, which will be shown to the public, and the behind-the-scenes tapping screen, which is only visible to The State and guards. He twists a knob, and the room is filled with sound.

"Ladies and Gentlemen, please direct your attention to your monitors. The tapping is about to begin... Ladies and Gentlemen, please direct your attention to your monitors..."

Of my hodgepodge group of friends, only Spyder and some of his mites are eligible for tapping. I'm not eligible again for a few more years because I was released early. Mrs. Blank is too old. Em's too young—she'll be fifteen in a few months, which makes her eligible for next year's tapping. Spyder's gotten lucky the last few years. He made sure to take a blocker before we passed them all out, so he should be safe again this year, as should all the mites. Really, this tapping is about seeing whether we got through to people and identifying areas of the sector that contain possible supporters.

We'll monitor the areas to see which have the fewest tapped. Those are the places where people likely used blockers. Spyder, the mites, and I will make follow-up visits to those areas in the next several weeks. From there, we'll stage several large-scale accidents over the next several months to wipe a few more people off the network. But we'll have to figure out how to avoid the guards, first. What happened last night can't happen again. Those who are with us now will have had time to train, and we can work the next groups of recruits through more gradually.

"Here we go," the Professor says.

"Welcome to the annual tapping." A soothing robotic voice comes over the speakers. "The worthy among the other sectors will be removed, trained, and report to guard duty within your sector within the next several months. Recruits from Sector Keystar will be selected in just a few moments. If you are between the ages of fifteen and thirty-two and eligible for tapping, please pay attention to your monitors. Those selected with an ankle monitor will see a red light flash. If you are chipped, you will feel a slight buzz in the shoulder where the chip is located. Due to immediate need in other sectors, there will be limited time to wrap up affairs within the sector. All Recruits must report by nine o'clock tonight to the transpo center."

We've heard for years that we must serve as guards in the other sectors to protect them, and that they take the good folks out so that they can have a better life as guards in our sector. Things must be getting really bad in the other sectors if they need the tapped to report to duty so quickly. I got three days before I had to report. Maybe other sectors have their own resistance movements.

On The State screen, lights start going off on the map. They're already tapping. Hopefully people put the blockers on at the very start of the announcement.

"Your monitors will be flashing in three...two...one. Congratulations to the newly tapped. Enjoy this day with your families. We thank you for your continued service."

"It worked." I breathe.

The Professor claps. Doc kisses him. Em runs among all of us, hugging us alternately. The map blinks in the background behind us. The areas around us have a few scattered red dots, but most are concentrated in Happytown and the work district. We've stopped the tapping for a majority of the sector.

The speakers crackle, and the robot voice comes on again. "Next year's tapping will occur within the season of preparation. Future announcements will follow as the date approaches."

The robot voice starts his closing remarks. "Certain events within and outside our borders require the special dedication of our forces. In addition to the normal tapped force, The State will be tapping some additional Recruits this year to respond to that need."

"What are they talking about?" Em directs the question to me, but I have no idea what's happening.

This can't be anything good. They've devised some last-ditch response to combat the map selection.

"As with your regularly scheduled tapping, the recruitment of special additional forces will be done by lottery. We require a special skill set for select missions, which necessitates an expansion of the tapping parameters."

Em tugs on my sleeve. "I don't understand."

"Hang on."

"Would all citizens please direct their attention to their chips or ankle monitors. Selections will be made in three...two...one."

The map lights up in areas that were previously dark. Our area of the sector flashes so red, the screen is bleeding.

"Bree." Em is crying.

"It's okay. It'll be okay. They couldn't keep their blockers on that long. There were bound to be some tapped in this area." I can't believe they tapped more. What will they do with the extra forces? Suppress our resistance, of course. Once again, The State is multiple steps ahead of us.

"Bree," Em says again.

"Not now." I can barely think, and the room seems too small.

Maybe we could just cut monitors en masse. The State already knows we have something in the works. No, but that would give them confirmation. They can't take a major action against us without proof. The guards wouldn't stand for that. My mind is racing, trying to figure out all the possibilities.

"Bree..." The Professor interrupts me this time.

I look over. Doc holds Em close as she sobs. I have no idea what's going on. The Professor points to my leg. Through the light green fabric of my pants, a flashing red light makes my whole ankle glow.

"By the VM." This can't be happening. I'm not eligible. I almost didn't survive last time. I reach for the table for support. My hand grasps at the air, and I sink to my knees.

"Oh, honey," Doc says, rocking Em.

I look at them, really look at them. Tears leak from Em's eyes. Doc wipes at them as fast as they come down. My own eyes begin to mist over. This is really hurting Em.

"I'll be okay, Em. I promise."

Through the haze of tears, she makes eye contact with me. Slowly, she pulls up her pant leg. A bright ring of flashing red encircles her ankle. She chokes out the words that break my heart.

"But will I?"

---

## 47

I don't remember reporting for tapping. Not the first time, and now, not the second. When my memories were partially restored, I had flashes of waiting for a bus and that first meeting in what I later learned was an old gymnasium. I puzzled through some of the chronology of my memories in the time I was with Dr. Fire, but I never fully remembered.

I'm in a bunk, and I know this is the present and this is real because I'm on the top bunk, and last time I'm pretty sure I was on the bottom. The ceiling is familiar—dizzyingly high, with metal crossbeams and dangling cobwebs that glitter and sway in the buzzing electric light.

Good morning, Training Quarters. Time for me to save Em.

My boots are in my bunk with me. I lace them tight and swing over the side of the bed, dropping a few feet to the floor. The thud echoes eerily through the chamber. Rows and rows of empty bunks in the long building confuse me as I walk to the door. There aren't even mattresses on most of them. The smell is wrong, too. Instead of the musty smell of weeks of training, there's...nothing.

I walk out of the building, onto what should be a gravel path to the mess hall. Instead, I step onto smooth, scuffed tile. What was once sterile-white has been polished to pale gray by time and hundreds of State-issue boots.

I recheck the door. Still looks like quarters in there. But this hall has the distinctly unpleasant citrus antiseptic odor of a health center.

My heart starts to race, and I try to take deep breaths to calm myself. I don't know where I am, what I'm doing, how long I've been here, or how I got here.

I am Bree. I am certain of this.

Make a plan, Bree. Make a plan. The where. I will figure out the where first, and the rest from there.

I'm almost to the end of the hall when a noise stops me—a slow clap that echoes in the emptiness.

I see his hands first, clapping, coming around the corner. Light flashes from his silver-blue ring.

"Congratulations," he says.

I cover my ears. I want to drop to the floor, but I force myself to stand.

"Brave little soldier. Not quite the greeting I was expecting."

"'Klahome yourself. Is that better?"

"Such...spunk. I had high hopes for you."

"Sorry to disappoint you." I spit on the ground, aiming for his shiny shoes.

"On the contrary, my dear. I couldn't be more proud. You stayed the longest."

The longest?

"Yes, the longest."

Did I say that out loud? I don't think I did.

"Come with me." He gestures in front of him, like I'm going to lead the way.

I stand still. Pain floods my head. The worst headache I've ever felt cripples me. I lean against the wall for support and close my eyes. The wall is unbearably hard. Imperfections in the concrete dig into my spine and tear through my clothes into my skin. My clothes—they're too heavy, and they burn when I move. I don't know what to do. I can't do anything because it hurts it hurts it hurts.

Someone stabs me with a sword. The pain would be unbearable if the pain weren't already unbearable, and death by stabbing is a good release.

"There you are." Sarge withdraws a long needle from my thigh.

"Get away from me."

"Sensory overload is common at first. That will help you acclimate." He steps away from me, thank the VM. "Why don't you take a few minutes to let that take hold. Meet me down that corridor when you're ready." He gets close to me again, too close. "And that is an order, soldier." He spins on his heel and marches away.

I spit again, aiming for the spot where he stood next to me.

I'm NOT sure how much time has passed when I finally walk down the hall and into the only room I find.

"Bree, so good to see you." Dr. Fire greets me. "Come in, come in."

"*Sit down, soldier,*" Sarge screams, inches from my face.

I flinch and regret it instantly. What's worse, I comply. I shuffle to a single chair in the middle of the room—big, with heavy leather straps. Since I can barely stand, sitting seems like the best option. I try to make myself believe sitting is my choice.

Sarge paces up front. He presses a red button on a large machine and begins to speak in a normal tone.

"Our objective in this meeting is to review the experiences of Guard Bree Carter during her mission in Project Praetereo and to assess her readiness to return to duties as assigned. Attendees are myself, Dr. Fire, and Guard Carter.

"Guard Carter, please place your arms through the straps on your chair and touch your palms to the metal plates on each arm."

"Sir," my reply to his directive is automatic, though I do not move. Sarge has not looked at me once since I entered the room.

"Dr. Fire, please assist as necessary."

Dr. Fire walks over to me, shrugs, and pulls each of my arms through the strap. She tightens them down enough to immobilize me, but not so tightly that they cause me pain. I guess I'm glad she's touching me rather than Sarge.

"Guard Carter is in position on the device, but let the auditory record show she required Dr. Fire's assistance. At this stage, I am unable to determine Guard Carter's level of compliance. She has received a moderate dose of sedative to mitigate side effects upon awakening."

He spins to face me.

"Guard, what is your name?"

"Bree Carter." I control the urge to roll my eyes, but cooperation is my best chance at survival until I can clear this painful fog from my brain and figure a way out.

"What is your home sector?"

"Sector Keystar."

"What is your term of service?"

"I served a year and a few months, but then I was released. This term's just started, so I guess I have about three years left."

Sarge clears his throat. "First tapping only, please."

"My service started on the second in the season of preparation, seventy-three years since the uprising. I was released sometime the next year, during the season of growth."

"What is your duty station?"

"I...I don't know."

"Dr. Fire?"

Dr. Fire walks to the corner of the room with the big box and turns some knobs. A sheet spits out of the side with a graph in the middle.

"Good, good. We have baseline," she says. "Proceed."

"Guard Carter, your duty and service to The State compels you to speak the truth. I have every confidence in your loyalty and service, but measures are in place to ensure the accuracy of your statements for record-keeping purposes. Do you understand?"

"Yes," I say.

They've hooked me up to a lie detector.

"Circumstances being what they are, I will forgive this lapse in protocol. Do you understand?"

Perfectly. "Yes, sir."

"Before your," Sarge clears his throat again, "second tapping, where were you?"

"In Sector Keystar."

"Where in the sector?"

"A lot of places. Mostly Undergroundland."

"What were you doing there?"

"Trying to remember."

"Remember what?"

"What happened to me. How I got there. It didn't help that you were chasing me."

Sarge smiles, faintly. "I see. Did I catch you?"

"Obviously." I flex against the leather restraints.

"Watch your tone, Guard."

"Did you resist?"

"Yes, sir." I can't keep the sarcasm from my voice, and I pull again on the leather.

Sarge gives Dr. Fire a nod. She consults her readouts and inclines her head.

"What are you most proud of from your time in Sector Keystar?"

The question throws me. I'm quiet for I don't know how long. "Guard Carter?"

I hesitate. Trying to stop the tapping was a colossal failure. I couldn't care less about the speeches I gave. Finally, I answer, truthfully. "Finding a home."

In a decrepit building with Charley, with Em and Doc and the Professor and Spyder, maybe with Lex if we'd had more time. But I leave out those details.

Sarge furrows his brow. Clearly not the answer he was looking for. "What did you do with your time in the sector?"

"Mostly tried to figure out ways to kill you." My answer is direct and sort of truthful. I will do my best not to provide any details on the Riverine Resistance movement. They still have a chance, even without me. Maybe I'm an even bigger figurehead now that I'm gone again. Maybe they're doing even better without me.

"What did I ever do to you?" He leers. There's the Sarge I know and hate.

"Tried to kill me, multiple times. Killed innocent citizens in my sector."

Dr. Fire holds up a hand. Sarge turns his back to me. It rises and falls as he takes huge breaths. I'm getting under his skin.

"Did you try to kill any other State forces during your time in Sector Keystar?"

We're treading on dangerous ground. I keep my answers as short as possible. "Not really."

"Did you engage State forces in combat?"

"Yes, sir."

"Why?"

"Necessity, sir."

"Why was it necessary?"

"To preserve and protect. Preserve. Protect. Kill." The old guard motto.

Sarge spins to face me. "The duty of the guards is to preserve and protect The State, even from its own people. Especially from its own people. Do you not agree with that?"

"I agree with the motto. I don't agree with your interpretation."

"Let me spell this one out for you, Guard Carter. Did you attempt to incite rebellion in Sector Keystar upon your release from duty?"

I weigh the options and choose my answer carefully. "No, sir." If anyone incited anything, it was The State itself, treating its citizens like disposable resources to feed its military machine. I merely fanned the flames.

"Yet you freely admit to engaging in combat with State-appointed guards and attempting to kill an officer of The State."

"Yes, sir."

Sarge picks up a folder and thumbs through the contents. "Guard Carter, you are released from Project Praetereo."

I lean back in the chair, stunned. "Sir? You're releasing me? Again?"

Sarge tosses the folder back on the table. He loosens the bindings on my arms, practically giddy. "Oh, no, Guard Carter. Not again. For the first time. You seem to be under the misapprehension that you left the service of The State for some time."

He lowers his voice to be inaudible to the recorders as he says, "My dear," then raises it to add, "You never left. This mission briefing has concluded. Guard Carter is to return to barracks to complete training, 0800 tomorrow."

"But sir—"

"Details of this mission are classified. Dr. Fire will provide you with final information and instructions before your departure. Thank you for your service to The State."

And with that, he leaves. Dr. Fire and I are alone. Well, I guess my massive headache is keeping us company.

∿

I'M AT THE TERMINAL, with my duffel between my boots. My personal effects, such as they are, amount to training uniforms, a toothbrush, and a small drawing Em made for me when I was tapped the first time. The only time, apparently. But I guess the good thing about that is that Em's safe. She's safe, as safe as she can be, in our sector.

Everything I experienced, everything I went through in the sector, was a lie. Doc, the Professor, Lex, all creations of my imagination based on reports they somehow fed into my brain about insurgents in the sector. Spyder and Em, projections from my brain to keep me connected to reality. Dr. Fire explained everything to me. Oh, and she was there in my memories of the sector because my brain incorporated her into the world it made, first as my therapist and then as the doctor who sent me to the sewage plant. Since she was overseeing the real experiment, my subconscious picked up on her and fit her into my universe.

She wouldn't tell me anything about the real experiment, only how my brain reacted to it. Too classified. Too dangerous.

My thoughts were in some weird loop, and my brain protected me from myself by chalking up any discrepancies or inexplicable challenges to memory blocks. Didn't I wonder why the same sorts of things kept happening to me? Why the guards kept chasing me? They were a representation of reality trying to confront me, whatever that means.

My memories from training, from the Bridge, those were real, but the timing was off. My brain pocketed them away to avoid contradictions. Because to be confronted with contradiction would lead to insanity. Apparently, my mental self-protection is one of the reasons I lasted the longest in the treatment protocol. So Dr. Fire says.

They're going to restart my training with the next group of tapped. I'm not fit for regular guard patrol duty just yet, and they want me monitored medically in case of side effects from Project Praetereo. Daily appointments with the doctor on the training base, then eventually weekly appointments, then once they're sure I'm okay, none. The schedule feels eerily similar to my time with the therapist Dr. Ableworth, who the good, good Dr. Fire tells me my brain created. I guess my brain is smarter than me.

An old diesel bus sputters around the corner. The bus slows to a crawl in front of me and stops a few feet past me. With a cough and a groan, the doors open. I sling my duffel over my shoulder and board. The bus is empty. I give the driver a nod. He ignores me, and I shuffle to the back of the bus.

I put my duffel against the window, and the bus rumbles down the dirt path. Leaning against my bag like a pillow, I watch the empty landscape, dotted with the occasional scrubby tree that resists the rain—or just gets lucky—and persists in this hard world.

I want to believe that Em is safe, that all the people of my sector are safe. I want to believe that my service means something. I want to believe that I will train, that I will be posted for duty in some sector somewhere, and that I will go home. There's just one problem:

I don't believe in anything anymore.

# ABOUT THE AUTHOR

K. E. Landry is the author of The Riverine Resistance series. You can find out more about her online at KELandry.com. If you'd like to connect with her, find her on Facebook or on Twitter. If you prefer to email, you can contact her at K@KELandry.com

# ALSO BY K. E. LANDRY

**The Riverine Resistance**

*Quiet Vapor,* a prequel novella to the main series

COMING 2019: *Heavy Water, Book 2 of The Riverine Resistance*

Made in the USA
San Bernardino, CA
27 December 2018